D1521731

holly freakin' hughes

kelsey kingsley

© 2017 Kelsey Kingsley

All rights reserved. No portion of this book may be reproduced in any form without permission from the publisher, except as permitted by U.S. copyright law. For permissions contact:

thekelseykingsley@gmail.com

Cover by Danny Manzella

For Diane Cornetto

I promised.

PROLOGUE

T HE LIMO WILL BE HERE in a few minutes, Jules," Brandon said, walking from the living room into the small bedroom. A wave of nervous nausea rolled over his stomach, as he fumbled with the cufflinks, biting his lip as he struggled to get them fastened. "Christ, I am not cut out for this shit. Tuxedos and cufflinks, and whatever the fuck this thing is." He touched the cummerbund at his waist.

He checked the mirror over the dresser he and his fiancée shared. His hair—God help it—had reached an awkward stage and the waves seemed to have a mind of their own. Brushing against the tops of his ears, the strands flipped in this way and that, and he groaned to himself, as he tried to fix it by pushing it back with both hands.

"Babe! I need some of that hair stuff you— Jules?" He glanced into the living room to see his fiancée, the tall, blonde bombshell of a woman, emerging from the bathroom. His eyes narrowed at the sight of her long legs; not because he particularly cared to stare—although there certainly was that, made evident by the stirring inside his uncomfortable pants— but she was still wearing those little shorts she wore to bed. "Uh, why aren't you dressed?"

Julia was silent, and she didn't bother looking at the man she had spent eleven years with as she dropped herself onto the old garage sale couch. Her hand reached for the remote and tucked her legs under her bottom, making herself comfortable to spend a night watching TV.

"Jules, what are you doing?" She continued her vow of silence, as the behemoth of a man approached her in that *stupid* tuxedo. She twisted her lips in disapproval when he snatched the remote from her hands. "I *said* the limo is going to be here in a few minutes."

She sighed, rolling her eyes up at him. Standing over her, she saw the beautiful face of the man she lived with. Chiseled jawline, deep blue eyes in the dim light of the seedy apartment, straight nose that would have been perfect had it not been for that deviated septum; a feature that she had once overlooked, but lately it screamed at her as a spotlighted imperfection. But still, there was no denying that he was gorgeous, and her body agreed with her mind with a rush of passionate warmth between her legs.

The chill in her heart was another story.

"I decided I'm not going," she announced, reaching to wrench the remote from his hands.

"*What?*" Julia watched as Brandon's face fell with immediate concern, and he eased himself down on the arm of the mismatched recliner. "Are you okay? You feel alright?"

"Yes, I'm *fine*," she replied. Her voice carried an edge that brought him to wince.

The room was brightened by the blue glow of the TV; the flat-screen he had bought a few years ago, with one of his checks from FIT. He had landed himself a pretty good deal as a nude model, one the girls and gay guys could appreciate. Julia remembered a time when she would laugh at his stories of being hit on, and she would swell with pride, knowing he had come home to be with her.

She couldn't remember when it was she began to wish he'd stop coming home altogether.

Brandon reached over to touch the back of her slender neck. She flinched at his touch, and he noticed with a bite of his lip, but he said nothing.

"You know this is a big deal for me." He spoke gently, ignoring his rapid heartbeat. "I really need you there."

Julia snorted a laugh. "Oh, I think you'll manage just fine."

He recoiled, holding his hands in his lap. His brain raced, trying to remember the last time she smiled at him. "So, are you going to tell me what's wrong, or …?" How many times would he ask that question before he finally got a response, he wondered, and ran a hand through his annoying hair.

Little did he know, he was about to get his wish.

Julia shot a stone-cold look at him, her mouth twisting with bitter anger. "If you stepped outside of yourself once in a while, then maybe you would know what's wrong."

"I'm not a fucking mind-reader."

"Well, that's for damn sure."

He looked to the ceiling, regretting he ever brought it up. The limo would be there to pick him up at any second, and he'd have to leave. Alone. *Goddamn her,* he thought, as his fists clenched on his lap. The Julia he once knew would have never asked him to do something like this alone. "Is it … Is it the wedding? Are you stressed out about that, because I told you, I'd—"

"For fuck's sake, Brandon, it's not the goddamn wedding, okay?" She catapulted off the couch and stomped toward the bedroom, where she proceeded to slam the door that never quite closed. It boomeranged, opening as soon as it was shut, and she growled in frustration as she threw herself on the bed. "Goddamn that fucking door!"

He stood up, walking slowly into the room and examined the door. "It'll be nice once we're in our new house, right? I swear, all the doors close." He smiled down at her weakly, hoping that she could find the strength to smile back. "I checked."

She gripped the edge of her pillow, and her mouth twisted around the angry words that felt so good to say. "*Your* new house, Brandon. I didn't sign a fucking thing."

His mouth fell open with a sudden realization. "Is that what this is all about? The money? 'Cause Jules, I told you, it's—"

He was verbally poking her; prodding, probing for the information he was desperately seeking. He wanted to fix things. He wanted to see her happy. He wanted her to smile again. He wanted her to talk to him. He wanted to shower with her, to have sex that didn't feel like a chore, to eat dinner that wasn't shrouded in silence.

He just wanted *her*.

"I don't *want* to be supported by *you*!" Julia bolted upright in bed, shooting daggers in his direction with eyes that were once filled with so much love. "Maybe if you weren't so fucking busy kissing the ass of your precious publisher, you would know what *this* is all about."

Brandon's eyes squinted at her, shaking his head with disbelief. "Kissing ass? What the fuck are you talking about?"

"You and your little seven-figure book deal." She spoke the words with sour rage, staring right at the beautiful face that appeared so ugly under her veil of envy. "It was supposed to happen for *me*."

It was as though a lamp had been turned on somewhere, and his bright blue eyes widened to take in the light. "Julia, we were *supposed* to do this *together*, and that includes when one of us—"

"No! Nobody can convince me that your *Dungeons & Dragons* bullshit is more deserving of *this* than my work. You probably fucked that bitch. I saw the way she looked at you. You probably—"

"Jesus Christ, Julia, you know that's—"

"Shut up!" Julia's fist contacted the lumpy surface of the unmade bed, startling him and bringing his mouth to clamp shut. "You want to know something? You want the *truth*? Here you go—I *never* wanted this for you. I *humored* you, and I *pitied* you, and now . . ." She shook her head with a short burst of laughter, and he continued to stare at a woman he no longer recognized.

"You're jealous of me," he stated in a low voice. The limo honked from the street below, but it no longer seemed important. All that mattered in that moment was the realization that everything he had ever wanted had destroyed everything he had needed.

"*Jealous?*" Julia laughed, shaking her head in protest, although that was exactly how it was. She *was* jealous. She had been jealous ever since he received that letter almost a year ago, and that jealousy grew as it became more and more evident that his success was only just beginning—but hers? She still couldn't find a job that didn't involve waiting on tables. "No, Brandon. I'm not jealous of you. I *hate* you. I hate you and I hate everything that is fucking happening for you, because *you* don't deserve it. And you know what else? You and your little dragon books don't deserve *me*."

The knife twisted in his heart, and his eyes watered. He told himself he wouldn't cry, he told himself he was stronger than that, but when she pulled the ring off her finger and threw it at his chest, a tear wriggled its way out and slid through his stubble. The *clink* seemed to resonate through the little apartment, and he stared at it, lying between his feet. He saw it then as all that had held his relationship together. Now, with the bond severed, his mouth twisted with anger.

"Fuck you." He managed to speak around the boulder in his throat.

In the eleven years they had been together, he had never once wished he could slap her—until that moment. He wanted to use his size, shove her against the wall, and whip his hand across her beautifully ugly face. But he was a good man, and control kept his hands from wrapping around her neck, as she stood from the bed defiantly and walked right up to him.

Her eyes looked up to him, as her finger prodded his chest, and she found it amazing how easily she could act upon the hatred she felt so deeply. "No, Brandon. Fuck *you*."

He grabbed her hand, startling her. For the first time, she saw the seven inches he had on her as a threat, and she pulled herself from his grasp and took a step backward toward the bed.

His eyes looked to her, through his eyelashes, and his lips curled into a snarl. "Get the fuck out of here right now."

With a smirk, she knelt beside the bed, reached underneath, and pulled out two bags she had already packed. How had he not noticed that? He swallowed at his tears.

"Don't worry, babe," she said condescendingly, her blonde brows lowering, "I'm leaving."

Despite the February chill, she shoved her feet into a pair of sandals—the only shoes she hadn't packed—and pushed her way past Brandon in that *stupid* tuxedo. She didn't bother asking him for help with the two large suitcases, nor did he offer as he continued to stare unseeing into the bedroom. She grabbed her coat, throwing it on over her pajamas, and turned to look at the life she was leaving. The stack of books on the little table—those goddamn books—stood as a symbol of what her life could have been; the beautiful house, the luxury cars, the celebrity friends, the rich lifestyle she always felt she was destined to have.

But what did it matter if it wasn't her name on the *New York Times* list of bestsellers?

"What are we going to tell everybody?" Brandon called from the bedroom, and he emerged with his hands stuffed into the pockets of his pants. "The wedding is—*w-was*—in two months."

Julia cocked her head to the side and feigned a pout. His eyes fell upon her bottom lip, remembering all at once the thousands of times he had bitten it, and his heart seemed to lurch to his throat.

"You seem to be doing fine on your own. You'll figure it out," she said, and she opened the door.

"So, this is it?" He took a step forward, hoping he could keep it together for just a few seconds longer. "Ten minutes' worth of fighting, and you're just going to call it quits after eleven years?"

She laughed, shaking her head. Tears stung her eyes, and he was grateful to see that there was still something human left inside her. "Oh, Jesus Christ, Brandon. I called it quits a long time ago. You were just too busy to notice."

Brandon hung his head and ran a hand through his hair. He thought about all those people waiting for him at the release party; the big PR bash his publisher had insisted was necessary. He thought about the wedding he alone had to cancel and all the people he was going to disappoint. He thought about the career that he had so desperately wanted his entire life, and how it had pulled the only person he wanted to share it with out from under him.

He decided then that he was alone, and forever would be, because if he couldn't have Julia, who else was there?

Then, the door slammed, and the limo continued to honk.

1

holly

"A NTONIO'S @ 8? I'LL MEET U THERE."

Stephen was asking me to dinner at my favorite restaurant in the entire city. The same restaurant he reserved for special occasions only—but why? I flipped through the archive of dates stored away in my memory, trying to narrow down what we could possibly be celebrating on an eyeball-melting day in July. I mean, five years of pre-marital bliss had accumulated quite a few memorable dates, so it took a while to determine that, nope, there was nothing to celebrate.

Unless ...

My eyes were glued to the phone while my heart began to thump a tune rivaling a Metallica song. The little voice in my head tried telling me there was no reason to get excited, that Stephen had insisted he wasn't the marrying type enough times for me to be convinced that he was serious. But it didn't take too long for my heart to hammer that conservative little voice right out of there, though, and the naysayer was replaced with the type of excitement that caused me to clap a hand over my mouth and utter a guttural "oh, my God!"

It made sense, though, after a half decade of being the epitome of cute couples. I mean, what else was there? We had the apartment, we had the cat, the matching pajamas … So, wasn't marriage the obvious next step? I had been trying to tell him that for years—three out of the five, to be exact—that there really wasn't any reason *not* to get married. I love him, he loves me, my family loves him, his family loves me …

It. Just. Made. Sense.

Of course, he would always tell me there were millions of reasons not to get married (an obvious exaggeration), like not needing a paper to solidify his devotion to me, but dammit, weren't my feelings important enough?

Well, apparently, now they were.

Holly freakin' Hughes. Soon-to-be Holly freakin' Keller.

***

I walked through the bustling city and although I wasn't even close to being a fashionista, I knew I looked pretty damn good. I had worn my finest little black dress and my best red strappy stilettos—Stephen's favorite. I couldn't exactly walk gracefully in them but hey, we all have to make sacrifices in the name of looking good. My hair was curled and pulled to one side, cascading over my shoulder with *Disney Princess* perfection and leaving my slender neck exposed for the whole world to see. To top the look off, I had spent damn near an hour perfecting my smoky eye, and I knew I could have passed for a freakin' model.

I wasn't really one to leak self-confidence through my pores or anything, but that night I could just feel the eyes of every horny man and every jealous woman following me as I click, click, tripped my way towards the restaurant.

I finally made it to Antonio's without falling flat on my ass in those heels. I stopped myself before going through the door, to try and collect my nerves before facing the man of my dreams and the dazzling rock that was about to sit on my finger.

It hit me then how nervous I was and I quickly glanced around to locate the nearest garbage can. Just in case.

A million thoughts raced through my head all at once, and chasing them left me feeling a little woozy. How was he going to propose? Was he actually going to get down on one knee in a restaurant full of people? How long after proposing would we be married? How long after getting married would we have kids? Did Stephen even want kids? Why had we never talked about kids?

Whoa, Holly. Deep breaths, deeeep breaths ...

I gathered my courage, and with a breath of humid New York City summer air, I walked inside.

A classical rendition of Frank Sinatra's "My Way" tinkled over the restaurant's chatter-filled atmosphere, and a bubbly hostess greeted me with a cheery "table for one?" I involuntarily raised an eyebrow.

Did anybody dress like that to go out to dinner alone?

"Uh," I began, feeling a little self-conscious that this girl thought I was some saucy lone diner, "no, I'm actually meeting someone."

My soon-to-be fiancé.

I gave her the name of my future husband, and she told me to follow her "right this way" through the restaurant. Just as I had hoped, she led me outside to the terrace. And there, under the pergola, surrounded by planters of shrubs and topiaries with twinkling white lights, sitting at the little iron table with the mosaic top, was Stephen. My Stephen. My heart skipped so many beats, I probably should have died standing there, watching him nervously chew at the cuticles around his fingernails.

After taking a few big gulps of air, I started my way towards him. Time seemed to slow to the crawl of a romantic movie as I pushed one foot in front of the other, and when he turned to look at me ... Christ, I swear it was in total Jack-and-Rose ala *Titanic* fashion, especially as he stood, extending a baby smooth hand towards me. I took a hold, gripping on for dear sweet life, and I was pulled into his arms.

"Stevie, this is beautiful," I gushed, gazing upwards at the sparkling slats of the pergola.

Stephen didn't speak a single word, but his lips brushed against my cheek before he released me from his hold and walked around to pull my chair out. Like a true gentleman.

If he was trying to make the night perfect, he was succeeding marvelously.

Maybe he'll let me sleep with him tonight.

We sat in unison, and I made an attempt at fixating on his eyes—those comfortable brown eyes—but no matter how hard I tried, he never seemed to meet my gaze. He just stared at the flickering candle in the center of the table with an expression that might've suggested someone had just kicked the bucket.

He's just nervous. My poor baby.

My arm stretched across the table to take one of his hands, freeing him from his cuticle picking. I admired his attempt to look his absolute best, taking note of his freshly cut hair and clean-shaven face. I have to admit, I preferred him with a little scruff; the baby-smooth look made him look a little too childish for my liking. I like my man to look *manly*. Not lumberjack-manly, per se, but I would have gladly taken Paul Bunyan over the boyish look sitting across from me.

I'm going to instate a rule that he's not permitted to shave once we're married.

Stephen's eyes continued their staring contest with the dancing flame. He didn't look up at me until I spoke his name, and when he did, I smiled the most genuine smile I think I've ever smiled in my life. But he didn't smile back. He just went back to looking at that damn candle.

Taken aback, I let my face fall and I dropped the hand I was holding, giving him silent permission to continue tearing his cuticles apart, except his thumb flew to his mouth to resume the even more disgusting chewing.

The waiter approached, asking if we were ready to order, and before I could shoo him away for a moment so that I could weasel my way into Stephen's brain, that's when Stephen finally spoke. He requested wine, my favorite red, and as soon as the waiter turned to retrieve the bottle, his fingers were back in his mouth.

"Stephen, you're drawing blood." I pinned my lips between my teeth as my excitement faded into impatient agitation.

"Oh." His hands clenched into fists as he brought them down to the table, willing himself to not gnaw the skin right off his bones.

I couldn't stand it anymore. "Stevie, what's going on?"

There was a long, dangerously painful silence. At the sight of his knuckles turning white, trembling slightly with the tightness of his grip, I can honestly say I have never been that worried in my entire life. In all of our five years of being a couple, I had never seen him act that way and it scared the absolute hell out of me.

The waiter brought over the bottle, hastily filling our glasses before leaving the bottle in the center of the table, and promptly walking away—a skilled master at reading the room. I grabbed my glass, and just as I was about to bring it to my lips, I noticed Stephen's trembling bottom lip and the big fat tear rolling down his annoyingly smooth cheek. His hands—bleeding cuticles and all—shot across the table, gripping my free hand and squeezing tight. I had to put my glass down, making the assumption that I didn't need it after all, and with both hands, I squeezed back.

"Oh, Stevie." I stroked the palms of his hands with my thumbs, allowing myself to smile just a bit. "I love you so much, you know that?" Of course he knew that, and as he nodded, a few more tears slid down and onto the table. "It's crazy how many memories we have here, right? Remember our first date? You brought me here, and—oh God, remember you ordered the most expensive wine on the menu because you wanted to impress me but you had no idea it was five-hundred dollars, so you had to put the whole dinner on credit? You were so broke back then. It took you months to pay off one freakin' date."

I smiled warmly at the memory, reminiscing momentarily on how far he had come in such a relatively short period of time. He had only been with his graphic design company for a few years when we had met. It had just barely taken off, but after five years of a lot of work and an equal amount of luck, the list of celebrity clientele had grown significantly and so had his paycheck. It was more than I could say for my own growth at *Teen Queen*, after working as their advice columnist for nearly ten years, but it was going places. I could just *feel* it. Together, we were well on our way to being considered one of those power couples. I just needed to catch up a bit on my end.

Stephen's gentle crying had built up to a steady blubber, and okay, yeah, he was starting to embarrass me a little bit. I mean, it was sweet that he could be that sensitive, but the guests inside were starting to look at the sobbing man in the nice suit.

"Stevie, please stop crying, baby. I know you're nervous, and that's okay, but—"

"Wait, you knew?" Stephen's watery eyes widened and he finally released my hands to wipe the tears from his face. A sob wracked through his body, and I hoped it was the last one.

Finally, able to gaze lovingly into his eyes, I said, "Of course, sweetie. I'd have to be a complete idiot to not realize what's going on here."

His tears were drying, thank God, but I couldn't detect even the slightest hint of a smile. "Holly, I've been wanting to do this for so long. I just … I didn't know how to even bring it up. I've been *such* an asshole …" His voice trailed off as his eyes dropped to that damn candle again. I was ready to blow the freakin' thing out.

"Well, that's a *little* harsh," I muttered. I mean, he certainly dragged his feet, but I'm not sure I'd call him an asshole for it. He shook his head in response, staring off beyond me. I released his hands and took a gulp from my wine. After downing half of the glass, assuming I was going to need it, I reached over the ever-appealing candle and stroked Stephen's smooth cheek. "Honey, don't beat yourself up for taking so long, okay? Sometimes these things take time."

He swallowed hard and cleared his throat. "I really appreciate how understanding you're being about this, Holly. I—" His eyes flitted over my face for a few brief seconds. What was he looking for? I casually picked at my teeth with a fingernail, just in case. "I just don't know how you could possibly know. I thought I had hidden it pretty well."

I laughed, because let's be honest, he had. I hadn't the slightest clue there was any possibility he was going to propose to me until earlier that day when my delusional mind forced those pieces together.

"I just don't understand one thing." Stephen downed his glass in two swift gulps. The wince reminded me that he was never much of a wine drinker. "Why haven't you said anything? Hell, why aren't you *mad*? You—You should be mad."

I gawked at him with a laughing smile pulling at my lips. "*Stevie*, why would I be *mad*? I mean, I've wanted you to propose for *years*. You know that. And yeah, maybe it's taken *way* longer than I wanted it to, but—"

With his eyes widening to the size of golf balls, Stephen held up a hand to stop me from continuing any further. Once my voice had trailed off, he covered his face and began a mantra. "Oh God, oh God, oh God." Over and over again.

"Holly, I'm not proposing to you." His voice was so flat, so matter-of-fact, and if I had known better, I could have sworn my heart had dropped right out of my body and onto the floor. His face remained expressionless and he was facing me, but he wasn't really looking at me. I'm not sure he even saw me there. I guess he didn't want to really see me when delivering the news he was about to drop down on top of my damn head.

And that's when I understood his grim demeanor.

This wasn't a beginning. It was a funeral.

I sunk into my chair again, finally removing the blanket that had been covering my eyes. Stephen took the bottle of wine from my hands and filled my glass like a good boy before continuing with his eulogy. Yet, there was no amount of wine that could have numbed me against the bomb that was about to hit.

Stephen scooted his chair around the table, sitting directly next to me, and I felt his hand gently touch my knee. He hadn't even broken my heart yet, and his touch felt wrong. Poisonous, even. "Holly, I love you so goddamn much, and I never want you to forget that. I will *always* love you and no matter what happens here tonight, you will always be my best friend."

Best friend.

"But?" I whispered through the tears that had already begun to fall.

***

And you know, the mind is a really funny thing. It has this way of protecting itself from horrifically traumatizing and upsetting experiences. It tries so hard to make us forget the moments that hurt us, and you know what? That moment in which Stephen broke my heart is one big blur.

Of course, that may or may not be due to the two very expensive bottles of wine I drank mostly by myself.

I *can* tell you there were tears—many, *many* tears. I *think* there was some yelling. I mean, it's pretty safe to assume there was, but I couldn't begin to tell you what was said. There *might* have been a few breadsticks thrown. There could have been a few sympathetic diners that came rushing to my aid when I threatened to impale myself on a sugar spoon (or so I've been told).

But really, I can't be too sure about the course of events that night. There was only one thing I was absolutely certain of.

Stephen was gay, and he was in love with somebody else.

2
brandon

ER BREATH CAME HOT AND heavy against the thin flesh of my ear lobe as her fingers crept their way over the shoulders of my leather jacket, and down along the lapels against my chest. I felt her breasts, heaving against my back, and with a giggle that seemed to tickle the tiny hairs leading down to my ear canal, she asked if I'd like to show her "my sword" back at her place. Why we would travel somewhere else and not up to my hotel room, I didn't understand, and with an impatient sigh, I told her that, *no*, I wasn't interested in checking out her apartment, and *no*, I wasn't interested in playing Show & Tell.

"I don't *really* think you have a sword," she laughed through the however-many-drinks she had consumed. "I *meant* I want to see …" Her muddled voice trailed off as she made her way around my bar stool, her hands diving for the fly on my jeans.

And that was my cue.

Before her hands could fumble their way through the difficult task of unzipping my pants, I stood up from my seat, placing my hands firmly on her bare shoulders to keep her from tipping over.

"So, that's a yes?" she asked me, her eyelids only half-open as she gazed up at me. "I've *always* wanted to have sex with *the* B. Davis."

"Always, huh," I muttered absentmindedly, fishing my wallet from my back pocket. I pulled out a few bills and threw them on the bar.

"Oh, m'God, *yeah*," she breathed, her breath laced with alcohol as her eyelids folded over in a slow blink. They opened partially, gazing up at me with enough hope to break my heart. "*You* are the *ha-hottest* man *ever*," she said sloppily, jabbing a finger in the center of my chest.

My eyes looked to her with sympathy, and for just a fragment of time, I gave myself permission to appreciate her beauty. A youthful face, untouched by the harsh reality of age, while her body possessed the curvature brought on by just enough maturity to make her supple and seductive. Successfully ignoring my screaming male instincts, I wouldn't allow my eyes to make a spectacle of traveling down her hourglass figure, but I knew it was there, remembering her from earlier at the bookstore. With the amount of people I met, it was a wonder I remembered anybody at all, but I always seemed to remember the ones who found me later on. The desperate ones. The ones that needed to find themselves between the sheets of their bed or mine; it didn't matter which, as long as that was the end result to their efforts. All of those hours spent doing their hair and makeup and picking out the right outfit, it all had to amount to something, but it never did.

It never would.

"Where do you live?" I asked, speaking slowly, and through her excitement and slurred tone, I got her address and wrote it down on the pad of paper I kept in the pocket of my jacket. I helped ease her onto the stool I had just been sitting on and made sure she was sitting steadily before removing my hands from her shoulders.

As I was busy asking the bartender for a couple cups of coffee, the blonde with perfectly tousled hair slipped a finger through one of the belt loops on my jeans and tugged in a failed attempt to pull me between her spread thighs. Her dress had gathered, putting the skintight garment just somewhere below groin level and I kept my eyes forward as I watched the bartender pour the pot of coffee into a couple of mugs I hoped were clean.

"But I don't *need* coffee, baby." She walked her fingers up the front of my t-shirt before tracing the neckline with her sharpened nails. "I just need to pull that hair and ride your—"

A welcome interruption cut in as the bartender slid the mugs over to my waiting hands. "Here you go, Mr. Davis. Can I get you anything else?" He eyed the blonde with narrowed eyes. "Security, perhaps?"

"Actually, if you could call a cab for this young lady here, I would really appreciate it. Make sure she gets in safely." I handed him the piece of paper with her address along with a hundred-dollar bill.

"Of course, sir," he said with a curt nod and promptly picked up the phone.

I turned back to the pouting young woman, who looked more and more like a child with the ticking of the clock, and handed her one of the mugs.

"But t-they said that you did this," she whined, scowling up at me. "And I don't *like* cof-coffee."

"Just drink it," I instructed, and as though I possessed the tongue of Houdini, she did as I demanded. "Who's 'they'?" I inquired, but I knew all too well who "they" were.

"They," as she began to sloppily iterate, were the ones my team referred to lovingly as, *The Crazies*. The fans that took to the internet while hidden behind their computer screens, to blast the message boards and various social media outlets with the things they wished were true. Rumors that I was dating someone of note, or more commonly, that I had bedded a legion of fans after a signing, or some other event. These convoluted, and untrue, stories were the reason for the occasional hotel visit from a hopeful fan looking for their own bragging rights.

"What's your name?" I gently asked her, after she finished telling me about the women she had befriended on Twitter.

"T-Tracey," she said in a quiet voice. The brazen vixen that previously sat there had wilted, leaving behind someone's little girl. Her legs had closed as a hand struggled to tug the garment into a more appropriate position.

"Tracey," I parroted. She looked up at me from her empty mug. Her big hazel eyes held an innocence that chipped away at my rock-solid heart. "I guess *they* neglected to tell you I like my women dressed-up like cowgirl Orcs, huh."

She bit on her lower lip, a barely-visible line appearing across her forehead. Her chin tucked to gaze disappointedly at the skintight dress she had chosen for the night's expedition. "You do?"

I rubbed a hand over my eyes, releasing a heavy sigh. "Good Lord ... Don't believe everything you read online, okay? I think you're smarter than that, and I also think you're better than *this*."

"How do you know?" The shame dripped from her voice like molasses, coating and suffocating.

"Because," I said, barely touching my hand to her shoulder, "if you weren't, you wouldn't have needed all that booze to come down here."

She cracked a little smile. "So, if I wasn't drunk, you would have slept with me?"

"Oh, hell no," I stated incredulously and watched the fleeting optimism wash from her face. I put my own empty mug down on the bar as the bartender came over to tell us the cab had arrived. "But hey, I also wouldn't have sat here drinking coffee with you, and I definitely wouldn't have made sure you got home safe, so I guess there's that."

***

I felt a twinge of shame for my bluntness towards the girl. Tracey, I reminded myself as I walked toward the hotel's lobby in search of the elevator. She had been young—*too* young—and I normally would have treated her with something resembling kid gloves, but I couldn't shake the idea that I would have wanted someone to treat my own daughter with the same harsh crack of reality. Had I been so lucky to have a daughter. Or a son, for that matter.

Another me, another life.

"Thank God I got her home before someone else could get to her," I muttered to myself as I passed through the lobby's entryway. The thought of some asshole with fewer morals and a lack of self-control getting their hands on her brought me to shudder.

"Would you like me to accompany you to your room, Mr. Davis?" An older gentleman with salt-and-pepper hair and a security uniform suddenly appeared by my side.

The lines on his face had initially been deceptive as I took a brief look at his build, assuring me that, yes, he could undoubtedly kick someone's ass if need be, and I shook my head with a polite smile.

"No, I'll be fine. Hotels at night aren't usually a threat. Well, unless this was the Overlook. In which case, I might be pretty screwed, right?" I waited for a laugh, or a smile at best, but he rewarded my lame excuse for a joke without so much as a twinkle in his eye. "Oh, come on, you know. Stephen King? *The Shining?*"

The security guard barely twitched an eyebrow. "No, sir, I'm not familiar."

I cocked my head slightly, blinking back my disbelief. "Wow, really?"

"Yes, sir."

The man would have made an excellent guard for Buckingham Palace, I decided, as I noticed that his face seldom changed expression and his voice remained in the same deep monotone. I was sure that he could not only kick someone's ass, but if I had needed him to, he could have murdered a man successfully with a paperclip.

"Well, huh, I wouldn't recommend you read it, or watch it for that matter." I dramatically grimaced before pressing the Up arrow for the elevator. "But anyway, thank you again for the offer, but I'll be fine."

He bowed his head. "Yes, sir. If you do require assistance, don't hesitate to give the front desk a call." His shoes tapped away to continue his rounds, his hands clasped behind his back and chest puffed out.

My eyes fluttered towards the doors of the elevator. "I would *not* fuck with that guy," I mumbled under my breath.

The elevator dinged its arrival, and I was about to step on when a group of guys in their early-twenties shouted for me to hold the door. They ran across the black-and-white checkered marble floor of the lobby right toward me, sneakers smacking and squeaking against the stone. My arm grew weary holding the elevator doors open waiting for them to slide their way into the enclosed space, but before I knew it, we were packed in like sardines with me manning the button panel. I caught a glimpse of the old security guard, eyeing the group of guys, almost assuredly considering the possibility that the hotel's one celebrity and current claim to fame could very well wind up dead at the hands of a gaggle of sorority brothers. I shot him an enthusiastic thumbs-up before the doors slid closed, locking me inside with my unlikely killers.

"What floor, guys?" I asked them, breaking the rousing conversation about plans for an upcoming road trip to Comic Con.

"Oh, uh, fourteen, I think," one kid said and reached into a pocket and then another, searching for his card key. "Here, uh, it's twelve. Thanks, man."

"No problem," I said with every ounce of pleasantry I could pull together while I silently cursed slow elevators and not being on a lower floor.

The whispers began shortly after the elevator began its climb, as though my elbow wasn't wedged between the ribs of the shortest member of the group.

"Is he ... *you know*?"

"I don't know, dude. Looks like him to me."

"Ask him."

"No, *you* ask him."

"Come on, don't be a pussy. You do it."

The hushed exchange between two of the four friends passed until I finally took the liberty myself of turning my head and said, "Guys, I'm practically standing *inside* you." I watched their expressions drop with horrified embarrassment, and I smiled. "Allow me to introduce myself." I extended my hand to one gawking kid, and he reluctantly accepted. "B. Davis, but people who are usually this intimate with me call me Brandon, so please—call me Brandon."

The four friends all turned towards each other, their faces taking on a shocked expression at the acknowledgement of sharing their journey in the elevator with a celebrity. As I waited for one of them to gather the courage to say something, I raised my tired eyes to the blinking numbers lining the top of the elevator doors and sighed. Floor three, eight to go.

"This is fucking awesome, Mr. B. Dav—I mean, Brandon. The two of us," he gestured towards his short friend, "we love your books. I keep telling *these* guys to give your shit a chance, but they're kinda illiterate."

One of the other two gawked at him as he punched his buddy in the arm. "I am not, you asshole. I just have better shit to do than read." And suddenly embarrassed, he glanced in my direction, avoiding any eye contact. "No offense, man. I'm sure your books are great."

"None taken," I said with a genuine smile. Honesty was better than false flattery any day. I tried turning my body more towards the two young men who were actual fans. "Were you guys at the signing today?"

"Nah, man. We wanted to, but our flight was delayed. We didn't get to the bookstore in time to reserve our place on line," the talkative one said, disappointment prominent in his voice, momentarily forgetting the unique position he had found himself in. And then that reality hit again as a grin spread across his face. "But *dude*, this is *so* much better. This is … it's an honor, actually."

"Well, hey, I can sign something now." I took a Sharpie from my pocket, as they scrambled to open their backpacks, both of them revealing one of my books.

I asked their names and learned that Chris was the outspoken one while Rob was still silent and possibly star-struck (the two non-fans were apparently Drew and Matt), and I set to work signing their books.

Very rarely was I given the opportunity to personalize autographs; my signings were more often than not hectic cluster-fucks that required heightened security measures and a strict time table. It was often done as an assembly line – shake a hand, take book, scribble name in book, hand book back, next. I rarely got to even ask their name, let alone take the extra two seconds to scribble a nice personalized message along with my signature. Nick always told me it was better that way. He said that personalized messages caused the book to depreciate in value. "And besides," he would say, "what if it's a gift?" I had always understood his point, and as my agent, I normally listened. *But fuck it*, I thought, as I scribbled into Rob's book.

To Rob – I like the strong, silent type. – B. Davis

These guys would have a fun story to tell their buddies and have a message in their book to go along with the memory, and if they could only get a couple hundred bucks off of it on eBay, so be it. I handed the book back to Rob, and took Chris's from his shaking hands.

Chris – The honor is all mine, man. – B. Davis

As I passed Chris his copy, I noticed the elevator was just about to arrive at my floor, I announced that it had been fun, and meant it. They asked if they could get a picture, and while normally I would have been anxious to get the hell out of there and back into my room, I reminded myself that this was a whole lot better than worrying about a drunk girl named Tracey. I took one of their phones, extended my arm and angled the camera lens down at the five of us, and snapped the shot just in time for the elevator doors to open. I wished them all a pleasant night and listened as they all tried to get their "thank you's" in before the doors could close and muffle their voices.

In the silence of the long repetitive hallway, I held my breath and shut my eyes, taking in the nothingness that surrounded me for the first time that day. Somewhere further down the hall came the therapeutic hum of an ice machine, and I listened intently through my meditative state, just enjoying the lack of voices. The lack of grabbing hands. The lack of every semblance that made me B. Davis. It had been a long and tiring day, and although I had another couple of weeks before the conclusion of the even more long and tiring tour, I was ready to cross the New York state line and head back to my small-town life and the house I managed to call a home. I was ready to return to my life, where nobody bothered me.

I was ready to be *me*.

The quiet was broken by the opening of a heavy hotel room door. With a jolt, I snapped my eyes open, hoping whoever it was hadn't seen me standing motionless in the hallway, only to find my best friend slumped against the doorframe. His hair was mussed in a way only sleep could accomplish and his eyes, without his glasses, squinted in my direction.

"Welcome home," he said in a drowsy mumble.

"Jesus Christ, Nick. How the hell did you know I was coming up?" I asked, startled by his apparent telepathy.

He grumbled, scratching at the fine hairs on his bare stomach. "I had gotten up to take a leak and heard some kids yelling in the hallway."

"And if it hadn't been me, you would have scarred someone for life with this whole *Slenderman* thing you have going on here," I said as my hands gestured toward his pale, lanky figure.

"What's a slender man?" Nick squinted at me before his face was taken over by a yawn that was indeed contagious.

After the reminder that I was running on fumes, I pushed him back into the suite, afraid that someone else would enter the hallway and be blinded by his pastiness. The door had barely clicked into place before I dropped myself onto a couch. Nick sat down at the other end and ran his hand back and forth over his short hair.

"So, you hooked up with someone?" He spoke with clarity, the sleep leaving his voice. I shook my head at the question, glaring at him through the strands of hair that had fallen out of place. "Oh, yeah? Then explain that."

I followed his accusing gaze to the lipstick on my neck, a temporary souvenir from Tracey. I hoped she had gotten home without decorating the backseat of the cab with the night's fruitless adventure. "One of the girls from the bookstore decided to get bold and drank herself into coming down here."

"She got past security?" Nick raised a concerned eyebrow, and for good reason. It was a wonder there hadn't been others getting into the hotel to track me down.

I shrugged, too tired to care. "I guess so."

"Humph. I'll have a word with the hotel manager." Nick sighed, tracing the outline of the couch's arm with his twiggy fingers. "Well, anyway, last night here, man. You could have gone with her, or I could have made myself invisible."

"She was a *kid*, Nick."

"Define 'kid.'"

"Do you just *forget* that you have three daughters when we're on the road?" I sighed with a pang of irritation that lasted only a moment as I rubbed the lipstick from the crook of my neck, its tackiness clinging to my skin. "Anyway, how many times do I have to tell you that I'm not going to just whisk them away to my bedroom simply because they're willing? What kind of asshole would that make me?"

"The kind who hasn't gotten laid in half a decade," Nick said in jest, but quickly realized he wasn't getting a laugh from me. Then it was his turn to sigh. "Hey, you're right, okay? But it might not kill you to open yourself up to the idea of actually being with someone. And you never know when one of these girls could be *someone*, you know?"

"Another me, another life," I grumbled.

"Whatever you say, bro." Nick continued to manipulate his hair while I wondered if he ever got tired of pushing me.

Running a hand through my hair again, the long strands sliding between my fingers, I stared at the intricate design of the ceiling in the living area, decorated with white crown molding against a backdrop of light grey. Just a few feet away was the open door to my room; a lavish spread of exquisite furniture, a flat-screen TV, and a bar that was anything but mini. I pictured the en suite bathroom--with its sunken tub and spa-like shower that could comfortably accommodate an orgy—and I sighed wearily.

I turned to Nick, my eyelids suddenly feeling heavy. Gesturing out towards the room around us, I said, "*This* is what they want—not me." He looked around curiously. "Come on, Nick, you're not stupid."

"You're more than just *this*," he tried to reason, ruffling his hair absentmindedly. His eyes suggested he was ready to go back to his room and sleep before our three-hour road trip the next day.

I nodded slowly. "*Right*, but these women that you insist could be *someone* don't see that. They don't *want* more than *this*." They didn't want the man who couldn't cook to save his life, or the guy who would rather eat at a diner than a four-star restaurant. They didn't see me as a fan of rock music, a drinker of black coffee, a lover of cats, or the devourer of sitcoms. None of them have any desire to acknowledge that person could even exist under all of the glamour they see on TV, because that person was ordinary—no different than any man in any store they might bump into on any day. "They want *B. Davis*, Nick, because he has fancy hotels and party invitations. Why the hell would they trade that to be with *Brandon*, a sarcastic bastard with a cat and a Keurig?"

I wished they only wanted the sarcastic bastard with the cat and the Keurig.

3

holly

B UT I DON'T WANT TO fall!' Maple shouted, dangling from the branch he grew up on.'" A very cheery middle-aged woman by the name of Jessie flashed the page before swiveling in her chair for the collected children and smiling parents to see, and read the next line. "'I like it here!'"

Flash. Swivel. Repeat.

The little girl at my feet stirred for a moment as she clutched her stuffed giraffe (whose name was Giraffe, for obvious reasons) closer to her chest, and settled once again into a deep slumber. With some quiet time to myself, I would have loved to take the opportunity to dive into the romance novel I had brought along—a real scorcher between a colonial settler named Christine and her rebel Red Coat, Thomas—there was something about the downer of a story Jessie had chosen that left me reminiscing on my own reluctance to let go. I slumped further into the bean bag chair I sat in and stared off into the bookshelves behind Jessie until I could see the life I had left behind in the city.

It was funny how quickly things could change. Just when you think it's all going so well for you, or decent at the very least, an atomic bomb lands itself right on your head. Stephen announcing he was gay hurt, and being single for the first time in five years was more difficult than I thought possible. And *then*, as though the entire world was working against me, my boss at *Teen Queen* had fired me just days later, adding serious insult to an already serious injury. Apparently, according to that bony witch, a thirty-one-year-old woman was "too old" and "too out of touch" to give effective advice to teenagers. As though a whole lot had changed in the ways of teenage romance since I was of the more appropriate age. Right.

Needless to say, without a steady paycheck, it was the nail in the coffin to keeping my precious apartment—my *home*—and after a phone call to my younger sister on Long Island, it was decided that I was moving in with her and taking over as her daughter's babysitter.

A single babysitter at thirty-one. Living in my baby sister's house.

Holly freakin' Hughes. Living the dream.

Speaking of dreams, a little boy decided it would be a good time to start screaming for no apparent reason, and abruptly woke Anna in the process, bringing her immediately to tears. With a groan, I stood up and dropped the untouched book in my bag before reaching to pick Anna up and quietly excused myself from the group.

As I juggled the crying little girl and my bag in my arms, the owner of the store—an older guy named Bill with a particular love for argyle—took note of my struggling. He had been standing nearby, hanging up mangled-looking paper cutouts of leaves attached to fishing line on the ceiling. The leaves had been a project I had seen him working on for weeks and the progression had been nothing short of disastrous. Particularly the time he stapled one of the leaves to his own thumb.

"Here, let me help you with this stuff," Bill said, stumbling off of his stepladder to catch Giraffe just as Anna released him. He also took the liberty of taking the sippy cup from my hand, leaving it free to hoist Anna up onto my hip.

"Thanks, Bill," I said through a sigh.

"Oh, it's no problem at all, Holly," he said in a hushed voice, eyeing his wife as she continued reading her stories to the rest of the group. "But don't let Jessie catch me not hanging up these leaves."

We walked a few feet to a child's size table, cluttered with books and oversized building blocks. I sat Anna down in one of the small chairs as she continued to sniffle even whilst she proceeded to play with the blocks.

I thanked him once again, taking the sippy cup from him and shoving it into my bag amongst the toys, spare diapers, fruit snacks, and hand sanitizer. Once upon a time, I could carry cute little bags from my favorite knock-off designer brands. Now I was lugging around an oversized vinyl tote bag my mom used on occasion for beach days, which was made obvious by the picture of *Winnie the Pooh's* very own donkey pal Eeyore moping on a mound of sand beside a lopsided sandcastle.

Holly freakin' Hughes. A vision in vinyl.

He passed Giraffe to Anna's grabby hands and smiled behind his eyeglasses. "Of course. I'll see you on Thursday?"

"You know it," I said with a smile and as he walked away to tend to his haphazard decorating, I wondered what the hell had become of my life.

"Come on, Anna Banana," I mumbled to my niece. "Let's go home."

***

Home had transformed into a three-bedroom ranch-style house with a decent sized yard and a two car garage, a far cry from my itty-bitty studio apartment on the Upper East Side. The mortgage was just a little less than what my apartment had cost, but it had easily ten times the space. I mean, I wasn't blind to the fact that two bathrooms, a living room, and a separate dining room were a serious upgrade from one bathroom and one small room with a stove and refrigerator. But without Stephen, the place had yet to feel like home.

I turned the wheel of my Mom's ancient minivan into the driveway. Despite my protests to drive the piece of disintegrating scrap metal, she insisted on lending it to me until I could afford something else, as if that was going to happen anytime in the new future. She had said, "Holly, you're going to need something to get you around. What if you meet a nice guy and he wants to meet you somewhere?" I did agree reluctantly, but not because of the possibility of meeting a "nice guy." I agreed when I decided to take over as Anna's babysitter. I knew I needed some wheels and I couldn't afford to be picky, as much as I desperately wanted to be. It wasn't exactly my dream to chug along in a minivan held together by rust particles holding hands.

I glanced in the rearview mirror at Anna, sleeping peacefully in her car seat with Giraffe tucked safely beneath her chubby arm. With a moment of hesitation, I exited the car, closing the door quietly behind me, praying she would sleep for just a few more minutes, and I wandered over to the fence where a little old lady stood, her hair barely visible to me over the wooden slats.

"Hey Esther," I said with a heaving sigh, standing on my toes to see over the five-foot fence.

Startled by my voice, my elderly pal looked up from her daily yard investigation. "Oh, Christ almighty, Holly!" She clutched her chest and stared at me, wide-eyed with exasperation. "Do you *want* to kill me?"

"Sorry," I mumbled, tucking my lips between my teeth.

"Elder abuse, Holly." She glared at me, but I caught that twinkle of amusement in her eye. "How was Story Time today?"

I shrugged. "Jessie read a book about a leaf afraid to fall, and ultimately had to accept its impending death, so there was that."

"Lovely. Well, hey, it's something to do. That's why I come out here and pull these fucking weeds. I feel like I do this shit every goddamn day." She plucked another, using so much force that she teetered on her unsteady legs. "Gotcha, you little prick."

I bit back the laughter. "You *do* come out here every day— and that wasn't a weed."

She waved the piece of greenery in my face. "Then what do you call this, missy?"

I threw my hands in the air. "If I was a botanist, do you think I'd be babysitting for a couple hundred bucks every two weeks? I have no idea what the hell that thing is, but I know it's not a—"

"It's a weed," Esther stated flatly, ignoring the fact that her gardener had just been to her house days earlier. "But if you're so smart, you should be over here doing this for me. I don't know how you live with yourself, knowing your old friend Esther is over here, killing herself with these fucking weeds."

"Because they're not weeds!" I laughed, shaking my head.

"Harry's going to come over there and haunt you, if you don't watch your mouth," she threatened.

"Good. I'll tell him all about your invisible weeds."

"Uh-huh," she muttered, bending to peer down at another sprig of something protruding from the ground. It looked identical to the one hanging from her hand, but she left it alone. "Where's Anna? Sleeping in the car?"

I glanced back towards the van. "Yeah, she was rudely awoken at the bookstore. One of the other kids thought it would be a good idea to start yelling for no reason and woke her up."

She shook her head. "When I was a kid, if you pulled something like that in public, it was a hand across the face for you. And you know what? You thought before you did something like that again."

I stifled a laugh. "Well, you know, different times and all that." She grumbled in response. "Anyway, I guess I should get her inside, but really, do you need any help? After Liz gets home, I could come over and … "

She waved a bony, wrinkly hand over the fence. "No, no, if I needed help, I'd ask."

"No, you wouldn't. You'd just continue to moan about the weeds that aren't weeds, and lay on the guilt like you always do."

"Humph. Well, if you see me collapsed on a pile of *weeds*, assume I need your goddamn help."

***

Liz opened the carton of fried rice, spooning some out onto Anna's plate and then her own. "So, *then* Dr. Martin told me there was no way he could let me take my usual lunch break after that family of ten came walking in. Can you believe that? I had twenty minutes to myself today and then I was back in the office, helping this woman fill out insurance forms for eight kids."

If I'm being honest, I had absolutely no idea what she had been talking about before she opened the fried rice. My mind had wandered itself into memories of dinner with Stephen, grasping at the opportunity to remind me of everything I was missing.

Dinner was our daily ritual, the one guaranteed time of day when we would meet up together at the apartment and cook with the radio blasting. We would make eggplant parmesan with sauce made from scratch, and meat loaf with my own personal recipe, and pot roast rubbed down with Stephen's secret sauce. We would sing along with Lady GaGa, as he chopped and I sautéed, and we would dance around to Bruno Mars while we waited for the timer to announce that the barbeque ham was ready. On occasion, when there had been maybe a little too much wine flow, Stephen would wrap his arms around me and kiss me to the tune of Sam Smith, and if the Red Hot Chili Peppers were playing, *forget it*. There was no keeping my hands off him, and the lasagna would burn.

Holly freakin' Hughes. Horny sous chef.

I pushed the boneless ribs around my plate with my fork, wishing I could remember that one song we made love to on the kitchen counter that one time years ago. I don't remember ever giving any memories permission to disappear, as if they never happened. As if *we* never happened.

"Holly, are you even listening to me?"

My eyes shot up from my plate to see Liz staring at me, aggravation blending with concern on her face. "Oh, right, yeah, family of ten. That sucks."

Satisfied with my half-assed answer, she shrugged. "Well, I mean, it is more business for the office. Anyway, how was your day?" She took a bite of an eggroll, resting her chin in hand, eagerly awaiting my reply, and I thought about how lonely her life must have been before I moved in.

***

Moving from the city back to Long Island had been hard. Losing my job had also been hard, and becoming a babysitter at the age of thirty-one hadn't been a walk in the park either. But nothing had been harder than going to sleep every night knowing he was out there, sharing his bed with someone else, while I shared mine with empty space.

It was amazing how I could get through the day without so much as a watery eye, but once I closed the door to my room and laid down for the night, my heart still ached the way it did when he first left me. The wound opened up the moment I turned out the light, reminding me of just how sad and lonely I really was without my Stephen to wrap his arms around me in the darkness.

I curled an arm around Camille, listening as she awoke from her sleep with a gentle purr. Her sandpaper tongue raked across my hand and I smiled through my heartache, nuzzling my face into her fur, grateful that I at least had her. I mean, she didn't do much for me physically, but hey, I had my vibrator for that. And then, I found myself giggling, because well, I guess Stephen didn't do much for me physically either.

Actually, that wasn't entirely true. He was an attractive man, on the higher end of average with a few killer features that made him stand out. It was his eyes—those *comfortable* eyes—and smile that really clinched the deal for me at a meeting between my magazine and his graphic design company years ago.

I could still remember the first couple of years of our relationship. That delicious honeymoon phase when we could barely keep our hands off each other. Everywhere we landed was a place to make love. Everything we did inspired us to indulge in each other. Every moment, every look, every word was a reason to spread my legs and succumb to desire.

It hadn't been until one year into our relationship that he confessed he had been a virgin, embarrassed that I would've been turned off by that bit of info. I had laughed. Not because he had never slept with someone before me, but because he had more skill in pleasing a woman than my college boyfriend, who had slept with a number of girls before being with me.

God, and he really was skilled.

Oh, the irony.

I remember telling a few of the ladies at work the less intimate details of our sex life, more because I was so excited to have something so carnally amazing and less because I wanted to make them jealous. But the conversations would always end with them wishing he were with them instead, and I would have a reason to hold my head up high, with the comfort of knowing that he was *mine*.

But like all good things, the consistent amazing sex came to an end, and I assumed we had just gotten comfortable in the relationship. We fell into a routine, occasionally making love before falling asleep. Spontaneity was rare, but I chalked it up to normal relationship stuff. The kissing never stopped, the making out still continued on a fairly regular basis, but the sex had slowed to a snail's pace, and I told myself I was okay with that. Until it just didn't happen at all, somewhere around our four-year mark, and I had to resort to buying a vibrator.

But I kept telling myself it was normal, because we were *comfortable*.

I giggled again into Camille's fur, this time through my tears, and asked her how I could have been so stupid and blind. She could only purr her response; which I took as reassurance that I wasn't in fact stupid. Just a woman in love with a man she knew would never want her in the way she wanted him.

***

Esther and I sat on her front steps, keeping our eyes on Anna. She had given the little girl the exciting task of collecting out of place foliage from around the yard, and Anna accepted with the promise of cookies. As the bubbly toddler ran around the lawn, the birds provided the cheery soundtrack for the grueling topic at hand—my love life, or lack thereof.

"I thought about *You-Know-Who* last night," I cautiously mentioned as my hands twisted together. Esther's eye roll was all the response I needed. "I'm sorry," I said with a sigh, "but I needed to tell someone, and if I told Liz, she'd just tell me he's not worth it."

"And you think I'll say something different?" She cocked a bushy brow and smirked, a gentle reminder that she had spent many conversations calling him every name in the book. "I thought you were doing better."

My eyes followed Anna as she ran across the yard, squealing with arms waving. "I can't just turn it off, you know. It's only been a few months."

"Right, and torturing yourself is obviously doing a hell of a lot to help."

I threw my head back in frustration and groaned. "I don't know what else to do. I know I sound like a broken record, but Christ, I loved him for five years! I've told you before, I can't just act like all of that never happened."

"Nobody is saying to act as though none of it happened, but maybe you could give yourself a little nudge in the right direction. Have you even gotten dressed in the past week?" She motioned towards my yoga pants and sweatshirt.

"These are different pants," I fibbed.

"Mm." She twisted her lips, eyeing me skeptically, as she reached behind her to retrieve the plate of cookies. "Have one."

They were oatmeal raisin—my favorite—and they were still warm and chewy from the oven. I took one without hesitation and practically inhaled the damn thing. I could focus on my extra weight some other time, when Stephen wasn't weighing so heavily on my mind.

I called to Anna, asking if she wanted to accept payment for all her hard work.

"Shock-lit chip?" She picked one up to inspect with the intensity of an FBI agent. I stared in disbelief at her and told her to "just eat it," and with the first bite, she grinned and uttered an "mmm" before sitting on the step below to finish chowing down.

With a nudge in my ribs, Esther leaned closer. In a whisper, she said, "Maybe you should, you know, find yourself a handsome man and get yourself laid."

With a roll of my eyes, I shoved another cookie into my mouth with little care that my yoga pants were feeling tighter by the second. "Oh, right. That's *exactly* what I need," I groaned.

She shrugged "Hey, sometimes a jump back in the saddle is the best way to get over someone. Get some of the ol' confidence back when you find you can still—"

"Esther!" I looked to the little girl sitting on the step below me, her pudgy fists wrapped around two halves of a second cookie. It had been easy for me to advertise myself as a successful advice columnist for a leading teen magazine, but what kind of man would find anything remotely enticing about a grown woman babysitting for a few hundred dollars a month?

4

brandon

HOME, SWEET, HOME.

The bags dropped to the marble floor of the foyer with a sound that echoed up to the vaulted ceilings. A pile of mail sat on a table next to the door, along with a Tupperware container full of my favorite double-fudge brownies, made specially for me by Nick's one-and-only, Ashley. A quickly scribbled note welcomed me back to my less-than-humble abode. It also let me know that I was now low on cat food, and if I didn't want Tolkien to feast upon my eyeballs while I slept, I better get to the store.

With an appreciation for my eyesight, I decided it would be wise to heed her warning. I took the opportunity to not face the rest of the house awaiting me just yet, fully aware that I wouldn't want to leave once my head hit the pillow.

Clutching my keys in hand, I locked the door with the comfort of knowing I would be returning shortly to my bed, where I was determined to sleep for a week. The floorboards of the wrap-around porch creaked the tales of their vacation from me under my heavy boots as I walked towards the steps, and before making the descent, I looked out onto the lake not twenty feet from the edge of my front yard. A rippled landscape of diamonds glittered in the early autumn sun—a sight that had been the deciding factor when buying the house years before, but the intent had never been to enjoy the view alone.

I climbed into the Mercedes GLS SUV that had been unloved for far too long, and enjoyed the deep breath I took once behind the wheel. The sense of independence was always overwhelming after months of being surrounded by Nick, security, press, and fans. Freedom was a sweet thing often taken advantage of, and while I was guilty of that myself, I had planned on reveling in just simply being alone for at least the next twenty-four hours. After I got the cat food, of course.

Turning the corner onto Main Street, I caught a glimpse of my favorite local bookstore and felt its gravity begin to pull me in. It didn't take much convincing to do my best job at parallel parking at the front of the store, and I headed in, greeted immediately by the familiar welcome of the jingling door.

Bill sat behind the counter with bifocals slid halfway down his nose. A cup of coffee seemed fused to his hand as he turned another page of the book nestled in his lap, never looking up even as I stood directly in front of him and leaned against the counter's ledge.

"Hey Bill," I said with a smile, attempting to pull him from whatever world he was currently living in. "Reading anything good?"

"Mm, the new Koontz. Just got it in. Not bad." He spoke in the broken sentences one strings together when neck deep in an engrossing story—my favorite kind.

"Oh yeah? Maybe I'll check it out. Haven't read any of good old Dean's work since he killed off Odd Thomas. Not sure I've forgiven him for that yet, though, so …" I drummed my fingertips against the counter, my eyes looking through the wide picturesque storefront windows, decorated festively for autumn. In fact, I noticed, the entire store looked like Mother Nature had exploded with shoddy kindergarten craft projects, and I knew instantly that Bill had been, once again, the head of the decorating committee.

I watched the Main Street, bustling with the lunchtime crowd on that Thursday. A small-town world where everybody knew everyone else. Shop owners and restaurant chefs greeted most by name, inquired about those they didn't, and treated each other with the nosy respectful cattiness you would expect from your stereotypical American hamlet. Everybody had their part to play, even if that role was simply to be a customer at the new pizza place, and mine was Hometown Boy Turned Local Celebrity. Most everybody knew me, everybody of note took care of me, and everybody else respected my desire to be left alone.

The town was my security blanket, even down to the street fairs and corny decorations that littered the lamp posts for every important holiday, and it felt good to be back in its easy embrace.

I cleared my throat as I rested my gaze back at Bill, still sucked into his book. With a sudden realization that he was behaving poorly towards a potential customer, he shot upwards as he placed the book somewhere beneath the counter. He straightened the hem of his famed argyle sweater vest and looked up to face me. It took a few moments before he focused, and then he smiled in a way that felt like coming home—because that's exactly what it was.

"Well, if it isn't my favorite author! You just get back today?"

I folded my leather-clad arms over the counter's wooden surface, surveying the small displays of locally made bookmarks and candles, and nodded wearily. "Yeah, just a little while ago. I figured I'd stop in and say hi before falling into a coma." The very mention of sleep brought forth a body-consuming yawn, and I apologized for my lack of composure.

Bill waved a hand, dismissing the apology. His face suddenly lit up, his eyebrows raising with his apparent stroke of brilliance. "Hey, Jessie just finished up with Story Time if you want to crash on a pile of bean bag chairs. I'm sure she wouldn't mind the company."

"Tempting, but I'd need a better reason to fold myself into one of those things." I laughed at my own expense, vaguely remembering a time when it was a piece of cake to crouch that low to the ground without hitting myself in the chin with a knee.

"Then can I interest you in a cup of our new Tahitian Vanilla Roast? I'm sure Scott wouldn't mind taking care of that for you," Bill said with a tantalizing smile.

"Oh, come on, Bill." I groaned, tossing my headful of hair back to look at the ceiling. "Don't tell me you're in on Mission: Kill Brandon with Sleep Deprivation, too."

"We have decaf."

"Well," I said as I straightened my back, "now you're talking my language."

I walked through the maze of shelving units and mismatched chairs, laid out haphazardly over a canvas of various rugs. The store was relatively small and whimsical, taking up two storefronts on the main street, but the amount that was squeezed into the space made it feel so much bigger, albeit confusing. Bill's wife Jessie was putting away her books from Story Time in the children's corner—affectionately titled The Book Nook—when she spotted me. Her face lit up and dropped the book she held before hurrying over to me, her long colorful skirt billowing behind her.

"Oh, Brandon, I've missed you!" Her arms stretched to wrap around my neck, hugging me as though I had been gone for much longer than three months.

I reciprocated as I bent to wrap my own arms around her waist. "I missed you too, Jess."

The bottle-red-headed woman backed away, her hands pressed to the sides of my neck. "Get yourself a cup of coffee and come sit down, hon. I *have* to tell you what happened with that Taco Bell that's going in next to the funeral home. I'm telling you, that Debbie Jefferson is going to get it from me one of these days, if she doesn't learn to keep her big fat mouth shut. She thinks she has her hands in everything around here, but *ohh*, did I prove her wrong when it was *my* vote that put that darn Taco Bell through." She grinned with enough sinister malice to leave me feeling momentarily disturbed. "Come—sit and I'll tell you the rest."

My hand flew to my hair, raking through the strands. "I'd *really* love to, Jess, but I am pretty sure I'm actively dying of exhaustion."

"Oh, but *B.*, you just got here," she protested with a pout.

"Let the man leave, Jessica!" Bill's voice bellowed from the front of the store, and I coughed on a laugh.

Jessie nodded through the hurt, and I assured her I'd be back soon—I always was, even if only to write outside of my own office—and I would hear all about her plot to take down Debbie Jefferson. Satisfied, she left me with another hug before returning to her work in the Book Nook, and I continued my walk through the bookstore's labyrinth to the café, managed by Bill and Jessie's son Scott.

I found him sorting through cups and lids of varying sizes, singing along a little too loudly with something playing through the headphones he wore over his grey slouchy beanie. The stringy strands of his long hair stuck out from underneath the hat, giving him the appearance of a misplaced scarecrow.

He caught a glimpse of me out of the corner of his eye, startled for only a moment before excitement took over, just like his mother. Pulling the headphones off, he exclaimed a "hey dude" before rounding the counter to shake my hand, finishing with a hearty clap on my back.

Scott wasted no time getting a cup of their latest blend brewing for me, and I reached for my wallet. "Come on, dude. You know we don't accept your money."

"Doesn't mean I won't try," I grumbled, and slipped a few dollars into the tip cup on the counter when his back was turned.

I had grown up with Scott. Both of us lacked siblings and being three years his senior, I played the part as an older brother to him during the years when our families were inseparable. The bond had remained solid well into our teens, and then I had gone off to college, fell in love and settled into my own life, separate from the one I had at home. Our parents had remained close, but Scott and I let the tethers holding our bond together disintegrate with the changing of our lives. More specifically, he had developed a taste for marijuana, and I was busy being in love with a judgmental woman who didn't care for his choice of habits.

It wasn't until I was single once again that our friendship reignited, no longer under the control of the woman who claimed my heart for too long, but eleven years was a long time, and I had to settle for the unfortunate fact that it would unlikely ever be the way it had been when we were kids. The painful proof was in the way I stood there, without a clue of what to say.

"So ..." I began, as I rifled through the small-talk-topics at my disposal, coming up empty while my fingers traced the outline of the cash register.

And as though the universe could sense the awkwardness hovering around the barista bar, I felt myself struck in the side of the leg by a moving object. The edge of my kneecap pulsed with pain as my assailant crashed to the floor with a wail, and I looked down to find myself staring at a little girl; blonde and frantic with hands clutched to her face, a stuffed giraffe laying at her side.

Instinctively I knelt down, preparing to assess the situation.

"I-is she okay?" Scott asked, suddenly standing over me, his hands nervously working inside the sleeves of his oversized sweater.

I glanced up at him incredulously. Of all the stupid questions.

"Sweetheart, are you hurt?" I asked in a gentle voice, hovering my hands over her with caution, undecided on what I should do with them.

She continued to cry in hysterics, and I noticed a trickle of blood coming from underneath her hands. Although my mind raced with the possible lawsuits I knew absolutely nothing about, I asked without panic, "Can you move your hands, and let me take a look?" When she refused, I took a chance and gently pried her hands away from her face to reveal a bloody nose and a fat lip.

Scott rushed to grab a few napkins, handed them down to me, and went to fetch some ice for her lip. Perhaps feeling a little too at ease with the little girl, I pulled her up into a seated position and wiped up the blood that ran over her lips. Gently tilting her head back, I pinched the bridge of her nose. Her hysterics had subsided into controlled sobs, and her wide brown eyes watched me with caution. Evidently, the Stranger Danger had settled in.

I lifted my head to quickly look around the store for any sign of a person missing a child. "Honey, where is your mommy or …"

"Anna! Oh, my God!"

I was startled by the sudden voice of a disheveled woman. She fell to her knees beside me, more of her dark brown hair falling out of her already messy ponytail. Her hands immediately went to the pudgy cheeks, turning her face unintentionally out of my fingers' grasp, and the little nose went un-pinched. A slow drop of blood appeared at the entrance of her nostril, and I reached over to hold her nose shut again, not bothering to wonder if I should keep my hands off this woman's daughter.

Scott returned with the icepack and handed it to the woman. Through her frazzled panic, she looked at it curiously in her hands. Understanding the worry she must have gone through, only to find her child bloodied and screaming on the floor, I spoke to her gently and instructed her to use it for the girl's lip. That's when she finally acknowledged my presence, turning to face me. If there was ever a moment to strike me breathless, it was that one, and it did.

She was a pale beacon of effortless beauty, without a mask of makeup to enhance or disguise. The delicate plains of her high cheekbones radiated with the natural flush of excitement from losing her child, while a set of full lips appeared red and bitten, and in the center of it all was a slender nose that came to a perfect point. I caught myself gazing into the melted chocolate pools of her eyes, clouded by a sadness I was all too familiar with, and I realized, had I believed in love at first sight, I had just fallen face first into it.

But I didn't believe in love at first sight.

"U-uh," I stammered, catching myself staring at her, and diverted my gaze to the child, desperately trying to pull myself together as I found my voice. "She ran right into me. Hit my knee pretty hard. I don't think her nose is broken, but I'm also not a doctor."

Surely she was aware that I was a writer, and yet, despite my lack of a PhD, the woman seemed to emit a sigh of relief, placing a hand on my arm before applying the icepack on Anna's lip.

"Thank you so much. She just ran off. God, she *never* does that." She squeezed her eyes shut, letting out a long sigh. "It's just been one of those years, you know?"

The dark circles under her eyes suggested she was in dire need of a stiff drink and a long, uninterrupted nap. I suppose I could have asked her out for a drink, or at the very least bought her a cup of coffee. But I bit my tongue, telling myself that it would never end well, and instead nodded.

"I've had those before," I said with a smile.

She smiled at me warmly, pushing the sadness aside for just a few moments, and touched my arm once again. "Thank you," she repeated.

She turned her attention to Anna. I removed my fingers from her nose, and took the ice pack from her lip. It appeared that she would survive the ordeal when she immediately reached for the raggedy giraffe and hugged the floppy body to her chest.

"You ready to go home, Anna Banana?"

Anna nodded eagerly, and I couldn't say I blamed her after all the excitement. She climbed into the arms of her mother, nuzzling her battered face into the hollow of her neck. Ignoring the shameful jealousy I immediately felt, I stood then, extending a hand to help pull the woman to her feet with the little girl in tow. As she laid her small hand in mine, I imagined that a current of electricity passed from her body into mine, bringing me instantly to life, as though I had been dead for too long.

A moment passed with us standing awkwardly. I realized that maybe fate had granted me another chance to throw myself out there and ask her out for a drink, but it dawned on me that she was more than likely married. Rejection seemed like a horrible way to start my time back home.

Another me, another life.

"Thank you again," she finally said, for a third time. She looked up at me, at least a foot from where she stood. "Say thank you to the nice man, Anna."

Nice man. I basked in that brief moment of anonymity, of being just an ordinary person in an ordinary store—of being a *nice man.* Maybe, I realized, she really didn't know who I was, and how arrogant it was to assume that she had in the first place.

"Sank yew," Anna said softly, as she looked out for a second from her hiding spot against the skin of her mother's neck.

"You're very welcome," I said with a smile, and then my eyes settled once again in a spot within hers—the woman I was dying to know the name of, but wouldn't dare to ask. "Maybe I'll see you around."

With a quickened smile and a turn of her heel, she was gone. I turned to Scott, who handed me the coffee I had since forgotten about, and he asked why I hadn't just asked her out. I was embarrassed that he could sense the stirring of emotion I felt for the woman I had just met, and maybe some time ago I would have gone into an explanation on why I hadn't. But all I could do was shrug and tell him I must have just been too tired to think, and began to walk away with coffee in hand, leaving Scott with his headphones and music.

"Actually, I have a question," I said, turning around as a thought entered my mind. "Have you seen her before?"

As he lowered the headphones again, Scott raised his brows with knowing eyes. "Yeah, she comes in a couple times a week for Story Time. Moved here from the city a few months ago."

"Hmm." That explained why I hadn't seen her before. And although I wasn't a fan of hanging around a corner full of strange little kids, that was subject to change. "Thanks, man."

"Uh-huh," Scott teased, his mouth curling into a taunting smile beneath his ratty beard, and he pulled the headphones back up.

I went through the rest of my day as normal as my normal got. I went to the grocery store and bought the cat food I initially left the house for. I picked up a turkey club sandwich from the diner, bumping into my favorite waitress Birdy in the process and received yet another hug, and headed home.

I sat on the bed I missed so much, sharing the sandwich with my four-legged friend with a rerun of *Frasier*. Afterwards I took the longest, hottest shower I had taken in two months, without Nick's rushed words telling me I needed to be somewhere to sign some things for some people. With my hair soaking wet, too physically and mentally beat to bother squeezing the water out of its length, I flopped down on my pillow, wrapping myself in the blankets at an hour that would've made an old man proud. I closed my eyes, breathing in the comfortable scent of my own bed clothes, and drifted into a deep sleep as I wondered what name could possibly be worthy of the most beautiful woman I had ever seen.

5
holly

THE WEEKENDS SINCE STEPHEN AND I ended had become painfully uneventful. This was no thanks to Anna being with her father and leaving me without any work to do, and I couldn't tell if Stephen alone had made me an exciting person, or if the breakup had really taken a toll on my own personal desire for fun. Or maybe it was both.

Probably both.

That Saturday wasn't much of an exception, and after lounging on my bed for hours with a book in hand, I announced to Camille how I planned to spend the rest of the weekend. Stay in my pajamas, watch *Frasier* reruns, indulge in a little wine from the box in the fridge, enjoy the company of my vibrator, and nap until it was time to go to bed again. It seemed like a sound plan—one I could easily stick to without putting much pressure on myself—and I rolled out of my bed to find that box of wine.

My feet shuffled along the slick wooden floor of the hallway into the living room to find my mom and Liz sitting there, apparently shocked to see me out of my room before five.

"Wow, you're up early," Liz gasped dramatically, checking her watch. "Wow, Holly, it's only four in the afternoon. What brings you out of your cave?"

Feeling an obligation to socialize, I slumped into a puffy armchair and rolled my eyes in her direction. "I thought some sunshine would do me some good, but then I saw you, and that's basically the same thing."

"Yeah, whatever. Mommy and I were just thinking about going out for some dinner, and then maybe hitting a couple stores afterwards. You interested?"

I pretended to think about the offer for a few split seconds before declining. There was no way I was sacrificing a day of *Frasier* and wine. That required getting dressed and at least giving the appearance that I wanted to be there, and neither seemed like the wisest way to spend my time.

Liz groaned as she turned her concerned attention to our mother with that "can you believe her?" look on her face. "I *told* you she hasn't gotten any better."

"You really do have to get out once in a while, Holly," Mom said in her stern Mom voice. "It really isn't healthy to be like this. What ever happened to going out every weekend? You always did stuff on the weekends, remember? You were always too busy to come out here and see us because you had stuff to do."

I let the guilt run off of me as I uttered a disgusted sound. "I *do* get out. I go to the bookstore and, um, Esther's house ..."

She sighed, her tone suggesting that I was driving her straight to a slow and painful death. "Just do something as an *adult*, for crying out loud. Sleeping your weekends away isn't doing you any good. You should be out, meeting people and having fun. Stephen wasn't your only ticket to a social life, you know."

Except that I think he was, I thought of mentioning, but kept my lips sealed.

She leaned towards the coffee table and shoved a stack of envelopes in my direction. "These came to my house, by the way. You might want to change your address if you expect to get your mail."

Little did she know, I didn't particularly care to receive credit card bills and house insurance offers from scammers. Still, I nodded my agreement to avoid another lecture on why it was beneficial to my being a responsible adult, and I reached for the pile to skim through them. Bill, junk, junk, bill, junk, and then, there was a large envelope. The address was handwritten and the return address was somewhere in Manhattan from a name I didn't recognize. I saw Liz and Mom exchange a concerned look as I eyed the envelope.

"It's gotta be from one of my old friends," I assured them, as though saying it out loud would help me to convince myself.

"You haven't heard from your friends since—" I shushed Liz with a pleading look. There was no need to remind me that my friends had mysteriously vanished with the demise of my relationship with Stephen. I remembered well enough on my own.

With mild curiosity and moderate confusion, I tore into the envelope, finding that it was made of very thick, expensive cardstock, and I found myself excited. But when I pulled out the ribbon-and-damasked piece of heavy paper, my vision went immediately blurry as I struggled to read the words embossed at the top in big spiraling calligraphy. My breaths came in heaving gasps as I waited for the tears to start, and—oh, did they ever.

"Holly!" I realized Liz was shouting at me. She got up from the couch and rushed over to me, taking the card from my shaking hands. I curled up on the chair, struggling to breathe as I sobbed into the cushions.

"*Oh God,*" she whispered, sitting at the edge of the chair. "Holly, I'm … I'm so sorry." She passed it on to my mom, who was convinced at this point that someone had died, and while she was technically wrong, I felt as though perhaps *I* had.

"They're *engaged?*" Mom stared at the invitation to Stephen's engagement party. "'Please join us in celebrating the engagement of Mr. Anthony Stevenson and Mr. Stephen Keller.'" She sent it floating to the coffee table. "Can you imagine? Stephen Stevenson? Karma is cruel." She shook her head, covering her mouth with a hand. "Not cruel enough, that's for damn sure."

"Why the hell would they invite her to their freakin' *engagement* party?" Liz snapped angrily. She glared furiously at our mother, directing her anger at the only other person in the room, because the person we were all truly angry at lived exactly 55.1 miles away, and who the hell really wanted to travel that far just to punch him in the balls?

That's right. I did.

"Does he even realize what he's doing to her? Look at her!" Liz shouted. She picked the invitation up and shook it in Mom's face before dropping it back down. "I could … I could—oh, my *God*! I could fucking kill him. Holly, do you want me to kill him?" she asked soothingly, with a hand on my back.

I nodded with a sob, because him being dead seemed like a really good idea at the time. Dead and out of my life for good.

For good. Oh God.

My arms curled around my body as another bout of tears poured over my cheeks.

Mom shook her head, signaling with her hand for Liz to cut the crap because she clearly wasn't helping. "Holly, nothing I can say is going to make this better, but—"

I sat up and pushed past Liz. "Then please. Don't say anything at all," I choked through the waterfall coming from my eyes, and hurried down the hall to throw on any pair of yoga pants I could find and my sweatshirt.

And suddenly, I was more than ready to take my mom's advice about getting out—alone.

***

But the only place I knew to go was Reade's. Sure, I could have gotten deliriously drunk at one of the two bars on Main Street, or maybe grabbed something greasy from the Golden Carousel diner, but second-nature brought me to the bookstore.

Holly freakin' Hughes. Creature of habit.

I pulled into the parking lot, removing the key from the ignition of Ol' Rusty, and just sat there behind the wheel, staring into oblivion at a life I was never meant to have. A man that was never really meant to be mine.

I suppose I had subconsciously been holding onto the hope that Stephen would come back to me. My heart had foolishly convinced my head that he was out there, thinking about me as I thought about him, and those thoughts were going to bring us back together. But that invitation in my hand had been a death sentence to every last inkling of hope I possessed, and in that moment, Stephen really was dead. The Stephen I knew.

Straight Stephen.

After snorting a bitter laugh, I squeezed my eyes shut and broke down behind the wheel of the van, beating my fists against the plastic as I mourned. I cried until my stomach hurt from the gut-wrenching sobs that had escalated, and I opened the door to vomit, only to dry heave just as someone was exiting the store. I continued to cry without abandon, despite being stared at by a total stranger, as guttural noises came from my body that I wasn't even aware I could make.

"Ma'am? Are you okay?"

A vaguely familiar and cautious voice came from just a couple feet away, and he walked closer. I looked up and through tear-stained eyes saw the man from the other day, the one Anna had run into. His eyes, a stormy blue in the sunset-dimmed parking lot, seemed to widen at the sight of me.

"It's you," he said almost in a whisper, and he rushed over to me, as though he knew me. Kneeling down beside the van, he looked up at me perched in the driver's seat and placed a hand on my knee. "Are you okay?" he repeated, with more concern and less caution. His tone was gentle, the deep voice wrapping around me like a hug.

As I hastily wiped away the tears that he had just witnessed, I managed to speak through my relentless sobbing. "Y-yes, I'm … f-f-fine." I sniffed, then coughed, all while trying desperately to maintain some semblance of composure in the presence of this all-too-kind stranger.

Kind and attractive, I then noticed, taking in the strong jaw line dotted with what was probably a permanent five-o'clock shadow. His almost-black collar-length hair was brushed back off of his face, the wavy ends curled under his ears to lightly embrace his face and neck with their wispy ends. It was obvious that he was either incredibly skilled at keeping himself groomed, from his facial hair to his eyebrows, or he paid someone to do it—and they did it well.

In the dimly lit parking lot, I couldn't see what he was wearing other than a black leather jacket and a dark pair of pants. But my other senses were intact, and I could smell the expensive cologne radiating from him. I knew it at first spicy whiff, even through the snot that packed my nose: *Tom Ford Tobacco Vanille*. It just so happened to be one of my favorites, and I caught myself breathing a little deeper, just to catch the notes carried by the fall breeze.

His mouth curled into a warm, knowing smile. "Okay, you don't have to tell me the truth, but you're *obviously* not fine. Let me buy you coffee, at least."

I wrinkled my nose at the thought of drinking coffee for anything but a hangover, and then realized how rude I was being. After all, he had been needlessly nice to me, and I quickly added, "Actually, I'm more of a tea person."

"I guess I can deal with that."

He laughed a deep throaty chuckle and stood up, reaching a hand out to help me from the car. I wasn't usually in the habit of taking the hand of strangers, and I certainly had never been in the habit of accepting invitations to have any kind of beverage with a man I didn't know from a hole in the wall. But he had been so kind, and there was no reason to believe he was in the habit of abducting unsuspecting women in parking lots. So, I listened to my gut and took his hand for the second time in just a few days, watching as my palm was engulfed by his long fingers, and I was pulled onto my feet.

***

"Okay, wait a second." The dark brows knitted together as his large frame leaned forward, arms crossed against the tabletop. "Just so I know I'm understanding all of this, answer something for me."

I nodded and gestured for him to continue, seizing the opportunity to take a long sip of my second cup of lavender Earl Grey.

"*So.*" He closed his eyes and pinched the bridge of his nose. "Your ex-boyfriend cheated on you for years, finally confessed he was in love with someone else, and then sent you an invitation to his engagement party just a few months after breaking up?"

"After years of telling me he would never want to get married," I reminded him, before taking another sip.

With a nod, he dropped his hand to the table again and worked his jaw from side to side. "Right. So, uh, stop me if I'm out of line here, but—why the hell would you allow yourself to waste a minute being upset about this?"

My mouth dropped open, stunned by the blunt question from the mouth of a man I had only just learned the name of. "Uh, yeah, I would say you're *way* out of line."

Brandon placed a warm hand over mine, and I hoped he hadn't noticed my body stiffen under his touch. "Okay, yeah, maybe, but you have to know—this guy *is* an asshole."

I opened my mouth to protest angrily, narrowing my eyes at him, because how dare he insult the man I had intended on spending my life with. But Brandon held up a pointer finger. "While he was busy screwing around, as far as you knew, it was still just the two of you. He might have been over you a long time ago, but the fact is that, right now, you're *not* over him. And he has the audacity to send you a goddamn invitation to *celebrate* his engagement to the guy he allowed to help ruin your relationship?" He leaned back in his chair, sending his blue gaze upward as he shook his head. "Gay or not, *that* makes him an asshole, Holly, and it makes me feel …" He bit his lip for a moment, as though he were searching for the word. "*Sad*. I feel sad for you that you would waste anymore of your time feeling depressed about this when he clearly doesn't really give a single fuck about how you're doing."

As I quietly wondered to myself if I should storm out of there, I said, "You have no—"

"Oh, so he's called you then?" He interrupted me with a cock of a brow. "Or is he more of a Facebook guy?" I shut my mouth immediately. Brandon tilted his head with a smirk that I would have slapped from his face, had I not been too busy crossing my arms defensively. "That's what I thought."

"Wow," I breathed, unable to say anything else. My eyes dropped to the table, my hands turning the empty cup absentmindedly.

I knew I should have given him a piece of my mind, or better yet, walked the hell out of there. But the truth in what he had said hit harder than how inappropriate his comments had been. Somewhere inside, I felt that I had needed to hear someone say those things, and nobody had. Everybody else had been too close to truly and honestly slam me in the face with the reality of the situation, but not him.

He squeezed his eyes and blew out a heavy breath of air. "I'm sorry. I shouldn't have said anything. I just—"

"No, um …" I stammered, trying to find my words.

"No, I was out of line. I don't even know why I …" He stopped himself, and with a bite of his lip, he gave his head a quick shake. A few of the long strands of hair fell from behind his ear to lie against his cheek. "Wait, I have to say something else, because I really wish that someone had said this to me once upon a time." He covered my shoulder with one of his hands, and I fought myself to not find too much relief in the warmth. "*I'm sorry* this happened to you. It sucks. It sucks a lot, and I can tell you it's probably going to suck for a while. But I promise that one day you're going to wake up, and you're not going to remember when it stopped hurting so goddamn badly. That's the day you'll realize that this was never worth your pain in the first place, and I hope that day comes sooner for you than it did for me."

The emotions swallowed me, but for the first time in months, sadness wasn't one of them. Grateful. I was grateful beyond contemplation for his words, and for his time. Time that he was under no obligation to give to me, and not knowing what to say, I leaned over and wrapped my arms around his neck, finding my cheek comfortable against his shoulder. A hesitant arm came around my back, stiffly hugging me against his body.

"Thank you," I said, my voice muffled by the leather of his jacket. "I really needed that."

His hand pressed tensely against my back, and I heard him inhale, holding his breath before relaxing and exhaling completely. "I know," he said, his breath warm against my ear.

The hand against the middle of my back began to rub gently, moving only an inch or two in a soothing circle, and Brandon leaned his cheek against the top of my head. It was comforting, and for just a second, I relaxed against his shoulder and allowed myself to enjoy the relief I felt in that hug.

And then, as suddenly as it began, the movement of his hand came to a halt as the sound of loafers approached.

"Um … Brandon." It was Bill and his voice was timid, suggesting that he was interrupting something not meant to be disturbed.

I hastily unlocked myself from his embrace, feeling oddly the same way I did when my dad walked in on me practicing my kissing techniques on a Backstreet Boys poster. How had I forgotten that there were other people there? I suddenly noticed Scott singing ridiculously loud to something blasting through his headphones, and Jessie was pushing around a cart of books, sliding them onto shelves as she went, and then, of course, there was Bill doing whatever it was Bill does. He was currently holding a broom, which might have suggested he was sweeping, or at the very least making himself look busy to keep from getting yelled at by Jessie.

"Yeah, what's up, Bill?" Brandon said, turning to face him.

"Hey, I see you're getting to know Holly here," Bill noted, his face lighting up. "She's one of Jessie's new regulars at Story Time, you know."

"Is that so?" Brandon turned his striking blue eyes on me.

I nodded, my hands busying themselves on my empty cup. "Yeah, Anna and I are here every Tuesday and Thursday. She's the little girl you battered," I reminded him, with a teasing smile and a nervous laugh.

"Ah, that's right. Your daughter with the stone head. My knee is still feeling the effects of that one. Just stopped limping yesterday."

My hands flew from my cup, startling them both. "Oh, God, no. *No*. Not my daughter." They both looked at me with brown and grey eyebrows knitted with confusion, and I realized I had never had any reason to tell anybody what my relation was to her—nor had I ever alluded to anybody that I was actually a babysitter. "She's my niece," I said in a small voice.

"Ah, very nice," Bill said with a smile, as though that explained everything. "It's nice you kids are getting acquainted. You make a good match." He winked at Brandon, who pushed his hair back in response.

Bill gripped the broom and grimaced regretfully. "Actually, I came over here to tell you we're closing in five minutes. I'd let you stay a little longer, but …"

With a shake of his head, Brandon grabbed our cups and smiled at Bill. "It's fine. We were just getting out of here, anyway."

"Well, I guess I'll be seeing you both soon then." With a clap on Brandon's back and a kind smile in my direction, Bill walked away, gentling pushing the broom every few feet or so, and glancing at Jessie as he went.

Had I really been out for that many hours? How long had I been sitting with him? I took my phone from my sweatshirt pocket, shocked to read that it was almost nine. I imagined Liz waiting by the door like a doting mother, wondering when her baby was finally going to return to the nest. So, while Brandon threw out our empty cups and shouted a friendly "good night" at Scott, I quickly composed a text to my sister.

"Didn't mean to stay out so late. Coming home soon. Hope you weren't worrying your pretty little head over me."

My phone promptly chimed in response.

"My pretty little head is fine. Hope you actually had some fun. For once."

***

The chilled night air hit me as we stepped into the parking lot where, just a few hours earlier, we were complete strangers. Now, as Brandon and Holly, we walked in silence to Ol' Rusty as I struggled to make sense of what happened that night. Time had flown in his company, and I found it both disconcerting and exciting.

I glanced up at him, standing over a foot taller than my petite five foot one, and caught the lopsided smile he wore. His head was held high, as he walked towards the car with something I read as confidence, and when we finally arrived at the door, he leaned his leather back against the side. I grimaced a little, wishing I had actually cared at all to give the grimy van a good washing.

Maybe it'll rain this week.

"So, niece, huh?" he finally said, and I eyed him suspiciously, confused by the sudden comment. "You said Anna was your niece," he reminded me gently.

"Oh, right, yeah." I took a deep breath, leaning beside him against the van. "After I lost my job for being *too old* and I moved back to Long Island, my sister offered me the job of being Anna's babysitter." I glanced over at him to see if he was making any judgmental faces of disgust. All I saw were lowered brows, and that was difficult to read, so I continued talking. "I mean, it's a fraction of what I was making before, and that really sucks because God, I really miss good wine, and living on my own, but it's something." I was breathing hard, unsure of when talking had become the equivalent to running a marathon. Brandon had turned to look down at me, his brows no longer sitting low over his eyes. He didn't look disgusted or judgmental at all, but I still felt the need to add, "You know, until I get back on my feet."

Whenever that is.

There it was. I had admitted to someone that I was a babysitter. At thirty-one. My God, I could only imagine what he was thinking, and I waited for him to make some joke or laugh condescendingly before wishing me a good night, never to me again.

"So," he finally said after a few exhilarating moments of listening to me breathe, "she gave you a place to live, food to eat, *and* a way to make a little bit of money while you work through this shitty thing you're going through." He glanced behind him at the van, and I shuddered. "And this?"

I shook my head, taking note that my palms were starting to feel clammy "Uh, no, this beautiful luxury vehicle was bestowed upon me by my mother. It was her excuse to get herself a nice little car to buzz around in while I got strapped with Ol' Rusty here."

He frowned then with disapproval, crossing his arms over his wide chest. "Well, damn, that's really rough."

My face lit up and I nodded, appreciating his sympathies. "Tell me about it."

"Yeah, I mean, it really sucks having a sister who would just … *give* you all of that when you're flat on your ass without you even asking, and then to have a mom who would *give* you a car on top of that? God, that must be *so* terrible for you." I looked up at him, and he cracked a little smile, nudging me gently in the ribs with an elbow. "That might be what you think, but *I* think you're pretty fuckin' lucky."

I swallowed a hard lump in my throat. "You don't think it's stupid that I'm an old babysitter?"

He laughed heartily at that. "Are you kidding me? There's nothing wrong with being *Mrs. Doubtfire*."

"*Mrs. Doubtfire* was a housekeeper," I corrected, "and made a considerable amount more than I do, I'm sure."

Brandon thought for a second, eyes glancing around to search for the answer to prove me wrong, and shrugged. "Whatever. What I'm saying is, there's nothing wrong with your situation. You were dealt a crappy hand, and you're lucky enough to have some help while you figure stuff out. Why would I think that's stupid?" He paused for another thoughtful moment, biting his bottom lip. "Hell, why would *anybody* find that stupid?"

I shamefully turned my eyes to the pavement, black illuminated by the glow of the lampposts. "I think it is."

He slumped against me as a friend would. His weight was heavy and comfortable against my shoulder. Good, I thought; he felt good, and he smelled even better.

"Well," he said in a deep, gruff voice, "that's something you'll have to make your own peace with."

Underneath that gnawing pit in my stomach telling me that everything was painfully hopeless, I felt an overwhelming sense of thankfulness for this night I had with Brandon. I wasn't exactly what I would consider religious, but I felt the need to thank the Lord then for dropping this guy in my path. The heaviness in my heart didn't feel any lighter, and I couldn't say the pain hurt any less. But for the first time in months, I could actually imagine there being a light somewhere at the end of the tunnel, and that was something.

"You know, I have to say, you've been thanking me all night, but I really feel like I should also thank you," he said, looking down at the scuffed boots he wore on his feet, before glancing over at me with sincerity brewing in his eyes. I asked him what for, allowing my head to tip toward him, feeling as though we had been friends for years—not hours. "It's been a long time since I've enjoyed being around someone, um, *new* this much."

"I don't think I was great company," I said apologetically.

"Nah." Brandon shook his head slowly, as he stared thoughtfully out into the parking lot. "This was good. It was *real*. I don't get a whole lot of that."

Silence then gave way to a tension that blossomed between us. He was so close, pressed firmly into my side, and while my mind tried resisting the magnetic chemistry that was manifesting between us, my body didn't seem to want to listen. I had been painfully aware of how otherworldly attractive he was—far better looking than any man I had ever spent time with—and I turned my head to look up at him. I pointed my chin skyward to trace the outline of his jaw with my eyes, and because of some sort of gravitational pull that happens between people in movies and apparently us, he turned to look down at me.

What was it Esther said about handsome men?

My body, my damn body, was rebelling against me as I continued to breathe him in. I took in the scent that had turned itself into something resembling sex, and really, didn't every woman dream of being that close to a man with the strong jawline of a Norse god? I absentmindedly bit my lip, as my eyes fixated on his mouth. It was a good mouth, I thought, as that familiar heated flame ignited between my legs.

"So, I guess I—"

I don't remember the moment when I had decided to kiss him, if it had even been a decision to make. He had started to speak, the depth of his voice melting in my ears, and I just acted with a sudden surge of lust, silencing him immediately as my lips met his. I had surprised him, sending a sharp inhale of breath through his nose, but when I cracked my eyes open just to make sure it was actually happening, I saw that his had softly closed.

Our lips moved together, a series of small kisses that became more profound when a hand reached over to rest against the side of my face, his fingertips tickling lightly against the edge of my jaw and the curve of my cheek. My lips parted boldly, fully prepared to coax his open with my tongue, when he pulled away and my eyes snapped open. His remained closed, but his brows had knitted in distress. His hand never stopped stroking my face.

"Maybe this isn't a, um …"

I could sense what was coming next. It was a mistake, he wanted to stop, he was disgusted by me, he was ready to leave and never see me again. Each possibility becoming worse and worse as they rampaged through my paranoid brain. But I kept still, waiting for him to make a move.

"Oh, fuck it," he said with purpose and thrust his open lips against mine.

He engulfed my mouth, his tongue dancing with mine under the lights of the parking lot, and *God*, it was everything a kiss should be and nothing like any kiss I'd had before. Slow and sensual, without sacrificing any passion or urgency. Our bodies turned in unison towards each other, and my arms looped around his neck, standing on my toes, as his hand slid down to the small of my back. His other hand went to meet the other, pulling me closer into him, and my body shivered with excitement at that familiar swelling that pressed against my stomach. I groaned my acknowledgment into his mouth, and wrapped my fingers around the long strands of his hair.

Against my wishes, he pulled away from my mouth with a groan. "Why are you so fucking short?"

"Or maybe you're just too—"

He hushed me with a bite against my lower lip before sliding his tongue back into my mouth, and without breaking the feverish lock our mouths had on each other, he pushed my back into the van and reached down to wrap an arm around my thigh, lifting me with impressive ease. Instinctively, I wrapped my legs around his waist, and didn't complain when the kissing was accompanied by the grinding of his hips.

"Holly." With his forehead pressed against mine, he moaned my name, and I had never been so happy to share a name with a plant. "I want you so bad."

He didn't have to tell me, when the evidence of his desire was hard and pressing exactly where I wanted it, and my God, it felt incredible to be wanted. To hear him moan my name, albeit strange to hear it coming from a different man with a different voice with a different way of kissing—a different *everything*. A pang of guilt washed over me, remembering Stephen and the intimacy we had once shared, all the times he had said my name in the throes of passion.

He sent you an invitation to his engagement party.

The thought chased away any feelings of guilt, as I let my fingers run through Brandon's hair. "I want you too," I groaned, overtaken by the need to have him between my legs in the back of Ol' Rusty.

But to my disappointment, Brandon gave a little shake of his head. The thrusts of his hips came to a halt and he held himself there, pressed hard against me. The place between my legs, the one that had been ignored for too long, throbbed with desperation and anticipation, but I knew as he straightened his back with that faraway look in his stormy eyes that it was over.

My feet dropped to the ground as his hands flew to his hair, raking it all back forcefully as he took a few steps back, shaking his head.

"Goddammit," he said, shutting his eyes and pinching the bridge of his nose. "Fuck, I'm so sorry."

"What just happened?" I demanded to know through my frustration.

"I'm sorry," he repeated, shaking his head once again rapidly. His eyes opened, and I saw then a regret that almost broke my heart. "I can't do this."

"But *why*?" I questioned, shocked to find myself whining.

"I-I just can't. I'm sorry." He looked troubled, and I narrowed my eyes and wished he'd stop apologizing.

"Are you married?" I snapped, looking towards his hands to spot any rings or a sign that one might have been there. "Because if you're married, then ..."

He shook his head, lifting one corner of his mouth into a sad smile. "No, I'm not married." His voice was low and gentle, as though he were talking to a child.

"Then, *what*? Are you gay? Is that what it is? Because I seem to have that effect on men, you know. Maybe kissing me, you just suddenly remembered that, oh shit, you're gay." My hands hung limply at my sides, feeling empty and missing the soft mass of his hair. God, he had amazing hair. I could've curled up in that hair and gone to sleep if I had the chance.

That brought him to laugh. "No, definitely not gay."

"Then ..." I took a step towards him, reaching my hands forward to grab the open sides of his jacket. I planned to pull him toward me and rock his world in that parking lot in every way I knew how, but he shook his head.

His sigh was impatient. "Holly, I just can't."

"But I *want* you to!" I hadn't intended to shout, and I glanced around to make sure no one was around, luckily finding nobody within hearing distance. "Please, Brandon." I found myself pleading with him. "It's been so long since I've been with someone and I just need it. I *need* this. *Please*."

I'm begging a stranger for sex. Never thought that'd ever happen, but hey, here we are.

He smiled through his regret. "I guarantee it's been longer for me."

"Yeah, right." I ran my eyes over him briskly in silent judgement, and gave him an accusing look that he ignored. Instead, he leaned down to kiss me on the forehead before taking a few more steps back, putting too much distance between us.

"You deserve someone who will respect you. Someone who will make you feel important. Not some horny prick who will use you in a parking lot."

I pouted. "Well, maybe I *want* someone to use me. Maybe I want to have a night of hot, meaningless sex."

Brandon chuckled that throaty laugh that sent waves of frustrating pleasure through my body. "If that's what you want, then I'm not your guy, I'm sorry." He went to turn and walk away into the darkness. "I hope I see you soon, Holly."

So much for handsome men.

I rolled my eyes sarcastically, and wished him a good night. I opened the door to the van and hopped in, left alone to process everything that had happened throughout the course of the day, and honestly, I hadn't the slightest clue where to begin. But, I thought as I put the key into the ignition, the wine in the fridge seemed like a pretty good place to start.

6

brandon

THE GLOWING SCREEN OF THE laptop stared me down, the blinking curser of my word processor taunting my writer's block with every flash. For two whole hours since returning home from whatever strange phenomenon had occurred at the bookstore, I had attempted to work on the fourth installment in the *Breckenridge* series. My busy brain just wasn't having any of that nonsense, despite the urgency that Nick and my publisher had stressed on me just days earlier. They wanted the next book, they said. They wanted to keep the momentum going, they said. And while I understood all of that, I couldn't get myself fired up enough to add anything more to the already existing 50,000 words.

I blamed her. *Holly.*

Since the day we met, she had haunted my mind with the memory of her smile, whispering to me like a restless ghost. The sadness hidden in the golden flecks of her eyes begged for a reason to smile more often, cried for a reason to sparkle in the magical way they did when she laughed. God, to be the man to make sure she never stopped having a reason to smile …

With a discouraged sigh, I admitted defeat and closed the laptop. *Maybe I'm not cut out for this anymore*, I thought, and stood from the high-backed leather office chair. I took a quick glance around the circular room lined with custom bookshelves that hugged the walls before walking my way to the leather sofa in the middle of the floor. I laid across the length of the couch, shoving a suede throw pillow under my head and resting my feet on the arm rest. My eyes stared upward towards the wrought iron chandelier, the soft glow of the bulbs shining down upon me like the stars I seldom saw living in the heart of suburban Long Island, and my thoughts drifted to those minutes in the Reade's parking lot.

She had kissed me, and dammit, I kissed back. My own willing participation had shocked me. But what was more startling was I had been two pairs of pants away from having sex with her right there in the parking lot, and without a care of who might have been watching. A careless act of carnal behavior on my part, only stopped by my respect for her, and reluctance to feel for someone new; *not* the possibility of some cell phone photograph winding up on the internet the next day. Because with her, I realized, I wasn't B. Davis, famed author of a fantasy book series that rivalled the likes of Tolkien and Martin. This was blatantly apparent to me when I realized I hadn't once mentioned any of the personal details of my career to her. It wasn't a secret I had purposely hidden—just genuine forgetfulness that was perhaps a subconscious effort to keep myself from being anything more than Brandon the Nice Man.

God, what am I doing?

I knew that she was in the process of mending a broken heart and making sense of her fragmented life, and of course, I was more than aware that I was a troubled man on the verge of permanent celibacy, living in a vacant shell of a house. And while a small glint of optimism whispered to me that we could be exactly what each other needed to pick up the pieces and super glue them back together, that required so much work, and I wasn't sure I was prepared to put in the hours.

I pulled myself up from the couch and headed out of the room, taking another quick glance around the space—full of memorabilia, pictures, and books from throughout my short career—before leaving B. Davis behind, and I closed the doors.

I pulled the fitted t-shirt over my head as I walked down the hall, casting it aside on the floor of my bedroom before flipping on my nightstand lamp. Tolkien promptly jumped from the bed to sniff the garment. I watched her as I unzipped my jeans, and laughed when she backed away abruptly with repulsion. She turned to look at me with what I was sure was judgement, and oh, perhaps just a bit of jealousy.

"Don't worry. You're still the only girl in my life," I said to her, bending over to scratch her behind the ears, while ignoring the stirring in my heart that wished that weren't true.

On my way to the four-poster bed, I caught a glimpse of myself wearing nothing but my boxer briefs in the floor-length mirror. While I didn't fancy myself a vain man, I was never ashamed to admit that I was proud of the way I looked. It had taken years to achieve that amount of muscle definition, and hours of pain to earn the tattoos that covered much of my torso. But that had its own downfalls. It was also my appearance that had set me apart from other authors. Few of them had received countless modeling offers from various companies, and I was fairly certain that most had never been made to pose shirtless for magazine covers. It was this type of publicity that I was convinced brought in the marriage proposals on social media and the grabby fans at various events, although Nick insisted it was the "killer jawline and the dreamy eyes." So, what did I know.

Tolkien jumped onto the plush comforter and turned herself around several times, kneading her paws into the fabric before she settled down for what was probably her hundredth nap of the day. I threw on an old t-shirt and a pair of flannel pajama pants before climbing into bed after her.

Left in darkness, my thoughts sprung back to life with a vengeance. I wanted nothing more than to flip a switch and turn my brain off, just long enough to allow for slumber to settle in. I could have dreamt about her and have been fine with that, just to have gotten some sleep, but God, I couldn't stop thinking about her—about Holly and her lips and her laugh—and I couldn't decide if I hated myself for it or not.

7
holly

S O, UH, WHERE DID YOU GO LAST NIGHT?"
I guess I should have expected I would be bombarded with that question once I had woken up the next day. I just wasn't anticipating it happening as soon as I stepped out of my room. Both Esther and Liz rushed at me, cups of hot tea in hands. I pushed past them as I walked into the living room. My groupies followed me through to the kitchen where I grabbed myself a refreshing bottle of water, which had a much lower alcohol content than I felt I needed. Grabbing a doughnut, I slumped into a chair at the table.

"So?" Esther asked as she and Liz sat in the chairs beside me. She clapped her hands together in prayer, and added, "Please tell me this story involves a handsome man."

"Your wish is my command," I grumbled, and began to tell the story, and it felt like just that—a story. Not something that could happen to me, and Liz seemed to agree with her mouth stretched into a dreamy smile. "And things ended before they could go too far." I hastily concluded the story about my night of sort of passion and gulped down some more water, wishing so bad that it had turned itself into wine at some point. Liz sighed, and I turned to her. "What?"

"It's just so perfect," she sighed again, resting her chin into the palm of her hand.

"Um, how? I made out with a stranger, and nothing came of it." It was so much less glamorous when I thought about it that way.

Liz shrugged, still wearing her wistful smile. "No, you made a connection with a guy, and there were fireworks. That's like something right out of a book or a movie." The wistful smile morphed into something I interpreted as smug. "You'll end up together, you'll see."

I rolled my eyes in response.

In my dreams.

"I'm just happy you took my advice and found a handsome man to sleep with," Esther chimed in.

"Oh, my God." I sighed heavily, covering my eyes with a hand. "I didn't sleep with him.

"Well, maybe you didn't, but at least you allowed yourself to have a little fun," she pointed out and nudged me with a bony elbow. "He *is* handsome, right?"

I threw my head back dramatically. "God, yes," I groaned before laughing. "Handsome isn't even how I'd describe him. He's more," I paused to sigh, "*beautiful.*"

Esther and I giggled together, and with the assumption that the topic had been dropped, I pushed myself from the table and prepared to stand up. That was when I noticed Liz with her chin still resting on her hand; she was glaring at me with a little smile and an accusing look in her eyes.

"What?" I asked, tilting my head to the side.

"So, you *do* like him?"

"What?" I repeated with exasperation. She raised her eyebrows and gave me that little telltale smile that told me she knew the deepest secrets of my soul. "I said he was attractive, Liz. I didn't say I wanted to marry him."

She shrugged and pulled her gaze away from me. The table was apparently more interesting. "Okay … but maybe you jumping his bones was a sign that you're ready to, you know, move on."

"Liz, I'm *not* ready. *Definitely* not ready. I think about Stephen too much to move on. I *miss* him too much to move on."

I expected maybe a bit of arguing from her, but I didn't expect for her to laugh. It was a condescending, sniffling sort of laugh. The kind that suggested she knew better than me. It was also the kind that made me want to pull her hair and run home to my mom, but I refused to stoop to that level of immaturity. So instead I asked what the hell was so funny.

"The thing is, I think you *are* ready and that's why subconsciously you decided to throw yourself at this guy." She watched me for a few moments, I guess waiting to see if I would explode in her face at the accusation. When I didn't so much as blink, she boldly added, "I think maybe you were hoping it would be a little more than just one little hook-up."

"Or maybe I just haven't gotten laid in a year and a half, and Brandon is obscenely hot," I pointed out.

"Ooh, it's Brandon now, huh?" Esther teased.

We both ignored the old woman while Liz went on. "Please, that's not you. You might want that to be you, but it's not. Even if in the moment you wanted to sleep with him, there was a part of you that really wanted the … I don't know—the companionship, I guess, of being in a relationship. I mean, you made a connection with him before you kissed him. You said you talked for hours. So, maybe you were acting more on *that* and not just the supposed fact that he's hot."

Oh, little sister, there's nothing "supposed" *about it.*

I shifted uncomfortably in my seat, touching my lips absentmindedly. I could still feel the coarse stubble of his facial hair raking against my skin as our lips massaged each other in a way that makes movie-goers breathless and long for something like that of their own. There had been something more there. Something that seemed to come from somewhere in my gut.

Something that said it was right, and not just because it felt so damn good.

Unless it was just something I had conjured up due to being so damn vulnerable, which was certainly a possibility—no, *more* than a possibility.

I sighed, dropping my hand to the table and rolling my lips between my teeth, erasing the ghost of his mouth on mine. Maybe Liz was right. But maybe, instead of a boyfriend, all I needed was a companion, a *friend*. After all, aside from him being an incredible kisser, the most memorable part of the night was the conversation. The way he talked to me as though he had known me forever. The way he listened as though I were the only other person on the planet.

He had made me feel important. When was the last time someone had made me feel that way?

Maybe he's exactly the friend I need. If we can move beyond our near-sex experience.

***

"'There once was a spoon named Spoony.'"

Anna was curled up on the floor at my feet, her head propped comfortably on Giraffe. She slept soundly, and thus granted me with a break that was more needed than usual.

Anna had started her day by rolling out of bed and onto the floor with a thud. I made an educated guess that the rude awakening was an indication of what the rest of our day would be like. And as luck would have it, I had been proven right shortly after, when she refused to eat anything for breakfast unless it was cake. I caved and compromised with a doughnut, hoping that she would be in a better mood once food was in her belly. But our morning had been filled with whining and a refusal to get dressed without an appropriate amount of struggle.

People don't give child care providers enough credit.

With my own book laid out on my lap, I found myself spacing out and staring blankly ahead of me at the walls of shelves, stuffed with books. Each one seemed to melt into the other as I drifted peacefully into a memory of Stephen taking me on a hunt for a book he wanted to buy for his brother's birthday. It was such a trivial memory, painfully mundane, but those were some of my favorite moments with him. I could still see the playful smile as he leaned in to kiss me between the shelves, the way his hands slid along my arms to interlock his fingers with mine. The smile had never left his lips when he backed away, his hands still holding mine. He looked into my eyes, said, "Holly, I love you more than anything."

Stop it, Holly.

I shook my head, tossing the memory away with a determination to keep him from plaguing my mind. I picked up my book with a determination to stop torturing myself by enjoying some dirty talk between the big-bosomed Caroline and her well-endowed stable boy.

A large hand on my shoulder pulled me from the pages, and with a startled jolt, I turned to see Brandon kneeling next to me with two cups from the café balancing in his free hand. A pair of Ray Bans were shielding me from seeing his mesmerizing blue eyes, but that was just as well, I thought. Between the raunchiness of the book and the memory of my hands in his hair, I wasn't sure I'd be able to stop myself from crossing *Have Sex on a Bean Bag Chair* off my Bucket List.

"Are you stalking me?" I laughed nervously, surprised by his seemingly impeccable timing.

"Is it that obvious?" he asked with a smile. To my surprise, he handed me one of the cups. "I saw you sitting over here. Thought I'd grab you a cup of your leaf water."

I thanked him with a playful roll of my eyes. I was touched, and took a sip from the steaming cup: lavender Earl Grey. "You remembered."

"I have a good memory," he said, and shoved a hand through his hair.

My eyes narrowed as a smile played on my lips. "So, uh, you're here a lot for someone I've never seen before."

"I was away for a few months, so that's probably why you never saw me before," Brandon said casually, sitting down with his back against the shelf behind us. He outstretched his long legs, crossing one over the other, and took the glasses off. "I probably left just as you were moving in."

He was making himself comfortable, I realized, and I eagerly stuffed my book in my bag. "So, you're *not* stalking me?"

"Nope," he said with a slow shake of his head, and pushed a hand through his hair.

"Very convenient," I said in a low voice before taking a sip of my tea.

"Hey." He pointed a finger at me, the corner of his mouth twitching. "Seizing the opportunity to spend time with you does not constitute as stalking."

"Fair enough," I laughed, and let the topic die.

Jessie droned on with the book she had chosen about a handful of utensils on an adventure to the dishwasher. Would I have been rude to pull my book back out, I wondered as I yawned. Brandon noticed, and stifled a laugh.

"So, you love this as much as she does, huh?" He gestured towards Anna, still sleeping peacefully at my feet.

I snorted, already aware of how absurd it was that I spent forty minutes in a bean bag chair while she slept. But, I explained, it was a guaranteed nap for her and a surefire way for me to get some time to myself, even if it did mean being trapped in one spot while I listened to some of the worst stories I had ever heard.

"So, you're saying you don't love the classic tale of Spoony and his trusty companion Forky?"

I laughed at that, harder than was necessary, and told him a monkey could write a better story. A few of the other adults turned to shush us and we whispered our apologies before silently giggling like a couple of misbehaving kids. For another ten minutes, we sat there together, listening intently and making faces at each other at the cheesier parts.

When Story Time was adjourned, we stayed there on the area rug as the other kids and their accompanying adults fled the scene. Anna was still sleeping, and instead of waking her up as I normally would, I decided to take the time to enjoy his company.

Brandon combed a hand through his hair and completely against my will, my mind replayed a moment where I did that very act to those very strands of hair.

"So," he said, as he pulled his legs to his chest and clasped his hands together around his knees, "I wanted to talk to you, but I really suck at crap like this. I didn't want to make things awkward, so I'm just going to come out and say it, and we can go from there, okay?"

"Okay …" My chest tightened, and I expected the worst.

His brow was furrowed, squinting his oceanic blue eyes in frustration while my stomach practiced its cartwheels. "I don't want to make a big deal out of it, but I did want to say I'm sorry for what happened the other night. It *definitely* shouldn't have happened."

I turned away from him, pretending to check on the sleeping Anna while my self-esteem cracked a little deeper. I mean, I didn't think I was *that* horrible of a kisser, for crying out loud, and he certainly seemed to enjoy himself while it lasted.

But let's not forget that Stephen is now gay.

"Well," I said coldly, keeping my eyes on the rise and fall of Anna's chest and trying not to feel too hurt by someone I hardly knew. "I'm not sure how to take that."

Brandon turned to me then, a line forming across his forehead, and if I hadn't known better, I would have thought someone just slapped him across the face. I felt my mission had been accomplished. "Oh, come on, Holly. You know what I mean. I was out of line. You were vulnerable, and it shouldn't have … It should not have gone as far as it did."

I turned to him, softening my expression. "Well, it wasn't like I didn't enjoy it while it lasted," I said with a playful smile, lightening the atmosphere. "And don't forget, I kissed you first."

He surprised me by blushing, averting his eyes to the floor. With the opportunity presented, I allowed myself a quick glance at the soft lips I had the pleasure of enjoying just a few nights before. I smiled to myself, knowing that I was going to always remember the time I made out with a man who could have passed for the hottest member of a popular boyband.

"I remember," he sighed, looking back at me, and that little half-smile made an appearance. He raised his cup of coffee. "Friends?"

I tapped mine against it. "Friends."

And there it was. The nail in the coffin. I couldn't help feeling the whole thing was a little bittersweet, in a pathetic sort of way. I barely knew him and I was actually sad that I would never kiss him again or tangle my fingers in his hair. But the conversation continued with him moving right into asking me what I was reading, and I settled into the comfortable way I could just be with him. He teased me for spending money on drugstore romance novels, and with a roll of my eyes, I thought, this is a good thing.

No, scratch that.

The best thing.

8
holly

I STARED ANGRILY AT MY PHONE'S CALENDAR.

It had been four months since Stephen had left me. It was almost funny to me that I could so vividly remember the day he crushed every semblance of my self-worth, self-confidence, and self-esteem, and yet … I could hardly remember the sound of his voice or the way he smelled right after a shower. My entire life with him had become some faraway land that had stopped feeling real. Nothing more than hazy memories, maybe even dreams, and it was awful not remembering what I still missed so much.

Camille climbed onto the bed to flop down on my chest, licking my chin once she had settled. I smiled sleepily, scratching behind her ears.

"At least I have you to kiss me good morning," I mumbled, my voice weighed down by the lingering sleep.

Rolling out of bed, I left my room and headed into the kitchen to find Liz sitting at her laptop with her hands wrapped around a steaming mug of tea. She looked up through her thick-rimmed glasses and gave me a bright smile.

"Wow, you're up! Good morning," she said cheerfully.

I grumbled my reply, temporarily hating her for possessing the ability to be chipper in the morning. I slumped into a chair next to her at the table and spotted the box of doughnuts.

Without bothering to use my words, I pointed at the box and by means of sister-to-sister telepathy, she knew exactly what I meant and grabbed the very doughnut I wanted.

"Thank you," I said through a mouthful of iced pastry. "Anna happy to see her dad?"

"Well, of course, because he's the *fun* parent," she said nonchalantly before taking a long sip of her tea and then proceeded to smack her lips. "He and Heather are taking Anna to that new trampoline place today. I warned him about giving her anything to eat beforehand, but let's see if he actually listens." She snorted a laugh and fidgeted with a strand of her blonde hair, probably fantasizing about Anna throwing up all over Mark's new Nikes. "I should've told Heather instead, but she was busy with Jacob. God, he's getting so big."

I never understood how Liz could so easily carry on a relationship with her cheating ex-husband and his mistress-turned-wife. She had once told me it was because of Anna, but I sometimes questioned if they would've remained friends regardless.

Some bonds can't be broken, even after they've gotten a little bruised and ugly, and seeing the grin on her face, I wondered if I could ever reach a point of being friends with Stephen again.

I snorted a laugh to chase that ridiculous thought away.

"Anyway," Liz said, "I saw Esther outside and told her we'd help pull some weeds for her today."

I shot her a disbelieving look as I popped the rest of the doughnut into my mouth. "Is she okay with that?"

Liz grunted a laugh. "Oh, hell no, but I'm afraid she's going to break an arm one of these days with the way she yanks at those things, and I don't know about you, but I'm really not up to helping her apply her bunion cream."

"Or the hemorrhoid cream," I added with a shudder and left the table to get dressed.

***

Esther's backyard had been off-limits to her for years since realizing she could no longer handle the stairs off her back deck. When I told her that my dad is a carpenter and perfectly capable of whipping up a nice ramp for her, she shooed the very concept away, insisting she wasn't old enough for a fucking ramp and that she wouldn't even know what to do with a yard that big, anyway.

So her enjoyment of the outdoors was limited to the front yard, where she kept a few raised box gardens against the front of the house full of perennial plants her son Robert had brought over for Mother's Day one year. Her lawn and shrubbery were meticulously kept by a gardener Robert paid monthly, keeping the place looking neat until the next time. But it was the time in between that was the problem.

"Esther, I'm not seeing any weeds," I whined from my hands and knees, looking underneath a large juniper bush.

"Oh yeah?" She jabbed the tip of her cane towards something next to my hand. "Then what do you call that?"

Sighing, I held the maple leaf up. "A leaf, Esther. I call it a leaf."

She let out a huff. "Get rid of the damn thing. That Ricardo always misses *something*. I don't know why Robert wastes his money. I tell him there's always leaves all over the place after that man has left." Liz and I exchanged a look after searching the yard for any other rogue leaves. There were *maybe* two, and that was including the one I held. "You girls want some cookies? I have a fresh batch inside."

"*Of course*, she does," Liz whispered to me, pouting as she pinched at her nonexistent muffin top.

"Oh, yes, you're so fat," I mumbled, not bothering to mention that my heavily elasticized yoga pants were starting to cut into my sides.

We followed Esther into the house, making sure to smile at the picture of her late husband Harry hanging above the TV. I had once forgotten to and she threatened to send his spirit to haunt me while I was trying to shower. Harry was apparently quite the pervert and wouldn't argue with that type of arrangement, she insisted, and to spare myself the possibility of seeing apparitions in a foggy bathroom mirror, I never forgot to acknowledge the man of the house again.

Walking through her dated house, her furniture potential candidates for a display in the Smithsonian, we entered the dining room as she tottered into the kitchen to retrieve the cookies. We waited without a single word, each of us taking a seat at the old wooden table that seated more people than she saw most months out of the year.

Esther loved telling tales of how she would once host family get-togethers on a regular basis for her sisters, her husband's siblings, and all their families. But once everybody started leaving, whether in death or a change in location, the get-togethers slowed to hardly ever at all. Even her son would pick her up and take her out to his place in Brooklyn whenever the family did get together, so her home sat, full of memories without any hope of creating new ones.

"How's work, Elizabeth?" Esther said, carrying in a plate of oatmeal raisin cookies.

Reaching to take them from her, Liz said, "Oh, you know, the usual. Dr. Martin recently took on a whole new set of patients after I told him to put that ad in the paper; which is good, except Debbie decided to leave after having the baby. So, I've been handling these new patient files and these different insurance companies, and I know it doesn't *sound* like a big deal, but I think I might be going insane." She took a bite of her cookie and with a shake of her head, she added, "I'm actually regretting the whole 'ad in the paper' thing."

Esther shoved a napkin toward Liz as the crumbs dropped to the table's surface. "Elizabeth, I just wiped this table down." My sister hurriedly apologized and swept the cookie debris into the napkin. "If Debbie left and you're taking on her workload, doesn't that mean more money for you?"

"My hours haven't changed so, no." Liz sighed with a roll of her eyes. "Dr. Martin promised that I'd be getting a raise at the end of the year, but we'll see about that."

Esther waved her hands in the air. "Oh no, honey. If your workload is changing because that tart Debbie went and got herself knocked up, never to return to work again, then you deserve more money. Put your damn foot down."

"She's not a *tart*, Esther. She's been married for a few years now."

"But is it her husband's baby?" Esther eyed Liz with a raised wispy eyebrow, and I choked as I took a bite of a cookie she must have baked just for me. Esther knew how much I loved oatmeal raisin.

"I'm not asking for a paternity test," Liz groaned. "But anyway, I know you're right. I just like my job. I don't want to piss Dr. Martin off."

"You won't," Esther insisted before turning to me, deciding that Liz's work discussion was no longer of interest to her. "And you. What's going on with that guy?"

Liz turned to me with her mouth hung open, suddenly remembering she had forgotten to bring Brandon up with me again. "Oh, that's *right*. Have you seen him? What was his name?"

My eyes rolled. "His name is Brandon, and yeah, I've seen him. I saw him the other day, and I was declared a friend, which is what I wanted, so … The end."

"So, what's your next move?" Liz asked, resting her chin in the palm of her hand.

"I don't have one?" I questioned, unaware that my love life was meant to be treated like a game of chess.

The truth was, I didn't exactly know where to go from there. I wasn't exactly able to get out of the house and meet men who weren't already married with children, and I had no interest in that scruffy barista Scott. Brandon had declared we were to be friends, and not the kind with benefits, and I wasn't too keen on the idea of cruising the bars on the weekend in hopes of getting lucky.

Check mate.

Esther shook her head with disappointment. "I would have at the very least made sure I got my hands in that guy's pants. Men don't turn down sex if you're persistent, or at least in my experience, and he sounded like a good one to take for a ride."

"Oh, my *God*," I groaned, never looking away from Liz, as though ignoring Esther's grotesque comments would get her to stop.

"You're disgusting," Liz shot at the woman, who only shrugged in response and made sure her dentures were securely in place before grabbing a cookie. "*Anyway*, have you thought about checking the internet? Debbie found her husband on there a few years ago, and that was a one-and-done deal. She met the first guy that messaged her, fell in love with him, and they were married within the year."

"Sounds like settling," I mumbled skeptically.

Liz rolled her eyes with a tired sigh. "It happens, Holly. Sometimes you just *know* when it's right, especially when you're older. You stop wanting to waste time—and hey, at least they're happy. That's more than I can say for you."

I had been hoping she wouldn't mention the internet. I knew it was becoming more and more common, and I had known people at *Teen Queen* who had met their significant others on various websites, but there was something that just didn't sit right for me. It seemed like a pathological liar's playground, or a wonderful way for a serial killer to lure his victims into his dingy old van before trucking them away to some remote dungeon.

"I don't know," I groaned. "It'd be my luck to set myself up with a guy who uses a picture of Ryan Gosling but really looks like a hairy potato."

Liz eyed me through her long eyelashes. "You *know* what Ryan Gosling looks like. You wouldn't willingly go out with a guy who used his picture."

"Who's Ryan Gosling?" Esther chimed in, her ears pricking at the sound of a man's name. She rubbed her hands together as though she were about to feast on a fine meal. "Is he handsome?"

"I think Esther's the one who needs to get laid, not me," I laughed before taking another bite of cookie. Liz laughed with a nod.

"You're right about that," Esther agreed with a disappointed shake of her head. "The sex isn't nearly as good since Harry became a ghost."

***

"I don't know about this," I groaned to myself, staring at the screen and suddenly feeling nauseated by the lovey-dovey mushiness staring back at me.

The website in front of me displayed a slideshow of happy couples. One smiling couple shared a milkshake while sitting side saddle back-to-back on a carousel horse. Another pair were clearly on a camping trip, roasting marshmallows; their hands overlapping on the same stick. It was cheesy, and while none of those particular activities enticed me to the point of jealousy, I had to admit I wished I had someone to at least hold hands with. Just maybe not on a sandy beach with a sundae.

Under a banner encouraging single men and women to sign up, there was a big glowing button reading "CLICK ME," and I suddenly felt like Alice after making her grand entrance in Wonderland. But despite my reluctance, I clicked. I half expected for the page to load with a caterpillar smoking a pipe, asking "huh-ooo" I was, which would've been a lot more exciting than the questionnaire that popped up instead.

First name: Holly.
Last name (optional): I opted out.
Date of birth: 1/28/1985.

Have you ever been married? No. No thanks to my ex-boyfriend and his lover.

Do you have kids? Want them? No and yes.

Where do you live? Long Island, NY. No way in hell I was putting down the town I lived in for these nut jobs to come find me and leave hair clippings on my front stoop.

What is your ideal first date? I'm not into bars, clubs, carousels, or walks on the beach, but I really like a good book and a good cup of tea, so a bookstore and a café sounds like a plan to me. I figured that would really reel the guys in.

Tell us a bit about yourself: I'm a 31yo woman living on Long Island with my sister and her kid, because my ex-boyfriend decided I wasn't man enough for him and left me for his boss. Oh, work? Nah, I don't do that either, in the conventional sense. My ex-boss fired me because I'm apparently too much of a grandma to write romantic advice for teenagers, so I babysit my sister's kid full-time in exchange for room and board. Fun work stories? Probably not gonna get 'em from this gal. I had a good chuckle at my own expense, and knowing that wouldn't do a whole lot for me, I hit the backspace key until the space was empty once again. *Hi, I'm Holly. I'm 31 years old. I hope there's someone out there who loves sitcoms, cats, books, and tea as much as I do. Could that be you?*

After submitting the form, the site prompted me to upload a picture of myself (also optional), and to create a username and password (mandatory). I found an old college picture of me dressed as a witch for Halloween. Lame, but hey, it's what I had on hand and it was better than me making some pathetic attempt at taking a decent selfie.

The final step was to create a username. I thought about it for a moment. It seemed so important, like this was the finishing touch that would seal my fate. Would I find a prince, or would I find a toad? Would I make myself enticing or would I find myself a place at the bottom of the barrel? There was so much pressure and I couldn't decide, so I just picked my old AOL username: HollyCatLover28.

"You're gonna be a hard one to sell," I laughed to myself as I completed my profile, and waited, not bothering to hold my breath.

9
holly

I HAD SCOURED THE PAGES upon pages of men, browsing as though they were shoes. Except instead of shoes, I was looking at countless pictures of usually half-naked men. Some of them really should have kept their shirts on, while others I was convinced didn't *really* look that good, and James had been one of the latter.

His picture looked like a professional headshot of a successfully dishonest politician, and convinced that he was *somebody*, I checked out his profile. I learned that he was the owner of a few local businesses, restaurants namely, and apparently loaded. Although I wasn't convinced I would be the type of person he'd go out with, I decided in a moment of optimism to give it a shot and messaged him.

To my surprise, he replied and asked if I'd like to go out with him to Bankers, one of the fanciest steakhouses on Long Island, and I said yes without hesitation.

Bankers is not just any steakhouse. It's a "fifty dollars for a steak the size of your eyeball" type of steakhouse. Only the wealthiest people on Long Island could afford to eat there on a regular basis, and the rest of us just had to settle for gathering around the back door of the kitchen to savor the wafts of searing beef. But not this girl. No, this girl was going to check it out first hand, and a hot stud named James was going to make that happen.

Assuming he's really a hot stud and not a troll taking the day off from tolling bridges.

"What do *you* know about online dating?" I had rolled my eyes at Brandon earlier in the day, after he had scoffed at the sheer thought of me having a date.

"Uh, enough to know that you could be going on a date with the Zodiac Killer. I hope you're at least packing pepper spray," he said as he took a sip of his coffee while I stared with horror. "Oh, I'm sorry. Should I trust that this guy is *really* a rich business-owner with the looks of a dashing Disney Prince? That's a pretty cliché story to tell to lure gullible women into his house of horrors."

"*I'm* not gullible," I stated defiantly, more to convince myself than him.

"Whatever you say, pal." Brandon took another sip of coffee.

While I had wanted to laugh and get back to a dirty scene between a French maid and the Duke she served, I couldn't shake the idea that maybe he was right. I had been so excited by the prospect of a date with an attractive, successful man that I hadn't stopped to wonder if I was setting myself up to die in a basement torture chamber.

Brandon had opened his own book but caught my distressed expression before he began reading. Laughing, he said. "Holly, relax. I'm joking."

Jessie had sat down in her chair and was preparing to read her chosen stories. Anna was well on her way to La La Land, and as soon as I lifted my book to begin reading, I placed it back down in my lap, unable to let it go.

"No, really, do you think I should be worried?"

Brandon reached over, barely touching my hand, and I scolded myself for melting just a little at his touch. The intense sincerity held within his eyes wasn't helping either. "No. I think it'll be just fine, and if it's not, I promise I will kick his ass."

"Oh, I'm not sure you could. You haven't seen what he looks like." I had laughed, feeling a little more at ease again, as though his promised protection could keep me from being shackled to the walls of a cellar.

"I don't give a shit what he looks like. I will kick his ass if he so much as looks at you the wrong way."

That's all a woman needs to hear to swoon, and oh, I did. But just a little.

I thought about his comments about killers and houses of horror when Esther had tottered over later on, with mugs of tea in hand. I gave her the juicy details about the date, as her eyes wrinkled up in delight at the thought of dining at Bankers. She treated it as though it were a magical, far-off land, and I guess for many of us, it was.

"Well," Esther said, finishing off the last of her tea. "It's time for me to hobble my way back home. Have fun on your date, and by *fun*, I mean ..." She winked, and I rolled my eyes to the ceiling. "Hey, he's rich," she stated, as though that made a difference.

"Oh, my God," I groaned and pushed her out the door. "I don't think him having money has any effect on how well he performs in bed."

"Christ almighty, when he stinks of money, it doesn't matter how well he *performs.* Have I taught you nothing?"

***

"Okay," Liz said, clapping her hands together. "We need to find you something to wear. You can't just go in yoga pants and a sweatshirt. You need a dress or something."

A perk of being one half of a kind of, up-and-coming "power couple" was having the privilege of attending my share of black tie events, where it was necessary to wear gowns that could have comfortably been worn by Kate Middleton. I held onto them after my move back to Long Island, and one happened to be this stunning floor-length black satin dress with a sweetheart neckline. Black Swarovski crystals were sprinkled over the bust line, falling into a gradient towards the waist.

It might have been just a little too much for Bankers, but fuck it. It was my first date since Stephen, and I was going to rock the hell out of it in any way I could.

Once I had managed to shimmy my way into the dress, I stood back and admired myself in the mirror. Camille purred her agreement as I mumbled, "Wow, I look freakin' hot right now." I did a little twirl, careful to not step on the dragging hem and dammit, I felt like royalty.

Step aside, Middleton.

Princess Holly freakin' Hughes is in the house.

There was a nagging memory trying to pull its way into the spotlight of my mind. The memory of the last time I had gotten myself dressed up for an occasion—the night I was meant to be engaged to Stephen. But just as it reared its ugly head, I pushed it back down with everything I had. I wasn't going to let this night be ruined, and especially not by *him*.

With my strappy black stilettos buckled up and my makeup done just right, I emerged from my room and walked down the hall to find Liz and Anna standing there in the living room, wearing smiles from ear to ear. If I had gone to prom, I imagined this is probably what it would've felt like. For a moment, I felt like my parents were missing some momentous occasion and thought maybe we should call them over to take some embarrassing pictures for the family photo album.

"You look so pretty, but …" Liz hurried to fuss with my hair and all I could do was roll my eyes. She pinned my hair up into a messy French Twist, insisting that the messy look was sexy and would guarantee me a spot in his boudoir.

"You people are obsessed with me getting laid," I noted.

Liz shrugged. "I just want to see you happy, and if that's what's gonna do it, then—" She shrugged again. "Now, go. He's going to be waiting for you."

Liz rushed me out the door and waved as I made my way to Ol' Rusty, my chariot for the evening. Where was my fairy godmother to turn that thing into a golden carriage pulled by unicorns?

I released a long, heavy sigh and realized there was no turning back now. My stomach did a flip in response and I prayed I wouldn't throw up.

***

So, there I was, puttering along Main Street; the muffler announcing my presence before the van was in view of anybody. I prayed to God I could find a parking space far, *far* away from the restaurant, and I could just walk there. I mean, I had lived in the freakin' city for over a decade, for crying out loud. I could handle a little clumsy walk in some heels. There was just no way this guy was going to see me driving this hunk of metal that was more than likely evaporating by the second under my own ass.

I pulled around back to see if there was any parking available that wasn't too close for the van to be an embarrassment, and just as I spotted a space, a young man knocked on the window.

With the touch of a button, the window groaned its way down, and for some reason, I felt compelled to speak to him as though I were someone of importance. I had the sneaking suspicion that my ride was blowing my cover. "Yes, my good man?"

He smiled apologetically. "Sorry, ma'am, I didn't mean to startle you." I wasn't sure I gave the impression that I had been startled. "I'll be taking your minivan from here."

The kid just had to remind me that I'm not sitting in a Porsche.

I felt my cheeks flush with humiliation. "What do you mean? Where are you taking my car?"

He smiled again, this time with amusement. I suddenly felt stupid. I was going to be that lady he laughed about later with his buddies, I just knew it. "Valet parking, ma'am. You can't go beyond this point, but if you just leave your keys with me, I'll park for you. I'll give you a ticket with a number, and—"

"Yes, I think I know what valet parking is, *thank you*," I snapped. Did he think I just crawled out from under a rock?

But, I realized, my tone had been harsh, and I muttered a brief apology. It had been a very long time since I blew the dust off my "first date" card and I was stressed.

"It's okay, but, uh, ma'am?"

Gripping the steering wheel tightly, my knuckles turned white, and I glanced in the rearview mirror to see a line forming behind me. My eyes widened in horror.

God, now they'll all see me get out of this damn thing and they'll know that the lady in the long black satin gown is driving a rusty old Mom Mobile. What if one of those people behind me is James? What if I don't get my pea-sized gourmet filet mignon?

The young man cleared his throat awkwardly and I turned my attention back to him, faking a smile and pulling the keys from the ignition. Slowly, I opened the door and as I tried to carefully exit without falling flat on my ass, I stepped on the hem of my dress, almost pulling the thing down off my chest. Before I could suffer a serious wardrobe malfunction, I quickly remedied my situation and adjusted my dress.

Bless his heart, the kid pretended to not notice.

Taking the keys from me, he smiled politely and handed me a ticket. "Just give this back to me when you're ready to leave."

I glanced back at Ol' Rusty. "If I slip you a fifty, will you pretend to steal this thing and drive it into a ditch somewhere?"

***

The smiling hostess asked me if I was meeting someone.

"Oh, uh, yes," I said absentmindedly, as my eyes rolled upward to look at the chandelier above my head. She asked if I had his name. "His name? Not his last name, no…"

The smile never left her face. "Well," she said, looking down at the list of names in front of her, "do you have a first name?"

"Of course, I have a first name," I chuckled, marveling at the multicolored crystals. "I'm Holly."

"Holly, Holly, Holly …" she mumbled under her breath, her finger scanning the names down the list. "I'm sorry, there's no Holly listed here …"

My stomach flipped, and I felt the beginnings of panic settle in. "W-what?"

"Do you have the first name of the man you're meeting?" She spoke slowly, obviously thinking I was a fool, and she would have been right.

"Oh! Oh, yes. His name is James."

I vowed to never enter a fancy restaurant again as she scanned the list once again.

"Ah, yes, here we are. He's already been seated, so if you'll follow me please …"

I checked my dress, making sure it was still sitting comfortably on top of my chest and not below it as she guided me through a pair of stained glass French doors into a room more dimly lit than the one before it. The sounds of clanging utensils and clinking glasses filled the room as we weaved through what felt like dozens of tables, and then, I saw him, and my heart decided to wedge itself in my throat.

Now, you know those books that will just prattle on about how gorgeous some guy is, and after you've read seventeen descriptive paragraphs about his beautiful hair and perfect body, you just start to skim because first of all, no man could possibly be that good looking, and second of all, oh my God, you get it already?

Well, if someone decided to write a freakin' book about this guy, they could have written seventeen *chapters* about how gorgeous he was, and it would have been totally justified. I would have read every single word, and I would have agreed with every sentence of it, because I had never seen a man more beautiful than that one right there.

He was ever so slightly sun-kissed, enough to give him some color, and I was silently grateful that he wasn't sporting one of those nasty orange fake tans. His dark brown hair was slicked back, and my God, he was so much better looking than his picture.

The hostess extended her arm, allowing me to walk ahead of her towards the table, as she said with a smile, "Your server will be with you shortly. Enjoy your meal."

I quietly thanked her and turned my attention towards the table. I shook away any last bit of doubt and inadequacy, and sauntered my way over to that table, making sure to exaggerate the sway of my hips. I was going to win this man over if it was the last thing I did.

Once I was standing next to the table, I could smell the heavy musk of his cologne. I wasn't a fan of men who liked to bathe in the stuff, but this only seemed to add to his masculine aura and made him just that much more attractive. I wanted him to feel the same about me so desperately, and I leaned over just a little, exposing as much cleavage as humanly possible. I felt just the slightest bit desperate, but if all this night resulted in was a good roll in the sand, I would've been satisfied with knowing that I had a one-night stand with God's actual gift to women.

That was when he looked up, and sweet Jesus, his eyes were the iciest shade of blue I had ever seen. I was almost scared that, as he stared at me, he was really sucking my soul from my body through his eye sockets. But then again, I was also kind of okay with my soul belonging to him for all of eternity.

I gazed into his eyes as a big smile slowly stretched across my lips. I leaned forward just a little bit more, bringing my face a little closer to his, close enough for me to feel his breath on my face. I could have kissed him right then and there, because I was apparently in the habit of kissing strangers. But I just lingered there for a moment before saying in my huskiest and sexiest of voices, "You must be James."

His eyes stared into mine for just a few seconds before scanning my body. I felt like the sluttiest version of myself as I slowly stood up straight, allowing him one last chance to stare at my less than impressive cleavage. He brought his hand up to rub the scruff on his chin in exaggerated thought as he looked me up and down one last time, as though he were buying a mare from an auction, and tingles were sent down my spine.

But as exhilarating as those moments kind of were, I wasn't totally sure what I should be doing. Was I supposed to pull out my own chair and sit? Was he going to get up and do it for me? Should I have just told him to skip dinner and go straight for dessert back at his place? I had jumped in feeling overly confident, but I hadn't thought this far into the plan.

I waited for what felt like an eternity while he continued to eye every inch of me, and my surge of sexy confidence quickly faded into discomfort. Was that my fault? Did I lay it on too thick? Was I too hot for my own good? I had no idea, but I knew I had enough of the mental undressing, so I began to pull out my own chair.

That's when he finally spoke, and I was startled by how deep and raspy, yet somehow smooth, his voice was; it suited him perfectly. He could have sold me a pile of dog crap with a voice like that.

I was so taken aback by just how perfect he was that I didn't hear what he said.

I smiled again and asked, "What was that?"

He held his hand up, signaling me to stop what I was doing. "I *said*, no need."

I chose to ignore his impatient tone and sharply inhaled as my stomach suddenly erupted in a swarm of butterflies. I knew what this meant. He wanted to skip dinner and go straight to dessert. I asked myself if I was ready for this kind of thing to happen, to which I answered, *yes*. This was exactly the kind of thing I wanted to happen.

I took my hand from the back of the chair, resting it on my hip. "And what do you mean by that, mister?"

Mister?

He pushed his chair out, plopped his cloth napkin on the table when it was just moments before in his lap, and said, "I *mean*, there's no need for this to continue."

Sexy Holly left in an instant, leaving Plain Ol' Holly in her place with her mouth hanging open in shock. "But ... but why?"

"*Well*." He cleared his throat and straightened his tie, and before speaking, he sighed impatiently, like I was an annoying little kid. "If you *really* must know, I wasn't too thrilled about taking a *babysitter* on a date, but I thought you were kind of cute." He looked me over again, then twisted his face into one of sheer disgust with a quick shake of his head. "Let's just say, your picture looked better. Now, if you'll excuse me ..."

He walked right past me, purposefully averting his eyes from ever landing on me again. He left me standing there, with my heart feeling as though it had broken all over again, and all I could do was pull out my chair and stare blankly at the space across from me. When the waiter came to take my order, I opened my mouth to ask him to please go away, but all that came out was the beginning of an onslaught of tears. I watched him awkwardly rush away on lanky legs to get some help for the crazy woman at table #14.

The hostess arrived at my side a few moments later, and taking my arm, she quietly asked for me to come with her to the bathroom. We sat on the couch in the sitting area of the ladies' room, with her arm around my shoulders, and it turned out that Judy with the constant smile was a good listener, almost as good as Brandon minus the parking lot make out session, and I greatly appreciated that.

I also appreciated the complimentary slice of layered chocolate cake.

Thanks, Judy.

10

brandon

MY LAPTOP SAT ON THE aluminum table top in the café of Reade's. Scott had brought over cup after steaming cup of black coffee to keep the fire burning, but what he didn't know was that I didn't even have the kindling to get the flames going in the first place. With every delivery, he asked how it was going and every time I grinned with feigned enthusiasm. "It's coming along, man," I'd say, and send him on his way, not having the heart to tell him that not only was I struggling to get anything down but I really would have preferred he just left me alone.

Nick had continued his badgering, because it was his job. When he asked what the hell had been wrong with me, I just told him I was finding it harder to find the inspiration to write. But the truth was, I had found an entirely different type of inspiration that made me want to push the story in a different direction, but I couldn't have found it at a worse time.

I leaned back in the chair, tipping it on its back legs. With my fingers laced behind my head, I glared angrily at the words I had typed that night. All of them felt like puzzle pieces that had been forced to fit somewhere they weren't supposed to go, and through my frustration, I angrily held down the backspace until they had disappeared entirely. That left me at 81,236 words, and dammit, what I would have given to have my bottle of Scotch magically appear before me in that moment.

The sound of the front door jingling open provided me with a welcomed distraction, and I turned to see the bane of my existence walking toward me in what I could only describe as a death march. She was a vision of vampiric elegance in the black dress; a jolt struck me in the heart and other neglected places of my body at the hint of milky white skin through the slit that went up to her thigh. Her hair framed her face in darkness, and I couldn't remember if I had ever seen it out of a ponytail.

I wanted nothing else than to take more than a moment basking in her enigmatic beauty, but I couldn't draw my eyes away from the makeup streaked along her cheeks as my blood reached a point beyond boiling.

Acting as the Knight in Shining Armor to her Damsel in Distress, I stood up to impulsively wrap my arms around her. Pressing my cheek against the top of her head, my thoughts ran angry circles around that instinctive part of my brain, screaming at me to protect her.

I will kill him. I will throw my entire fucking life away and kill him. I will find him and break every fucking bone in his body and I. Will. Kill. Him.

She took a step back after several moments, wiping her hands against her face frantically before wrapping her arms around herself with a shiver. Her shoulders and back were exposed, and I took my jacket off to drape it over her. She thanked me, pushing her arms through the sleeves, and when they had a moment to focus on the sight before her, her dark eyes widened.

"Wow," she said breathlessly, sniffling the last bit of her tears, looking over the tattoos that I realized she had never seen. "How many do you have?"

I struggled a laugh, still seething. "I've lost count."

Her hands went to my arms; a grateful disruption to whatever was happening in her mind, as she rolled the short sleeves of my t-shirt to the shoulders. I felt frozen with excitement as her hands ran over my bicep, and I saw her lick her lips before letting them part.

She swallowed, and moved her hands away, stepping back to stare for a moment. "Do you only have these?"

Aware suddenly of Scott's boisterous singing from behind us, I glanced over my shoulder to see him with his back turned, buffing away at the espresso machine. I pulled the collar of my t-shirt down just a bit, revealing a little peek of the stone lion's head that encompassed the right side of my chest, and then turned around and lifted the hem, exposing half of the piece that blanketed my entire back. I had to remind myself to breathe as her eyes stared at the skull that covered most of my lower back; the lower jaw disappearing under the waistband of my jeans. My heart jumped and my flesh goose-pimpled, startled by the touch of her hands against the sensitive skin, and dammit, my pants strangled my groin as she pulled my shirt up further, giving her a full view of the raven carrying a crown in its talons, spanning the width of my upper back and shoulders.

It was the closest I had gotten to a woman disrobing me in over five years, and my cheeks flamed with the reminder of how exhilarating it could feel to be touched.

"*Jesus*," she said quietly with awe. "Don't take this the wrong way, but um, you look ..." She cleared her throat and swallowed. "You look really good."

Oh, but I wanted to take that the "wrong way," if there was such a thing, and after hearing the compliment countless times before, it had never sounded sweeter.

"Thanks," I said with haste, covering myself before Bill or Scott could ask why I was undressing in their store. I turned back to her to find her face flushed, knowing mine was as well. "You like tattoos?"

She nodded, wrapping her arms tightly over her chest. "I've always wanted them, but ..." She shrugged, her eyes wandering toward something off to the side. "Stephen didn't really like them, so ..."

"He didn't let you?" My mouth twisted into a frown.

Looking back to me, she shook her head. "Oh, no, I just never got them, because I, uh, thought he wouldn't want me anymore if I did." She snorted a sorrowful laugh, dropping her gaze to the floor. "Oh, the irony, right?"

"Well, hey, if you wanted to go get matching butterflies or something, I'm game." She silently rolled her eyes up at me, and I took that as my cue to change the subject. "So, um, do I really want to ask what happened tonight?"

She bit her bottom lip to keep it from quivering as her watery eyes looked everywhere but at me. I felt guilty, as though I had jinxed her with my jokes about him being a psychopath. I hadn't meant anything by it, of course, even though it would have thrilled me to find that he had snagged a picture off of the internet to call his own. I had secretly hoped that he was really a basement-dwelling goblin of a man without a penny to his name. Maybe he would have even left her with the tab—shame on me.

The truth was, I selfishly didn't want her to have any other man to turn to, to sit with and read during Story Time, to receive cups of tea from. I didn't want another man to be lucky enough to hear her laugh and see her smile; to be the *reason* for that smile. It was wrong of me to assume I could hold her from a romantic life, especially after I had vowed to never make another move, but having her so close to me almost felt like enough. Almost.

But when she told me that he had implied that she wasn't the most beautiful woman he had ever laid his snobby eyes on, I instantly regretted ever hoping for anything but wedding bells as I clenched my fists on my lap, out of her view.

"So, wait, you haven't even eaten dinner yet?" I asked. My heart pumped hot blood through my veins, each one of them threatening to burst under the pressure. She shook her head, and without a moment of hesitation, I stood up from the table, grabbing the closed laptop and taking her hand in mine.

"Where are we going?" she asked with surprise, wobbling on her stiletto heels as she stood.

I led her to the door with anger fueled determination. "You put in all of this effort to go out to dinner, and dammit, you deserve that."

***

Turning the black Mercedes into the parking lot of the Golden Carousel diner, I felt the shame of taking her somewhere so lack luster when she had dressed for a place of class and wealth. But despite the casual destination, like a gentleman, I rounded the car and opened the door for her, enveloping her hand in mine to help her out. She curtsied as best as she could in the dress with sarcastic pleasantry.

"Why, thank you, kind sir," she said, followed by a giggle that awakened every nerve in my body.

Playing along, I bowed with more grace than even I expected, holding my opposite arm behind my back and I brought her delicate hand to my lips.

"It is my most honorable pleasure, milady," I said with sincerity, looking at her through my lashes before lightly kissing her knuckles.

"Wow." Her giggle was nervous, and a light flush rose from her chest to her cheeks. I caught her bite against her lower lip, and I tried with great difficulty not to let my ego inflate. "You're smooth," she said with a blushing grin.

"It's how I woo all the ladies," I said, unable to fight my own laugh, and straightened my back to offer her my arm. "Shall we?"

She accepted graciously, and we walked along the sidewalk and up the steps to the aluminum adorned doors as the late October wind whipped cruelly against the thin material of my shirt, but with her close at my side, I couldn't find it at all possible to feel cold.

"Hey B.!" A raspy voice called from inside the diner, and my favorite grey-rooted waitress Birdy bounded her way over to us. "I can't wait for you to try this new pie I've been working

101 | P a g e

on. It's peach with—" Her eyes opened in shock at the sight of Holly on my arm, and she gave me a suspicious look. "Well, well—who's this?"

"Birdy, this is my *friend* Holly," I said, giving her a stern look and hoped she got the message, and as I should have predicted after thirty years of knowing the woman, she didn't.

Birdy dramatically clapped her hands over her buxom chest and grinned from ear-to-ear. "Oh, *Brandon*, your mother is going to be *thrilled*. Absolutely *thrilled*! Honestly, she never thought you would ever meet anybody, especially after …" She grimaced before shooting a look in Holly's direction. "Well, anyway, she's always so worried about you, hon. Every time I talk to her, she says, 'Brandon needs to meet someone soon or I'm never going to meet my grandchildren.' Can you believe that? I always tell her, 'Carole, you raised a good, successful, *handsome* man and sooner or later, the right girl is going to come along and sweep him off his feet. You'll see.'"

"Mom needs to relax," I grumbled at the plump woman.

"Oh, honey, she's your *mother*. She can't relax. She knows you need someone to take care of you." Her bauble-adorned hand patted my arm gently as she turned to Holly. "You know he doesn't cook for himself? If this diner didn't stand, I'm convinced he'd starve."

Holly looked up at me through her smudge-ringed eyes. They twinkled with amusement, and that instantly made the teasing worth it.

"You'd starve, huh?" She hugged my arm tighter against her and treated me to her smile, and I felt a sliver of affection poke through my humiliation.

"I wouldn't *starve*," I insisted, glowering down at Birdy. "I'm capable of using a microwave, you know."

Birdy waved her hands, dismissing my comment as unimportant. "B., I can tell you found a good one here. She's absolutely stunning, and that *smile*!" She paused to take a hand from each of us in hers, squeezing tightly as though I had just burst through the metallic doors with the announcement of our engagement. "I'm just … I'm so happy, I could cry—Oh! But I won't, I won't, don't worry. I just … Oh God, I can't wait to call your mother …" She turned, letting the excitement in her voice trail off as she hurried to grab a couple menus from the rack, and walked ahead of us down the aisle of booths.

"Does *everybody* know you?" Holly asked in a whisper.

I leaned down to whisper in her ear. "She and my mom go way back. She actually used to babysit me back in the day, and—*Jesus*." I cupped a hand over my mouth, lost for words. "I'm sorry. I really didn't think she'd react like that."

I expected her to look up at me with a panicked expression, but I was relieved to find her grinning. "No, it's fine. I actually think it's sweet." She tightened her grip on my arm once again, and my heart swelled against the skeletal confines of my chest. "I can play along. I mean, I wouldn't want to disappoint your *mom*."

We met with Birdy at my usual spot, hidden behind a wall of frosted glass bricks. Unhooking her arm from mine, Holly excused herself, but before leaving for the ladies' room, she craned her neck and stood on her toes to kiss me on the cheek. My breath was instantly entrapped in my lungs, and I closed my eyes at the sensation of having her lips touch my skin again.

"I'll be right back," she said softly, and walked away in the direction of Birdy's finger.

My eyes followed every step she took as I sat down into my usual seat, entranced by the steady but fluid rock of her hips, barely visible beneath the length of my jacket. The exuberant woman leaned close to me. She was absolutely beside herself with glee and the ruby red grin didn't hide that fact one bit. I cringed to imagine the phone call she would be having with my poor mother. I cringed again at the thought of having to tell the hopeful woman it was all a ruse.

"So, you love her, huh?" Birdy blurted out.

My heart might have stopped at her question; I couldn't be sure because in that moment, my entire body had seemed to come to a functioning strike. I held my breath, my body stiffened, and the only sign of life that remained was the perspiration that collected along my brow.

If my mother's old friend could hear the secrets of my heart, how was I supposed to keep Holly from listening?

I remained still, as if I could cease to exist, but instead of taking the hint and walking away to busy herself with another customer, Birdy cocked her head with a knowing smile and squeezed my shoulder. The expression took me back to when I was a child, sitting in her living room while she and my mom visited; I would sit on the floor, writing stories in composition notebooks for hours. When Birdy would ask if I wanted a snack, I'd decline the offer, too polite to beg for a slice of pie. And she'd give me that look, seeing through the lies told by a well-mannered kid, and off she'd go to fetch me a piece of her latest baking adventure.

She shifted her weight, jutting a hip to the side in a position of attitude. "Does she know?"

With nowhere to hide, I raked a hand through my hair and shook my head. "No," I said dryly, but I softened immediately, letting myself relax into the childish comfort I felt in her presence. "I'm really not sure how I feel about her."

She nodded knowingly. "I know, hon. It's tough. You know, admitting you could feel that way about someone new."

My mouth fell open to protest, but to protest would have been to lie, and what was the point in that?

I abruptly turned to her, impassioned by a sudden surge of panic. "You cannot tell my mother. *Please*."

"Oh, my God, but *why*?" she whined with desperation. Forty years of smoking caused the higher pitches of her voice to sound akin to squealing tires.

Much to my relief, Holly walked back to the table, fresh-faced and smiling. She slid into the seat across from me and picked up a menu. Birdy straightened up and shook her head at me with disappointment, but she didn't need to. I was already disappointed in myself.

"I'll be back to get your order, kids. Take your time," she said, still glaring directly at me with her mouth forming a thin, tight line before turning to bound her way down the aisle towards the other diners.

Holly put down her menu and leaned closer. "What was that about?"

I shrugged. "Who the hell knows?" I brushed it off, hiding myself behind my own menu, just grateful that the prying into my soul had stopped.

"So, you never answered my question," she said, turning the laminated pages.

"What was that?"

"Does everybody know you?"

I laughed, putting the menu down, knowing already what I was going to order. "It's a small town," I reasoned with a shrug.

She shook her head. "Yeah, but I mean, you seem to have these close relationships with people, or at least from what I've seen."

I pursed my lips and scratched against my chin. "No, you're right. I just have a tendency to go where I feel comfortable, I guess." I had a thought and chuckled at the realization. "Actually, you're the first *real* friend I've made since … Shit, college, maybe."

There was only a handful of people I had met over the years that I could consider myself friendly with, but could I sit in a diner at ten o'clock at night with any of them? The realization hit me with lonely clarity, and I waited for Holly to flash me a sympathetic look.

But she only smiled, looking up from her menu. "Me too."

***

She was ravenous, and she seemed to inhale the hamburger loaded with bacon, lettuce, and tomato. I couldn't recall the last time a woman had eaten in front of me without the slightest hint of self-consciousness getting in the way of their enjoyment.

My God, it was so refreshing.

"This is *so* good," she groaned through a mouthful of food. I tried to hide my amusement, but she caught me and rolled her eyes. "You have *no* idea how sick of take-out I am. This isn't even a *real* home-cooked meal, but it's the closest thing I've come to it in months." She took a long sip of iced tea before resuming her assault on the burger.

"Well, hey, if you ever want to come over and cook me dinner, don't let me stop you. I can't cook to save my life," I admitted before stuffing a fry into my mouth.

"I heard," she teased, sending a quick glance over at Birdy.

"Julia was the cook, so when she left, I stopped eating like a normal human being." I talked absentmindedly, and as what I had said settled in, I stopped my chewing and a hand flew to my hair.

Holly shoved the last bite of her burger into her mouth. "Who's Julia?" She asked innocently, completely unaware of what it truly meant for me to openly talk about her to someone. "It's amazing you even have hair, by the way. You do that *thing* so often."

I sighed ruefully, looking up towards the low-hanging light that hovered above the table. "Julia," I began, letting the name pass through my lips slowly, savoring the bitter taste, "was my fiancée."

"You were engaged?" She was clearly shocked by the news and unsure of if she should be expressing pity or not.

"Yep," I said shortly, annoyed at myself for inviting the conversation.

Holly's eyes dropped to the table and danced over the surface for a few painful moments, her jaw working from side-to-side. With her eyes still glued to the table, she finally spoke in a timid voice. "What happened?"

I wasn't wanting the topic to linger for long, and I quickly ran through the different ways to explain what had happened. To tell the whole truth meant telling the whole truth about myself, and I wasn't ready. I clasped my hands on the table, resisting the urge to rake my hair right out of my scalp.

"She and I had been together for a long time—about ten years or so—before we were engaged."

Holly held her hands up, keeping me from moving forward, and dammit if I didn't have the slightest bit of aggravation niggling at me. "I'm sorry, but you were together for ten *years* before you were engaged? Jeez, and *I* was mad at Stephen that he hadn't proposed after two."

"Well, we never shied away from the idea of getting married, but …" I sighed, already feeling as though I was delving further into the topic than I wanted. I drummed my fingers anxiously against the table. "We had started dating in our first year of college, so when we had come to the realization that we wanted to get married one day, we decided to wait until after graduation. But then graduation rolled around, and we got busy with finding jobs, finding an apartment, then … life just gets in the way sometimes, and before you know it, ten years fly by."

I shook my head, feeling a few hairs fall against my forehead, but I didn't bother pushing them back as I nudged a fry on my plate. "I used to wonder if that was part of it; maybe we had just waited too long. But …" I avoided noticing the way she looked at me by shoving the fry in, and I continued, talking around it. "We were only two months away from the wedding, just closed on a house, and she just, uh, decided she more or less despised me and no longer wanted anything to do with me."

"Holy shit, I'm sorry," she said apologetically, her eyes dropping to the table, as though I would snap at her if she dared to look. "I don't even know what else to say."

"It's fine, and you don't have to say anything. It was a long time ago."

"Well, I'm sorry," Holly repeated, this time in a whisper. She looked to me again, the familiar pain overshadowing the golden flecks in her eyes.

She was sad for me, but without the pity so many others had felt when I called to tell them the wedding was off. No, she was sad in a way that told me she understood what it was like to have love and be forced to give it up. She understood what it was to not be enough for the person you thought you needed more than the world. She understood in a way that brought my heart to release any residual ache it had been holding onto, and it felt good. It felt warm, it felt alive, and it felt a lot like love.

I shook my head slowly, dismissing the apology. "It doesn't matter anymore," I said in a low voice, and cursed myself for not sending the fear along with the pain.

***

We drove in silence back down Main Street, and I fantasized about the bottle of Scotch lying in my desk drawer. I accepted I was going to need it that night. I also accepted that there was little chance of getting anymore writing done. I silently apologized to Breckenridge, feeling guilty for already stifling his voice for too long.

Holly shifted in the heated seat, a distressed sigh passed through her lips and into the quiet of the car. I glanced quickly at her, to see if she was all right, and her eyes met mine.

"Thanks for tonight," she said with a little smile and another sigh. "I'm just not exactly looking forward to going home and having to work tomorrow, just so my little mundane life can begin all over again."

"Yeah, well, at least you won't have the phone call I'll have waiting for me once I get back to my house," I grumbled, knowing damn well that Birdy had called my mother once we had left. I could just hear my mother's excited voice, leaving message after joyful message on the machine.

Holly laughed. "God, that's right. Hey, I could come with you and talk to her. Really solidify the whole thing."

On the surface, the idea wasn't a terrible one. My mother would rest easy for once, believing her little boy was happily involved with a respectful woman, and I could, at least for a while, avoid any further conversation about my relationship status. But when I dug deeper, the sheer thought of her being in my house kicked my anxiety to an unbearable level. Having her exposed to so many secrets, as well as my bedroom, told me that the idea was not only a bad one, but a dangerous one.

I gave my head a little shake. "Nah, I'll suffer on my own, but thanks," I said, smiling my appreciation.

"So, she used to babysit you?"

"Who, Birdy?" Holly nodded as I turned the wheel into Reade's parking lot. "Well, my mom was a hairdresser by day, waitress by night, and Birdy would babysit me until my dad could pick me up after his deliveries were done." I glanced at her, pleased to find myself divulging a little information without any apprehension. "He used to drive a delivery truck for Entenmann's."

I parked the car next to her van as she asked, "What do they do now?"

"Well, a few years ago, they both decided to retire, sold their house, and moved down to a condo in Florida. So basically, they sit on a beach all day and play shuffleboard at their fifty-five-and-over complex," I laughed with the acknowledgement that the smile on my face was one of bitter sweetness.

"You miss them," she stated, and I nodded. "Why don't you live closer to them?"

I considered the question, biting my bottom lip. God knows my parents had asked me that question countless times since I helped buy their condo on the Atlantic coast. They reminded me often that there was nothing holding me to New York, that I had enough money to fly back when I needed to, and I retaliated with my distaste for a state that seldom saw more than a sprinkling of dusty snow.

Not long ago, that was all I had. A single weak argument holding me to a home that left a bitter taste on my tongue. But there, in my car with my heart relearning the words to a long-forgotten song, I had something so much more than the weather to hold onto.

"New York is home," I said nonchalantly, drumming my fingers on the steering wheel.

"Where *is* home?" She was on a roll, and so was I, satisfying her with the town name. "You *actually* live in Brightwaters? Where?" I told her that I lived around the lakes. Her expression suggested she was impressed. "Wow, then you live in a beautiful house."

I caught her smiling wistfully as she looked into the distance, at somewhere faraway and out of her reach. "You know, when they were alive, my grandparents lived a few blocks over from that area, and I would go for walks around the lakes—feeding the ducks and whatever. I would fantasize about one day living in one of those houses. There was one in particular that I just … Oh, my God. I loved it so much." I resisted the urge to ask which one, because what did that matter? "I didn't really have any plan of *how* I'd end up in one, because I was just a stupid kid, but I would just imagine what it would be like to wake up in the morning and look out my window at that. I mean, it's gotta be beautiful."

My throat felt constrained by the loose collar of my t-shirt. "It is," I confirmed, my voice sounding unused and hoarse.

She shook her head. "It's funny, because I would imagine these amazing things happening to me. You know, meeting a guy who loved me as much as he was rich, moving into a gorgeous house, having a beautiful wedding, maybe having a couple kids of my own. But then sooner or later, I just started to accept that maybe all I was destined for was a guy who never touched me and a studio apartment in the city, and now …" Her voice faded as she looked downward at the leather sleeves covering her hands. "Now I just feel like it's all too late, you know? I'm going to be thirty-two in a few months, and my freakin' clock is starting to sound like Big Ben. I think I went out with James tonight because he said he was rich and successful, which is *so* horrible and shallow—but I thought if things had gone well, then he might have been the guy from my fantasies, and then I wouldn't have to worry. But …"

Holly sighed a shaky breath that had me praying she wouldn't cry again. "I was so stupid to think a guy like that could want someone like me."

She was killing me. I hadn't been sure up until that point, but I knew for certain then that she was in fact killing me. How cruel it was to meet someone so perfect in every way imaginable, and not have the courage to reach out and hold onto them for dear life.

"You think I'm stupid," she stated, and she couldn't have been more wrong.

"No." My voice came out as one I didn't recognize—gruff and strangled. I cleared my throat, staring at the steering wheel, as if it could read my fortune like some overpriced Magic 8 Ball. "But I do think you're too hard on yourself."

I looked over to her, and saw her dark eyes had flooded; they resembled the mysterious depths of the ocean, undiscovered by mankind. I wanted to dive in and drown in them, to swallow all her pain and make it my own. If only I possessed such power, power that I could only manage in the stories I told and not in the real world.

"I'm a fucking babysitter, Brandon. That's not even a real job, and a guy like that—" She shook her head and snorted a watery laugh. "A guy like that wants a woman with a real job and a real salary. Guys like that don't want someone who would rather be in yoga pants and a sweatshirt than this stupid thing."

"I like your yoga pants," I said defensively, as I held a fist to my mouth. The image of her ass in those tight black pants came to mind, and I had to squeeze my eyes shut to scold it away.

She scoffed. "You're not a guy like *that*, though."

With a surge of defiance, I nodded my head with purpose. "Yeah, that's right. I'm not a fucking asshole."

Holly shook her head and twisted her lips around bitter words before spitting them out. "No, you're not, and I cannot understand why a guy like *you* would want to spend so much time with me either."

I couldn't bear to hear her criticize herself any longer. I reached across to grab a hold of her hand with just the right amount of force to shock her into closing her mouth, and I looked her right in the eyes.

"Listen to me, okay?" The stern tone of my voice caused her body to tense, and I was pleased to have her attention. "You told me that you used to answer teenager's questions for a living, and you think *that's* a real job?" With a slight nod of her head, she shrugged her shoulders momentarily, and then they sagged with the weight of her sadness. "Okay, so let me get this straight. A job in which you told girls how to pick up a guy they're not going to care about in a week is a real job to you. Yet, now, you have this new job where you are enriching the life of a little girl every single day, in ways that she will carry with her forever, and you think *that's* demeaning? Fuck, I don't know, Holly. You have a right to your own opinion, but in *my* opinion, there's really no contest as to which one of those is the real job."

I squeezed her hand gently. She reciprocated, and it was as though she squeezed my heart. "Nobody should ever make you feel like less of a person because of what you do, Holly, and anybody who feels they are able to do that is the lesser person— not you." She nodded her understanding finally, and wiped a hand hastily over her eyes.

"You've never told me what you do," she sniffed, glancing at me.

I gave her my best lopsided smile, and said, "I do the same thing as you. I enrich lives."

She laughed, shaking her head. "You're ridiculous."

"It's part of my charm." I shrugged, and leaned over the center console to nudge her with an elbow. "Actually, I'm a writer."

I was on the ledge, ready to dive off, ready to tell her everything. Her face contorted into one of genuine interest as her eyebrows raised with curiosity.

"Well, you're certainly not a struggling one." The gears turned in her head, trying to fit together the pieces. I wanted her to miraculously know who I was. I wanted her to suddenly exclaim that I was that guy that wrote those books. "So, what kind of writer are you?"

I laughed at that, ignoring the panicked churning of my stomach. "Sounds like you already have your answer."

Opening my door, I went to her side. She climbed out without my help, too deep in thought to pay attention to the hand I had lent her.

"Well, what do you write?"

"Books," I teased, resting my back against her van.

"What books?"

I was close, *so* close. I stood at that ledge, ready to take the plunge, but I made the mistake of looking down at those uncertain, rocky cliffs. I saw myself dead, floating at the water's surface, and I took a step backward, recoiling with terror.

"I'll tell you one day," I said, hoping that would be good enough. She cocked her hip, visibly annoyed by my answer. "I promise," I emphasized, hoping she could tell that I meant it, and I did.

"Is being a mystery part of your charm, too?" she asked, the hint of a smile playing on her lips.

"Well, is it working?" I asked, and she rolled her eyes and reached out to pull me into a hug. My arms wrapped around her shoulders, and I added, "I'll take that as a yes."

With her face pressed into the hollow of my chest and her arms around my waist, she sighed happily. A few moments passed with my chin sitting atop her head, looking out into the open spaces of the parking lot. I sat on the edge of being disappointed with myself, angry with my weakness, but the scent of her hair and the soft expansion of her chest against my middle left me hovering in a place of peaceful elation.

"Can I ask one more question?" she asked.

"Hmm," I replied, floating in the daze of tranquility with her in my arms.

"What's your last name?"

I paused, my sense of serenity drifting away with the autumn wind that nipped at the naked flesh of my arms, and I bit my lower lip in consideration of the question. It was almost too personal for comfort, but if she knew, she could feel free to Google my name and find everything out for herself, and it would be all out in the open. Whether that would be a good thing or not, I could leave up to fate, and I decided to bite.

"Davis," I said, and asked for hers.

I felt her smile against my chest. "Hughes," she said.

It was a silly thing; how learning even just a small fact about someone could make you feel closer to them, and I found myself smiling along with her. *Holly Hughes*, I thought, feeling that I couldn't have made up a better name for her myself. Endearing with a touch of quirky sadness, like the heroine in a romantic comedy.

And I wished on the nearly-invisible Long Island suburban stars that I could be her happy ending.

To my disappointment, she pulled away and began to take the jacket off. I insisted that she didn't have to, if she needed it for warmth, but she assured me she would be fine once she got the heat going in the van.

About to open the door, she turned to me and thanked me again for making her night better. There was a moment of looking down at her in the dim light, and I felt the shove to kiss her hard on the mouth and claim her as mine. Of course, I didn't, but I did lean down and felt my lips against her cheek, inhaling the scent of her hair deeply to accompany me during the lonely night ahead.

"Good night, Holly freakin' Hughes."

I love you.

11
holly

BRANDON DAVIS.

I smiled, despite feeling mildly freaked out that he called me Holly freakin' Hughes. That was my thing, and it took a moment to convince myself that he wasn't in fact living in my brain.

Brandon freakin' Davis. Mind reader.

What a bizarre turn of events, I thought, as I drove back to Liz's house. I mean, I had set out that night to see James, and I ended up at a diner with Brandon. I hadn't admitted it to him, but I had gone to the bookstore with the purpose of finding him, not knowing where else to look. I had been in desperate need of a comfort that--let's face it—I wasn't going to get from anyone else. Liz would have hugged me and busied herself with something else, Esther would have told me to get back on the horse and find some handsome man to take my mind off of it, and Anna would have continued watching some dancing vegetable on TV.

No, what I needed was him, and there he was, as though he were planted exactly where I needed him, when I needed him.

He always is.

Pulling into the driveway, I sighed at the dark house. I imagined my sister cuddled into her bed with my niece sleeping in the room next to her. I could see the little room I called my own, with its small bed, Stephen's old dresser, a desk from Ikea, and a TV. The sadness of it all made me think of it more as *Harry Potter*'s little cupboard of a room underneath the stairs, and I wondered if I could ever have that life I had described to Brandon. The luxurious life of living in a Brightwaters house on the lake and a couple of kids. I mean, it happened to people, didn't it? But then again, I assumed a man like that looked for a trophy wife, and well, that sort of explained why Brandon only wanted me as a friend.

Holly freakin' Hughes. Consolation prize.

I entered the house, closing the door behind me softly and undid my heels before tiptoeing to my room. Camille slept peacefully on the bed, only stirring a little as I sat down next to her in the dark room. The dress felt as though it were strangling me, clinging to every unfortunate roll and imperfection that James clearly noticed right away, but I couldn't be bothered taking it off. All I wanted was to lie down and let my head hit the pillow after an exhausting night.

***

Hands shook my shoulders a hair below what I would considered violent. My lids flipped open to see Liz standing over me. Her face displayed a look of concern and anger, and at that moment, the memories from the night before came rushing back to me all at once. I glanced downward, taking note that I was still wearing the evening gown.

Holly freakin' Hughes. Total freakin' wreck.

I sat up, suddenly alert. Liz was running late for work, no thanks to me, but she insisted that I tell her what had happened the night before. I managed to fit it all into a very small nutshell—a pistachio, really—and it wasn't all that hard to do. All I had to say was the douchebag saw me and high-tailed it the hell out of there.

"Why would he *do that*?" she asked, her perfectly plucked brows knitting together with question.

"Because I'm hideous." I finished my tale of woe with a heavy sigh and Liz wrapped her arms around me. "And I'm a babysitter. Who the hell wants a thirty-one-year-old babysitter?"

She assured me that I wasn't in fact hideous. "In fact," she stated, "you're one of the most beautiful women I've ever known." I appreciated the sentiment, but come on, she was my sister and one of my best friends. She *had* to say things like that out of obligation.

"Besides, he's only one guy. I bet there are tons of others online that would *kill* to be with you," she said with a little too much optimism.

Except, I neglected to add, I was finished with online dating. One failed attempt was enough; just like one cheating ex-boyfriend was plenty, thanks.

"So, what did you end up doing then? You came home pretty late," she mused, lifting an accusing eyebrow.

"Oh, I just spent some time with Brandon," I said nonchalantly.

"Mm-hmm," she said with a smirk, "I figured."

There was nothing wrong with spending a crappy night with a friend to cheer yourself up, and I chose to not honor that comment with a response as she finished getting her things together.

After she had finally made it out the door, an hour late for work, Anna and I ate a delayed breakfast of pancakes and bacon. She thought it was a special treat, and sure, I suppose it was, but it was more for me than her. A bad date deserved a good breakfast.

We amused ourselves with three rousing games of Candy Land (all of which Anna graciously won), and then it was a lunch of peanut butter and jelly. We watched a few episodes of *Dora the Explorer* and *Peppa Pig* before it was time for her nap, and as she slept, I wandered outside with the baby monitor to see what Esther was up to. I brought along my Styrofoam to-go container concealing my complimentary dessert from

Bankers. We ate the rich and delicious chocolate cake on her steps while I told her about what had happened on the date.

"What a disgusting prick." She pursed her thinned lips and lowered her wispy brows into a look of sheer rage. "I could shove my cane *right* up his gorgeous ass. I'm so sorry, honey. People can be such assholes sometimes." I shrugged sadly, nodding. I guess Esther took that as my surrender because she quickly added, "Oh, but honey, there are so many men out there. You've only been on one date." She smiled as though she had just said the magic words to turn this whole thing around. "And remember, you did get that one guy to make out with you. That's something."

"Except it was nothing but a way to land me in the friend-zone," I pointed out. Esther shrugged her response. "And I am done finding guys online. I can't handle another date like that."

"Because running away is a great way to solve things." She shook her head with a scowl.

"Yeah, well, better to run away than run head-first into another night of tears and greasy diner food." I flashed Esther the baby monitor, showing her the stirring Anna. "I gotta head back."

"Ah, yes, must attend to your duties and leave me sitting here alone. I might be dead tomorrow, you know." She wagged a finger at me.

Eye roll. "Uh-huh."

I kissed her on the cheek and began the long walk home to find the cherry that was to be on top of my no good, very bad day sundae.

Somewhere between Esther's front stoop and Anna's room, Anna had ripped her Naptime Diaper off and I found her sitting in the middle of her room, completely naked, and covered in poop—and I mean, *covered*. From head to toe. *Between* her toes. In her hair. In her—oh, *God*, in her nostrils and ears and—

Jesus Christ, it was in her mouth.

I wanted to die. Right there in that room. I wanted to just collapse and die.

Three thoughts instantly hit me all at once.

One, how could something so little produce that much crap?

Two, how could she be giggling at a time like this?

Three, what the hell would possess a three-year-old to cover herself in poop like some tribal war paint?

"Anna, *why*? Why would you do this?" I pleaded with her, feeling my delicious chocolate cake rising in my throat.

"I twied to cwean my butt."

"Well, thank you ever so much, but next time, leave that to the authorities."

I gagged and heaved my way through the clean-up from hell, with Anna taking it all very much in stride. The one and only time she showed the slightest bit of resistance was when it was time for her bath, because God forbid I insist she didn't walk around caked in her own crap. She shrieked for forty minutes as I dumped her in the tub, and scrubbed her until she sparkled like a 21st century vampire.

Liz walked into the bathroom just as I was toweling her off. "Holly, why does my house smell like crap? And why are you killing my daughter?" I turned to her and there was no need to speak. My eyes, my angry, angry eyes, said it all. "You know what? You obviously have this handled, so I'm just going to get the table set. I brought home Chinese."

***

Once Anna was asleep and Liz had retreated to her bedroom for the night, I headed over to Reade's to get myself a cup of tea from the café before closing time. I had become pretty accustomed to the lavender Earl Grey and decided it was only right to treat myself after the crappy hell I had been through. Pun totally intended.

I walked through the small shop towards the café, greeted by a cheerful Bill busying himself by rearranging a display of books near the entrance. I found Brandon sitting at a table with his laptop and a notebook, pen tucked behind his ear. He smiled and gave me a little wave, and I took that as a signal to bother him. I pulled a chair out and practically threw myself onto the seat.

"Another day in Paradise, huh?" He laughed and held up his cup. "I need a refill. Earl Grey?"

I know I shouldn't have just assumed he would always use his connections at the store to get me free drinks, but he offered, so I accepted. He left the table to give Scott our order, leaving behind his open notebook and pen. Feeling a little bold, I grasped the opportunity to take a gander at the book. I couldn't make out much of what had been scribbled down; the guy's handwriting was atrocious. But they appeared to be notes, something about a war and something about swords. Out of the corner of my eye, I caught him walking back to the table and I quickly looked away from the book.

"It's just some research." He winked at me, and I blushed. For good measure, I apologized for looking. "Oh, it's no biggie. Anyway, how are you doing? Better than yesterday?"

God, why did he have to bring that up? Pressing my hand into my forehead, I groaned. He apologized for rekindling bad memories, and I shook my head.

"No, it's not that," I began, before telling him about how I had overslept, making my sister late for work, and then moved into telling him about the diaper disaster with Anna. I looked up to find an amused smile plastered on his face, as if my misfortune with the diaper was the funniest thing he had heard all day. I crossed my arms defensively over my chest. "And you find this amusing?" I scoffed.

He shook his head, a few strands of hair falling out of place. "I'm not laughing at *you*. I'm just—" He chuckled, his smile widening. "I'm just thinking about this one time I babysat for my best friend's kids. His wife was going into labor with their third daughter, so he called me over to his place to keep an eye on the other two until he could get someone, um, *more qualified* to take over." He looked up toward the ceiling, pushing back in his chair to teeter on the two back legs. His smile never left his face, and my God, he was adorable.

"So, what happened?" I asked, folding my arms on the table.

"Okay, so I had very, *very* limited experience with babies at the time, and the youngest was something like a year old; the oldest was somewhere around three or four—I can't remember. Point is, they were little, I had no clue what I was doing, but I figured, how hard can it be? I just had to keep them safe until someone else got there." He leaned forward again, covered his face with his hands and groaned. "Holly, I swear to God, those were three of the most eye-opening hours of my life. The oldest one—Lynn—had started the day off by coloring all over the brand-new *beige* couch with a fucking *Sharpie* she found in my jacket pocket. And in the three seconds it took me to notice this had happened, Sarah crawled over to the cat's dish and proceeded to pick away at the food like it was the perfect mid-morning snack." He dropped his hands onto the table. The grin had consumed his face, crinkling the corners of his eyes. "And that was within the first ten minutes of me being over there."

"You would *die* in my job," I laughed, suddenly feeling that my one poop incident wasn't all that bad.

He took a sip from his coffee, and swallowed with another chuckle. "Hey, I've gotten better since then. They actually like the rare occasion I watch them by myself, so I guess I do something right." His head shook as I secretly gushed over the idea of him hanging out with little kids. "But fuck, kids can be such unpredictable little psychos."

"Tell me about it. Anna freaked out the other day because I didn't *place* her cup down on the table with Minnie Mouse's face actually looking at her. She dropped to the floor and cried for a solid ten minutes." I smiled at the ridiculous memory then, but God, it had *not* been funny at the time.

"Well, duh." Brandon crossed his arms over his chest with a convincing expression of disapproval, teetering on the back legs of the chair again.

"Oh, my God, shut up," I laughed, crumpling up a napkin and tossing it at him. Brandon ducked, and the napkin landed on the floor somewhere behind his chair. "Oops."

"Hey, come on, no throwing in my café," Scott scolded teasingly from the barista counter, putting a pause to his singing.

Brandon responded by flashing him the middle finger. "It's your dad's café, and your dad doesn't care." Scott muttered a few obscenities under his breath before throwing a lid over in our direction and continued his obligatory singing.

I couldn't control my smile as I took another sip of my tea. "So, I take it you don't want kids, huh?"

Brandon cocked his head, twisting his lips. "Well, no, I didn't say that. I *said* they're psychotic, but I didn't say I wouldn't like to have a few of my own psychos running around." He picked his coffee up and brought it up to his lips. "I'd have awesome kids," he mused before tilting the cup back into his mouth. "And they'd be hilarious, because I mean, come on." He gestured towards himself with that half-smile, and my ovaries ached just a little.

"What about you?" he asked. "Now that you've washed crap off a toddler, you think you could have your own?"

I sucked in a gust of air and exhaled loudly, rubbing my hand against my forehead. "Oh, well, that was always the plan, but you know, my eggs are just shriveling up into nothingness at this point, so who the hell knows."

"Ah, come on, you're not that old."

I rolled my eyes. "I'm almost thirty-two. That's pretty old."

Brandon's jaw dropped. "Hey, fuck you. I'll be thirty-seven next year."

I glared at him through my eyelashes. "It's different for you. You can have kids forever, but me?" I waved a hand in the air, dismissing the idea. "I still have to lock a guy down to give me his seed anyway, and we both know where *that's* going right now."

He sighed. "It shouldn't be that hard."

"Yeah, okay. Just look at me. I look like I crawled out of a hole somewhere."

Brandon laughed. "You mean guys don't normally like this living dead thing you have going on?" That made me giggle a little bit, and he smiled. "But really, I'm sure you'll find that lucky guy who wants you and your shriveled-up eggs. And hey, there's always artificial insemination, right?"

We sat in silence then. Brandon had turned to the notebook again, fervently scribbling something down with a determined look on his face. Shamefully feeling a little ignored, I sipped my tea and glanced around the near-empty store. It was a few minutes before closing and it was only a matter of time before Bill or Scott came over to kick us out. I would go home to Liz's, he would go to what was undoubtedly a beautiful house in Brightwaters, and we would sleep alone. *God*, I didn't want to sleep alone. Not when my shriveled eggs were so fresh in my mind, and I just wanted to be held in someone's arms as they told me everything would be okay.

He seemed to be the only person who could make me believe it.

Brandon stopped his scribbling, closed the book, and as he looked up at me, a few strands of hair fell into his eyes.

"You okay?" He put the pen down, focusing entirely on me again

Not even a little bit.

I forced a smile that I hoped said I was doing just swell, and said, "Yeah, but I should probably get going. They're going to close soon."

"We could hang out longer, if you want to. We could go to the diner."

I shook my head, knowing the temptation would've been too great if I did. Somewhere along the line, I'd ask him if we could go back to his place, or if he wanted to come see my lame little room back at my sister's house, thanks to my ovaries that I was suddenly very aware of. Maybe there wouldn't be sex, but there very well could have been if I had my way, and I needed to just stay away from that.

So, we both stood from the table. Empty cups were thrown into the trash can, and Scott wished us a good night. Brandon walked me to the minivan and opened the door for me. He leaned down to kiss my cheek, but on his way to touch his lips to my skin, I thought there was a moment of hesitation when his mouth was just inches from mine. Or maybe it was just my imagination, my own subconscious wanting to see something that wasn't there. That's what I told myself while I got into Ol' Rusty and watched him walk to his fancy-shmancy Mercedes, and I felt okay with that.

That is, until we drove our separate ways and I remembered the cold bed I was going home to and the warm friend I was leaving.

12
holly

ANNA SPENT EVERY WEEKEND WITH her father. That was no different on this particular weekend, but what had set it apart was that she was being dropped off on Monday, as opposed to being picked up the day before. Mark and his wife had taken Anna and their one-and-a-half-year-old son Jacob to Sesame Place for a Halloween show. A very nice little trip that I had found myself feeling jealous of, despite the destination being full of singing, dancing puppet people.

I took pleasure in the morning alone after Liz had left for work. I had been determined not to think about anything but me while I ate my yogurt parfait in peace, watching a *Frasier* rerun. Once I had eaten, I allowed myself to indulge a bit with a nice, hot bubble bath accompanied by the romance novel of the week. When the doorbell rang, I was already dried and dressed, savoring the last few precious seconds of quiet as I walked to the door.

Mark, Liz's ex-husband, stood on the other side with Anna in his arms, sporting a frown that told me my morning was going to be extra appreciated by the end of the day. It was an odd thing, seeing him for the first time in years. Liz had always been around to deal with him, so I never had to—boy, did he ever feel like a stranger.

"Hey Holly," he said with a civil smile. "It's nice to see you."

"Yeah, you too," I said, returning the gesture.

And really freakin' bizarre.

It was funny to me that during Liz's relationship to him, I had never thought about him at all as being a decent looking guy, but now that they were divorced for three, going on four, years, I couldn't help but notice that he wasn't half bad. I took note of the short sandy blonde hair that blew gently in the breeze, the definition of muscles underneath his t-shirt, and the smile that was a little too white.

Or, you know, I could have just been desperate. Either way.

We stood in the doorway for a few painstaking moments; the discomfort became more and more evident between us. Was I supposed to invite him in? Did I actually have to socialize with this guy I never really socialized with, even during the years that he and my sister had been together? Was that in my job description?

Come to think of it, I wasn't entirely sure what my job description even was.

"Uh, do you want to come in?" I finally asked, still feeling unsure of the proper protocol when handling my sister's ex-husband-turned-friend.

Seeming grateful for the offer, Mark smiled politely. "Oh, yeah, thanks. I won't stay long."

Well, thank the baby Jesus for that.

I stepped aside, allowing him to enter, and I closed the door.

"How was Sesame Place?" I asked, sitting on the couch.

Mark put Anna down next to me and helped unzip her coat as he said, "Oh, it was great. The kids had a blast. Heather and I, on the other hand, are exhausted from chasing them around and I nearly had a coronary when I saw how much an F-ing bottle of water cost—*eight* bucks! Most expensive weekend I've ever had."

"Yeah, I bet. I have it made with the places I take her. Like Story Time? Free."

With a stiff laugh, he excused himself to grab Anna's stuff from the car. I turned to her, and she remained silent. "Hey kiddo," I said, helping her to take off her shoes. "Did you see Elmo?" Anna kicked her feet out of my grasp and crossed her arms just as Mark came back in. "Wow, she's a little cranky today, huh?"

He sighed, putting her bags and Giraffe down on an armchair. "Yeah, she was sad to leave. But I told her that it's okay, and that it'll still be there in the summer. Right, Peanut?" Anna responded by sticking out her bottom lip, and it wiggled fiercely. "Come on, sweetheart. Daddy is leaving soon and he doesn't want you to cry."

Anna apparently didn't care what Daddy wanted. Fat tears rolled down her cheeks as she jumped off the couch wearing only one shoe and ran to her room. I waited for the door to slam behind her, as she sometimes did in the throes of a tantrum, but it never came. I stood to go tend to her when Mark stopped me from leaving.

"So, hey, Holly. Liz told me you were dating."

For a second, I really did think he was making some creepy pass at me. But once it dawned on me that he was genuinely making conversation at the most inopportune moment, I was suddenly perplexed that Liz would even talk to him about my love life at all. Was that something you would typically make your ex-husband's business?

"Uh—well, I went on *one* date. That's really it."

"Well, not to be weird, but I have a buddy who might be good for you."

Oh no, Mark. It was already weird, thanks.

Deep down I had been wondering when someone was going to play match maker, but I expected it to come more from, say, my mom. It wouldn't have surprised me in the least if she had approached me with the offer of going out with a son of a friend. Or if Liz had told me one of Dr. Martin's patients had recently been divorced and had a nice set of chompers. But I never would have expected my sister's ex to bring up a single pal after not seeing me for, oh, three years.

"Oh, um, th-thanks?" I stammered, speaking slowly. "I'm not sure I'm ready to see someone else. I didn't have the greatest date last time."

Mark shrugged "Well, hey, if you change your mind, let me know."

"Yeah, thanks. I'll do that." Or I wouldn't.

He saw himself out after that, air-kissing my cheek before heading to the door. I rolled my eyes as soon as the door shut behind him with the reminder to kick Liz's ass for discussing the private matters of my life with a total stranger. What the hell did Dr. Martin know about me? The fact that I hadn't washed my bras in a few months, perhaps?

I headed down to Anna's room, hoping that her fit would be a quick fix. A little bit of ice cream or a handful of cookies, maybe a trip to the park, and good as new. That was the typical remedy for a little tantrum, but walking into her room, it became pretty obvious it wouldn't be that simple.

She was lying in the middle of the room with the entire contents of her dresser strewn around her—like a nest. The fat tears continued to roll down her cheeks with accompanying sobs and hiccups, and for a second, I wished I still cried over things like Ernie and Bert. Simpler times and all that.

I approached with caution, crouching down next to her. "Anna Banana, you wanna tell me what's wrong?"

The backs of her little hands pressed against her eyes as she kicked her one shoed foot against the floor. "I wanna see … *Ewmo-oo*," she wailed, a hiccup breaking her sentence.

"Well, kiddo, Elmo lives at Sesame Place, and you live here. But you know, maybe we can go see him soon, okay?" I reached down to smooth her messy hair off her forehead. Mark was clearly in charge of doing her hair that day, and his skills with the hairbrush and hair ties were nothing to brag about.

Anna rolled away from my touch. "*No*! I wanna see Ewmo *now*!" She rolled into a pile of t-shirts and lying on her stomach, she cried into the clothes, continuing to pound her foot against the floor.

I went to grab her and cuddle her into me, thinking that maybe a nice big hug could keep her from losing her mind more than she already had. I grabbed her under her arms and picked her up off the floor, pulling her into me, and that was the precise moment she decided to arch her back like she had just been possessed by something straight out of Hell. Her skull made direct impact with my face, crashing into me with a terrifying thud and a blinding pain unlike anything I had felt before.

Well, at least it shocked her out of her tantrum.

We sat there frozen in time—both afraid that movement would make something happen. Pain, tears—*something*, but I soon found that no lack of movement could keep the searing pain from radiating through my cheekbone and eye socket. It also didn't keep my eye from swelling, and it didn't keep Anna from howling about the knot forming on the back of her head.

My face hurt. Oh, it hurt bad. It hurt worse than the time I broke my pinkie toe after running through the basement of my parents' house and bashing it into a metal filing cabinet. I couldn't walk on that foot for three weeks, and I couldn't imagine how horribly my face was going to hurt as the night went on, let alone looked.

Holly freakin' Hughes. Battered babysitter.

I couldn't focus on myself, though. I had to make sure Anna was okay, although I was fairly certain she was doing a whole lot better than I was. She made that obvious when she stopped her complaining and crawled off my lap to play with her toys, as if nothing happened. Still, I stood up on unsteady legs, afraid that the pain in my face would send me blacked out on the floor. I managed to walk into the kitchen to fetch an icepack for Anna's lump, and I returned with my battered eye completely swollen shut, only able to see through the other.

"Here, Anna. Let's put this on your—"

My niece turned to me and her eyes bugged out of her head, her mouth forming a panicked O. She scrambled away from me, backing into her bed and hugging her knees into her chest. What the hell, I thought, and glanced at myself in the mirror above her dresser, and—yeah, I would've run away from me too.

The entire socket had swollen to twice its original size and the horrific bruise had already begun to spread down towards my cheekbone and up to my eyelid. I reached up to gingerly touch it, pressing lightly, and the pain scorched throughout the entire left side of my face.

"Oh God," I groaned, and went to call my mommy.

***

Mom held the washcloth full of ice to my eye tenderly. "You know, Holly, it could be broken." Her hand held my chin still, glancing over at Anna playing calmly on the living room floor. "Is Liz on her way home?"

"I told her not to worry about it," I said, wincing at the pain. "I cannot believe how *bad* this hurts. That kid's head is made of fucking lead. Do you think I need to go to the doctor?"

"I broke my foot once stepping on a LEGO. Hurt like a son-of-a-bitch for weeks," Mom reminisced, placing my hand on the freezing cold washcloth before walking to the fridge for a bottle of water. She handed it to me, along with a pair of Advil. "Take these. I'll stay here with you until Liz gets home and we'll assess the damage then. You might be fine, though. I'm hoping it just looks worse than it is."

I mumbled something about it definitely hurting worse than it looked, and it sure as hell looked ugly.

I laid down on the couch while Mom went to fetch me another bundle of ice, and Anna approached me with fear and regret.

"I sowwy, Ant Howwy."

"Accidents happen, kiddo," I said, giving her a brave smile that sent daggers through my face. "I'll be fine."

She handed Giraffe over to me. "Make you bettah."

I clutched the smelly, sticky, raggedy stuffed animal to my chest, instantly feeling moved and for maybe the first time, I felt as though I had the best job in the entire world.

Broken face and all.

"You're the best kid an aunt could ask for, you know that?"

Anna smiled with her little gapped teeth and let out a laugh that would have been contagious had I not felt like my face might shatter if I so much as giggled. "I know," she said, stroking my hair the way a mother might touch a child.

Then, just like that, she took off to watch TV while I wondered if I'd ever be able to watch *Frasier* again through my swollen eye.

13
holly

GOOD GOLLY, MISS HOLLY! WHAT happened to you?" Bill asked, spotting me walking through the door. He was busy putting together a Halloween display in the window of the store, and in his hands was a Jack-o-Lantern cut out from a piece of plywood. The smile was lopsided and the eyes were different sizes—and it looked as though it were going to be the centerpiece.

Oh boy.

"Oh, I thought I'd get a jump start on my Halloween costume. I'm going as Rocky."

He stared blankly, the joke clearly lost on him, and I told him Anna had decided to use my face for target practice with her noggin, and he winced his sympathy. "Have you had that checked out?"

I had in fact. Mom did me the favor of driving down to the ER, where we enjoyed five hours in the waiting room before a doctor would see me. Among the puking drunks and occasional accident, I felt honored to be the only one there with a battered eye caused by the head of a toddler.

The doctor who eventually did see me got a good chuckle out of my misfortune. He gave me a smile as he poked and prodded at my injury, and proceeded to tell me about the time his now-grown kid jumped on his groin with so much force, he ruptured a testicle. Worst thing he had ever felt in his entire life, he insisted, and you know what? I was pretty damn sure he wasn't exaggerating.

The eye socket was indeed broken, but it was such a minor blow-out fracture, he sent me on my way with strict instructions to use icepacks and a prescription dose of ibuprofen every six hours while the pain lasted. He insisted it was a no-big-deal injury and that I wouldn't have any lasting issues—once the swelling had gone down and the healing began, that is.

For such a "no big deal," it felt pretty horrible.

It looked like absolute hell too. There wasn't any amount of makeup to cover that thing up, so I didn't bother. Instead, I hoped the book I brought would shield my face sufficiently enough to keep anybody from wondering if they needed to call the police.

Thanks to the efficient pain meds, Story Time resumed as usual. Being just days before Halloween, Jessie had selected a few appropriately themed books to entertain the kids while Anna played quietly with Giraffe until she fell asleep.

When Jessie had finished reading, I remained seated with my nose glued into the book I had brought—a steamy romance between a blacksmith named Maxwell and a saloon girl, Heidi. I had just gotten to a particularly saucy scene, when I heard the footsteps that I instantly knew to be Brandon's. Forgetting entirely about the bruise that consumed my face, despite the pain that continued to radiate from the spot, I looked up at him from the pages.

"Are they getting it on yet?" Brandon asked absentmindedly, as he sat down next to me, not yet taking the chance to look at me.

I rolled my eyes defensively. I had begun to say something about how it wasn't *all* about sex, that it was actually a very educational novel about living as a bar maid in the 18th century—and then, I saw the look of horror on his face.

"What the *hell* happened to you?" he asked with concern, speaking slowly to enunciate the words.

I was glad then that he had showed up late and couldn't cause a scene in front of the other parents and kids. His hand flew to my cheek, turning my face to get a better look. I tried swatting him away, but he was relentless, tilting my head back-and-forth and side-to-side.

"Come on, you're not helping," I whined, wincing and pushing his hands away.

"Did someone do this?" he asked. His eyes stormed over with murderous intent.

"Yes, someone jumped me to try and steal my millions, and now the police are on the prowl looking for the bastard," I said, and laughed at my own poorly made joke.

He didn't. "I'm serious. If someone hit you, I want to know." His hands balled into fists and dropped to his lap. He suddenly looked helpless—and angry, I noted, as his jaw set tightly in place.

I sighed. "No, nobody hit me. Anna bashed me in the face with her head," I said, suddenly wishing I had a better story to go along with an injury that looked so horrendously epic.

He shook his head and grumbled something about being right back, and he went to get something from the café. I saw him talking to Scott, who glanced over in my direction and it wasn't long before his face contorted into a look of shock. He disappeared beneath the counter, then reappeared, handing something to Brandon. He walked back over to me with an icepack in hand, and knelt beside me, holding it to my cheek.

"You're cute when you're protective," I said, teasing. "Thanks, by the way. I'm supposed to keep these things on my face pretty much constantly and I don't have one with me."

"*Cute*? I promise you, there'd be nothing *cute* about me beating the crap out of someone who laid their hands on you," he replied with a touch of agitation, and I thought maybe he was angry with me—but the gentle hand against the side of my face said otherwise. His eyes locked with mine. I wanted to look away to anywhere, just to keep myself from drowning, but he held me in place. "And … you're welcome."

Anna began to stir, and I pulled myself from his grasp, welcoming the distraction.

Saved by the kid.

"You're very lucky you're not a big bad man, Anna," I said jokingly, reaching to smooth the stray hairs out of her eyes. Brandon sniffed a laugh, but the smile was missing from his face. I assured him that I was only kidding. "I know you're just looking out for me," I said with sincerity.

"Is it broken?" He still held the pack against my face, and I nodded with as much of an eye roll as I could muster. "Holy crap. What is her head made of?"

"My theory is that she has a metal plate back there that we don't know about, but the jury's still out on whether it's true."

"Hmm, you might want to look into that before she does more damage," he said before standing.

He handed the pack to me and shook his hair out, letting it fall freely around his perfectly structured face, and I stared like a horny guy watching a wet t-shirt contest. I wondered if this was some sort of mating dance, because if it was, I could see how it could be very effective.

With his hands held to the back of his head, he caught my gaze and—there was that smile. The charming little half-smile that never failed to tug at my heart. "What?"

I sat there, stunned at the sight of him, and feeling as though I had never *really* looked at him before that moment. He stood with his long legs hip-width apart, his hands stuffed into the pockets of his jeans. Under his jacket, the white t-shirt he wore was just fitted enough to show off the definition of his chest, and I'd be lying through my teeth if I said I wasn't curious about how his stomach was fairing under there.

Without any care of how he would take the compliment, I finally replied, "I have no idea how you're single."

His jaw dropped with mock insult. "I am more than a pretty face, thank you very much."

"Exactly," I muttered, giving him a sidelong glance. I took another look at him and added, "You should give up writing and get into modeling before you lose your hair."

His eyes dropped to the floor as a crimson flush took over his cheeks. "Actually, I do model on occasion."

Jesus, take the wheel.

He rubbed a hand along his jaw, divulging the information without question. "Before I got settled into my job, I modeled a lot more often than I do now—mostly artsy stuff at FIT. It was another way to make extra money while I was bartending." Then with a shrug, he added, "I still do some from time to time, but not as much."

"Oh, of course," I laughed, floating somewhere in a dream world. "You're that unlikely guy the girl becomes best friends with in a chick flick."

"Doesn't she usually end up with him in the end?"

"Yes, but this isn't a movie," I pointed out, dropping my eyes to Anna as she climbed into my lap, reminding me again that she was there.

"This is true," he said with a unreadable twitch of his lips, shuffling his feet. "But, uh, best friend, huh?"

"Well, obviously," I said, suddenly shy as I adjusted the pigtails in Anna's hair.

Brandon crouched next to me. "Well, as far as ladies go, you are hands-down the best friend I've ever had, and coming here to do absolutely nothing with you is the highlight of my life." He took one of my hands and kissed my knuckles, bringing the fluttering of butterfly wings to life in my stomach.

God, I need to get laid.

"You lead a boring life." I giggled like a nervous little girl as he stood back up.

"If this is boring, then I'm not sure I ever want things to pick up again," he said, turning to walk away. "See you Thursday."

Shamelessly watching his ass in those beautifully fitted jeans, I made a mental note to let Liz know I wanted Mark to set me up with that buddy of his.

14

brandon

I WALKED THROUGH THE DINER feeling inconspicuous in my sunglasses as I usually did during daylight hours, much like Clark Kent feels that his flimsy disguise will hide his true identity. And like Clark Kent, the disguise always seemed to work.

I didn't have to wait to be seated, knowing exactly where I was headed, and I slumped into the secluded booth in the back. Nick sat across from me, looking both peeved and intrigued.

"You're never late," he stated, not looking up from a pile of paperwork.

"Lost track of time talking to Scott." I picked up a menu, hoping my casual demeanor would set him off the trail. It seemed to work as he nodded and pushed his glasses back up the slope of his nose.

A diner outing with Nick normally would have been casual. We would have bullshitted about this and that, he would've given me the lowdown on the wife and kids, and I would smile and nod, having not much to add to the conversation myself. But this was a business meeting, and Nick meant business.

He pulled a sheet of paper out from the stack, adjusting his glasses once again before peering down at his chicken scratch handwriting.

"So, there was a call the other day from Burberry. They want you for their Fall/Winter collection next year. It is—and I quote—inspired heavily by the sensuality of leather. I have no idea what the hell that might actually mean. Sounds a little kinky to me, but I told them we'd discuss details. Totally up to you if you want to go for it, but I think you should hear them out. It's been a couple years since you've done any mainstream modeling work, and it looks good for you. Keeps you in the spotlight. Keeps people talking."

Oh, how ironic, I thought, after just being involved in the modeling conversation with Holly.

"The sensuality of leather?" My imagination blazed a trail with every image I could muster from my curious college days with BDSM porn. "I'm not wearing one of those freaky masks."

Nick snorted a laugh, raising an open palm in the air. "Dude, I have no idea. I just answer the calls and take the notes. You could, you know, hire someone else to handle this shit. Like, oh, a publicist or an assistant or ..."

"Yeah, but that's part of my charm. Small town guy, small town crew."

"I didn't know that was a thing," Nick muttered.

"Oh, it totally is," I said, nodding insistently. "I don't need a circus of people when I have you."

"You're not going to have me after I have a stroke," he pointed out before reading off the other items on the laundry list of messages: I had pending interviews with *People*, *GQ*, and *Writer's World*. *Glamour* was naming me #16 on their list of *Sexiest Men*. Jimmy Fallon wanted to set something up. My publisher was throwing some big party for the five-year-anniversary of the first book's release, and then finally, of course, there was my current work in progress.

"So, how's that going?" Nick asked, shuffling the papers again and waving Birdy over to take our order. With a twist of my mouth, I wasn't sure how to answer. If I lied again as I had for months and said it was coming along well, he would expect it done sooner. My hands went to my hair, and he immediately shook his head before resting his furrowed brow into the palm of his slender hand. "You're fucking kidding me, right? You *said* it was going well, Brandon. The hell am I supposed to tell Patricia?"

"I don't like the direction its going in, man. It doesn't feel right." I scratched the stubble on my cheek, shaking my head. "I think I actually want to rewrite it. I'd need more time, though, and—"

"Fuck. No. Absolutely not." Nick waved his hands as if he were directing traffic. He did it well, and if he hadn't been so angry, I would've suggested that as his next gig when S&S Publications decided to send my contract to the shredder. "*You can't.* You've taken too long on this already. If you had told me that, uh, a year ago—or hell, even six months ago—then it would've been no problem, but dude, you don't fuck the hand that feeds."

"I didn't know I wanted to rewrite six months ago," I said through my own aggravation, chewing the inside of my lip. "You think I actually *want* to scrap something I've been working on for the better part of a year? Of course not. But I can't focus, man. I want to change things up. I have some new inspiration, and … maybe it's time for Breckenridge to settle down." I clasped my hands together on the table, shifting a little on the squeaking vinyl seat.

"You're writing a romance novel?" Nick eyed me, as though waiting for me to laugh and assure him that I was only kidding. When I didn't, he slid both hands over his head. "You really want them to kill me, don't you?"

"Talk them into giving me more time, okay? Work your magic. Say I had a family emergency or some shit, and I'll buckle down and bang it out in the next few months. They won't argue too much with me. I'm the reason they were able to send the whole team to Jamaica for two weeks, for fuck's sake, and where was my invitation?"

Nick opened his mouth to say something when Birdy bounded over, grinning with her ruby red lipstick.

"What can I get you, boys?" she asked, sliding into the seat beside me. I put an arm around her, taking in the heavy scent of cigarettes, and she reciprocated by resting her head against my shoulder. "No Holly today, huh?"

Oh, I could have killed her.

I didn't particularly care to look at Nick, didn't exactly want to know what little smirks his face was twisting into. But my eyes slowly made the shift, and I saw him with that teasing smile that I hated so much. The one he would always give to me before asking if I had "gotten any," and in that moment, I could only assume that he was guessing that I had, in fact, "gotten some."

I shook my head, struggling a smile. "Nah, she's working today."

"Oh, right. What does she do?" Birdy asked.

"She babysits her niece," I said, glaring at Nick as he held a fist to his mouth.

Birdy nodded as though this were the most interesting bit of information she had received all day—most likely because she would be using it later on in conversation with my poor, hopeful mother. I expected her to continue with another slew of questions, digging for more information to relay back to her master, but she left it at that.

She took our order, not bothering to jot it down in her notepad. After twenty years of serving us turkey club wraps and coffee, she had become a pro and committed it to memory. She turned on her heel to fetch mugs, giving Nick a whopping few minutes to interrogate me.

"*So* ... Holly, huh?" He folded his arms on the table and leaned forward with a sly smile that made him look like the sleazy wingman in an R-rated movie about a bunch of buddies looking to get laid. "Why haven't *I* heard about her?"

"Because it isn't a big deal. She's someone I hang out with at Reade's occasionally, and one time, we came here together as *friends*. Birdy met her, and of course she ran with it. But seriously, dude, we are *friends*—that's all." I crossed my fingers that he bought the friend bit, but to my dismay, he didn't. He knew me better than that, and for this, I cursed him and lifelong friendships.

"Not a big deal? Dude, you haven't stayed in contact with a woman since Julia left." Groaning, I leaned my head back to stare up at the tiled ceiling and raked both hands through my hair. Nick let out a triumphant laugh and pointed a finger at me, thrusting it across the table and against my chest. "Ha! I *knew* it! So, come on, who is she? A babysitter? Robbing the cradle, huh?"

"Shut the fuck up," I snapped, and he raised his hands in surrender with a mumbled apology. "And I told you already. I met her at Reade's, and we hang out a couple times a week." Nick raised his eyebrows, gesturing for me to elaborate. "What do you want to know?" I sighed with irritation.

Leaning against the table, Nick's eyes looked to the pendant lamp hanging above us and shrugged his shoulders up to his ears. "Oh, you know, when you met, what does she look like, is she good in bed ... You know, the usual shit."

Birdy bounded over to us with our water and coffee, the ceramic of the cups clattering against the surface of the table as she put them down with gusto. One red-tipped hand tapped against the aluminum edge of the bench seat I sat on, peering down at me. "What are we talking about, boys?"

"Hey Birdy, what does Holly look like?" Nick asked, mischievously wiggling his eyebrows at her.

She clapped a hand over her heart, her mouth dropping open in exaggerated awe. "Oh, Nicky, she's *gorgeous*. Dark hair, *beautiful* dark brown eyes... They'll have very attractive kids; I can tell you that." She nodded with confidence, resting a fist against a heavy hip.

A groan escaped my lungs as I shielded my face with the clammy palms of my hands. Taking the hint, Birdy squeezed my shoulder before walking away to tend to other diners. A second or two of silence passed, and my mind filled the darkness between my eyes and hands with pathetic visions of us as parents—together. I dropped them to the table when it became too much.

"So?" Nick said, sipping at his water. "Have you gotten laid?"

"Nope," I replied shortly, stirring my coffee despite it having nothing to stir.

"You have a girlfriend, and you haven't slept with her yet?" He pushed his glasses onto his nose, averting his eyes as he sat in bewildered judgement. "Is she seriously too young? Because man, I ... I really can't condone that kind of—"

"Holy shit, Nick." My patience was wearing thin. "I told you, she's *not* my girlfriend."

"Why the hell not?"

And that was when my tethers snapped, leaving the fragments of my sanity frayed and flapping in the wind. "Why the fuck *should* she be?" I crossed my arms and let my head roll to the side. "She doesn't even know who I am."

He looked at me suspiciously. "How the hell does she not know? Everybody around here knows who you are."

"Well, she's younger than us, for one thing, and grew up a few towns over, then lived in the city for a long time, and ..." I sighed, shaking my head. "Maybe she's lived under a rock for the past five years. I have no clue. But either way, she doesn't, okay? And the fucked up thing is, I *love* it. I really fucking love it. It feels so *good* to be absolutely nobody for once. But when she finds out—and she *will* find out—it's all going to blow up in my face. I fucked it up a long time ago and I'm just biding my time before it all goes to hell, okay? Now drop it." I set my jaw, the muscles trembling under the strain of my self-loathing.

Nick's excitement had faded. He took his glasses off, dropping them to the table with a tinny clatter and rubbed his temples. "Jesus, Brandon. You and your hatred towards your amazingly enviable, pathetic life." He pinched the bridge of his nose. "Okay, let me ask you something. Did you ever think that you might be somebody to *her*?" He dropped that ton of bricks over my head, and I felt them landing one by one onto my shoulders. Piling higher and higher until I couldn't breathe under the weight.

"Yes," I said quietly. She had told me I was her best friend. That certainly meant I was somebody.

"So, how exactly did you see this all playing out? I'm really interested to hear it." Nick leaned against the back of his seat, folding his arms over his bony chest.

"I don't fucking know, Nick. I guess I thought she'd find out one day, she'd get pissed at me for keeping it from her, and—" My voice dropped to a whisper in synchronization with my eyes, gazing at the table. "Yeah, that'd be it."

"*Holy shit*." Nick uttered, uncrossing his arms. "You *really* like her."

I sighed, shaking my head, and then I was swallowed up by a wave of unexpected emotion. Fighting hard against the constriction in my throat, I brought a hand up to shield my eyes; pointer finger and thumb pressing against my temples.

"No, I fucking *love* her, Nick," I said, and with an embarrassing intake of quivering breath, I felt the beginnings of tears prick at my eyes. I shook my head, rapidly blinking them away, and dropped my hand. "Dude, I'm terrified of telling her the truth. It's so fucking stupid, and I know it's what I have to do, but—*fuck*. What happens if she finds out and gets pissed off that I kept it from her? What if I tell her and all she sees is dollar signs? What if she goes to the press and ruins me? I guess I would deserve that, but—"

"*Or* … what if *none* of that happens? What if she loves *you*, for whatever fucking reason, and this is your chance at being happy?" I blinked my response, feeling foolish for never thinking of that as a possibility. "If you love her, it's not fair to either of you to not tell her."

Birdy brought over our meals, and gasped at the tail-end of the line she had overheard. "You *still* haven't told her? Brandon Alexander Davis, what in Heaven's name is wrong with you?"

she hissed at me, placing the heaping plates of food down in front of us. "Your mother is going to *kill* you, you know."

"Well, if you had kept your damn mouth shut like I had asked you to, Mom never would have known about any of this in the first place," I reminded her stiffly, rolling my eyes up to look at her.

The manicured hand that had sat on her hip reached out to grab my scruffy chin and forcefully turned my head to face her. My eyes met hers and saw not anger at my fresh talk, but compassion towards my well-being. I felt the stone walls of my heart begin to crumble.

"B., the whole 'reclusive author' thing doesn't work for you, so knock it off. Listen to your friend, and tell that girl how you feel." I grumbled a response, not committing or signing any contracts, and she released me with a gentle shove. "Okay, now I'm going to get a bag of food together for you. I'll send you home with another turkey club, and you want a chunk of this new blueberry crumble I tried out? The crumble is made of— get this—Cap'n Crunch. You want to try some?"

I swallowed at the lump in my throat. "Yeah, sure."

She clapped me on the back jovially, as though the serious turn in conversation had never been taken.

As Birdy walked away towards the kitchen, Nick salted his fries and I took a bite of my wrap despite not feeling at all hungry. The turkey rolling around on my tongue instantly turned sour, and I forced myself to swallow.

I turned my head to look out the window at the SUV I had custom-built for myself the moment I could afford it, and I thought about Holly's old rusty minivan. I thought about the old Victorian on the lake in Brightwaters, standing empty with the ghosts inhabiting its walls, cursing my name for leaving it empty for so long. I thought about how she could turn it into her dream home in any way she wished. I thought about how long it had been since I had eaten a home-cooked meal on a night that wasn't Thanksgiving or Christmas, and how big my bed never ceased to feel.

Finally, I thought about her eyes and how I found myself struggling to not disappear in their depths. My desperate need to protect her from anything that could cause her harm. Kissing her in the parking lot and the lack of self-control I felt for the first time in years. What kind of idiot would throw that away? Maybe this chance wasn't meant for another me in another life, but *this* me, *this* life.

I nodded to myself. A decision was made, and although I was scared shitless, I knew it was the only thing that felt right.

"So, hey, I have a question." Nick broke the silence, looking up casually.

"Yeah?"

"Holly … She's the inspiration, huh?" Nick asked, and I turned back to him. My expression seemed to say it all. "Okay, I'll see what I can do. Write your goddamn book, and I'll handle the rest."

And just like that, my shoulders felt a little lighter.

15

holly

THE BRUISE AROUND MY EYE had started to get better—and by better, I mean it was garish and a lovely shade of brown. According to Google, this was an obvious sign of it healing, and that it wouldn't go through any other color transformations; instead, it was now going to fade away until it was gone. But according to *me*, it was just as hideous as it was when it was red and blackish purple.

And while its appearance was apparently looking better, the pain of having a broken eye socket hadn't improved much in a little more than a week's time. I mean, I guess the constant throbbing had started to subside a little—but still, it was a broken bone, for crying out loud, and I wasn't blessed with supernatural healing powers.

What I was blessed with, however, was a date with Ben, the buddy Mark had distastefully mentioned to me on that fateful day when his daughter cracked my face. So, I guess in a way, he owed me.

Liz had known exactly who the buddy in question was, and she seemed excited enough for me to go out with him. But when she asked what had suddenly changed my mind, I neglected to tell her that my romance novels were starting to get the better of me at Story Time. Making me feel things I wasn't wanting to feel for friends and all that. So instead, I told her that

I was ready to get back in that saddle again, and I guess it wasn't entirely a lie.

With a date coming up and a fresh desire to look like a human being and less like an extra on *The Walking Dead*, I talked Liz and Esther into going out with me to get our hair done. It wasn't difficult to twist Liz's arm, but Esther was a whole other story with her insisting that Harry was fine with her looking like an old used Q-tip.

"Come on, Esther," I had pleaded, "don't you think your creepy ghost husband would love to see you with a new 'do?'" She did begrudgingly agree to going, but only for a trim and nothing more.

Liz and I had gotten our hair colored; a lightened blonde with honey highlights for Liz and a deep auburn for me, giving my already dark hair a nice reddish hue. Esther was left to badger the receptionist about the offensive smell of the place. Liz and I exchanged mortified glances, listening to our friend threaten to call her attorney to question him about elder abuse. Luckily, she refrained from calling any lawyers and once we all sat to get our haircuts, her crabbiness changed to something sort of resembling excitement.

"Esther, you look *adorable*," Liz cooed, admiring the poufy pixie Esther's wispy hair had been cut into.

"Oh, knock it off. Old people hate being called adorable, like we're fucking kittens or something," Esther snapped, but I caught that little smile on her face as she studied her hair in the mirror.

"Oh, hell no, Esther. You're no kitten—you're a *cougar*," I teased as I went cross-eyed, watching the stylist cut away at my new set of bangs.

"The hell does that mean?" Esther asked, and Liz and I laughed along with the giggles of our respective stylists.

Liz had her long mid-back length hair chopped to her shoulders in a cute layered bob with angled bangs that framed her rounded face perfectly. The rest of my hair was trimmed to a few inches below my shoulders and I asked for long layers with some angled pieces around my face, and I'd say the job had been done sufficiently. I could have cried looking at the sleek glossiness of my hair, giving life to something that had turned so dull.

I hoped Ben would like it, despite not having the slightest clue who the hell Ben even was or if I'd even like him in the first place.

We paid, treating Esther to the treatment we had talked her into, and she insisted on treating us to lunch. Remembering the burger I had eaten at the Golden Carousel, I made the suggestion as our dining destination. Without any other cravings among the carful of women, they agreed that some diner food sounded good, and Liz traveled down Main Street until we came by the shiny exterior and she turned her Explorer into the parking lot.

Birdy welcomed us when we walked in. I recognized her immediately, but thanks to my new hair and the lovely blackened-brown bruise that seemed to swallow a quarter of my face, she didn't seem to recognize me at all. Not even a double take, and I thanked God for that.

She sat us in a booth and doled out the menus, giving us a grin and a few minutes to look over the menus.

"I haven't been to a diner in years," Esther mused with a smile, sliding a thick pair of glasses onto her nose before looking the menu over.

"Esther, have you gone *anywhere* in years?" Liz teased, peering at her over her own menu.

"Robert takes me out to Brooklyn for the holidays, Elizabeth. You know that. Don't be a wiseass." Her voice suggested she was irritated, but she smiled and looked up at us, her eyes magnified at least four times through the lenses. "This has been a really nice day, girls. Harry's going to *die* when he sees my hair."

I thought about pointing out the obvious, but …
Nah. Not worth it.

After several minutes of silence with our noses shoved in the laminated pages of our menus, Birdy returned to the table and asked if we were ready. We ordered three unsweetened iced teas, two turkey club wraps, and a chicken salad sandwich—all with fries on the side, thank you very much.

Birdy beamed at the order and slipped her note pad back into the pocket of her apron. "An easy one. Thank you, ladies. I'll be right back with your drinks."

She turned and as she walked towards the kitchen, I heard her voice, shrill with excitement, as she greeted someone that had just walked in, and dammit if my stomach didn't do a somersault. But it wasn't Brandon, I noticed, pretending to stretch my neck out to the side as I looked to see who had entered. Close call.

Or was it?

I mean, did it *really* matter if he walked in that very second and noticed me sitting there with my sister and friend? Did it *really* matter if they met him and had a face to put to the name? The more I thought about it, the more it actually didn't seem like the worst thing to happen. When I thought about it even *more*, I found myself actually wishing he'd show up. That he could just walk in there as I willed him to, walk up to the booth, and beam at the sight of me in the way that he did

But in the span of forty minutes, Birdy brought our food over, we ate through vibrant conversation, and Esther paid the bill; never once did he walk in. The disappointment was hard to ignore as we left the diner, and because my life had been proving to be the plot of a romantic comedy, we turned the corner to find ourselves face-to-face with the very person I had been hoping for. His own companion gabbed his ear off as he fell silent at the sight of me, and a smirk curled at the corners of his mouth.

"You have to be kidding me," he said, bringing his friend to silence with the raise of a finger. "So, you're telling me that not only do I have to find myself a new bookstore, but I have to find a new diner too?"

"Maybe, but I was here first, so it sorta looks like *you're* the stalker, actually." I apologetically grimaced, and smiled when he stepped forward to kiss me on the cheek. "Hello to you, too."

The man he was with raised an eyebrow to Brandon, silently exchanging a look that I recognized, *"Who the hell are these people?"* Oddly enough, the two ladies flanking my sides were giving me a very similar look, narrowed eyes passing between Brandon and me.

Speaking up first, Brandon turned to the lanky man with the beak-like nose and beady eyes hiding behind a little pair of wire-rimmed glasses. "Nick, this is Holly. Holly, Nick."

I watched as the man's expression changed from one of suspicion to one of instant knowing as his mouth dropped open, nodding slowly. *"Ohh, riiight."* He turned to me, and extended a hand with some of the longest fingers I had ever seen. "Very nice to meet you. Brandon talks about you." His hand engulfed mine, and we shook as he added, *"A lot."*

"Thank you very much for that, Nicholas," Brandon said with a flush of his cheeks.

At the mention of his name, Liz and Esther simultaneously turned to look up at him, uttering what could have been a rehearsed "ohh." I knew my cheeks had to be burning brighter than a goddamn tomato on fire. I introduced them to him and he graciously shook their hands with a smile that could have made any woman swoon, and they undoubtedly were.

Esther noticed one of Brandon's tattoos peeking out from the sleeve of his leather jacket. She reached out with wrinkled old hands, sliding the sleeve up as far as it would allow, while his crystal blue eyes widened with shocked amusement. I stood there, completely mortified, as she peered up at him and asked, "You got any others?"

"Indeed, I do," he said, glancing up at me with his half-smile.

"Oh, yeah? Well, let's see 'em," Esther said, as she dropped his hand and looked up expectantly.

Nick and Brandon both laughed with surprise, and he replied, "Sure, but you have to buy me dinner first."

She smirked with a nod, and turned to me. "Yeah, I like him." As if I needed her approval. Then with a wave of her hand, she motioned for Liz to follow her. "Take me to the car, Elizabeth. My ass is freezing out here, and my blood thinners aren't appreciating it."

Liz nudged me in the ribs and whispered, "Wow." She turned to smile at Brandon and his friend before taking Esther by the arm. "It was nice to finally meet you," she said, and hurried off to the car; the two of them giggling like teenagers all the way.

Nick took that as his cue, and told Brandon he'd get their table, and with a gallant little bow, he mentioned again how nice it was to meet me. "I hope I see you again," he added, and with that, he was hurrying into the diner.

And suddenly, we were alone.

"You had your hair done," Brandon mentioned immediately, cocking his head slightly as he gazed down at me. "It looks nice," he added, stuffing his hands into his pockets.

"Thanks," I said with a smile, automatically touching the soft ends of my freshly cut hair. "I have a date," I blurted out, feeling suddenly that he deserved an explanation for my sudden change in appearance.

I was bothered to find myself disappointed when Brandon didn't so much as flinch. "You might want to do something with your face first," he laughed, gently touching my cheek. "Still feeling shitty?"

I winced a little, and he pulled his hand away apologetically. "Yeah, but hey, that's what drugs are for, right?"

"Or booze, but hey, pick your own poison." He laughed with a little shuffle of his feet. "Anyway, I should get in there, but I'm glad I bumped into you. Small towns have their perks."

"Yeah, they do," I agreed with a smile, and with another kiss on the cheek, he took off at a jog around me to hurry into the diner.

I made my way back to Liz's SUV and climbed into the passenger side to the two of them glaring at me. "What?" I asked, immediately on the defense.

"Let's just say," Esther began with a little clearing of her throat, "when you had told us about that time you got down and dirty with that guy, neither of us had expected someone quite like *that*."

I glanced toward the backseat at her, and then over at Liz. "What do you mean?"

Liz laughed. "You said he was beautiful, but you do know he's *seriously* gorgeous, right?"

"He's okay," I said a little too casually, buckling myself in.

"Oh, yeah. Just *okay*." Liz smirked with a knowing glare. "And—I don't know. I mean, I guess I didn't expect a guy who genuinely liked you."

"What, you thought I was hanging out with some douchebag or something?"

Liz shrugged with her hands raised. "I don't know! I think, at least for me, I assumed that he was some sleazy guy." I guess my expression had suggested I was insulted by the accusation, and she touched me lightly on the arm. "But he's really nice, and he obviously likes you a lot."

"He's a good friend," I said, mostly to myself.

Liz and Esther maintained a vow of silence as we drove through the varying side streets, making our way back to Liz's house, and a rather annoying paranoid little voice told me they weren't convinced of that.

A good friend.

Holly freakin' Hughes. Ignorantly oblivious.

16

holly

I REALLY THINK YOU'LL LIKE this guy," Liz said, standing in my doorway with her cup of tea held tightly in both hands. "You always like those dorky types."

"Stephen wasn't dorky!" I laughed. "He's a real man's man."

"Oh, yeah," she snickered, raising the mug to her lips. "Clearly."

Liz told me that I was meeting Ben for mini golf. No fancy restaurants to get dressed up for, thank God. It was relaxed and actually sounded like fun, and I found that not only was I looking forward to it, but I was nervous as all hell. It was a legitimate set-up with a guy that my sister's ex-husband was buddies with and saw on a regular basis. What happened if it didn't go well and the dynamic between them was forever awkward?

After I had gotten dressed for the date in a pair of leggings and a sweater, I noticed my palms growing clammy. I wiped them against the scarf I was about to wrap around my neck, silently telling myself to chill the fuck out. I left my hair down—a habit I had been easing myself into since getting my hair done—and I swept some mascara and eyeliner on in an attempt to make my face look at least a little more put together.

"Remember what I said about sleeping with handsome men, honey," Esther called over her fence before I got into the van.

"Oh God," I mumbled, flipping her my middle finger as I got in.

***

It wasn't long before I got to the course; a little sleazy hole in the wall that I immediately assumed crawled with high schoolers on any given weekend. I half expected to see beer bottles and condom wrappers hiding behind one of the several billboards leading up to the place, and my expectations of the date began to suffer. I parked the van close to the gated entrance, in the event that I needed to make a quick run for it. If he seemed at all like he was going to conveniently slip something into my drink, I was going to high-tail it the hell out of there.

It seemed like a sound plan, as I climbed out of Ol' Rusty, and that's when a younger looking man approached me.

"Um … Holly?" he asked with a worried expression on his face, and in his hand, I noticed a picnic basket. He seemed adorably unsure of himself and reminded me of a lost kid who had packed his lunch before he ran away from home, and dammit, I smiled.

My stomach flipped with excitement as he stepped closer, the friendly twinkle of his eyes dancing in the light of the parking lot.

"You must be Ben." I extended my hand to him, hoping he didn't notice how it trembled, and he eagerly accepted.

"Oh, thank God. I have no idea how this blind date stuff works. I didn't want to come up to the wrong woman and scare the hell out of her, you know?" He was flustered, and God help me, he really was cute.

Ben was obviously a few years younger, and the slight hint of a goatee on his chin didn't help to make his baby face look any older. His dirty blonde hair was scruffy in a way that made him look simultaneously messy and put together. He was decently tall without the threat of killing me had a strong wind come along to blow him over, and from the looks of things, he had a pretty nice, slightly above average build. But what really made him stand out were his striking green eyes, and even in the dim lighting of the parking lot, they reminded me of lucid gem stones.

"Do you play mini golf?" he asked, feeling a little less flustered and a lot bolder as he took my hand in his, leading me towards the entrance of the golf course. I noticed that I felt nothing but his warm, slightly clammy hand engulfing mine. No sparks, no fireworks, no nothing that would set him apart from any other guy, but he felt comfortable. I could settle for comfortable.

I shook my head in response with a smile, feeling playful and shy and incredibly intrigued as to where the night was going to take me. At this, his eyes widened, as though it were totally inconceivable for someone to not partake in miniature golf on the regular. I half expected for him to say something about it being the most incredible pastime ever, that I was seriously missing out, and that if I was interested, I could join his league.

If there were, in fact, miniature golf leagues.

Instead, he asked, "Have you ever played?" I responded with a nod and a little smile, and he grinned. "Well, I hope you're ready to have your ass kicked, because I'm literally here every single weekend."

Well, that was certainly something to brag about.

I suppressed a sarcastic giggle as we approached the counter and a young man with the furriest brows I had ever seen acknowledged Ben by name.

"Ben! How's it going, man? What can I get you? The usual?"

He has a usual. At a mini golf place.

Ben smiled at me, and then turned to smile at Caterpillar Brows. "Well, I'll have my usual, and maybe a—hmmm, you know what?" He eyed me carefully, clearly calculating something in his head as his pursed lips moved from side to side. "Give me a purple handle. That might be good for Holly here."

"Holly, huh?" Caterpillar Brows said, glancing at me before giving Ben a wink that didn't exactly ooze class. He grabbed two clubs from behind the counter. "No Kaylee today?"

Kaylee? Who the hell is Kaylee?

I guess I was due to date a man-whore. I had dated a gay man and a world-class asshole, so why not add a player to the list? My stomach sank with disappointment as I shifted uncomfortably in my shoes.

"Nah, she's with my mother tonight," Ben replied, as though the idea of this guy just casually mentioning the name of another woman was a totally normal thing to do while on a date.

I felt nauseous. What the hell had Mark done to me?

Holly freakin' Hughes. The other woman.

Ben took the clubs, handing me the one with the purple handle and said, "See how that one feels to you. You might need something a little taller."

I took the club and positioned myself in my most professional golf stance, which was apparently all wrong. Ben laughed, a little attractive arrogance seeping through, and stood behind me with his hands over mine, moving them into the proper alignment to correctly hold the club. My back and shoulders pressed against his chest, his arms taut against mine. My lips parted, inhaling and exhaling loudly, as he helped me test it out by winding our arms back, moving with me, and taking a faux swing at absolutely nothing.

"How did that feel?" Ben asked, placing a warm hand on my shoulder, rounding to face me with his endearing smile and emerald eyes.

"W-what?" I asked, my cheeks burning from the rush of intimate contact.

He smiled, his own face turning a brighter shade of pink. "The club. Is it okay?"

Embarrassed, I bobbed my head rapidly, confirming his original assessment and hoping the shaking would knock some sense into me. Who gets turned on by mini golf?

Me. That's who.

Ben confirmed the club selection with a squeeze of my shoulder and a thumbs-up to the furry-browed kid behind the counter.

Caterpillar Brows handed us two balls. "Okay, guys, have fun," he said. "Tell Kaylee I said hi."

***

And so, we played mini golf.

Honestly, I wouldn't be the right person to describe a game of golf in proper golf terminology. I couldn't even properly hold a golf club until Ben so expertly showed me how. But I will say that he *did* kick my ass. Apparently the fewer the hits, the better, and Ben only told me this after I jumped up and down with child-like glee when I saw how high my score was. At least he let me down gently. He could have really rubbed it in and made me feel like crap, but instead he squeezed my shoulder, looked into my eyes, and told me that, no, I wasn't winning but I was still "doing great."

A liar, but a sweet one.

While I was busy losing miserably, I had learned a bit about Ben. Like that he was a widower, and Kaylee? His five-year-old daughter. Two little details I wish I had known about before venturing on a date with him. Maybe then I could have spared him the shocked look on my face, and the lingering discomfort that hung in the air long after the game had ended.

"So, you didn't know about Kaylee, huh?" he asked, as he pulled a Tupperware out of the picnic basket, along with a couple paper plates and plastic utensils. "I hope you like lemon chicken and rice. It really is incredible what you can do with a crockpot."

I inhaled deeply as he opened the lid. "Real food sounds amazing, thank you." He raised an eyebrow in question. "My sister is the take-out queen."

"Ah, right. *Liz* … Single working parent. I totally understand." I had also learned that Ben was a new veterinarian at his father's animal clinic with a full schedule. "Kay and I used to live on McDonald's and Taco Bell until my Mom got me the crockpot. Now, it's crockpot dinners every night. Crockpot meatloaf, crockpot stew, crockpot baked ziti …"

He spooned chicken and rice out onto the plates, and as we set out to eat, he repeated, "You didn't know about Kaylee."

I took a bite of chicken, closing my eyes to savor the lemony zest. "This is *so* good," I groaned.

"Thanks," he said with his dimpled smile, "but are you purposely avoiding this conversation, or …"

I placed the plate in my lap and breathed out heavily. "No, I didn't know that you have a daughter," I said, avoiding his eyes by poking the rice around with my plastic fork.

The truth was, I was downright annoyed that I hadn't known. Mark certainly had, and I was sure Liz did as well. It would have been nice to be aware of that little factoid before considering him as my rebound. What if we really hit it off for a while, and then decided to break up? How could I break the heart of a little girl, especially if she was to the point of calling me Mama Holly or something? I wasn't sure I was prepared to handle that kind of baggage when I already carried too much of my own.

As though he read my mind, Ben shook his head. "Look, I'm not looking for anything serious right now. I'm not going to be introducing you to my daughter anytime soon." I breathed a sigh of relief, and felt my cheeks flush at how obvious my apprehension had been. "Feel better?" he asked with a laugh.

"*Much*," I said, and felt that he could be exactly what I needed.

For a little while, at least.

We laughed, and I admired the emerald twinkle in his eyes. We talked and teased each other, and lightly touched hands and arms, and as the night went on, I felt that all too familiar tension growing between us. The more things progressed, the more I started to wonder if maybe I needed to slow things down. But it was hard to stop it, when he was so charming and nice to look at. I mean, the guy was a puppy and I wanted to take him home.

"What time is it?" I asked, glancing at the phone he had kept next to him in the event his mother had an urgent need to call.

He checked the time as per my request, and with a shocked expression, he looked sadly to me. "Late, and I have to rescue my mom soon, although Kay's probably sleeping, or at least I hope she is." He paused for a moment, our eyes meeting. There was a longing gaze, one that seemed to speak for itself. "But if she *is* sleeping, my mom wouldn't mind if she stayed over ..."

Oh God, oh God, oh God.

My stomach fluttered at the suggestive line, and I knew how my body wanted me to respond. It wanted me to go back to his place, strip it of all its clothes, and ravage him until we both passed out in a pile of lust and sweat. Judging from the way he stared at me, passion churning in his eyes, I knew that was exactly what he wanted too. I mean, of course it was; he was the one who brought it up, and if I needed any more proof of what his thought process might have been, he soon provided it by inching his face towards mine, staring into my eyes with every move.

I helped close the space between us by thrusting my mouth toward his, and all at once, our lips were acquainted. His were soft against mine and it didn't take many pecks before we escalated into a bundle of sexual rage; both of us reacting to a desire left untouched for too long. His hands were in my hair while mine fisted his jacket, and our tongues tangled, invading each other's mouths. His fingers traveled up and down my back, pulling at my shirt and everything else they could grab, and all I could wonder was how far away his place was.

And then, as Ben's hand was sliding its way up the front of my top, and I was preparing myself to have sex with a new man on an old blanket, his cellphone chimed. With fatherly concern, he pulled away immediately without a moment's hesitation and checked the screen, leaving me to adjust my twisted sweater.

"Oh *God*," he groaned as he turned to me. The fire in his eyes had been extinguished and it was replaced with guilt. "I'm so sorry. Mom is asking when I'm picking her up."

I shook my head and smiled. "Oh, don't apologize. It's fine."

Ben smiled a little through his embarrassment and said, "Well, I guess it's safe to say I'd really like to see you again."

"Good, because I'd really like to see you too."

It was the truth. I hadn't thought about anybody else all night, and it felt good. Refreshing. Safe.

Comfortable.

"Maybe next time I'll make you my famous crockpot spaghetti and meatballs," he said, and flashed me that dimpled smile.

And that was how I met Ben.

17
holly

I'M TRYING TO UNDERSTAND SOMETHING here. So, you had *another* handsome man all over you, and you didn't sleep with him? *Again?*" Esther asked in disbelief. The more time I spent with her, the more I began to see that Esther was quite the naughty one back in her day. It was a wonder she had stayed with her late husband for forty-one years before he passed.

"Oh, Jesus Christ," I groaned. I looked to Liz to come to my defense, but despite her straight-laced ways, she couldn't believe it either. What kind of person did these people think I was? "I don't need to sleep with every *handsome man* I meet, and it wasn't his fault. His mother texted him."

"Please, you could have insisted that you get in a quickie before he had to leave." Esther eyed me over the champagne flute before downing the rest of her mimosa.

"You didn't have any objections to begging *Brandon*," Liz pointed out, spearing a pancake onto her fork. "If he had gotten a text to pick up *his* kid, I bet you *still* would have begged him." With a mouthful of food, she added, "Not that I would've blamed you. I'd ignore the house burning down if it meant getting a piece of him."

Esther nodded, jabbing her knife in Liz's direction. "You know something? You're absolutely right. Holly would have woken up in *that* handsome man's bed if she'd had her way."

My hand clapped over my eyes. "Okay, first of all, if you say 'handsome man' one more time, I'm going to lose your dentures. And second of all, just because you do something once doesn't mean you do it again. Maybe I didn't push it with Ben because I didn't want to screw things up."

I swallowed my guilt immediately for ever saying that I thought what had transpired between Brandon and me had been anything but wonderful. I would have gladly relived that moment, and not just for the physical gratification but for the sensation of aptness that I got when we were tangled in the source of my fantasies. For the reminder of being a part of something so exciting, something so scary, and something so ... perfect.

My teeth bit against my bottom lip, as my inner voice yelled that kissing Ben was nice too.

"So, Brandon was a mistake, huh? That's not what it looked like when we saw you guys together," Liz teased as she bit into a piece of bacon.

Moving back to the topic of Ben, Esther threw her hands up. "I just don't understand how you could have a strapping young man all over you and you just ... let him go."

As Liz brought her glass to her lips, she replied to Esther with, "That's what I told her, Esther. And you should see him. He's *nice*. Maybe not Brandon-nice, but he's still nice to look at. I've always thought he was kind of cute, but you know, I was married, so ..."

I gave my sister an unnoticed sideways glance, and I could see a hint of a jealous flush. I tightened my lips, pressing them together in an attempt to keep my mouth from running as I cut up my pancakes.

"Actually," she continued, "let me see, maybe I can get a picture of him up on Facebook." She grabbed her phone, and after her fingers flew across the screen for a few moments, she handed the phone over to Esther. "Okay, here you go. Can you see this? Do you want me to make it bigger for you?"

Esther snatched the phone away from her. "Elizabeth, I'm *old*. I'm not fucking *blind*." She squinted at the phone, bringing it about an inch away from her face. Liz tried to reach around to help, but Esther swatted the hand away. "I'm *fine*—oh, Mother of Christ, Holly. You let this get away? If you don't want him, I'll take him. I'll show him what a real woman can do."

Groaning, I grabbed the phone from her, finding myself looking at the sweet and charming man I had spent my night with. The picture, taken outside at what looked like a backyard barbeque, showcased his more characteristic assets; his eyes namely, and the dimples of his smile. The sunlight turned his eyes a paler shade of green, a color that I could really only describe as breathtaking. I took note of his arms, on display thanks to the short-sleeved t-shirt he was wearing, and—shame on me—I couldn't help but compare them mentally to Brandon's; tattooed and sculpted with hard muscle, and undeniably sexy. Still, Ben's were pleasantly average with the slightest bit of definition. I looked at his eyes and the dimples of his grin, and I couldn't help that little prickle of regret coming from somewhere inside of me.

There was only one thing to do.

"So, how do I get in touch with him?" I asked, trying to sound casual as I handed Liz the phone.

Seeing through my façade, Esther nodded, wagging a bony finger at me. "You're regretting not getting a piece of that. I can see it in your eyes."

Liz got up to grab a pad of paper and a pen. "Well, you're in luck," she said, "because I have his number, and he said to call him any time."

Esther clapped her hands together in celebration of this grand discovery, and my nerves kicked into high gear as I took the number from Liz and grabbed my own phone. I felt the eyes of Esther and my sister burning holes through me as I swallowed my fear and dialed the number.

One ring, two rings, three …

"Hello?"

I willed my stomach to hold down my brunch of near-expired Bisquick and mimosas.

"Hi Ben, it's Holly. You know, from the other night?" My voice came out trembling and panicked, and I rolled my eyes at how ridiculous I was being.

He laughed. "You didn't think I forgot you, did you? Did Liz give you my number? I had—yes, honey, you're staying over Grandma's tonight." Did he slip that in there purposely? "Sorry. My daughter. Anyway, I was wondering if you were ever gonna call. I had given Liz my number on Facebook the other day, but ..."

I got up from the table to escape from the two pairs of ogling eyes, and hurried to my room. I closed the door and flopped on my bed, feeling like I was back at my parents' house, talking to my middle school crush (his name was David and he had a PlayStation before anybody else, which obviously made him the coolest).

I relished in the sensation of feeling young again.

"You there?"

"O-oh! Sorry, I had to get out of the kitchen. Liz and my next-door neighbor were driving me insane."

He let out a throaty chuckle that made my spine tingle. "Can I interest you in getting out of the house altogether?"

Oh God, he was smooth. I could feel his jacket under my hands and his scent in my nostrils and his taste in my mouth. I didn't even think before I blurted out, "Yes!" I clapped my hand over my mouth, surprised by how eager I was. Either Esther was rubbing off on me too much or I was letting my hormones talk before consulting with my brain.

I heard a door close, and then he whispered, "I don't mean to be too forward here, but I haven't been able to think about anything else since the other night."

Somehow, I found my voice, albeit only a fragment of what my voice actually was. It came out as a strained noise not unlike a hurt dog. "Me neither."

Was this really happening? Wait, what exactly *was* happening? Was I really *planning* to hook up with someone? That was certainly a first. My fingers found Camille, and they nervously tangled themselves in her soft hair.

"Kaylee!" he shouted, and I jumped, startled by the sudden noise. "I will be out in two minutes!" Back to a whisper, he grumbled, "Sorry about that again. I do love my daughter; I swear to God. Anyway, can I convince you to come over?"

"W-what? Now?"

"If I'm being too pushy, say so. I just really …" His voice went down to a whisper I could barely hear through the phone. "Holly, I want you so bad," he growled, bringing the skin on my arms to goosebumps.

I had to close my eyes to let the words sink in as my face burned something fierce, and fanned myself with a nearby romance novel. He sounded pained, like his life depended on a night of wild fornication, and I found myself desperate for the same remedy.

"I want you too," I whispered into the phone, then clapped my hand over my mouth again as Ben groaned.

"Thank God," he said with a relieved sigh. "Six? Does that work?" He sounded nervous beneath his sexy and vaguely confident exterior.

I didn't bother checking my schedule. I was free. Even if I wasn't free, I'd make sure I was. "Six works fine."

He was relieved, and gave me the address. I heard pounding from his end, and before he had a chance to scold his daughter for attempting to break down the door, we hung up. Instantly my body was filled with butterflies and anticipation for what the night had in store for me, and I hoped to Christ I still remembered how to be good in bed.

***

"Now, remember to call me after. I need to know *everything*," Esther said. She and Liz flanked me as I walked to the van, and I decided they were both way too involved in my life.

"That's definitely not happening," I replied, getting into the car.

Liz smiled like a parent sending their baby off to kindergarten. "I'm so happy for you, Holly. This is a good thing. I can feel it."

Esther stopped me from closing the door. "Speaking of feeling things, tell me—"

"You're both sick, you know that?" I laughed, trying to hide the jitters I was feeling. "I'll see you later—or tomorrow?" I grimaced, not knowing where the night was going to take me, and closed the door.

Driving to his house was proving to be a difficult task, and I wondered where confident uninhibited Holly had run off to. I figured it was because I was driving towards something I hadn't had in a long time, not to mention with someone I hardly knew, and—well, what if I had forgotten? What if my skills in the way of between-the-sheets activities had faded with my love for wearing anything but yoga pants and sweatshirts?

My stomach was in thousands of knots and my thoughts weren't helping any. Alcohol would have been welcomed, but I was driving and needed all my senses intact, so tea would have to suffice.

I pulled into Reade's parking lot, parked Ol' Rusty, and ran inside. I passed Bill with a smile and a wave, not bothering to say anything and risk being pulled into a conversation about the Thanksgiving decorations he was creating at the front counter. I hurried to the café and asked Scott for a large lavender Earl Grey, and then waited impatiently for my order to be filled.

Nervously I checked my phone, played with my hair, and just as I was about to check the little bit of makeup I had slapped on, there was a hand on my back and a kiss on my cheek. Not expecting the interruption, I quickly turned, prepared to attack my assailant, only to find myself face-to-chest with

Brandon. And for the first time since meeting him, I wished to God he had been anywhere but there.

"Oh, God, it's you," I said, breathing a sigh of relief as I looked up to his face. He looked a little confused, maybe hurt, by the comment. "Sorry, I thought you were some … pervert or something."

Brandon smiled and leaned against the counter with his arms crossed over his broad chest, the leather of his jacket creaking as he moved. "Well, for you, maybe I could turn into one." I rolled my eyes in response.

Where was that attitude when I needed it?

"Scott, is my drink ready?" I asked, and he held up his pointer finger as he continued to bop his head along to the song blasting through his headphones. My fingers tapped against the barista counter impatiently, when my drumming was interrupted by Brandon's throat clearing.

"Um, so I wanted to talk to you about something, if you're not busy." I looked back to him, seeing the smile had faded to give way to something much more serious. Regretfully I told him I was on my way somewhere, and his face fell. "It's really important, Holly, and I promise it won't take long."

A good friend would have stayed. A good friend would have listened to him, but I wasn't a good friend in that moment. I was a horny friend, one that was sick of being lonely in bed. "Can it wait?"

"Uh … Yeah, sure. I guess so," he said, attempting to hide his disappointment and failing miserably. "So, um, where are you going?"

I blushed at the question. "Well, actually, I went on that date the other night—the one I told you about—and uh, I'm seeing him again."

Brandon's body grew rigid and his tight jaw worked from side-to-side as a hand went to run through his hair. "So, it went well, huh? You didn't tell me that."

"I'm not *obligated* to tell you everything, Brandon," I unintentionally snapped at him.

His blue eyes widened at my tone. "Okay, that's fine," he replied cautiously. "Where is this guy taking you?"

My cheeks were on fire and I diverted my gaze. "Scott, can you please hurry up?"

Brandon grunted a sarcastic laugh. "Ah, say no more," he said as he pushed himself away from the barista counter and turned to leave.

But he couldn't just walk away, of course. He had to turn around. He had to open his mouth—his stupid, beautiful mouth. "I just hope you're not doing something stupid simply because you're lonely and want to be with someone. You're better than that."

I spun around, an anger brewing somewhere deep within. "Better than *what*? You have no idea who this guy is."

"Oh, and you do?"

The hypocrisy in the scenario pained me, as my breathing escalated heavily, burning my lungs with every deep inhale. I glared right up at him with my hands firmly on my hips. "Well, I sure as hell know more about *him* than I knew about you when *we* made out." His eyes widened as his jaw locked, his face reflecting the shock he felt, and the victory pushed me further. "Hell, I probably know more about him than I *currently* know about you. I know what he does for a living. I know exactly where he lives. I know about his family and his his, uh, his crockpot. What *exactly* do I know about you? I mean, really, Brandon. If you were going to try and talk me out of doing anything with someone, why couldn't it have been us?"

"Holly," Brandon said in a gravelly voice, his fists clenched as he struggled to speak in a calm tone. "You don't mean that."

"Stop." I thrust my hand up in front of my face, standing my ground. "You have spent the past several months opening your mouth with your opinions on how I live my life, and I've been listening, but now *you're* going to listen to *me*. You're *not* allowed to have an opinion about this. And you will *not* make me feel badly about it, just because *you* have chosen to be nothing more to me than *some guy* I sit with a couple times a week."

My eyes dropped to the floor, unable to look at how I had made him feel with the ambush of words that I never meant to say. I noticed Scott's headphones had been pulled down to sling around his neck, and he reluctantly handed me the cup of tea I had been waiting a thousand years for. I snatched it from him and shoved past Brandon, keeping my eyes on the floor as I hurried. My flats plodded hard against the rugs strewn throughout the store, which turned into concrete and finally asphalt as I headed to the van. But somewhere during my hurried walk, the anger I had felt dissipated and I was left with gut-retching guilt for lashing out at him.

What the hell did I just do?

I stopped and considered walking back inside, just as he came out of the store and started to walk purposefully to his car, his head hanging low.

"Brandon, wait!" I called to him, and I envisioned him ignoring me and leaving without saying anything, just like I had almost done. But the guy was unlike anybody else, and he walked towards me.

"I'm so sorry," I said as he leaned against the van. "I didn't mean that. I don't even know why I blew up at you like that." I laughed a little through my humiliation. "I'm just nervous about tonight, and—"

He sighed, cutting me off. "I'm sorry too." He paused, dropping his gaze to the asphalt beneath his feet. "But you did kind of mean what you said, and that's okay."

"No! You are so much more than just *some guy*, and I shouldn't—"

"Hey," he interrupted, turning so that he faced me. His eyes were a deep stormy blue, reflecting his mood accurately. I felt a large hand grab onto one of mine, holding tight as though he were scared to let go. "You're right in that I made a choice, and I have to live with that."

"What does that mean?" I asked, my voice trembling in a hoarse whisper. My eyes searched his face for any hint of an emotion I could grab onto, to decipher what he wasn't saying.

His dark blue eyes dropped to the hand he held, and forced a smile. "It means that I hope you have a good time tonight. I hope you don't run away from something that could make you happy." His fingers squeezed gently around mine, his thumb stroking along my knuckles. "And I hope he doesn't hurt you, because if he does, I can't promise I won't kill him."

I decided then that I wouldn't go to see Ben if Brandon had just said the word. I would have gladly spent the rest of the night sitting with him, doing absolutely nothing, instead of finally getting much-needed physical attention. All he had to do was tell me not to.

But he bent to kiss me on the cheek, gripping my hand all the while, and lingered for a moment before standing upright again. He took a deep breath, puffing his chest out, squeezing my hand once more before dropping it on his exhale.

"I, uh—I'll see you soon," he said, and walked backward for a pace or two, almost as if he were memorizing the way I looked in that moment, and he turned to hurry off to his car.

And all I could do was get back into Ol' Rusty and head over to Ben's, in hopes that I could forget another moment in Reade's parking lot.

18
holly

WHEN I PULLED UP TO Ben's house, my nerves switched into high gear and although I hadn't forgotten about whatever the hell had just happened with Brandon, I was hoping that Ben could help me with that.

The ranch-style home wasn't the most inviting from the outside. The lawn appeared dry and dead in the hazy glow of the light hanging next to the front door. There was little landscaping to speak of with the exception of a few low-lying shrubs that could've passed for tumbleweeds. But it was well lit inside, and while uninviting from its exterior, it wasn't scary, and I got out of the van to walk up the cracked concrete of the driveway, shivering at the constant tickle of the broken-through weeds against my ankles.

Esther would have a stroke out here.

Standing outside the door, I inhaled and exhaled slowly before knocking, making a conscious effort to clear my brain of anything but excitement for the night ahead. I told myself that Brandon didn't want me, Brandon was only a friend, and with a final deep breath, I knocked.

As if he had been waiting right on the other side, the door flew open. There to greet me was Ben and three large tail-wagging Labrador Retrievers—two black and one yellow. The three beasts pushed past Ben, tripping up his legs as they rushed toward me; pushing against me with their huffing black noses and slobbering mouths.

One of them—the biggest of the black dogs—jumped up to rest his heavy paws against my chest. A thick tongue lapped out of his wide mouth to slurp over my face. My eyes squeezed shut through the sloppy assault, hovering somewhere between amusement and panic.

After regaining his balance, Ben grabbed the dog by the collar and gently pulled him back to the ground. "Jesus, Rocky, that's not how we make friends," Ben told the dog, crouching next to the excited animal, mushing his snout affectionately with his hands before standing to flash me a genuine grin.

"Hey, I'm sorry about that. We don't get too many strangers around here. I hope you're not afraid of dogs," he said, apparently noticing the way I clutched my hands to my chest in an attempt to guard myself from the watering mouths of his hellhounds.

"O-oh, no, I, uh, I-I …" I closed my eyes, taking a deep controlled breath. I opened them again to Ben scratching the ears of the dog named Rocky, and I smiled then. "Let me try that again. No, I'm not afraid of dogs. I just wasn't really expecting that to be the first kiss I got tonight, but you know … here we are."

"Rocky just has a thing for the ladies, but here—let me make it up to you." And before I knew what was happening, he was standing and snaking an arm around my waist. He pulled me into him to press his lips firmly against mine for all of a couple seconds before backing away with a dimpled grin. "Better?"

"Much," I said with a relaxed smile.

Brandon who?

"I thought you might've gotten lost," he said, releasing his arm from my waist and stepping aside.

I walked into the house, petting the dogs as I went. "Oh, Liz wouldn't stop talking about work stuff," I lied, and took a look around the living room, taking note of the Barbie's and kitchen play set that seemed to be part of the décor.

He caught my gaze. "I bet Liz's living room looks a lot like this," he said with an apologetic smile.

"Comes with the territory," I laughed politely.

My eyes scanned the rest of the room, they fell upon pictures of his little girl—some current, and some of her as an infant—and then pictures of who I could only assume was his late wife; a young woman with a slight bone structure and stick-straight blonde hair. She was beautiful with a catching smile, and one of the rare people I would've considered perfect.

He had caught me looking, and as he scratched his head anxiously, he said, "Ah, yeah, that was Cassie. Sorry about all the pictures. I keep them around so that Kaylee can feel like her Mom is still with us." He faltered a little, and then added, "And, uh, me too." He diverted his eyes from me, ashamed of the confession.

"Oh, of course," I said, immediately taken aback by the apology.

"Anyway," he quickly changed the subject, placing a hand at the small of my back, the tips of his fingers lightly grazing against the upper slope of my butt. A shiver of excitement trailed through my body as he led me towards the kitchen, the dogs following us every step of the way. There on the table was the famed crockpot, a basket of sliced garlic bread, and a bottle of wine with a candle flickering in the center of it all. "I hope you like pasta. Sauce and meatballs are two of the things I cook best."

"Thank you. This is … great," I said, breathless with sudden emotion.

It was more than great. Here I thought I was heading over for a night of meaningless sex, and instead I was presented with an endearing romantic gesture.

Ben pulled out a chair, inviting me to sit before dimming the lights and rounding the table to his own chair, and we began our meal.

The food was delicious, and he had been right—he really could cook a mean sauce and meatball. The conversation, however, wasn't what I would call lively or even comfortable, but I chalked it all up to being in his home. I questioned if perhaps the setting had been almost *too* intimate, and maybe that was the reason why so many people opted to run away to the disconnected confines of hotel rooms.

"So, um, see any cool animals this week?" I asked, glancing up briefly from my plate.

Ben chopped a meatball with the side of his fork, then poked at the pieces distractedly. "Hmm … Yeah, I guess so. A, uh, a lady came in with a Chinook. Never seen one before, so that was cool."

I made an attempt at being remotely interested. "Oh, what's a Chinook?"

It sounded like maybe a rodent from some faraway arctic land, one that required intensive exotic care, and my mind conjured up a veterinary clinic that specialized in the strange and unusual. I sniffed a laugh with a little smile at the thought of someone waltzing through the door with a warthog in a harness.

"A Chinook," Ben said in between bites of meatball, "is a dog. One of the rarest breeds, I think, or at least the last time I checked."

And just like that, my visions of an exotic animal emporium fluttered away. "Oh, that's cool," I muttered without enthusiasm, but I smiled nonetheless because it seemed to be of some importance to him.

"So, uh, how's Liz been?" Ben asked, taking a sip of wine.

I hadn't expected the conversation to steer towards my sister, but at least it was something I could talk about without falling asleep. "She's good. Working at the dentist's office."

He nodded. "I haven't seen her in … God, it's gotta be years. We're on Facebook, but we don't really *talk*, you know? So, I was pretty surprised when Mark mentioned setting me up with her sister."

That made two of us. "How do you know Mark?"

"I went to school with his brother. You know Josh?"

I wobbled my hand in the air, squinting one eye. "I met him at the wedding, but I don't *know* him."

"Oh, *yeah*, I guess you would have been at the wedding. I was in the wedding party," Ben mused with an excited smile.

I tipped my head slightly, trying to place him. "You were? I was the Maid of Honor. I don't remember you."

He grimaced with a shake of his head. "Yeah, you probably wouldn't. I was eighteen and very, um, skinny with black hair."

My mouth and eyes opened in shock, remembering the gothic-looking kid who spent the entire night sulking because he couldn't legally drink anything.

I pointed at him across the table. "Oh, my God, I *do* remember you," I laughed.

"Yeah, yeah." He waved my amusement away with his hands. "Anyway, Josh and I would hang out after school every now and then. I met Mark one of the times I was over there, and we really hit it off. Been good friends ever since. He's a great guy." I unintentionally snickered. "Well, to me, anyway."

I nodded my apologies. "No, I know. It's just, uh, the history with my sister. I'm a little biased."

"Oh, yeah, I completely understand. Liz did *not* deserve the shit he put her through, that's for damn sure. He had a good thing with her and he royally screwed that up." Ben rubbed the stubble along his upper lip, drifting off somewhere away from me. "I always thought he was an idiot for throwing that away."

He looked into the flickering candle flame, hooding his eyes in the light with his finger crooked around the curve of his lip. The room filled with silence, aside from the gentle snores from the dogs coming from the adjacent living room, and the awkward atmosphere returned again. I thought about asking where he had gone, what he was thinking about, but something told me I probably didn't care to know.

"So, um, anyway, I wanted to ask you a sort of personal question," he said after a few moments of silence, and I urged him to continue. Anything was better than the uncomfortable quiet. "Don't be offended, but you were with a gay guy for five years, right? How did you *not* suspect anything?" he asked with a laugh that I interpreted as facetious.

"Well, it's not like it was something I thought to ask," I stated wryly before taking a long sip of wine. "How do you even know about that? *I* didn't tell you."

He shook his head, reaching across the table to take my hand, and for reasons I couldn't understand, an image of Brandon jumped into mind. Ben's hand enfolded over mine, gently rubbing his thumb along the ridges in the back of my hand, and I focused on his touch, with hopes that I could erase the notion that it felt …

Wrong. This is wrong.

"I'm sorry. Mark had mentioned it," he said with sincerity, and I made a mental note to slaughter Mark. "I was just genuinely curious, but I didn't realize you were, uh—"

"Hung up on it?" I asked accusingly. He briefly winced and looked off to the side, shrugging. "I'm not, *really*," I insisted, and mostly meaning it. "But I don't like talking about it."

He nodded, looking back to me with those big green eyes. "It isn't easy to lose the most important person in your life—no matter how you lose them."

I was so embarrassed that he would liken the death of his wife to my break-up, but I managed an appreciative smile. What I couldn't shake was the thought that passed through my mind at his comment. He had referred to Stephen as the "most important person in my life," and when he said those words, I found myself chewing on my lip with the nagging feeling that he had been horribly wrong.

My lip trembled, remembering suddenly that Brandon had wanted to tell me something and I had blown him off—and for what? For dinner and meaningless sex with a man I had absolutely nothing in common with?

My shame and guilt pushed a tear out of my eye, and I wished that Ben hadn't seen it, but of course he had. In the glow of the candlelight, that one single tear probably shown like the sun, reflecting the colors of the rainbow off the walls like the freakin' Northern Lights.

Without saying a word, he stood from the table and took my hand, pulling me up from my chair. "Here, it's okay," he said softly, wrapping his arms around me.

He was so warm and welcoming and instinct told me to wrap my arms around him, and before I knew it, my face was buried in his chest, and I shed a few more tears. I allowed Ben to think that I was crying over the loss of my ex-lover, while I internally beat myself up over making Brandon feel any less important than he was.

The most important person in my life.

His hands rubbed my back and he kissed the top of my head. It wasn't meant to be seductive, but every second that went by, I was feeling more and more aroused by his need to hold me, and I remembered why I was there. I let my hands run the length of his back, the soft fabric of his worn-in t-shirt gliding under my fingers.

"Ben," I mumbled against his chest.

He pulled away, so that there was only just a whisper of space between us. I lifted my head, tilting my chin upward, looking into his eyes. He bent his neck, his mouth barely touching my lips, and he hovered there.

"Your ex-boyfriend is an idiot," he whispered, his eyes gazing into mine.

There was something in the way he spoke, or maybe it was the flame reflected in his eyes, but whatever it was, it was the final straw. With a lust that traced from my fingertips all the way down to the soles of my feet, I thrust my lips against his, needing to forget about everything but how desperate I was to feel wanted.

Within seconds of frenzied passion-driven kissing, I felt Ben's hands reach down to cup the two halves my ass, hoisting me up and I wrapped my legs around his waist. A vivid flash of memory came through of leaning against the side of the van, but

I shoved it away, focusing entirely on Ben and continuing my assault on his mouth as he carried me off to—well, somewhere in his house. Somewhere that I soon discovered was his bedroom.

Ben broke the continuous kiss to gently lay me on the bed, easing his larger frame on top of mine. I sighed as I felt him pressing against me, finding myself comforted by his weight, grinding his hips against mine as we resumed the tango with our tongues.

His kisses left my mouth and trailed down my neck, his tongue hot and wet against my skin. His erection pressed against the heat between my legs, and I shifted slightly, reaching my hand down to investigate. But just as I was seeking my destination, just as he inhaled sharply at the feeling of someone aside from himself touching the most intimate part of his body, I felt something else. Something even more hard and far more painful poking me right in the ass.

"Ow!" I shouted, scrambling to get up against his weight and he jumped right off the bed.

"W-what? What's wrong?" His hand frantically reached over to a wall and flipped on the light. "Oh, goddammit, Kaylee," he muttered, pulling a Barbie doll out from where I had been laying. He sighed and suddenly, he sounded tired and much older than he was "I'm sorry. She leaves her crap everywhere."

I saw in his eyes for the first time how exhausted and frustrated he was, having to do so much on his own. And maybe I was just trying to rationalize what we were about to do, but I felt that we both needed this; if for nothing else but for some kind of release that nothing else was capable of providing.

I knelt on the bed, wrapping my arms around his neck. "Shh, it's okay," I whispered into his ear. His arms went to my waist, burying his face in my neck. His stubble scratched roughly against my skin in a way that was sure to sting the next morning, but it felt deliriously good in the moment, and I sighed.

The night took us from a feverish desperation for release, to a sense of present belonging in each other's arms, while the bed beneath us played a tune I had missed more than I thought I ever could.

My eyes had remained closed for all but one moment, and in that one brief moment, I found him looking down at me and the fervent movement of his hips slowed in pace. I felt everything from the beating of his heart against my chest to the hairs of his legs against my inner thighs, and it all became real. Before that one single moment it could have been nothing more than a memory with Stephen, or one of my hot dreams with a young Tom Selleck. But in that moment, when my eyes met his, I was with Ben.

"God," he breathed, looking unblinking into my eyes. One of his hands crept up to brush my tangled hair from my face. "You are so beautiful."

The moment was sweet—typical Ben—and I wished I could have kept gazing into his eyes, to feel everything, but I couldn't bring myself to delve deeper. Instead, I dug my face into his shoulder, closing my eyes against his sweat dampened skin, and let myself fall back into my fantasies with Tom and tried to convince myself that it would be this way with anybody different and new.

19
holly

HIGHER!" ANNA SHOUTED GLEEFULLY FROM her perch two feet above my head.

I sighed through my responsible nerves. "Anna, if I push you any higher, you're going to flip over the swing set and Mommy won't like getting a call from the hospital."

"*Higher!*"

Grumbling, I gave her a forceful shove, sending the toddler swing only a few inches higher, but it seemed good enough judging by her delighted screams.

It was unseasonably warm for November on Long Island, with the temperature hovering somewhere around the mid 60s. The forecast was calling for a frost come the end of the week and I figured I'd treat Anna with a trip to the park before the weather became too unbearable. It wasn't common for me to bring her to the little park in the quaint town of Brightwaters, because she had a perfectly good swing set in the backyard that she rarely had the desire to use. But on that particular day, I thought it would do us both some good to get some fresh air.

Another woman seemed to have the same idea, sitting on a nearby bench while her two small children played on a seesaw. Whenever the kids made a noise that would suggest they were having less than a good time, she'd glance up from her phone and scold them with disgust before looking down at the screen.

"Higher!" Anna shrieked, giggling as she outstretched her arms, spreading her fingers into the air.

"Seriously, Anna Banana, if I push you any higher, I'm going to launch you into space. I'd really rather not explain to your mother why we have to send your dinner to the moon."

As Anna giggled, my phone vibrated in my back pocket. Resuming my pushing one-handed, I pulled the phone out to check who had disturbed my relaxing day of shoving a toddler on a swing until my arms fell off, and I wasn't surprised to find that it was Ben.

"Hey babe, are you gonna be around during my lunch break?"

It was now par for the course that he stopped by the house around noon on days that I didn't take Anna to Story Time. I made sure to have her tucked snugly into bed for her nap, and Ben snuck in like a teenage boyfriend to grace me with a quickie and a sandwich before heading back to work. Our relationship—whatever it was—had been going on for about two weeks and for the most part, it had been more or less enjoyable. More in that I had a regular sex life that I was relatively satisfied with; less in that we didn't seem to click otherwise—at all.

Ben, I learned, didn't read, so he didn't find any enjoyment in spending hours at a bookstore. He didn't particularly care for cats, despite caring for them every day of his work life, and didn't seem to find any interest in my job as a child's caregiver. Yet, while I found myself growing exceedingly irritated by this, I couldn't say I had been any better. I knew all of the things he didn't like, but I couldn't think of a single thing he enjoyed.

Well, besides sex, his crockpot, his daughter, and dogs.

Still, though, I kept reminding myself that neither of us had signed up for anything serious, and we were certainly having fun.

"I'm at the park right now, but I'll be home at noon."

The young woman with the two kids raised her voice, and I turned to find her standing over them. They sat on the wooden edge of a sandbox, their heads in hands, elbows on knees with pouts plastered on their little round faces.

"You *need* to stop! Do you understand me? If you don't, I am going to tell your mother that you were both little brats for me, and then she'll punish you. Do you want that?" she shouted at the kids—two little boys, who couldn't have been more than Anna's age.

I squinted in her direction, neglecting my pushing duties as the disgust rose in my throat. I couldn't recall the kids doing anything that would have warranted an outburst like that, and I couldn't imagine whatever was on her phone to be that important.

One of the boys began to cry and the apparent babysitter groaned, stuffing her phone into her pocket. "Oh, here we go with this now. I can't do this! I *can't*. We're leaving. Happy?" This announcement caused the other to start crying, and she grabbed them by the hands. "Come on, get up *now*. We're leaving."

"Excuse me, is everything okay?" I called before biting my tongue to keep myself from tearing her apart from the start.

She turned in surprise that someone else was there, and flashed me an obligatory smile. "Oh, yeah, everything is fine. You know how kids are—because like, you have one."

I flashed her my own wry smile. "Oh, I do. My kid actually broke my face about four weeks ago, and you know what? I would still never talk to her the way you just talked to those boys."

Her smile faded, replaced by guilt as she pushed her long dark hair from her face. "It's my first week with them and it's been a long one. My patience is nonexistent at this point." Her eyes fell to the two little boys attached to both of her arms and sighed, her lower lip puffing out.

"You want a tip?" I asked dryly, feeling only a sliver of sympathy for her. I understood long weeks. Hell, I understood long months, but that was no excuse to scold them for doing nothing.

She gave me a small nod, and I said, "Stay off your phone and pay attention to them. They'll respond a lot better to you and treat you with respect if you show them some."

***

"You should have seen me," I smiled, reminiscing as I clasped my bra and pulled my t-shirt over my head. "It was like I actually knew what I was talking about. I felt … I felt *proud*, for probably the first time in a long time, you know? I think that maybe I, uh—Ben?"

When I didn't receive a response, I glanced over at him, sitting upright with my blanket across his naked lap, his back against the headboard. His phone was in his hands, thumbs tapping the screen as his brows worked together, deepening the line between them.

"What's wrong?" I asked flatly, pulling my underwear up as my mouth twisted with irritation.

He put the phone down on the blanket and looked up, his forehead lining with surprise as though he had just remembered where he was and who he was with. "Huh?" I repeated myself, and he shrugged, "Oh, it's nothing. Just discussing Thanksgiving with my mom. She wants to know what we're doing."

"We?" I swallowed hard, taken aback by the sudden interest in possibly moving the relationship forward from having sex and eating lunch. After only a couple weeks of sleeping together, meeting his family for Thanksgiving seemed like an enormous jump when maybe we should have been considering a smaller step, like discussing what we were to each other.

"Yeah, *we*—Kaylee and me." He gave me a hard look as though that should have been obvious, and I realized my shoulders had tensed as they relaxed. Ben noticed then that I had gotten dressed and he pouted. "I have a half hour before I have to get back."

"Don't you want to eat something?" I balanced on the edge of the bed, too small to comfortably accommodate us both.

He placed a hand on my thigh, fingers sliding upward to the juncture between my thighs. "I'd be fine with this," he insisted, but I looked at him knowingly and he groaned. "Yeah, you're right. I'll be starving if I don't eat, but *shit*, I wish I got a longer break."

But Anna still wouldn't have a longer nap.

He threw the sheet off himself, revealing very plainly that he could've gone for another round. I could have maybe entertained the idea, providing that Anna had remained asleep, but since that panic stricken moment of thinking he wanted us to be a more serious item, I had lost any desire for rolls in the hay.

"Hey, uh, did you actually *want* to come to Thanksgiving?" Ben asked as though reading my mind. I hadn't been aware we had that type of connection, or any connection for that matter, and I gawked at him as he slid his scrub bottoms over his boxers. "I just didn't really think to ask, because we haven't really talked about, you know ..."

"Oh, well," I said, my voice carrying on a loud exhale. He turned to me, shaking out the long-sleeved shirt he wore under the top of his uniform. I had the sudden need to divert my eyes, looking distractedly at Camille on a pile of dirty laundry. "I don't really know."

"It's fine. I just didn't know if you expected it," he replied indifferently, pulling the shirt over his head and covering the chest I had only minutes before had my hands against. The top of his scrubs came next, and then the name tag he kept clipped to the front pocket. "Where are my sneakers?"

"Um, I think in the living room," I said, welcoming a reason to get out of the room that seemed to be closing in on me. I opened the door to abandon him in my room, my socks sliding easily along the floor of the hallway and living room, and I spotted his black sneakers next to the couch. "Got 'em."

Ben had followed me and leaned against the wall. "Are you alright?"

I had to resist the urge to roll my eyes at that. For two weeks I had struggled, trying to find some semblance of a connection to this man I was giving myself to willingly on a regular basis, and not once had he picked up on that. And yet, there he was, noticing that I panicked at the sheer thought of meeting his parents.

"Yeah, I'm fine. I've just had a weird day."

"Tell me about it," Ben said, walking towards me and wrapping his arms around my waist, pulling me to him.

I sighed irritably. "I already did, Ben."

"You did?" He rested a cheek against the top of my head as a hand came up to tangle in my ponytail. "Oh, wait, are you talking about that girl at the park?"

He had actually listened. I smiled against his chest. "Yeah. It just felt good, but I don't know what that means. I mean, I spent months feeling unhappy about this whole thing, but now I think I actually like it."

"Yeah, that's good." His hand continued to curl into the strands of my hair, and I took note of the tone in his voice. Distant and disinterested.

My arms unlatched from behind Ben's back, signaling for him to let go, and I walked into the kitchen to fetch the bag of deli sandwiches he had brought over. I pulled out the two wrapped rolls, and placed them on paper plates, while Ben grabbed a couple bottles of water from the fridge. We ate in silence at the table, checking our respective phones for news, until Ben spoke.

"This is really nice," he said with a smile, his dimples looking adorable. "I love that I can just sit here and be totally comfortable with not talking."

"Yeah," I said with a smile, and thought about the only person I truly felt comfortable doing nothing with.

I missed him.

20

holly

SOMEHOW A FEW WEEKS OF somewhat casual sex went by, and I found myself in Ben's minivan a couple days before Christmas.

We sat outside Liz's house, the endnote to our weekend together. He turned to me, grinning, and I had to smile back. My eyes lingered on his lips and I allowed myself to drift back to his place just an hour earlier. I thought about the pizza, and how he had allowed me to inhale four slices while he ate two and proceeded to devour areas of my body that would make my mother blush. The memory was a nice one, especially when it consisted of food that didn't come from his crockpot.

Reaching across my lap, he opened the glove compartment and removed a little wrapped box. "Here, I got this for you."

I held my breath in my lungs, silently cursing him for buying me a freakin' Christmas present. "Ben, I didn't get you anything," I admitted. We hadn't even considered ourselves *together*, for crying out loud.

He just shook his head, still flashing those dimples. "We never talked about gifts, it's fine."

He *said* it was fine, but it wasn't fine. Not at all.

Still, I awkwardly unwrapped the present, cursing him further at the sight of a velvet jewelry box, and I creaked it open to reveal a little teardrop garnet pendant attached to a thin silver chain. All at once I felt guilty, angry, ashamed, and touched at the sight of the glittering little stone.

"Ben, I really don't think I can—"

He held up a hand. "*Yes,* you can. I *want* you to have it."

"Thank you," I said in a choked mumble, unable to take my eyes off of the necklace. "It's beautiful."

Ben smiled as he began to stroke my hair with a gloved hand. For a fleeting panic-stricken moment, I thought he was about to ask for us to move forward; meet the parents, meet the daughter, and I knew I'd have to turn him down. What kind of awful person wants to do that right before Christmas?

But thank God, he wasn't making any suggestions that night.

"Come here," he said coyly, and I turned to him.

Yes. This is something I can do.

He kissed me softly, his lips barely touching mine, teasing me, before parting his lips. Mine followed his lead, allowing for his tongue to slip between them for just a few moments. And then he pulled away, flashing his dimples. "I'll talk to you later, okay?"

I left the car, feeling guilty with a dash of lust, and walked up to the house. Liz opened the door, waving to Ben with a big grin. She called a hearty "Merry Christmas!" to him before he drove away and out of sight.

"God, Holly, you're so lucky to have him," she gushed, clutching her hands to her chest, and I wished I could agree.

***

The next day Anna and I had busied ourselves with baking Christmas cookies—another bittersweet moment to add to the scrapbook. Just a year before, Stephen and I had baked them together, as we did traditionally, allowing ourselves a rousing duet of "Baby It's Cold Outside" and a lovely slow dance to "Have Yourself a Merry Little Christmas" while the cookies baked to perfection. We laughed over our tongue-in-cheek gingerbread men as "Jingle Bells" played, and we cuddled around the yule log blazing on our TV screen with cups of hot cocoa spiked with Bailey's Irish Cream, as an elevator version of "We Wish You a Merry Christmas" tinkled in the background.

As I rolled out the dough for Anna to squish her cookie cutters into, I caught myself feeling a little emotional, wondering if Stephen was baking his own cookies with Anthony and if he was thinking about me while he stuck little candy cane penises onto gingerbread.

I sighed through my festive sadness. Christmas always has a cruel way of reminding you of all the things you forgot you missed.

Liz returned home with a bag of presents from her co-workers at Dr. Martin's office. I had to admit I was a little jealous as she pulled out the tins of baked goods and token gifts, missing my own Christmas party at *Teen Queen*. Not that it was ever a particularly fun time; my former boss would hand out a scented candle to everybody, we'd eat some food, maybe have a few drinks, and go on our merry way. But still, it was a holiday party, and babysitters didn't get those

And as my thought process traveled through people and things I was missing, Brandon filled my mind, pushing everything else aside with his perfect hair, velvet voice, and expensive cologne. I had seen him only once since I started seeing Ben. It was as though he had been purposely avoiding me, and although he had insisted that wasn't the case, I couldn't shake the feeling that he was lying to me.

By all accounts, Ben should have filled the void he had left with his absence, but I missed my friend. I missed the way he always made me feel better without trying. I missed the way he could build me up to something when I felt like nothing. I missed the way he smelled, and the way his arms felt when he pulled me in for a hug, and the way his lips felt on my cheek …

I missed the guy I insisted was just my friend, and as *Alvin & The Chipmunks* crooned through the speaker in Liz's kitchen, I found that nothing had made me sadder than that.

***

Clutching a tin of Christmas cookies in my hands, I hurried into Reade's out of the cold, wishing my sort-of-wool coat provided me with a little more warmth against the winter chill. But within seconds, the ice around my bones thawed and my lips curled into a smile at the sight of Brandon, despite that he was clearly about to leave the store with a cup of coffee in hand. Seeing him walking in my direction was enough to lift my spirits away from everything else I had spent the evening missing with painful reminiscence.

"Merry Christmas, stranger," I said, just as our paths met.

His hug surprised me, after the way he had been not-avoiding me for over a month. But he wrapped his arms around me, holding me to his chest as a hand cupped the back of my head. He held me as though he had just returned home from battle, his heart beating hard but steady inside his chest and against my ear.

"Merry Christmas, Holly," he said with his chin resting on top of my head. He spoke in a low, gruff voice that made me shiver despite being wrapped in my coat and the warmth of his arms.

I reluctantly pulled away from him, but not before inhaling his cologne, and I asked him what he was doing for the holiday. All he said was that he would be spending it with Nick, and without thinking, I invited him to my parents' house. Clearly touched, his cheeks flushed and he thanked me for the offer, but that it was a little too last minute to blow off his friend—and yeah, I might have felt a little rejected.

"And I'm sure you're spending time with your boyfriend. Not sure how he'd feel about another man hanging around," he threw in, eyes narrowing with suspicion, and instantly my crappy coat was too hot for comfort.

I opened my mouth to tell him I wouldn't be seeing Ben, who wasn't my boyfriend, when I saw Bill approaching. He was wearing an incredibly loud Fair Isle Christmas sweater that blinked with colored LED lights, and with the smile he wore, I could tell it was one of the best things he had ever spent his hard-earned money on.

"Merry Christmas, Ho-Ho-Ho-lly!" he shouted, pleased with his creative butchering of my name. "Bet you haven't gotten that one before, huh?"

"Only every year since my dad thought of it," I whispered to Brandon before rushing to give Bill a hug.

"Are your parents' big fans of Christmas?" Bill asked, wrapping his arms around me tightly. "Because your name is pretty festive, isn't it?"

I laughed, and handed him the tin of cookies. "Anna and I made these for you," I said with a smile, "but you have to share them with Jessie and Scott. Anna insisted."

"We'll see about that," Bill laughed, and then his eyes floated upward and a cheeky smile spread across his face, emphasizing the deep-set lines at the corners of his bright eyes. "Hey, don't look now, kids, but I think you two are standing under the mistletoe."

And as though the woman had bionic hearing, Jessie came bounding over from the Book Nook to come see that, yes, we were indeed standing under the freakin' mistletoe.

"Ooh! I told that Debbie Jefferson I could get people under the mistletoe! She said, 'Jessica, there is no way you're going to get anybody to go along with that garbage, so get rid of it,' but look at you!" she exclaimed, clapping her hands together with enthusiasm, causing the bells on her wrists and sweater to jingle a tune that was simultaneously festive and irritating.

"Hey, I haven't committed to anything," Brandon laughed doubtfully, but he turned to me and cocked a suggestive eyebrow.

"Oh, but you wouldn't want to break tradition!" Bill exclaimed jovially, and Jessie reached to grip his hand, clasping it between hers.

Brandon twisted his lips thoughtfully, his eyes never leaving mine. "Well, now that would be a shame."

I could feel my cheeks burning as I looked up at him. "I *can't*," I hissed in a whisper. Ben and I hadn't discussed what we were, but we had also never discussed kissing other people under mistletoe. Together or not, the whole thing screamed "unfaithful" to me.

"I know, but …" He shrugged nonchalantly. "You wouldn't want to break tradition, would you?" Brandon took a step toward me, causing my breath to hold in my lungs. "Plus, we're just friends, right?"

The sad look in his eyes seemed to say something entirely different, but he smiled tauntingly as he craned his neck with a slight bend of his back, bringing his face closer to mine.

My eyes rolled in a regrettable display of indifference as I groaned, "Okay, fine," and my stomach lurched with the sudden onset of nerves, as I closed my eyes.

My mouth seemed to have a mind of its own as it formed a smile that I couldn't stop despite how hard I tried, in anticipation of feeling his lips on mine once again. With every painstaking second that ticked by, I found there was nothing I wanted more. But after a few moments of lingering and feeling the fresh, cool breath from his nostrils against my face, I opened my eyes, afraid he had decided to back down.

What I saw was the sparkling blue eyes staring back at me, while he wore a smile similar to my own.

Right. Just friends.

"Let's make this quick," he said, feigning a groan as I felt a warm hand on the back of my neck.

"Just get it over with," I whispered, knowing I wasn't tricking anybody when my voice caught in my throat at the touch of his other hand against my jaw, his thumb stroking the skin of my cheek, and with that, he pulled me towards him.

And you know, I thought that after months had passed since I first kissed him, that maybe the thrill would be gone and I would feel nothing. I thought that those sparks wouldn't have sprinkled behind my eyelids and the wobbly feeling in my knees would remain a distant memory from a time when I was desperate. I envisioned that, after experiencing his lips on mine one last time, I could put it to rest knowing that it was just a fluke, and we could continue as the friends we truly were.

But what happened instead was … something else entirely.

Our lips crashed together as I melted into his hands, and all I could do to keep myself from collapsing at his feet was to reach my arms up and around his neck. The small kiss between friends in the spirit of tradition, had quickly built to something intimate; our lips parting in unison and the tips of our tongues meeting somewhere in the middle with a tenderness that could only be interpreted as romantic. The bitter sampling of black coffee sat on my tongue, and even though I would have at one point been completely repulsed by the flavor, it tasted like *him*, and I had to fight myself from devouring it then.

But then … There was that ache, more pronounced than the scraping of his stubble against my chin. It began as a whisper and ended as a scream, telling me to not let him go, to keep him there in that moment with me, but before I could listen to myself, it was over. He pulled away, and it wasn't until that point that I realized I was on the brink of tears. My heart felt wrung out of all emotion, and for just a second, I was terrified of looking at him and seeing that he felt nothing, leaving me to drown alone. But despite my fears, out of necessity, I reluctantly opened my eyes to find his scanning my face as though they were searching for something.

They locked onto mine; moisture lined the rims, turning his blue eyes into prisms. "Holly, I—"

Swallowing hard, I asked, "What?"

I wanted to hear him say whatever it was that sat at the tip of his tongue. I imagined it being something to the effect of, "Leave him and be with me," and dammit, I would have done it.

I would have pulled my phone out right there and called Ben to tell him it was over. Whatever *it* was.

But then the world reappeared around us as Jessie sighed. "Oh, Bill … Wait until Debbie hears about this …"

And just like that, I remembered we were friends. I remembered the guy I had been semi-unfaithful to. I remembered that there were other places to be, even if that place was in my bed, alone with my cat.

I dropped my hands from Brandon's neck as he dropped his from mine. I composed myself with a clearing of my throat as Brandon ran his hands through his hair in what I guessed to be an attempt to put himself back in order. I wished the three of them a merry Christmas, and before anything else could be said, I hurried out of there, cursing Jessie for not listening to Debbie Jefferson.

21

brandon

OR MANY PEOPLE, WHEN ASKED what they consider to be the most romantic holiday, they would promptly respond with, "Valentine's Day." I supposed they wouldn't be incorrect in their feelings, given the day's amorous history and commercialized sentiment, but no, for me, it has always been Christmas Eve.

There was something in that intimate hush that lulled over the Earth, that momentary sense of peace that brought those Wise Men travelling through the desert all those years ago. The desire and need to be closest to those you care for most, the magical awe of the twinkling lights on the Christmas tree, and the sensual kiss of the fireplace against rosy cheeks. All of it combined, painted a picture of cozy warmth, one to fall in love with over and over again.

And to me, that was exactly what love should be.

But of course, that wasn't the type of love I had found myself in. I was in the torturous kind that left me lying awake when I should have been sleeping; tossing and turning through the stresses of wondering if her feelings for me ran as deep as mine for her. Wondering how I had allowed myself to get into such a predicament. Wondering how the hell it was I would confess my true identity to her. Wondering why the hell I had approached her in the Reade's parking lot all those months ago.

Brandon the Nice Man.

I had come close the night before, under the mistletoe in Bill's shop. The guilt of her not knowing had hit me hard in the gut after a kiss that had manifested into something of a tornado of emotion. I had been within millimeters of telling her everything when the world suddenly appeared around us, and the reality of her being unavailable drove a stake through my heart.

The Reade family urged me to run after her in some display of storybook valiance. I thought about it for a few moments, allowing enough time to pass for her to get into her car and drive away; subconsciously deciding that it wasn't the right time long before she had even reached the shop's jingling door.

But would there ever be a right time, I thought, rubbing a hand against my jaw.

My thoughts had left me entranced by the twinkling lights on the Christmas tree in Nick's living room, oblivious to the other guests around me. A far stretch from the one leading the Wise Men to Bethlehem, I wished upon the gaudy tinseled star that I could blink and suddenly be one of the few dozen couples jammed into Nick's house. With my arm around Holly's waist, gabbing about the new addition to our house or a new recipe we tried as our contribution to the holiday spread.

I blinked, and while I wasn't surprised to find myself still alone on that couch, it took a hard bite against my inner lip to keep myself together. I squeezed my eyes shut and pushed a hand through my hair, and wished for the lovesick teenager in my mind to give it a fucking rest.

The sound of a throat clearing brought me to open my eyes just as Nick's father nudged my boot with the toe of his loafer, pulling me from my wishful thinking—a welcomed distraction. He handed me a tumbler of what I could only assume was something alcoholic, and I accepted the glass gratefully. Anything to numb the ache that seemed to be a permanent fixture in my day-to-day living.

"You look like you could use a drink," Richard Bolton said, and he toasted with the glass in his hand. "Merry Christmas, son."

"And a merry Christmas to you, sir." I raised the glass to him before tipping it back into my mouth. The familiar warmth of Scotch slid down my throat.

"Here alone?" The man who acted as a second father for much of my life had asked me that same question on every occasion since Julia was no longer in the picture.

I smiled solemnly. "You know it."

"She's out there, Brandon," he said, nodding with certainty.

"I know," I replied, gazing into the therapeutic slosh of the amber liquid. And she's with someone else, I thought, and the Scotch turned to poison on my tongue.

He cocked his head and his forehead crumpled in thought. "Then go get her," he encouraged, leaning forward to gently tap my shoulder with the back of his hand.

"Wish it were that easy."

Mr. Bolton straightened his back, shoved his silver-rimmed glasses up the bridge of his beak-like nose, and pointed a finger at me. It struck me then that I was looking at Nick in thirty years, and the thought gently lifted a side of my mouth into an almost-smile.

"Never underestimate the power of a man in love, Brandon," he said. His finger wagged for a moment before he nudged his foot against my boot again, and off he went to schmooze with the other guests.

I sniffed a laugh before downing the rest of my own glass, and got up from the couch to find the kitchen sink. After weaving through the clusters of friends and family members, I found Nick and Ashley hustling to get Christmas Eve dinner out onto the buffet table. Lynn, the eldest of their three daughters, was carrying trays of food on unsteady legs as though she were performing on a tight-rope, and upon entering the kitchen, I hurried over to her before she could drop the aluminum pan of roasted potatoes.

"Thanks, Uncle Brandon." She exhaled a sigh of relief, dramatically wiping her brow.

I placed the tray among the other steaming dishes of food, and turned back to the eight-year-old looking way too old in her Christmas dress and high-heeled shoes.

"Why don't you go play with the other kids?" I reached out a hand to tuck a strand of her auburn hair behind an ear. "I can help these losers out with the rest of this stuff."

That brought out a giggle from her. She turned to her parents, asking to confirm that it was okay to abandon her duties as Kitchen Helper.

"Thanks, B. Now she'll be making it a point to call us her loser parents." Ashley groaned, turning to point her pregnant belly in my direction with a hand on her hip. "Go ahead, Lynnie. We'll put Uncle Brandon to work, but you owe him one."

"I'll settle for a hug," I said with a laugh, catching the worried look in Lynn's green eyes, perfectly matching her mother's. With a look of relief, the girl outstretched her arms up to me, and with a swift bend, I wrapped my arms around her waist and lifted her up, squeezing around her. With her arms tightly around my neck, I groaned with enthusiasm. "You give the best hugs. That's why you're my first favorite niece."

"First favorite gets the best presents, right?" She gave me a wide-eyed hopeful stare.

"Maybe, but don't tell Second and Third, okay?" I said, putting her feet back on the floor.

Satisfied, Lynn ran off to join her sisters and cousins in the basement playroom, leaving me alone with her parents in the bright country-style kitchen. Ashley shook her head, mumbling that I better not have spoiled them again, and I could only shrug with a little smirk plastered on my face.

Nick spooned candied yams into a tray and passed it into my hands. "So, how are things going with *You-Know*?" His voice implied that he was teasing me, while his eyes held something deeper. Something a little like hope.

With the tray securely next to the mashed potatoes and steamed carrots, I shook my head in response to his prying, and said that it was over. Nick's tone quickly changed to one of concern, and asked what the fuck had happened with an accusing touch that I didn't exactly appreciate. In as few words as possible, I mentioned that I had missed my window of opportunity the moment she had found herself a boyfriend. I threw in that I had been almost successfully avoiding her for the past month, but then the kiss crossed my mind. Try as I might, I couldn't fight the smile that stretched my lips as Ashley handed me a basket of fluffy warm biscuits.

"Hmm, I haven't seen *that* look in a long time. What's that for?" she teased with excitement, poking me playfully in the chest.

This was precisely the problem with knowing the same people for most of your life. They had plenty of time to learn every little nuance about you.

"Nothing," I said, but not convincingly enough. Nick shook his head, demanding I spill the beans, and so with nowhere left to run, I did. The short story was concluded with a duo of sighs blended with hopeless romanticism, and I said, "It really doesn't matter, though."

Ashley shook her head, rubbing the purple velvet over her engorged belly. "Why would you say that?" I once again mentioned the little issue of her having a boyfriend, but Ashley only shrugged, cradling the bump in her hands. "I'm not really sure that's an issue."

"And what makes *you* say *that*?" I implored, intrigued by the statement.

The little pregnant lady with the long wavy hair and green eyes sidled up next to me. "*Well,*" she slyly said, wrapping an arm around my waist, "would a woman who's happy in a relationship kiss another man like that? I mean, she could have stopped it before you shoved your tongue down her throat."

"I didn't shove—never mind," I muttered with a shake of my head. "You do make a compelling argument, though."

Nick sliced into the ham, the steam fogging up his glasses instantly. "Relationships end, dude. I'm not saying to sleep with her while she's with the guy, but maybe some incentive wouldn't hurt on your part."

"Sounds like he already gave her some incentive, hon," Ash threw in with a poke against my side, and I groaned.

Nick snickered with a laugh, and his face lit up as though he were just struck with sudden brilliance. "Maybe she's only with this guy because she's under the impression *you* don't want anything to do with *her*. You ever think of *that*?" He jabbed the knife in my direction.

"Stop pointing that thing at your pregnant wife," I laughed, shielding Ashley with an arm. "But that's a good point," I said thoughtfully, and I found myself startled by just how out of practice I had been in the department of romance and was quickly learning just how much better I was writing about it, rather than actually doing it.

Ashley took over with the slicing of the ham to let Nick walk from room to room with the announcement that dinner was about to be served. I insisted on taking the knife from her, giving her the gift of a few moments to get off her swollen feet and into one of the kitchen table chairs. The sharp tool sliced through the ham with ease and using my weapon wielding skills, thanks to research-required sword fighting lessons, I cut the meat with a precision and speed that made Ashley snort with laughter.

"Pal, you have that job from now on," she said, kicking off her flat sequined shoes. "So, Nicky told me you're rewriting the new book."

"Yeah," I confirmed and raised a brow, looking up at her from my carving. I was sure she had never read one of my books, simply because battle and carnage were never her cup of tea and to get through one of them would have been torture.

"Tell me about it," she said with a slight smile, hugging her arms around her belly as she closed her eyes, taking the moment to enjoy the quiet kitchen. "Start from the beginning. I know nothing about your shit," she laughed apologetically.

"Yeah, I figured," I grumbled, and took a deep breath.

"*Well*, Alexander Breckenridge begins his story as a nobody. He works in the stables at a Lord's castle but he always had dreams of doing something more. You know, something important that people would remember him by, so he practices with an old sword until he's a pretty kick-ass swordsman.

"Then, one day he finds himself recruited by the King's Guard to battle, after witnessing his unmatched skills with the sword. They've pulled him in to fight against a force they've never seen before, and because he's *so* damn good, they've assumed he's prepared to face whatever the hell it is, and long story short, he blows their socks off.

"Anyway, this more or less has placed him into a much more notable position, and he's found himself doing well. He's a Knight, the Lord of his own castle, has his pick of any woman he could possibly want and often has, has all the gold he could ever want, and he saves entire villages and kingdoms from both the natural and supernatural on a regular basis. He's happy for a while, but he eventually realizes that, although it's everything he's ever dreamed of, it's ..." I noticed that the knife had stopped moving; my eyes staring into and beyond the candied yams on the buffet table. "It's, uh, pretty fucking empty."

"Uh-huh," Ashley said with an adoring smile, gesturing for me to go on.

"He realizes that his heroic life means little if he can't share it with someone. He wants someone to wait for him. He wants a son to carry on his family name. He wants … something *he* cares about to fight for, because all of those kingdoms and people, they mean nothing but a paycheck to him at the end of the day."

"So, basically, he needs a damsel to save and love." Ashley batted her eyelashes, clutching her hands together for effect.

"Basically."

"And you have this planned out, right?" I nodded, and her face took on a smug expression. "So, I guess it shouldn't be that hard."

"What?"

"This whole thing with Holly."

With the ham successfully sawed off the bone and the meat piled haphazardly on a platter, I dropped the butcher knife and set to washing my hands with Ashley's smirking stare boring holes into my back. The evergreen-scented soap filled my nostrils, reminding me that we were there for Christmas Eve dinner and not to piece together the ruins of my love life.

Ripping a paper towel from the dispenser, I turned back to Ashley. "My real life is a little different than the life of a fictional character. I decide what goes on in his world, and I make it happen." I tossed the paper towel in the garbage with a smoothness that would make Shaq drool. "He needed a damsel, so I made one up and gave him the skills to woo her with his charm and impressive manhood. That's *not* how the real world works."

The sounds of four dozen people swarming towards the kitchen seemed to fill the surrounding area and we knew our time together was soon coming to a close. Ashley waved me over to her and with an arm around my back and a hand in mine, we together got her on legs that were immediately unsteady but within moments, she had regained her balance and waddled over to hastily drop serving spoons into the trays of food.

"I know nothing about your manhood—thank God—but you certainly have the charm," she finally said, pointing a spoon in my direction. "All I'm saying is, you needed a damsel, and the universe provided. All you have to do is decide what comes next, and make it happen."

When the room had filled beyond the point of breathing anything other than someone else's air, I slipped through the double French doors to the back deck, where I took a seat on one of the chaise lounges overlooking the lavish greenery of the backyard. A light dusting of fresh snow had sprinkled over the yard, and still recovering from the suffocating warmth from inside, the chilled air hadn't begun to affect me through the comfortable thickness of my sweater.

I looked towards the sky, the snowflakes catching onto my eyelashes and speckling my view of the stars. That hush had blanketed over the world—the one I had always perceived as being romantic. I allowed temptation to pull my imagination towards what Holly could have possibly been doing in that moment, and not surprisingly, the only fantasy I could conjure was one of her in the arms of some guy far better looking than I was, with a body I could envy. There was a backdrop of a roaring fireplace, a couple glasses of an expensive wine, but the details were unimportant as I watched his hands roam down her back, lingering on the ends of her dark hair before continuing their descent towards the ass I had watched walking away from me enough times to classify me as a pervert in the eyes of women everywhere.

Jealousy burnt a hole through my mind's projector, and I was looking at the sky again. The snow was falling at a steadier pace, and I wondered how long it would be before I could pass for Jack Nicholson's character at the end of *The Shining*.

I could always take Ashley's convoluted advice. I chuckled with mischief at the thought of stealing another man's woman. It had dawned on me that I had set out to do just that when I made the decision to kiss her under the mistletoe. Some ridiculous attempt to get her to forget about the boyfriend with my lips of sensual magic. A feeble attempt at taking a shot at her. I had given her that gentle nudge without even the tiniest bit of guilt, but a guy really up to no good would have chased her into the parking lot. That wasn't me, and if that's what it was going to take to steal her away from this guy, I wasn't up to the task.

"But," I said to the dancing snowflakes, "she isn't happy."

And that was something to hold onto.

***

"Merry Christmas, sweetheart." My mom's voice was strained with emotion brought on by another Christmas gone without seeing her only child's face. "I wish you would come down here and be with us for a while. There's no reason to spend Christmas alone."

"I'm not alone, Mom." I sighed, dropping the leather coat on the ornately carved banister as I climbed the stairs, not bothering to look into the darkness of either the empty kitchen or living room as I went.

"Brandon, you haven't had a Christmas with us in two years!" she pleaded, driving a painful stake into my heart poisoned with guilt. I heard the gruff voice of my father in the background, telling her to leave me alone. "Oh, stop it, Jack. I can ask my son to spend one holiday with me."

Crossing the threshold of my bedroom, I kicked off my boots and put my parents on speakerphone, freeing my hands to get undressed for bed. I sighed with irritation, listening to the two of them argue about who I did or didn't have to spend holidays with.

"You know," I chimed in, "you can always come up here for Christmas next year." There was a break in their bickering, and I shook my head with a smile.

"Well, I guess we could do that," Dad mused, and then mentioned, "We could meet your girlfriend's family."

"Oh! That's right!" Mom exclaimed. "You could have brought her down here for *this* Christmas, though …"

I pulled the sweater over my head, static collecting through my hair as I sighed again at the mention of her. I hoped I wouldn't have to tell them on Christmas that the whole thing was a farce.

"We'll see where it goes, guys. It's still early, you know?" I pulled off the red polo I had worn under the sweater, leaving my skin exposed to the cold air of the bedroom.

It was Mom's turn to sigh. "I know, but I'm just so excited that you're seeing someone. She must be really special to get your attention."

"And *keep* it," Dad chimed in with a chuckle from somewhere in the background, and I had to laugh.

"Yeah, she is," I agreed, undoing the buckle of my belt and sliding it through the loops of my pants with the soft hum of leather against cotton. I worked at the button and zipper as Mom asked how work was. It was a question I had always despised, and I often wondered if Michelangelo had been hounded much while painting the Sistine Chapel. "It's good. Slow, but you know ..."

"Hey, what if you came down here for a while? Just for a vacation to clear your head? With the new girlfriend, I bet you've got your share of distractions going on up there and maybe that's getting in the way of your work," Dad suggested, and I heard mumbles come through the speaker, and then he added, "Or you could bring her down if you wanted. *Okay, Carole?*"

I smirked at myself in the mirror, amused at how right he was without even realizing it. The offer was attractive. I could see myself on their condo's balcony with laptop resting comfortably on my knees, the ocean breeze gently whipping my hair away from my face and a glass of Scotch by my side to accompany the view of the Atlantic.

But then I remembered, she wasn't happy. How could I leave when there was still hope?

"Tempting, Dad. I'll think about it, okay?" I climbed under the flannel comforter. "I'm exhausted, guys. It's been a long night."

Dad sighed with a detected hint of disappointment. "Alright, kiddo. We'll talk to you soon. Give our love to Holly, okay?"

My head hit the pillow as my eyes watered at the sobering remark. An emotion-ridden huff passed through my lips and I looked to the empty space beside me, as though she had laid there a thousand times before and was supposed to be there then.

"Yeah, I will," I croaked, my voice breaking. "Love you, guys. Merry Christmas."

22

holly

NEW YEARS' EVE WAS NEVER a holiday I made a big deal
out of, but Stephen had always made it a point to find a
party for us to attend. I would have always preferred to
spend the night stuck at home with a bottle of wine and a good
old movie, but I always went along with his plans and dolled
myself up to spend the night with him.

It only hit me then that Anthony had always been at those
parties. I laughed to myself at how pissed it must have made
him to watch Stephen kiss me at midnight, not him.

Well, I guess he's finally getting his wish.

I had been excited that day to finally spend the New Year
doing nothing. Liz was taking Anna over to our parents' house
to bang pots and pans, and although I had been invited, I
cordially declined with a big ol' "hell no." I was going to enjoy
my night alone with Camille, plug in *Breakfast at Tiffany's*, and
snuggle up with Mr. and Mrs. Pinot.

After handing Anna Giraffe and her sippy cup, she waited
for Jessie to begin her story while I proceeded to open my book
to the spot held by my bookmark, eager to find out if the
voluptuous Clementine was going to finally get her gun-toting
cowboy Heathcliff to take her for a hayride.

I had drowned out Jessie's cheery voice and dove headfirst
into the long-awaited raunchy chapter, only glancing up

periodically to make sure Anna was still sitting in front of me. My loins were on fire, completely unaware that it wasn't the most ideal setting to be getting so hot and bothered.

Her hand slid over his rippled abdominal muscles, her fingers inching their way closer and closer to the pulsating length of his ...

"Hey there, beautiful," a voice floated into my ear before a kiss was planted on my cheek. I jumped at the sudden interruption and turned to find Ben on one knee beside me. The dimpled smile was the last thing I expected to see in what had become a sacred place to me, and my first reaction was immediate annoyance.

"What are you doing here?" I hissed at him through my teeth while glancing around to see if anybody was looking over at us. Too distracted by Ben being there, I closed my book without remembering to put the bookmark back in. "Goddammit," I grumbled, glaring down at the oiled-and-tanned skin of the lusty couple in cowboy hats on the cover.

Ben's smile wiped away instantly and was replaced with a look of defensive shock. "Well, I got out of work early, so I thought I'd come here to surprise you."

I knew I should have thought the gesture was sweet. The company should have been welcomed, and probably would have been had I not been a lousy person, but because that's exactly what I was, I could only stare at him with bewilderment plastered on my face while he pouted.

"Ben," I said, blinking rapidly, trying to form my words wisely. "I'm working here, and you can't just come in, and … and …" And what? I had nothing.

"Oh, because God forbid I want to spend time with you, Holly," Ben snapped back and looking over at him, I caught the hurt that had taken over, and I caught some quick glances from other people in our vicinity.

I stood up and grabbed his hand, pulling him along with me until we stood several feet away between a pair of bookshelves with a clear view of the unsuspecting, sleeping Anna.

"Ben, would you like me to walk into your dad's office and just start hanging out with you while you do your work? Would that be okay? You know, while you're sticking some dog with a vaccine or something, I could just barge in and say, 'Hey Benny, I thought I'd just come in and chill for a while.' Would *that* be okay?"

"*Job?*" He snickered on the word as it rolled out of his mouth. "Holly, you hang out with your niece all day. That's hardly a job." He smiled, looking down at me as though I were the most adorable thing on the planet, and I resisted my hand's desire to smack him across the face.

I looked to the little girl still sleeping in a ball on the area rug, hugging Giraffe. I hoped she wouldn't wake up to find that I was missing, and Lord knows what would have happened then. The longer I stood there with Ben, the more I knew I had to get back over there and the more I grew annoyed that he was keeping me from the job he didn't take seriously.

Turning back to him, I shook my head, ponytail wiggling furiously. "And you play with *dogs* all day, Ben. What's your point?" I snapped, knowing very well he did more than just play with puppies and kittens, but I also did more than *hang out* with a little girl all day.

He opened his mouth to throw another quip at me, and then stopped, scratching the back of his head. "Look, I didn't come here to fight with you. I just wanted to come here and ..." He sighed, gazing his eyes towards the ceiling.

In the two moments it took for him to divert his eyes, I spotted a very curious Brandon sitting several feet away in the café. I wondered if that's how he spent Story Time those days; hanging out in the café while I kept the bean bag chairs warm. Seeing him there, watching me with the man he had to know was the one I had been seeing, I felt a squeeze of regret around my heart.

With the risk of Ben noticing, I nudged my head towards Anna, hoping Brandon would catch my drift, and with two thumbs up, he headed over to take a seat behind the sleeping little girl. A small wave of relief washed over me once I was assured she would have someone familiar with her, in the event she woke up before I returned.

"Ben?" I asked, more out of impatience than anything. I mean, I didn't exactly have all day to stand there while he counted the ceiling tiles.

His eyes came back down from the fluorescent bulbs and scratched his forehead. "I wanted to ask if you would come over tonight and spend New Year's with Kaylee and me. I'm making crockpot chili and some rice, and maybe some other snacks if the mood strikes." He snaked an arm around my waist, as if we hadn't just been on the verge of killing each other, and pulled me toward him. "Then after Kay goes to bed, you and I can pop open a bottle of champagne … And maybe do a little more than kiss at midnight …" He leaned into me and the softness of his lips played against my earlobe gently, a move that had brought me to my literal knees on a number of occasions.

But instead of sinking to my knees, my stomach was cartwheeling the hell out of there, and it had been since he mentioned the *K* word.

The sheer possibility of meeting his daughter had been enough to leave me white-knuckled and nauseous. He had never mentioned it before, but I knew it had been bound to happen sooner or later, as long as we continued seeing each other.

"Uh …" I breathed unsteadily, willing myself to not succumb to his touch. "I actually had plans for tonight."

Ben looked up from his attack on my ear. "Plans? You didn't mention anything about plans yesterday afternoon when I came to see you." His other arm came around my back, pulling me further into him. "Come on, Holly," he pleaded, nuzzling against my neck. "You can't leave me stranded for New Year's. Who am I going to kiss?"

I turned my neck, glancing at Anna, relieved to find she was still sleeping. Brandon, however, had occupied himself with the romance novel I had left on my bean bag chair and I hid my smile at the flushed pink of his cheeks. I hoped he was enjoying it more than I was apparently allowed to.

"Ben," I pleaded, my tone softening under his persuasive touch. "Seriously. I have other stuff going on."

And the last thing I want to do is meet your daughter.

Holly freakin' Hughes. First-class asshole.

Ben sighed with disappointment. "I can't twist your arm?" I shook my head, standing firmly with my bottles of wine and movie waiting for me back at home. He shrugged, releasing my waist from his grasp. I could see the defeat picking away at the lines that sprouted around his furrowed brow. "I guess I should have expected this."

"Ben, come on. Please don't be hurt." I reached out to take his hand, and he pulled away.

"No, don't bother. It's my fault. I sprung this on you, because I thought that maybe ..." His voice trailed off as he shook his head, pursing his lips. "Never mind. Enjoy your night."

He took a few steps back, giving me a little wave before stuffing his hands into the pockets of his scrubs. With head hanging low, he shuffled his sneakers along the patchwork quilt of rugs. I didn't bother to watch him leave, and instead turned back to the Book Nook.

Not having the strength to pull over another bean bag chair, I dropped myself to the floor with an elbow resting on the chair Brandon occupied. My hand flew to my temple, fingers massaging gently, as I listened to the end of Jessie's story of choice. Something about a New Year's ball that was afraid of dropping. Turns out, he was afraid that he would cease to exist once the clock struck twelve, but the other balls assured him that he would go on to continue falling every year for the rest of his life. Seemed bleak, but he was pretty happy about it, and they lived happily ever after, the end. Jessie concluded the tale with a smile and wished everyone a happy New Year before leaving us.

On her way out, she walked past us, and I thought I noticed her smile.

Brandon, flushed cheeks and all, turned to look down at me and passed the book into my hands. He cleared his throat and crossed his legs. "Well, that was, uh, enlightening."

"You learn anything?" I laughed, stuffing the book back into my bag.

"Yeah, actually," he said, running a hand through his hair. "Women have very unrealistic expectations of most men." He raised his hands with air quotes. "'The sinews of his rippled chest.' Give me a break."

I smirked. "*You* have ripples."

"I said, *most* men, Holly." He looked down at me as his fingers nudged against my arm. "Hey, you okay?"

"Oh, uh, yeah. Just … having an off day, I guess," I muttered, taken aback. He widened his eyes, allowing the light to brighten the blue, and glared at me knowingly. "He just threw me off coming here. It's fine."

"Mm." He pursed his lips, and he knew I was lying. "Seeing him tonight?"

I shook my head and filled him in on my plans. "*Breakfast at Tiffany's* is already waiting in the Blu-ray player and my bottles are already on the back stoop, chilling to perfection." My fists clenched with my enthusiasm. "It's going to be *amazing*."

Brandon laughed, stretching his legs out. He clasped his hands behind his head before yawning. "Sounds good to me," he said, mid-yawn.

"Tired?"

He blinked his eyes slowly and gave me a sidelong glance. "Exhausted, actually. I've been doing a lot of work stuff that's wiping me out, but …" He shrugged. "Anyway, doing nothing sounds *amazing*."

"Really?"

"Oh, hell yeah. I've been to enough New Year's parties to know that I'd rather not be at one." His nose wrinkled as he shook his head with disgust. "Besides, what's the point if I don't have someone to kiss at midnight? I always get stuck sitting on the couch with the pet cat, watching everybody around me make out, and then someone's grandma comes over to try and con me into kissing *her* ..." He cringed while I laughed. "Yeah, no thanks."

And with that, he pulled himself from the bean bag chair, extending a hand down to me while visions of kissing him danced through my head. I grabbed a hold, falling victim just a little to the way my body seemed to instantly warm at the touch of his hand.

With a kiss on my cheek, Brandon wished me a good night and a happy New Year. Then he turned, preparing himself to walk away when he stopped short. He faltered a bit before turning around, his jaw working with determination before taking a step towards me.

"Hey, Holly? I know we both have crazy nights planned, but if you decide that being alone isn't all its cut out to be, why don't you give me a call?" And as if he had the whole thing planned, he pulled a pad of paper and a pen from his pocket and scribbled what I assumed to be a number. Extending the piece of paper to me, he shrugged and added, "You know, if you feel like watching *Breakfast at Tiffany's* with someone."

***

A musical rendition of "Moon River" played dreamily through the speakers of the TV, as Holly Golightly walked through the streets of New York City as the opening credits rolled. Holly, donning her oversized sunglasses and little black dress, stops at the window of Tiffany's, drinks a sip of her coffee and takes a gander in the other windows to marvel at the displays of jewelry she will never possess.

I feel your pain, sister.

Sprawled out on the couch, I held my bottle in the crook of my arm with my chin pressed against the gaping mouth of its opening. My one-woman party had begun before I had given the movie the okay to start rolling. In fact, it had started the moment Liz bundled Anna up and walked out the door. That was when I cracked open a bottle of beer and treated myself to a nice, warm bubble bath before taking the other two beers from the fridge to drink while enjoying an episode of *Frasier*; it was the one where Frasier's brother Niles proposes to Daphne.

"Nobody will ever marry me," I had said to Camille, curled up on the couch beside me, and I hugged my knees to my chest with a sorrowful sigh and gave the Blu-ray player permission to get *Breakfast at Tiffany's* going.

If I was honest, the night hadn't been picking me up the way I had hoped it would. I mean, it wasn't that I hadn't enjoyed my bath, or that the quiet house wasn't giving me the sense of independence that I had been missing from my apartment in the city. But looking around the house with the bottle of red hugged into my body, it occurred to me that what had made a quiet New Year's Eve so appealing years ago was that it had been outside of my norm to spend a cozy night with a bottle of wine in front of the TV. However, at Liz's house, *every* night before bed was a time to snuggle up with my favorite sitcoms and cuddly cat.

The bottle, instead of boxed wine, was the only difference and I was enjoying it maybe a little too much, because by the time I was meeting Holly Golightly's love interest, the bottle had found its way into my system.

"Don't worry," I mumbled to Camille. "I bought two."

I retrieved the second bottle from the back patio, and wrapped a throw blanket around my shoulders. With the wine dangling from my hand, I tripped my slippers along the front yard until I had reached my destination: Esther's door.

"Happy New Year!" I shouted, spreading my arms wide when she opened the door. "*That* i-is a … *lovely* mu-mu, Esther. You *really* have to take me shopping one of these days." I pushed past her into her living room and flopped down on the couch, taking a swig of my bottle. "Hello, Harry!" I saluted the picture hanging above the TV before drinking again.

"Holly, you're drunk." Esther planted her bony hands on her hips, her face scowling with disapproval.

"Yes. Yes, I a-am," I stated and pursed my lips contemplatively, as I rolled my eyes to the peeling paint of the ceiling. "Esther, your sky is falling."

Sighing, she craned her neck to check the time on her wall clock. "It's nearly nine, honey. I'm going to bed in a few minutes. Tell me what you want, and get the hell out of my house."

I sighed, still gazing at the shavings of paint, clinging desperately to the plaster. "I was all alone and I wanted to see my best friend." I snuggled my back into the cushions of her lumpy couch.

"Don't you have a boyfriend you should be seeing?"

My eyes rolled at the thought of spending a moment with Ben—poor, poor Ben. "*First* of a-all, that guy is not my boy … boyfriend, okay? He's one of your *handsome men* that I'm sup-supposed to fuck. And sec-second of all, I *definitely* don't want to see him tonight. Oh, no. He wants to drink champagne and sing 'Auld Lang Syne', and …" I waved my hand around, grasping for the word, coming up empty. "No. Just no."

"I thought you liked spending time with Ben?" she questioned, shuffling her feet towards the couch.

I snorted loudly. "I *like* Ben when we have sex, but you know, Esther, sex isn't a magic *thing*, okay? Sex doesn't … make you n-not *lonely*. Sex doesn't *fix* things. And besides, he does this thing with his toes, and …"

"Honey, I am way too tired for this shit."

Esther sat down next to me, raking her hands through her wispy white hair, and with that gesture, it hit me. I dug my hands into my sweatshirt pocket and pulled out the little slip of paper Brandon had given me.

"What's that?" she asked, glancing over as I eyed the digits scrawled onto it.

I took a small sip of wine. "Brandon gave me his number today. I've known the guy for *so long* and he g-gave me his number *today*. Why the hell would he do *that*? *God*, he's such a fucking …" My voice trailed off, looking at the number through booze-bleary eyes.

"Such a fucking, *what*?" Esther's mouth twisted into a little toothless smirk that told me she knew exactly what he was.

"He's just … a *fucking* good kisser. *God*, he's a good kisser. He should kiss Benny and … teach him." I smacked my forehead before taking another gulp of wine. "He kissed me last week. Did I tell you that?"

Esther kept her expression indifferent. "He kissed you again?"

I closed my eyes and nodded, emphasizing my movements. "*Yep*, he did."

"I thought he just wanted to be friends?" She raised an eyebrow.

My mouth twitched into a smile, and I opened my eyes to look at the number in my hand. "Yeah, well … Fucking m-mistletoe."

"Holly, get off my couch and out of my house."

"Why?" I whined, snuggling into one of the throw pillows with every intention of falling asleep.

"Because," she said patting my leg, "you're going to go call him and leave me the hell alone."

23

brandon

A CHOIR OF CLACKING KEYS filled the dimly lit room, providing an added musical element to the Red Hot Chili Peppers album blasting through my laptop's speakers. My fingers danced across the keyboard as I watched the blank spaces of the word processer fill with the story brewing in my head, and hot damn, it felt good. I couldn't yet decipher if what I had been writing was any good or if my editor would later tell me to chuck the entire thing into the fire and set it ablaze, but the important thing was that I was writing and *that* felt good.

I glanced over at my empty mug, put my thought process on hold, and pushed away from the heavy wooden desk. I walked across the rug, and took the curved staircase two steps at a time, turning the corner into the dark kitchen, illuminated by only the streaming light from the porch.

Already plugged in and ready, I shoved my mug under the spout of the Keurig and gave the machine the OK to start brewing. While waiting for my liquid nourishment to fill the cup, I took my eyes for a trip around the gourmet kitchen to a soundtrack of pumps and grinding from the coffee machine. It felt impossible to walk in there and not instantly be struck with the morose heaviness of the stale air. The granite countertop was cluttered with boxes; things I had always meant to put away, now weighed down by years of dust and bitter neglect. The cabinets hung empty, the refrigerator held nothing but takeout leftovers, and I couldn't begin to explain how to actually use the electric stovetop—because I never had.

The Keurig spurted the remainder of the boiling hot coffee into my cup, and that was my cue to leave until the next refill, all too eager to go.

With mug in hand, I stepped onto the bottom step's tread, all set to get back to work on the long-awaited love life of my truest friend, when a vibration came from the pocket of my pajama pants. I waited to see if the vibrating persisted or if it was just the one-time buzz of a text message to be ignored until I felt like answering, but it continued. Intrigued by receiving a phone call on my personal number, I fished the phone from my pocket, initially surprised that I didn't recognize the local number and then remembered that I had given Holly my number.

Without another moment of hesitation, my thumb swiped across the screen and the phone went to my ear. "Hello?" I sat down on the second step, looking ahead at the heavy wooden door and its stained-glass window. My gut buzzed with nerves, waiting for a reply on the other end, and I put the mug down next to me, freeing my hand to run through my hair.

"It *really* fucking sucks drinking alone."

As predicted, Holly's voice came through the speaker, sounding farther away than I knew she really was.

"Yeah, I could have told you that," I laughed uneasily. God knows I wasn't a stranger to the old One Man Drinking Party. *Another me, another life* ...

"So, you busy?"

My heart jumped, and I glanced upwards towards the office, envisioning the glowing computer screen and imagining Breckenridge cursing me for once again tossing him on the backburner. "Nah, not really."

"Do you wanna come over and watch *Breakfast at Tiffany's*?"

She didn't have to ask me twice. I bolted upright at the invitation and leaving my mug on the bottom step, I ran back up the stairs. Despite my hurried actions, I kept my tone from sounding too eager. "Sure, but what about your boyfriend? I'm not sure he'd be too thrilled with you spending your night with another man."

"Oh *God*, fucking *Ben*." She said the name with a disgusted emphasis, and I had to say my thoughts reflected her tone as I fit the man she had been talking to with his name. "He's just so *stupid* with his kid, and oh *God*, the crockpot."

"Crockpot?" I laughed, hoping that it wasn't innuendo for something else.

"Yes! God, why did anybody have to set me up with a guy with a kid? Why does he want me to even *meet* the kid when we agreed to be nothing serious? And then, *then*! He told me today that my job isn't a job. My job broke my freakin' face, *Ben*." There was a pause. "That's why *you're* the good friend. You don't say my job is stupid. You don't make me dress up and go to stupid parties, like a doll. You like me for me, like that song. Who sings that? Blessed-something, right? I liked that one …" She sighed. "And you know what?"

"Yeah?" I stopped at the doorway of my bedroom. Her slurred words suggested that she was drunk.

"You're a better kisser," she giggled, and the very thought brought a stirring from below my waist. "Oh *God*, you're a *way* better kisser. Ben sucks at kissing, and sex with him is so *boring*. If sex with you is anything like kissing you, then …"

She broke into a fit of giggles, and with that, my better judgement told me that perhaps it would have been best to just stay home and continue my writing. Being at her house, I couldn't guarantee she would behave herself, and there was certainly no guarantee I'd have the willpower to stop her from trying.

But, I reminded myself, I was sober with my faculties intact, and it was now my responsibility to keep her from getting hurt in some drunken accident.

I threw a t-shirt over my head and stuffed my feet into my boots. "Where am I going?"

***

The house was dark aside from a small bit of blue light flashing in one window, and I parked the car at the curb before heading up the walkway. Before I could reach the door and extend a fist to knock, Holly threw the door open and I couldn't fight the smile that threatened the corners of my mouth at the sight of her in pajamas with the blanket tied around her neck like a cape.

"Does Holly live here?" I asked, looking around her into the dark house. "She didn't tell me she lived with Wonder Woman."

She groaned, grabbing my hand and pulling me into the house, slamming the door behind us. "Do you want a drink? I think there's something … somewhere. I was going to save you some wine, but," she held up the bottle, dangling from her hand, "I acci-accidentedly drank it all."

She spoke with purpose as her eyes blinked slowly, only opening halfway, and her breath was heavy with the heated scent of alcohol. She reminded me of the girls that ventured out to find me in hotel bars, but I found my heart swelling with warmth, not pity, and when she pulled me to the couch, I obeyed without a single complaint. Nor did I complain when she sat next to me, or when she immediately pressed her head against my chest and wrapped an arm around my stomach.

"How much, exactly, have you had to drink?" I asked, glancing around the dark room for any visible evidence.

"Mm-what? Oh, three beers and this bottle." She held up the empty bottle of wine still glued to her hand. "And there was another one, but *shhh*, don't tell Liz."

"You drank two bottles of wine?"

She held a tired hand up with four fingers extended. "And three beers."

I felt better about my decision to come as I curled an arm around her shoulders, and dared my hand to gently smooth the flyaway hairs from her rosy-cheeked face. She didn't protest; hell, she didn't say anything. I felt her breathe softly against my chest, and for a few minutes I thought she had fallen asleep to the scene of Audrey and her companion Fake Fred spending the day together in New York City. I allowed my hand the joy of stroking against the soft skin of her cheek, running my fingers along the delicate line of her jaw as I fell into a sense of relaxation—the one I only felt with her.

"I was named after her." Her voice surprised me, and I moved my hand away hastily. "Don't stop. It's nice." She spoke with surprising clarity, although sleepy, and I hesitated before resuming my fingers gentle stroking against the side of her face.

"So, are your parents' huge fans or something?" I asked, suddenly aware of how dry my throat was.

She hummed a sleepy laugh that vibrated through my ribs. "This damn movie was playing while my mom was pushing me out and they hadn't decided on a name for me yet. So, when I was out and the doctor was like, '*Oh*, it's a girl,' and my dad was like, '*Hey*, what about Holly. That's a *great* girl's name!'"

"It is," I confirmed, trailing my fingers from her jaw to her temple and back again. "Have you always wanted something from Tiffany's too?"

Holly moved to lay her head in my lap, and looked up at me. Her arms pulled one of mine to her chest, hugging it to her. I had to bite my lip, to keep my thoughts from drifting to the more impure corners of my mind, and I hoped my tortured discomfort would go unnoticed.

"When I was in college, right, *all* the girls had these bracelets from Tiffany's. I thought about getting one, but then I was like, fuck it, because if I got something from *Tiffany's*, it would have to be special, right? I mean, it's fucking Tiffany's!" Her eyes widened with enthusiasm and she waited for a reaction from me, so I nodded my agreement. "Like a *ring* or something.

Tiffany's makes *beautiful* en-engagement rings. Have you ever *seen* them?"

"I can't say I have," I said gently. An image of the glittering diamond ring I had bought for Julia popped into my mind at the thought, but it didn't matter.

"Oh my *God*, you *have* to! I used to go online and just browse for hours, and I would point at them and look at Stephen and be like, hey, buy that for me. But fuck, he could never afford that shit, right? Do you think *he* has a Tiffany's engagement ring? That'd be perfect, right? Then he really could have everything, and I get ... nothing."

I caught myself staring at her with her stray hairs fanned out against my plaid thighs. She gazed beyond me towards the ceiling as she spoke, her eyes misting with the influence of her night of solo drinking. Her skin was porcelain perfect in the dim glow of the television, not a blemish or bump to be seen, and I found myself reminiscing to the first time I had laid eyes on her. That faraway moment when I didn't know her and she didn't know me, and I wanted her more than I needed her. I never would have expected to find myself there on her sister's couch, watching over her in her drunken state, and still wanting her more than I needed her.

But then again, I needed her more than anything.

"Hey Brandon?" she asked, pulling me from my thoughts. Her eyes focused back on me, the pain in her eyes making itself known.

"Yeah?" I asked, wishing I could have pulled that pain out of her soul and carried it with me instead.

"Do you think I'll ever get married?" she asked me, her chin quivering just a bit. The hand belonging to the arm she clung to came up to rest against her cheek.

"Of course I think you'll get married," I insisted. My opposite elbow found a comfortable spot on the armrest of the couch and I rested my cheek against my fist. "Why do you ask?"

She shrugged. "Why don't I want to marry Ben?"

"Does Ben want to marry you?" I asked, raising an eyebrow.

"No, but I knew right away that I wanted Stephen. Ben … No. But I *like* Ben. Ben is good at buying san-sandwiches, and he's sort of good at sex." I bit my lower lip to keep from snickering at the comment. "But I don't want to *marry* him. You don't *marry* because of sandwiches and sex. I wanted to marry Stephen, and he never wanted sex ever because I don't have a dick. Do you think if I had a dick, Stephen would've wanted to marry me?"

I glanced down to my arm, resting between her sweatshirt-covered breasts, and—shame on me—I momentarily wondered what they looked like outside of their usual garments. I let the image of possibly exaggerated perfection, remain in focus for two blips before pushing it away and looking back at her face. It was impossible to ignore the tear that trickled towards the flannel of my pants and I felt my heart twist in a way that could only be described as torture.

"Holly." I sighed, turning away from her moist eyes to look at the hands that gripped my arm to her chest. "Stephen didn't want to marry you because he knew you were wrong for him. He knew that somewhere out there, some guy was wandering around, wondering where the hell his damsel in distress was. He had to let you go, and you had to come here, just so that guy could find you."

She smiled, dreamily looking up at me from her spot on my lap. "Not Ben, though, right?"

My thumb betrayed my original intent of behaving myself and boldly caressed the curve of her lower lip. "Not Ben."

I hadn't a clue who Ben was, aside from seeing him for a total of five minutes at the store, and I felt a little guilty for throwing him under the bus, but all I needed to know was that he was the guy she had been sleeping with for a month, and that in itself made him my mortal enemy.

"Do you still want to get married?"

The question startled me, and I thought for a brief and foolish moment that she had actually asked me if I'd marry her. "What?"

"You were engaged before, right, and you ob-obviously thought she was *the one*, and it all ended. So, after you went through that, do you *still* want to get married?"

"More than anything," I stated, looking up toward the blinding TV screen without any intent of focusing on the movie.

"I think … I think you'd make a good husband," she said in a whisper, and her quavering breath drew my attention back to her face.

"And I think you'd make a good wife," I replied before pinning my lip between my teeth.

The darkness engulfed us, reminding me of how very alone we were. I knew just how easy it would have been to open my mouth and tell her that I was a famed author, a notable public figure, and that I was more in love with her than any one person had the right to be. There was nobody there to make any interruptions; just us, and Audrey Hepburn about to send her trusted cat companion out the door of a moving taxi into the pouring rain.

I looked down at her, at the face I had allowed myself to envision too many times while lying solo in bed after a night of writing. Her long lashes gripped onto a few drops of moisture, the light from the TV playing off them like diamonds in the moonlight, and my lips parted with every intention of finally making my grand confession. My mouth was dry as her breathing quickened in her chest, my arm moving with the rise and fall of her breasts at a more rapid pace, and I felt it impossible to breath in the suffocating tension.

"Brandon," she swallowed, sitting upright, and I was so sure it was in that moment that she would confess why she really invited me over there, convinced that it somehow involved us naked in her bed. "I think … I think …" My impatience was getting the better of me as she stammered, her head hanging loosely over her bent knees.

"What is it?" I gently prodded, my heart thumping against the walls of my chest as I placed a hand firmly against her back.

"I think I'm …"

And with those three little words, she threw herself over me, reaching for the wastepaper basket next to the couch, and hung over my lap as she threw up into the bucket. Immediately, my hands gathered the stray hairs haloing around her head, holding them out of the line of fire as her body purged itself of the night's indulgences.

After several minutes, she draped her arms over my leg, turning to face me with flushed cheeks and bleary eyes. Her nose sniffled as she wiped a hand over her eyes, under her nose, and across her mouth before resting her cheek against my thigh, breathing a bit unsteadily after the few minutes' workout.

"Feeling better?" I asked, pressing my cheek into my fist while rubbing her back through the thickness of her sweatshirt.

Her dark brown eyes squeezed shut. "Not really, and I probably *look* like shit." A hand came up to cover her face.

What I wanted to say was that even then, even with her hair looking like birds could nest in it and the clamminess of her hands seeping through the fabric of my pants, I had still never seen someone I found more beautiful.

But I bit my tongue and lifted her, standing as I asked where her room was. She pointed a lazy finger down the hall and I followed her lead, finding the dark room and without bothering to find the light switch, I threw back the covers of her small bed and laid her down gently. My hand smoothed the hair off her face, lingering for a moment on her cheek before grabbing the comforter at her feet.

As I pulled the blanket up over her shoulders, she said through a mouth of fuzz, "Don't leave yet." And pulling up the blanket that I had just laid over her, she beckoned me to join her. "Please. I hate sleeping alone."

"I don't know if that's such a good idea, Holly," I said honestly, fully aware of what could happen between two adults lying in bed together with little more than a bit of fabric between them and even less self-control.

But she pleaded with me, rolling over as far as she could in the small bed without sending herself over the edge and patted the surface next to her.

"Fine," I sighed, caving under the pressure and climbed onto the bed next to her, curling an arm around her shoulders and pulling her into me. "But once you fall asleep, I'm gone. I don't need your sister calling the cops."

"Uh-huh," she mumbled, nuzzling her face into my chest and wrapping an arm around my waist.

Her leg came up, curling around mine and pulling it against her, and as I nestled my cheek against the top of her hair with the heaviness of my eyelids reminding me of just how tired I was, I thought to myself, *I hate sleeping alone too.*

24

holly

HOLLY!"

My eyelids struggled to flicker open at the sound of Liz's voice bellowing through the house, followed by the giddy banter that could only come from Anna. I groaned as an ache came from somewhere deep inside my skull, leaving me disoriented to the point of not knowing where I was. I mean, the cat was there, coiled between my legs as usual, and I recognized the feeling of my lumpy bed beneath me, and there was certainly no mistaking the sound of Liz's currently overpowering voice; the sound ricocheted through my head like a bullet in a room made of plexiglass.

But none of that accounted for the man snoring softly above my ear with a pool of what I assumed to be my dried drool collected in the middle of his t-shirt. His arm was wrapped comfortably around my shoulders while his head rested against the top of mine, laying there as though this were the most natural position for us to find ourselves in.

What the hell did I do last night? Did I have sex? Was it good?

The wave of nausea rolled over me like a bulldozer as I brought a hand up to cover my eyes, shielding them from the sunlight that streamed through the open blinds of my room.

"Oh, my God," I groaned with a mouth full of cotton. My voice didn't sound like it belonged to me; it was husky and hushed without even trying.

"Holly! Are you in here?" Liz knocked on the door to my room, sending my head into a fit of pain.

The man beneath me awoke with a start at the sound of Liz's voice and pounding.

"Holy shit," he moaned, speaking with the voice of Brandon and in that instant, the fragmented memories of events from the night before came back to me with a groan and a smile. "I stayed here last night," he mumbled, reminding himself of where he was.

Clearly, he was as disoriented as I was.

But he bounced back quickly, and his hand found my hair and stroked absentmindedly as he nuzzled his cheek into the top of my head. "How are you feeling?"

"Like hell," I croaked, wrapping my arm around his waist, vaguely aware of how unusually comfortable it was to wake up with him. My nostrils opened to the sour smell of vomit. "Ugh, did I puke last night?"

That brought a rumble of a laugh against my ear. "Uh, yeah, I'd say so. A few times." He teased the ends of the ponytail I could only assume looked like a Brillo pad. "You owe me a new shirt, by the way."

I pulled away, covering my face with my hands. "Ugh, I'm sorry." I peeked at him through my fingers to find him smiling with a heavier shade of stubble peppering his jawline. "You took care of me," I stated, dropping my hands to my lap, squinting in the light.

"You really didn't leave me with much choice," he laughed, bringing a hand up to tuck hair behind my ear. "It was either that or leave you alone, and I couldn't live with myself if you had gotten hurt or …" His voice trailed off as Liz knocked on the door again.

"Holly, are you *alive*?"

I rolled my eyes. "Yeah, I'm miraculously still a member of the living," I called to her through the door, wincing at the volume of my own voice.

The door flew open. "Are you oka—oh, God, I'm sorry. I didn't realize you had, uh—" Liz stood in the doorway, stammering at the sight of Brandon. Her eyes dropped to the floor, unable to look at him as though he were lying there unclothed.

"You remember Brandon." I shielded the blushing of my cheeks with my hands.

Brandon lifted a hand with a polite smile in some attempt to hide his own embarrassment. "Hey Liz."

"Oh, right. Guy from the bookstore. Hi." Liz waved with an awkward smile that unsuccessfully disguised her excitement, finally looking at him but for only a moment, and then turned her attention back at me. "Um, Holly, do you have a minute?"

Reluctantly I slid my feet off the bed. "I'll be right back," I said to him, in mild disbelief that I was leaving him lying on my little bed as I walked into the hall.

Anna played in the living room, the clattering of her toys against the floor crashing like thunder in my head, and I reacted by pressing my palms against my temples. Liz's expression had changed from one of awkward discomfort to one of confused astonishment as she leaned in close and began whispering with excitement.

"Um, okay, two questions." I nodded my reply, wincing as the world spun. "First, why is that ridiculously hot guy in your bed? And second, does Ben know about that?"

Oh God. Ben.

"Ben knows nothing," I said, massaging in little circles against my temples, praying for the strength to not throw up again. "I think I'll call him today to … to end things."

Liz nodded, not seeming all that surprised by the news. "*Oookay*, that's my second question. What's up with the guy in your bed?" I told her my side of the story, what I could remember of it, and she flashed me a look of skepticism, cocking an eyebrow. "So, you're telling me this guy stayed over all night with you drunk and throwing up, and he didn't once try to make a move? He just took care of you?"

"That's the gist of it, yeah." I wrapped my arms around my stomach, nauseated and not from the hangover. I dropped my voice a little lower and leaned closer to her. "Who does that?"

Her mouth stretched into a wide grin and shrugged. "Someone who really cares about you, I think."

I entered the room again and smiled at Brandon, who had preoccupied himself with petting Camille and flipping the pages of a romance novel I hadn't yet read. He looked up from the paperback, spotting my sister and I standing in the doorway.

"Are you ladies done whispering about me?" he asked with a knowing simper. Liz flashed me a sideways glance, and he sniffed a laugh. "If you want to talk about someone, don't do it right outside the door."

I walked into the room, sitting down next to him with the sensation that the world was falling around me. My hands grabbed at my head, and I felt the gentle touch of his hand against my arm, pulling me down to lay against his hard, sturdy body. I found a comfortable place in the crook of his arm, resting my head on his shoulder as my eyes closed. There wasn't any more spinning or mind-splintering headache; just the stability and ease of being with him.

Now this… *This is right. He's always been right.*

I had forgotten Liz was still standing in the doorway. "Um, okay. I, uh … I'm just going to take Anna out to, um, run some errands," she said before closing the door behind her.

I knew she was making herself scarce after witnessing whatever she thought she was seeing, and I would be lying if I said I wasn't grateful as I listened for the sound of the front door.

"Are you enjoying your book?" I said with a smile, listening as the pages turned.

"Mm," he mumbled before clearing his throat. "Oh, yeah, it's great. You wanna know what's happening?"

"Sure," I grinned, snuggling into his shoulder. "But can you talk quietly? My head is fucking killing me."

"Oh, right," he said, bringing his voice down to a gruff whisper, causing the hairs on my arms to stand on end. His arm wrapped tighter around my shoulders. "Okay, so right now, this guy Raoul is meeting with his housemaid Angeline in the water closet. He's apparently very wealthy and she's been trying to seduce him for a long time, because she wants to marry rich, but she never thought she'd fall in love with him. So, they're talking about what it is that's happening between them, when he forcefully kisses her full on the mouth, running his tongue along her full bottom lip, and ... Jesus."

"Did you open *right* to this part?" I laughed, and I pretended to not notice the way he readjusted himself.

"Oh, of course. I think most of these have convenient breaks in the pages at the good parts. Unless ... *you* put some extra creases in the spine ..." His voice was teasing, but his hand continued a gentle stroking of my arm that did nothing but soothe me into a drowsy comfort.

"It does get very lonely here all by myself," I half-joked.

"Well, hey, if you want really good book sex, you should check out some fantasy books. You know, if you're into elves and orcs." I heard the book close and drop back on my nightstand. His other arm crept around me into a full hug,

"Hot. You'll have to recommend some to me." I sighed, knowing I was well on my way to drifting back into sleep and not sure I wanted to fight it from happening.

The stubble on Brandon's cheek rubbed against my hair as he got himself comfortable. "I could definitely do that," he said drowsily, "but first, I think maybe a nap is in order."

"We just woke up, though," I protested without making any effort to show I cared.

My hand smoothed over his t-shirt, finding a place on the side of his chest. My fingers stroked lazily, opening and closing against the fabric and the contours of the muscles beneath it. Without putting any thought behind my actions, that hand slid up and over his collarbone, over the side of his neck, and up into the thickness of his hair. My hand slid between the strands, separating them with my intrusion. I tangled my fingers in it as I gently massaged his scalp with my fingertips, rubbing in a way to soothe myself without any conscious attempt to be at all sensual.

I felt him move against the top of my head, and without a single thought to prevent me from doing otherwise, I tilted my chin up in hopes that my lips would somehow make their way to him. With my fingers still manipulating his hair, my nose nudged against his and our lips grazed; not kissing, but just … there, daring the other to make the move.

"Holly." His breath was hot against my mouth, and the sound of my name passing through his lips was enough to make my toes curl. I heard him swallow hard before he spoke again in a voice that suggested he was just as tormented as me. "Call Ben."

I pulled my hand from his hair, laying it back down on his chest, and my head moved back to his shoulder. My eyes opened to see him looking down at me, the clear blue irises emphasized by the still-painful rays of sun streaming through the window blinds.

"I don't want to," I stated in a whine, all of a sudden wishing Mom could be there to call him for me.

"I know it sucks," Brandon sympathized, "but you're doing it. It's the right thing to do."

I groaned, crawling off the bed. I walked to the dresser to find a shirt he might fit into. "Do you have any objections to this?" I asked, holding up an old band t-shirt.

He grinned. "I'll never say no to the Foo Fighters." I tossed the shirt over to his open hands.

"Remind me why it's the right thing to do," I whined, clutching my stomach.

Brandon laid the shirt out in front of him and without looking up at me, he said, "Because you're keeping yourself from being happy." And whichever way I interpreted the statement, I knew he was right.

"You want me to make you some coffee?" I asked, obviously stalling.

"Oh no, *I'll* get it," he insisted with a knowing smirk, as he sat up straight to pull the dirty t-shirt over his head, "and *you* can call Ben."

I didn't intend to let my eyes linger, but I found it impossible not to stare at his tattooed flexing muscles. Men looking like that belonged in the pages of magazines or on TV, and not on my puny little twin-sized bed after spending the night holding my hair back.

What the hell is he doing with me?

Brandon looked up to catch my gaze. The corner of his mouth twitched. "What?"

I shook my head, diverting my eyes to the TV on the dresser. "N-nothing," I stammered, overcome by a rush between my legs.

"Oh, come on. Now you're just watching me in the reflection of the TV," he stated with a chuckle before standing from the bed, elongating his torso and giving me a good look at his toned stomach before turning to showcase the mural that encompassed his back, leaving me breathless.

He was teasing me, I acknowledged, as he purposely flexed the muscles along his arms and down his spine before pulling the shirt down, and I couldn't say I minded all that much.

With it resting comfortably snug over the contours of his arms and chest, he straightened the plaid flannel of his pants before glancing in the floor-length mirror hanging next to the door and ran his fingers through the disarray of his hair. He glanced over at me with an effortless sexiness that sent a wave of heat over my body.

"Do I look like we had sex last night?"

If my mouth hadn't been dry before, it was then and my jaw dropped open at the thought of sleeping with him and forgetting about it. "We, um … What?"

Brandon shook his head and chuckled. "Holly, I'm kidding."

"We *didn't* have sex?" I confirmed, simultaneously disappointed and relieved. I'd want to remember if I had seen him naked.

He shook his head with a little crooked smile. "Being puked on and sleeping better than I have in years was the extent to our intimacy last night." I breathed a sigh of relief as I sat on the edge of the bed.

"Now, where do you keep your coffee?" I gave him instructions, navigating him through the kitchen, and he stopped me when I told him Liz owned a Keurig. "Say no more," he said, bending to kiss me on the forehead. "I'm married to my Keurig. I know my way around one better than I know my way around a woman's body."

"I'm not sure that's something I'd brag about."

His lips pursed and his eyes narrowed. "Yeah, maybe not."

With that, he headed out of my room with the purpose of retrieving coffee, while I crawled back up to my pillows, burying my nose in the one that had supported Brandon through the night. Tom Ford's Tobacco Vanille floated through my senses as I closed my eyes, protecting myself from the pain of my hangover that had since dulled with the thrill of seeing him half-naked. I listened as he opened cabinet doors, placed a pair of mugs down on the countertop, and got the Keurig fired up while mumbling his way through the process, saying things I couldn't hear, but he made me smile nonetheless.

Camille nuzzled against my hand, coaxing me to give her a good scratch behind the ears while I contemplated what was unfolding. It had only been a matter of time before I was buckling under my feelings for him, but whether he allowed himself to succumb to the same fate was a whole other story. It was ridiculous and wonderful, I thought with a smile, and I grabbed my cell phone and found Ben's number to let him down easy.

"Hey Holly," he said in a somber voice, immediately setting the tone for the talk he seemed to already predict. "Happy New Year."

"Yeah, you too. How was your chili?"

"Um, it was good. The rice was a little overdone, but you know … It was okay." He paused, a gust of breath hitting the phone's receiver. "I ended up falling asleep before midnight. There just wasn't a point to staying awake."

"Yeah, I didn't watch the ball either. I, uh, had a lot to drink last night." I tried to remember just how much, but the exact figures were escaping me and I figured it was better to just be grateful I didn't suffer from alcohol poisoning.

"So, uh, my friend slept over last night," I said abruptly. Why I thought this was the best way to lead into the conversation, I have no idea.

"Oh … Cool," Ben said with the slightest bit of suspicion.

I stood up from the bed and paced to the dresser and back again. "A *guy* friend," I said in a quiet voice, hardly believing it myself.

There was a heavy awkward silence before Ben finally said, "I see."

"Nothing happened," I blurted out, "but I don't think I would have stopped it if it had. I know that sounds terrible, but I, um …"

To my surprise, Ben laughed. Not a little bitter chuckle or a sarcastic snicker, but a real knee-slapping belly laugh. I stared at my reflection in the mirror, my expression perfectly matching my thoughts.

What the fuck?

"Oh my God," he finally breathed, attempting to catch his breath between giggle fits. "Holly, I've been thinking about breaking up with you for a couple weeks now."

"But the necklace …" I thought about the sparkling little garnet sitting in a box on my dresser. "And … last night …"

Ben sighed. "I know. I just thought you deserved something nice, and just because I don't want to be with you doesn't mean I don't *like* you. I know I should have ended things sooner, but I guess I felt bad ditching you after everything you've been through. That's why I invited you over last night. I thought … I thought you wouldn't want to be single on New Years' Eve."

Despite the sting of knowing he was with me only out of pity, a sigh of relief passed through my lips, my shoulders instantly feeling lighter at the sensation of being free. "Are you serious? I've been ready to break up for … a while," I said, not wanting to give him the exact answer, because telling him that I wasn't feeling him the first night we slept together seemed cruel.

"I have feelings for someone else," he stated without warning, and I felt lighter still. "Nothing has happened while we've been together, I wouldn't do that, but I've been ignoring my feelings for a while, and—yeah, I think it's time."

I smiled at that, sticking my head out the door of my room to see Brandon in the kitchen, poking through the refrigerator. "I know the feeling."

Ben let out a light and airy laugh. "Holy crap, I'm so *relieved*—but hey, what we had was okay. It was fun. I think I needed it to jump back into the whole relationship thing."

"Yeah, me too," I sighed with a smile, sitting back on my bed. "Well, good luck with her. I hope everything works out for you."

"You too, Holly."

The heavy footsteps came down the hall just as I was hanging up the phone.

"So, you find yourself single once again," Brandon mused, handing me a mug before taking a long, thoughtful sip from his own.

I nodded my confirmation before taking a long, slow sip of the steaming hot black coffee. "How much did you hear?"

"Enough to know you're single," he said with a lopsided smile. I took another sip and grimaced at the bitter taste. "I actually have no idea how you take your coffee," he mentioned apologetically. "You're always drinking that damn leaf water."

I laughed. "Black is fine."

"Yeah, well, it doesn't look fine but thanks for saying so." He reached his fingers out to run them over Camille's back, and she immediately arched in appreciation at his touch. His breathtakingly blue eyes looked into mine, sending an icy chill down my spine as they seemed to beg me with a sadness I couldn't quite pinpoint. "Spend the day with me, Holly."

"What do you want to do?" I asked, never once considering no as my answer.

"What should have happened months ago."

***

A grocery store.

That's what he had in mind.

I mean, I wasn't entirely sure what to expect when I had finished my coffee, chasing it down with the appropriate amount of Advil, and Brandon instructed me to get dressed. When I asked what I should wear, because I hadn't the slightest clue what the dress code might've been wherever we were going, he looked at me as though I had just sprouted four additional heads.

"Wear whatever the hell you want," he said with a laugh before heading off into the kitchen to make himself another cup of coffee.

With determination to prove to him that I owned something other than yoga pants and sweatshirts, I dug my way through drawers of clothes that hadn't been touched in six months at the least and prayed to every power I could think of that, after my shower, I could still squeeze my ass into the leggings and sweater I had chosen.

I brushed my teeth (twice), coated my lashes with too-old mascara, managed a quick sweep of black eyeliner, slapped on a bit of lipstick, and dusted my cheeks with a little blush. I even raked a brush through my hair a few times, apologizing to the knots that once had big dreams of becoming dreadlocks.

When I felt I had sufficiently cleaned myself up enough to make a lasting impression, I zipped an old pair of boots over my calves, a bit startled that they didn't fit as well as they once did. I walked down the hall to find Brandon lying comfortably on the couch with his head and feet resting on opposite armrests, his thumbs tapping wildly across the screen of his phone.

He's huge.

The thought popped into my head, stating the fact as though I hadn't been previously aware of it.

"How tall are you?" I asked, startling him from his texting.

"Six foot four," he replied with a warm chuckle, turning his head slightly before looking back at the screen.

He was wearing the Foo Fighters t-shirt I had given him, and his pants had miraculously changed from his pajamas to a pair of jeans that had been worn almost completely through to the knees. I thought about asking if he were a wizard or just anticipated spending the night, but I didn't have to.

"I had them in my car from an overnight business trip." He stood, slipping the phone into his pocket before taking a moment to observe my thrown together ensemble. "You're not wearing your uniform."

My eyes rolled playfully. "I do own something other than yoga pants and sweatshirts, you know. Remember the dress?"

"I do, and I remember it fondly, but I had the illusion going in my mind that your wardrobe consisted of too casual and too formal with not much in between." He reached over to grab his leather jacket from the arm of a nearby armchair. His eyes never left me as his arms pushed into the sleeves. "But you look very nice."

A little too nice for the grocery store, I soon found out, stepping out of his car and staring up at the Stop & Shop sign. "This is what you had in mind for today? Grocery shopping?"

Sliding his sunglasses on and stuffing his hands into his jacket pockets, he rounded the car to stand beside me and extended his elbow for me to take. "*Well*, a few months ago you told me that you used to cook dinner when you had your own place, and if I recall correctly, you also mentioned it was one of your favorite things to do and that you miss it." I hooked my arm through his and we walked toward the store as he continued talking. "*So*, I thought I'd put you to work on your day off and ask you to cook me dinner, because I can't remember the last time I ate a home-cooked meal on a day that wasn't Thanksgiving or Christmas."

Stepping into the store from the cold, I hugged his arm to me, touched by his thoughtful and very likely romantic gesture. "Where am I going to cook, though? Liz and Anna will be back at the house, and that's fine by me, but—"

Brandon reached for a hand basket. "Actually, I know of a kitchen where you will have the freedom to do whatever you want. Just get everything you need, and leave that part to me."

25

brandon

I CANNOT BELIEVE YOU LIVE here," she said breathlessly, covering her mouth with a gloved hand. "This is *the* house. H-how can you ... I don't ..." The fragmented sentences spilled out of her mouth as her hands shook, her feet moving gingerly over the stone pathway to the porch of the Victorian.

I hurried ahead of her, the grocery bags hanging from one hand with the keys dangling from the other. I couldn't begin to explain how I could've lucked into buying the one house in the entire tristate area that she dreamt about as a kid. I attempted to wrap my brain around the unexpected coincidences, and wondered if they weren't coincidences at all. Maybe it was simply fate slamming the pieces of this puzzle into place in a blatant attempt to shove us together.

I slid the keys into the three locks, and pushed the heavy door open. "My humble abode, milady," I said, waving a hand inside.

She stepped wordlessly over the threshold, her boots taking silent steps into the empty foyer as she looked up with wonder, turning herself around underneath the chandelier in a sort of dance, illuminated by the light streaming from the open front door.

I had been given the unique and enviable opportunity to feast my eyes upon many women possessing undeniable beauty;

not on a screen, not in the pages of a book or magazine, but in person. Many women who flaunted their most prized assets with the support of clothing or makeup with the sole intention of being noticed by attractive men. Holly was not one of those. She was so unaware of how naturally beautiful she was, so completely oblivious to the delicate features that made up her appearance. It was enough to strike me speechless in the doorway of my house as I watched her, helpless to the surge of passion that sent my heart into speedy overdrive.

Her eyes swept the foyer; taking in the wood paneling and marble floor, the pocket doors on either side and to the back, and the heavy rail of the grand staircase. The shutting of the door brought her from the fairytale trance as she turned to face me.

"I can't believe you live in *this* house," she repeated, speaking through a veil of awe and disbelief. "I would pass by here *all* the time when I was a kid."

Her hand reached out to gingerly brush against the carved filigree of the banister's newel post as I smiled. Her lips stretched into a grin that reminded me of a kid on Christmas, receiving the gift they had waited all year for and were convinced they could never get.

"Oh, my God, I just can't believe this is *your* house," she said once again, as though saying the words would get that fact to seep in.

To my surprise, she wiped a tear from her eye, careful to not smudge the makeup she wore. I had a hard time grasping the idea of the house bringing her to tears after I had spent too many years treating the place like a harsh reminder of everything I had lost and everything I never got the chance to have. A tidal wave of guilt swept over me.

I left Holly standing dumbfounded in the foyer to slide open the pocket door to the kitchen. Looking around the room of piled dust, cobwebs, and boxes, I wished I had taken a moment to see a fortune teller. Maybe then I could have been a little better prepared to woo a woman with my crust-entombed gourmet kitchen. I dropped the bags containing the ingredients for eggplant parmesan to begin a quick clean-up around the room, feeling suddenly overwhelmed with not knowing where anything was. Holly cleared her throat from the doorway and I turned with my eyes wide with embarrassment, paper towels in hand.

"Wow, Birdy wasn't kidding," she said meekly, running a hand over the granite countertop. I slowly nodded my head, wondering if I should just chalk the whole thing up to another failure in my attempt at a romantic life, when suddenly she took the paper towels from me and began unfolding the flaps of the box tops. "Where do you keep your cleaning supplies?"

"I can't ask you to clean my kitchen." I scoffed at the idea, raking a hand through my hair. But seeing her dig through the boxes, removing the things I hadn't seen in years, I submitted to the idea of letting this woman help me to put the other pieces of my life back together. "Um, I think there's some stuff under the sink."

Opening one of the boxes to help her unpack, I pulled out a set of dishes my mom had bought for Julia and me; an early wedding gift to use when we got our own house. They had spent months on a shelf before being packed in a box, never to be eaten upon. I swallowed hard, thinking of all the forgotten belongings I would uncover. All the things I thought I would never see again, but glancing up at Holly, I saw them then as treasures I was ready to unearth.

She caught my gaze and smiled. "I have my work cut out for me, huh."

Sliding the dishes out of the box and stacking them in the sink, I laughed heartily. "Oh, you have absolutely no idea."

***

"This table," I announced, rolling the circular tabletop into the kitchen's breakfast nook to meet up with its pedestal legs, "belonged to my grandfather, and when he passed away, it belonged to my parents. I ate on this thing almost every night until they gave it to me a few years ago, and it's been living in my garage ever since." I looked down at Holly, standing next to me with her hands on her hips and her hair piled into a messy bun. "Now, it lives in here."

Holly ran her hands over the wooden edge of the heavy antique. "I like it," she said with an approving nod and a smile before heading back to her peeling at the island.

I set out to perch the tabletop back on its legs and screw it into place. After getting down on my knees with the electric screwdriver my father had gifted me years earlier, I stopped to glance over at the woman who had been through two hours of unpacking and scrubbing, turning the dingy hole of a kitchen into a place I felt proud to call mine. She had music blasting through the speakers of her phone, some poppy guy I didn't recognize, and her hips rocked as she sang, while skinning the eggplant with the peeler I had no idea I owned. She might be the death of me, but I would die a happy man, I thought, finding comfort in the expansion of my heart.

She caught my gaze. "What are you looking at?" she said with a little smile.

"Just you," I said softly before screwing the tabletop back onto its legs, and when the two-minute job was complete, I smacked the table's surface and nodded with pride at my brief stint with handiwork. "Yeah, I'd say I'm ready to put together some shit from Ikea. What do you think?"

"*Right*," she chuckled, shaking her head. "I'm not sure Ikea can handle you and your screwdriver."

"Hey, are you making fun of my screwdriver?" I leaned my forearms against the island, looking over the counter's surface at her. The corner of my mouth lifted into a teasing half-smile, and I saw the flush creep up from the neckline of her sweater.

"Oh, no, not at all." She smirked, beginning the task of slicing the eggplant. "It wouldn't be fair to make fun of something I haven't had the pleasure of meeting." Her dark eyes looked up at me from her work.

"Oh, please, don't let me stop you. I have it right over here. Maybe you could say hi."

"Maybe I will," she said, and I could have sworn I caught her eyes frisk over me before turning her attention back to her music and her eggplant.

I snorted a laugh with a tinge of hope that she'd actually follow through with that, but pessimism told me not to count on us actually getting that far in the night, despite my hopes of this being the beginning to my own happily ever after while Breckenridge got his.

I walked from the kitchen to the living room, suddenly needing a drink to take the edge off the nerves that were all at once making their presence known in the pit of my gut. I called to Holly, asking if she wanted something, to which she declined, but that wasn't stopping me from having a shot of Scotch.

Pouring the amber liquid courage into an etched glass tumbler, I noticed my hand shaking. *Get a fucking grip*, I scolded myself, picking up the glass and bringing it to my lips, sipping at it gently before turning to pull myself together on the couch.

I had made the decision to tell her that night. Sleeping with her helped to solidify the notion that I had to get it over with, but it wasn't until I overheard her on the phone with Ben, breaking up with him, that I knew for certain it had to be that day. I owed that to her after knowing part of the reason behind the breakup was me. I had to make it at least seem somewhat worthwhile on her end.

Pulling me from my thoughts, Holly walked casually into the living room, her hand hovering under a ladle of sauce, as she asked me to give it a taste.

An explosion of tomato, garlic, and onion burst into my mouth accompanied by a hint of red wine. "Holy shit. I can't tell if it's just been *that* long since I've had homemade sauce or if it really is *that* good."

Pleased with herself, she turned on her heel and headed back towards the kitchen, making sure to tell me that dinner would be ready in less than twenty minutes. Having a timeframe now made me feel like a prisoner waiting for his turn at the gallows, waiting to hear the executioner call his name, waiting for that rope to slip around his neck and end it all.

I rolled my drink around the glass, losing myself in its reflection. I could see it all playing out in my mind: we would have a nice dinner, possibly the best either of us had eaten in God knows how long, and I would fall further into my love for her with every taste taken and every word spoken. Maybe she would even realize then that she had fallen in love with me over those months of us lying to ourselves. The wine would go to our heads, and after completing the meal, before the dishes could be cleared, I would kiss her. I wouldn't be able to control myself any longer after a day of displaying more self-control than I ever thought possible, and I would kiss her long and hard. My hands would roam a little, testing the waters and seeing where she would permit me to go, and when it had been decided that *this is it*, we would take our hands and kisses to the living room or the bedroom or wherever the hell, it didn't matter.

But I would stop myself, unable to seal the deal without her knowing the truth, and I would tell her. I would crumble at the falling of her face at the realization that I had been hiding a crucial bit of information from her for months when I could have just come clean.

"And then ... it's over," I said softly to the glass before pouring its remaining contents down my throat.

26
holly

O KAY, I'M NOT JUST SAYING this, but this is the best eggplant parm I've ever eaten."

I bowed my head to the man sitting to the right of me. "I'll tell the chef," I said beaming, before digging in myself.

Oh, thank God, I haven't lost my touch.

I closed my eyes as I chewed the fried eggplant, perfectly crispy around the edges and smothered in mozzarella, and I tried to remember the last time I had eaten eggplant parmesan. I knew it had undoubtedly been with Stephen in our little apartment. I tried picturing his face and whether or not he enjoyed it, but glancing up at Brandon, I knew instantly that none of that mattered. Not when I had this new man, treating the meal like the finest cuisine he had ever rolled around his palate. I couldn't remember ever feeling quite that proud over something I had cooked, and I couldn't think of anybody I would have rather shared it with.

Brandon put his knife and fork down, and ran a hand through his hair before looking around the kitchen with the sadness he couldn't seem to shake all night. I wondered what was wrong, but fear told me not to ask; too afraid the night would end if I so much as mentioned it.

"Thank you for this," he said softly, taking in the organized countertops that were just hours before piled with boxes.

He hadn't asked me to clean or put things away, but seeing the shambles the kitchen had been in, I could sense that he *needed* me to step in and make it happen, to show him that he wasn't nearly as broken as his house would've had me believe. He had then proven that he wasn't when he quickly jumped in, putting things in cabinets as though he had always had a place for them in mind and bringing in furniture that had been in storage for years. All he needed was a gentle nudge in the right direction. Someone to show him he could, and I was pretty freakin' happy that I could be that someone.

"Next, we tackle the rest of the house," I laughed, not entirely sure I was ready to handle a job that big, assuming I even had a say in the matter.

We ate the rest of the meal in a state of comfortable chatter; talking about things that didn't seem overly important and yet somehow felt crucial to what was happening between us. It seemed difficult to get him to talk about himself at times, always seeming to want me to carry the conversation while he kept his gaze on me and his cheek against his fist, but when I did get him talking, I found it hard not to lose myself in his animated storytelling. He had me laughing through stories about him and Nick, mostly tales from their time in college, and he would grab a hold of my laughter and get himself going. The sound filled the kitchen, carrying over into the foyer, and up to the cathedral ceilings, and I would catch myself looking into the crinkled corners of his eyes with a swelling in my chest that left me feeling comfortable and content.

Oh my God. I love him.

The thought punched me in the stomach when he stood up to carry our plates to the sink. I panicked, trying to scan my mind for some sort of timeline that would've indicated when the hell that happened and why I hadn't stopped it. It seemed that it had been that way forever, but I knew that was impossible because I hadn't *known* him forever. There didn't seem to be a defining moment when I fell out of love with Stephen and *into* it with Brandon, but there I was, with the sudden knowledge that that was exactly what had happened.

"So, I thought we could maybe watch a couple episodes of *Frasier*," Brandon said, walking back to the table and finishing the rest of his second glass of wine. "Do you like that show? Nobody else I know likes that show."

I picked mine up, suddenly afraid that looking at him would cause me to fall even further in love with him, and I polished off the last drop, swallowing hard. "It's my favorite," I croaked, placing the glass back down on the table with a hand I wished to God would stop shaking.

"Get the hell out of here," he said with surprise. "It's like you were made for me or something." He took my shaking hand, sending a thousand lightning bolts up my arm, pulling me to my feet. I diverted my eyes from his, making my apprehension noticeable. "Hey, what's going on? Is something wrong?" His hands found my cheeks, holding my head from turning away from him.

"What are we doing?" I asked, startled by his hold on me. I wrapped my hands around his inked wrists, unsure if I should pull him closer or push him away.

His head inclined toward me, pressing his forehead against mine. "I wanted to see how things could be if we just ..." His breath caught in his throat, as his thumbs stroked along my cheekbones, coaxing me to look into his eyes.

"Oh God, Brandon, I don't think—"

My words were cut off by the sudden pressure of his mouth against mine. I considered that the wise thing to do would be to pull away, to not allow myself to start something new after ending a miserable excuse for a relationship, if you could even call it that. Yet, I found myself gripping the back of his neck and parting my lips, inviting his tongue to tangle with mine, allowing him deeper into my heart.

Taking charge, I blindly backed him into the foyer. His feet must have hit against the staircase, because the next thing I knew, he was somehow gracefully pulling me down with him to sit on the two bottom steps, never once breaking the kiss that I was certain would leave my tongue sprained by the end of the night. My hands left his neck to roam the length of his back, trying to memorize the tension of his muscles through the taught material of my old t-shirt, traveling over the ridges of his spine until I came in contact with the hem. I smiled against his lips, slipping my fingers under the material to brush my fingertips against the soft skin of his lower back and pulled upward.

Breaking the kiss to raise his arms, granting me permission to remove the shirt, I caught the hungry look in Brandon's blue eyes, darkened by the intensity of months of now-obvious passion.

"Oh, you're not going to stop me this time?" I teased, reminding him of the first time we had kissed in the parking lot at Reade's too many months earlier.

"I'm never stopping you again," he said, pulling the shirt off his arms and tossing it to the marble floor.

"Never, huh?" I said coyly.

He shook his head, and for just a second, the wanton desire left his eyes and was replaced by something beautiful and absolutely fucking terrifying. "Never."

Before I could react to that flash of change, he reverted back to desperation and I followed suit. My eyes feasted on the bulging muscles, accentuated by the tattoos, and it was enough to leave my mouth slack.

"My God, you're so fucking hot," I breathed, all sense of class leaving me as I inched my hands towards his chest, feeling like a horny teenager about to get to second base.

Brandon feigned a gasp, dipping his mouth to my neck, and he said, "I'm not sure my mother would approve of me kissing someone with a mouth like that."

I really did gasp then, with his mouth against my neck, kissing from below my ear to my collar bone and back up again. The kisses began lighter than air, painfully taking his time before gradually building up to a battle between his tongue and my skin. I leaned into him, burying my face into his shoulder without the strength to do anything other than moan and breathe him in, wishing for the torture to end. Preferably on my back, with him between my legs.

"Brandon," I panted, my hands maneuvering to the bulging, buttoned fly of his jeans.

"Hmm," he responded in a growl, muffled against my neck.

"I don't think we can be friends anymore."

27

brandon

I NEVER WANTED TO BE friends," I confessed, grasping onto her hands. "I've wanted *this* since I first met you."

Her dark eyes held mine. "Then why didn't you say so? Why did you tell me you couldn't be with me?"

I sighed, dropping my gaze from hers. "Because … Because I haven't felt this way in a very, very long time, and it scared the shit out of me."

I wondered if I should have taken the opportunity to spill the details then, but all I wanted was to selfishly enjoy that time on the staircase before bringing it all down on my head. I would tell her, but after I got to enjoy a few more moments as plain old Brandon.

She nodded, pulling her hands from mine and pressing them against my bare chest, sniffing lightly as her eyes watered. "It scares me too."

I smiled, my own eyes growing dewy under the heaviness of the emotional atmosphere. "For the love of *God*, please don't fucking cry right now."

We laughed together, the sound breathing fresh air into the room. Her hands moved from my chest to my face, a palm pressing against each cheek and instinct told me to mimic.

"You know, believe it or not, I was never really a crier," she said, her fingers tracing the line of my jaw.

I smiled, my eyes drifting to the lips that were only an inch or two from mine. "You sure had me fooled."

She giggled. Music to my ears. "You should take it as a compliment, actually. I rarely cry around other people." Her hands moved to the back of my head, her fingers tickling against the ends of my hair.

"Oh, gee, I'm so honored," I laughed.

She widened her smile. "You really should be. It's just kind of—"

"Holly."

"What?"

I pulled her towards me and my lips brushed against hers as I spoke. "Please, shut up."

My mouth was once again on hers, and it was a kiss like the others we had shared, but there was something new: *freedom*. The freedom to express ourselves without worry of how the other would respond. The freedom for her fingernails to rake along the contracting muscles on either side of my spine. The freedom for my eager hands to move along her neck and down to the bottom of her sweater. The freedom for my aching erection to press against her without any worry of how she might react.

My fingers curled under the soft hem, tugging gently to urge her to lift herself, and she responded with a gentle bite against my lower lip as her hips raised from the step with the simultaneous lift of her arms. I held my breath as I pulled the garment off her body, revealing first her supple hips and the softness of her belly; then the faint outline of her ribcage, her skin pulled taught over her lovely bone structure; and finally, the appearance of her bra, red and lacy in design. My arms raised with the sweater, pulling it along until it was free of her hands and I threw it to the floor, resting with the t-shirt I had borrowed.

I held her hands in mine, bringing them down to rest between us while my eyes took her in. I couldn't spend enough time memorizing every last inch of soft, alabaster skin; so perfect and statuesque, she hardly seemed real.

"I *really* don't feel worthy," she laughed, her cheeks flushing at my eyes' interrogation of her body. My fingers traced the length of her inner arms, lightly running their tips along the sides of her waist, bringing her to laugh, and over the ridges of her ribs until my hands could form to the underside of her breasts. She sighed, lolling her head slightly to one side. "Maybe I should join a gym. *Then* we could be even, providing I can stay away from the doughnuts."

My hands dropped from their new favorite place and I raised my eyebrows in bafflement at her remark. I shifted our bodies, positioning her against the nosing of the step and I was facing her, between the outstretched legs that boasted gloriously meaty thighs that gave way to slim calves. I knelt on the floor, holding one leg in my hands, and found the zipper that ran along the inside of her boot. I pulled it down, freeing one foot from the leather confines.

"Do you know how hard I have to work to look like this?" I asked her, pulling off the sock. Her lips twisted with disgust before giggling as I brushed my lips against the sensitive flesh on the top of her foot. "I have to take time out of almost every single day to make sure I get my ass into my gym, and I spend about an hour in there—sometimes more—just to look like *this*."

I placed her foot down on the floor, and lifted the other leg, resting her booted foot in the hollow of my neck while my hands took their time committing every last curve of her thigh, knee, and calf to memory. "Then of course I have to make sure I run, especially with the way I eat, so that's another chunk of time spent." My fingers had made their way to the second boot, and removed it with just as much ease as the first.

"It's not *just* your body, though," she replied softly. "It's everything. All of you is like ..." It was my turn to feel on display, her eyes working their way over every inch of me. "*Art*. I mean, your body is amazing, but it's the tattoos and the hair and—" She shifted uncomfortably on the step. "And you're obviously well off financially, and God … you treat me better than anybody ever has."

I laughed through my sudden stroke of bashfulness, and slid my hands over the outside of her calves, up the curvature of her thighs, and to the waistband of her leggings.

"I can't speak for everything. I didn't *ask* to be this devilishly handsome," I laughed and my fingers played with the thick cotton as she rolled her eyes. I gave the pants a gentle tug and I was rolling them down, my eyes immediately falling on the lacy red panties that matched the bra she wore. "But everything else is the image of many hours of work—and I treat you the way you *deserve* to be treated. There's nothing special about that, but you …"

I pulled the leggings off one leg at a time and threw them aside. Shamefully, I had a glimpse of Julia in my mind's eye—the last woman I had slept with more than five years ago in the past—and perhaps my memory had been purposely putting an ugly spin on the way things were, or perhaps I was simply blinded by the strength of my feelings for the woman lying before me. But in that moment, all I knew was the greatest painters the world has ever seen would have felt blessed to have had the opportunity to lay her imprint upon their canvas.

All I knew was I had never felt my heart threaten to burst under the pressure of being so much in love with someone as it did in that moment—and I was the luckiest man alive.

"You," I continued, leaning forward and holding onto her hips, "don't have to do anything." I placed my lips against the inner thigh of one leg, and then the other, bringing her to utter a sound somewhere between a whimper and a moan. "You can wake up in the morning and throw your hair into a ponytail without even brushing it." I kissed against her lower belly, just above the waistline of her panties. I was rewarded with another moan, deeper and throatier than the first, and a hand on the back of my head. I ignored her protesting groans as I went further up along her body, to bring myself face to face with the breasts that were rising and falling with anticipation of my next move.

"You can throw on a pair of yoga pants with holes ripped along the seams and a sweatshirt with way too many stains." My lips brushed against the top of one breast, lingering a little against the pillow-like softness before moving to the next. "You can have on smudged makeup from the day before because you forgot to wash off."

I kissed along her collarbones and up the delicate architecture of her neck to her ear, where I allowed my teeth to take part in the fun, before raising up on my arms to look into her eyes. "You can do everything you possibly can to make yourself invisible to everyone else, but my eyes will always find you and I will always see the most breathtakingly gorgeous woman I will ever look at for the rest of my life."

I hadn't intended to make her cry, but the tears flowed down the sides of her face freely, and I asked her what was wrong as I tried to keep up with their falling.

She smiled, taking my face between her hands, and shook her head. "I've never been enough for anybody. Fuck, I wasted years of my life on a relationship with a man who wouldn't even touch me. He needed to find a man to finally get what he wanted." She laughed between sniffles. "If all I had to do was throw on some dirty clothes and maybe shower once in a while, I would have done that a long time ago."

I lost myself in the ocean of her watery eyes, my hands gripping the back of her head, tangling my fingers in the net of her hair without any desire to set myself free. And not knowing what moment could ever come that close to being right, I bent my head forward, resting my forehead against hers. "Can I tell you something?"

The question brought another burst of nervous laughter. "Yes."

It all felt like a dream suddenly, or something of an out of body experience. I held her hands in mine and bent my head to kiss her fingertips, treasuring each of the slender digits with the acknowledgement that it might not all last forever, but Christ … I could hope.

Our near-naked bodies pressed against each other on the stairs, warm with anticipation and affection, and I hovered my lips over hers, so close I could taste the remainder of wine on her breath. "Holly freakin' Hughes ... I'm very much in love with you."

"What?" she asked, her breath coming in short gasps. She forcefully used her hands to move my face to look me in the eyes, as if trying to seek the truth in my words, as if the only reasonable explanation was that I had to be lying. "Are you serious?"

My response was to sit up and pull her with me, kneeling between her bent legs. I grabbed a hand, and brought it to my chest, placing it over the heart that seemed to only beat her name. "This," I said, pressing her hand firmly against my chest, "is *yours*. It has been yours from the moment I first laid eyes on you, and no matter *what* happens tonight, it will be yours until the day I die."

Her arms flew around me, nearly knocking me off balance. I enveloped her in the strength of my arms and buried my face in her neck. "Oh, my *God*, Brandon," she mumbled against my shoulder, her lips moving against my skin. "I love you. I love you *so* freakin' much. I don't even know when that happened, but ... oh God, I love you."

I held her to me and focused on the pounding of my heart, beating against the flesh of her chest. *She loves me*, I kept telling myself, and I knew that to be the truth. Tiny tremors worked their way from my chest to my throat as it settled in that she not only meant the world to me but I to her, and what a fucking idiot I was to have held it all off for so long.

"I have to talk to you about something, Holly," I croaked through a dry throat. My mouth moved against her neck, and she sighed at the touch, working her hands into my hair. My body responded to the gentle tugging and despite the deep breathing I had been exercising, I couldn't fight back the part of my body that didn't agree with having a conversation that could prevent what it had been waiting months to do. But still, I said, "It's serious, and I think it should happen now."

Against my neck, she shook her head. "No, you've been calling the shots for too long. Tell me whatever you want later, but I want *this* now."

One hand left my hair and the fingers trickled like water around my neck, down my chest, and past the waistband of my jeans. I groaned inwardly at the soft warmth of her fingers against the evidence of my rock-hard desire to have her, and the grip around me warranted a sharp intake of breath into my lungs. My eyes closed with the immediate decision that she was right, I was wrong, and nothing was more important in that moment than burying myself between those legs.

With her hand slowly working against me, she pressed her lips against the sensitive flesh of my earlobe. "Okay, now, where is your room?" she asked huskily, drawing the sensitive skin into her mouth to nibble a little, and I responded with another groan as my eyes rolled upward.

28
holly

I TRIED REMEMBERING THE LAST time I had basked in the afterglow of an almost earth-shattering session of orgasms, and I came up with absolutely nothing. Zilch. Nada. Even the last time Stephen and I had sex, if I could recall that last time accurately, it had been nothing more than a ten-minute session to reach the inevitable goal. Almost a job, really.

How had I allowed myself to spend five years in a relationship like that? How could I have given myself permission to always come last, both literally and figuratively? How had I permitted myself to go so long with settling for anything less than what I had there in Brandon's bed?

But it had been so much more than feeling good. So much more than *sex*. It was as though I finally understood why they called it making love, with his eyes boring into mine while our bodies moved together and became one in a fervent ball of limbs and fistfuls of hair. We had created something amazing in those moments when my legs were wrapped around his waist, clutching his body to my chest in desperation while he sunk his teeth into my flesh, and it had been sealed with the simultaneous release of our rattle-the-bedframe orgasms.

I sniffed a laugh to myself as the cheesy thought crossed my mind, but I couldn't deny that that's exactly what had happened.

"Hmm?" Brandon questioned sleepily, the heat of his naked body pressing against me under the dark sheets of his bed. His hand was resting against the curve of my stomach, moving side to side lightly with his palm and fingers in a light massage.

"I'm just thinking," I said lightly, hugging my arms over my chest and sighing happily.

Holy crap. I'm actually happy.

"Are you going to elaborate, or do I have to use other methods to get it out of you?" His hand began a descent, tickling against the sensitive folds before slipping a finger between them. "My God, how are you still so wet …"

"Take it as a compliment," I said with a moan, and he pressed himself into my thigh, hardening with every stroke between my legs. "Gee, I'm honored."

"You really should be," he growled, as his hand continued its manipulation. He moved his mouth to my neck, his lips hot against my skin. "So, what are you thinking about?"

Pressing my hips against his hand, I sighed. "I was just thinking about how … I've never known … what making love feels like … until tonight."

He lifted his head from my neck, looking at me with an expression I couldn't decipher. His eyes flitted from my lips to my hair and then settled on my eyes, and the corner of his mouth twitched. "I thought the same thing," he said with astonishment, pulling his hand away from the wonderful torment to rest it again on my stomach as he leaned in to kiss me.

"Wait, you didn't tell me you were going to stop if I told you," I said, protesting with a laugh. A thought passed through my mind then, and I bit my lip before asking. "Weren't you engaged?"

"Yes, and you wanted to be," he reminded me before landing another soft kiss against my bitten lip.

"But he was my first love. It was … different," I said, wondering if I had ever actually been in love with Stephen when I had never felt for him the way I did then.

"And she was mine," he stated, his eyes taking on a dreamy gaze, as though revisiting her in his mind, and I at once felt a little prick of jealousy.

They were engaged. There was another woman he wanted to marry. Would there ever be a time when he'd want to marry me?

But a second later, he came back to me and looked firmly into my eyes. "That was nothing compared to this, though. I couldn't give everything up for her. She wanted me to and I couldn't do it. I wanted other things more at that point, but there is nothing I want more than this. Absolutely nothing."

My arms came down against my sides, suddenly warmed by the impact of his romantic babbling. "What the hell are you talking about?"

He remained silent, though, and I drew my own conclusions, remembering what he had said about her months before at the diner: she hadn't wanted him to be happy, whatever that meant. I assumed that meant he was willing to give up whatever it was that had made him happy, and with that assumption, my heart swelled.

Brandon was propped up on an elbow then, looking down at me as my eyes danced across the ceiling of the dark, masculine room. His gaze wandered my body sleepily, the little half-smile accompanying his stare. It wasn't a look of lust, nor was he sexualizing me at all in the way he stared, but it was a look of appreciation and adoration.

My hand reached to rest against his rough cheek, my palm cupping his jaw, and he turned his gaze to my face and smiled wider, both corners of his mouth lifting.

"What are *you* thinking?" I asked, remembering when I would ask Stephen that very question. His answer was always something mundane and typical, like that he was thinking about me, and I half-expected Brandon to say the same thing given the adoring look in his eyes.

He rolled over onto his stomach, hugging his pillow and resting his broad chin into it. His eyes were on the headboard in front of him, looking up towards the carved detail along the edge for a moment in thought.

"Well, actually," he finally said, and turned his face to look at me, his facial hair rasping against the pillowcase, "I'm thinking about how you are the only woman to ever be in this room."

I tilted my head back against the pillow and laughed in disbelief. "Oh, my God, stop it! Now you're just lying to make me feel better. Come on, it's okay. We're adults. I mean, I don't need to know how many women you've been with, but ..." The straight-faced expression hadn't left, and I could only open my mouth and gape at him. "Are you freakin' kidding me?"

"Nope." His hand reached down to grip one of mine, lacing our fingers together. "In fact, this is the first time I've been with someone in over five years." He brought my hand to his mouth, pressing his lips against my thumb. His fingers played over mine like the strings of a harp. "How'd I do, by the way?"

"Uh, I'd say you did pretty well." I laughed before saying, "But how the hell is that even possible? Have you looked in the mirror lately?"

Brandon chuckled and the hairs along my arms pricked up. "Oh, trust me, it's not as though women haven't tried. But I've never been able to bring myself to go through with it."

"Including with me, remember?" I teased, remembering that night months ago.

"Yeah, well, resisting you was like telling myself to quit breathing." He wrapped his arm around me, pulling me into the warmth of his body, and kissed me tenderly. "Obviously, I failed miserably."

I laughed. "That makes two of us."

His thumb traced my bottom lip as he said, with that hint of sadness he had been tiresomely holding onto all damn night, "I really don't want to leave this room."

My eyes closed at his touch, sighing at the thought of never having to go out and see the real world again. Just lying there for all of eternity with that impossibly wonderful man who was, for some reason beyond all explanation, in love with *me*. It was too hard to fight the smile that threatened my lips, so I didn't. My eyes opened, and I hoped to see him with a smile that equaled mine, because how could you not smile when you were *this* happy?

But I didn't see a smile anywhere on his face. Not on his lips, not in the crinkles at the corners of his eyes—nowhere. What I did see was his face pressed against a tattooed arm, biting the inside of his lower lip with an expression that told me he was fighting back a tsunami.

"What?" I asked, all traces of my smile wiping away as I imagined every possible reason for him to be looking at me that way.

Brandon's gaze caught mine, holding me there in an intense mental vice grip. "I love you, Holly."

I reached a hand to him, resting it against the dragon that wrapped around his bicep. "I love you too," I said, emphasizing every word

He nodded and exhaled deeply, his cheeks puffing out. "I, uh, I have to tell you something, and when I tell you, I want you to do me a favor."

"Okay …"

"I want you to remember what you just said, that you love me, and no matter what happens, I want you to remember that *I* love *you*." His eyes seemed to darken in color as he spoke slowly, appearing to me now as a stormy sky ready to break at any moment. "Okay?" I nodded quickly, suddenly needing the conversation to be over. Or better yet, not happening at all.

At that, he nodded, released a huff of air, and rolled out of bed swiftly, swinging his legs over the side and grabbed his boxer briefs that had found the floor a couple hours earlier. Stepping into them and standing to pull them up, I treated myself to what I suddenly felt was the last time I'd get a good view at his backside, committing the sight of his tight and shapely ass to memory.

Please, God, don't let this be the last time I see that ass.

He walked to a desk in the corner of the room and picked up a book, grasping it tightly in his hands as he headed back toward me.

"Do you know this book?"

I would have recognized the cover anywhere—a black-eyed dragon wrapped around the length of a sword made of bone. The picture had given me the freakin' creeps years before with its cold, dead stare, but Stephen had been a big fan when we had first started dating. So I read it to see what all the fuss was about and, yes, maybe to impress him a little by showing him I was more than capable of reading something other than a cheesy paperback romance.

I sat up and nodded. He seemed mildly shocked and raised an eyebrow with questionable curiosity. "Have you read it?"

"Yes." I nodded again, almost impatiently. "Why?"

Brandon sat down stiffly at the edge of the bed, still clutching the book. "Okay, um, so you know of the author then?"

What the hell is this? Twenty Questions?

"Sure," I said, not bothering to control my irritation.

His eyes narrowed. "You don't know what he looks like, though?"

"Why *would* I?" I snapped, instantly full of regret. I exhaled, releasing my tension and allowing my voice to soften. "I'm sorry. I just don't understand what you're getting at and I wish you'd just—"

And that's when my eyes fell on his arm, and the damn dragon tattoo. It was the mirror image of the dragon from the cover of that very book, complete with black eyes and a sword made of bone.

"Your tattoo," I said blankly, pointing at the arm.

"Yes," he said with a nod.

My heart knocked against my chest in alarm as pieces of the puzzle slid together. He had a beautiful house that undoubtedly cost a fortune, and a car to match. A flash of a memory entered my mind: He had told me he was a writer of books; a successful one. His clear blue eyes watched me with uncertain intensity, and I noticed my palms were sweaty despite the chilly room. I swallowed, wishing the constraining of my throat and chest would go away, and I finally choked, "You're, um …"

He nodded and flipped the book over, slid it over to me, and I felt the color drain from my face.

How did I not know?

A younger Brandon stared up at me from the book's jacket, leaning against a worn brick building with the thumb of one hand hooked through the belt loop of his perfectly tailored jeans; the other held the hilt of a sword, the point digging into the dirt his boots stood upon. The fitted black t-shirt emphasized a subtle outline of his pectoral muscles while the short sleeves showcased fewer tattoos than he had presently. His hair was shorter, dark and unruly, while his facial hair was kept at that stubble-length I loved.

Slowly my eyes drifted from the book back up to the real deal. My mouth hung open as I struggled to find words to express how I felt, but what was it that I felt exactly? Baffled? Amazed? Betrayed? Duped? Angry? Inadequate? All of the above?

"Holly," Brandon said, predictably pushing a hand through his hair. "Say something, please."

My jaw seemed to flap a few times in some feeble attempt to get a sound to come forth, and after a few tries, I finally spoke. "You're a celebrity," I stated, allowing the words to slide over my tongue and around my brain for a moment before swallowing hard.

Brandon faltered a bit before nodding. "Yes."

The reply was simple, and yet, it was enough to bring my hands to shake uncontrollably. I looked down at my naked body, suddenly appearing to me as a cellulite-ridden blob of shapes and fat glued together in a mad scientist's lab. I thought about my stained sweatshirts and ripped yoga pants, all of those times I cried in front of him, the time I tried having sex with him in the parking lot, and that one time—still fresh in my freakin' memory—when I threw up on him.

I threw up on a famous guy.

"I, uh …" My mouth was suddenly dry while the remnants of eggplant threatened to crawl their way up my throat and all over the sheets. Tears sprung to my eyes and I shook my head. "I … I don't belong here."

I wrapped myself in the sheet hastily, and ran down the hall, down the stairs in search of my clothes and my phone. I had to call Liz, I had to have her pick me up, I had to get the fuck away from that house. Away from a life I foolishly thought I had any claim to, and away from a man I definitely didn't deserve.

"*Holly*," Brandon called, and ran down the stairs after me just moments later. "What do you mean, 'you don't belong here?' What the hell does that mean?" He strained to keep his voice calm as he spoke; his fists opened and closed, chest heaving.

I didn't dare look at him standing there in his pajama pants. I didn't dare to remind myself that those arms had been wrapped around me, that his mouth had just explored every part of my body, that he had been inside me.

The tears streamed down my face as I picked my sweater up off the floor. "I am a *babysitter*, Brandon."

"Oh, my *God* … So *what*?!" His voice with its usual depth had taken on a tense, almost high-pitched tone that finally broke under the strain.

"I'm *nobody*," I said softly, clutching the sweater to my chest.

"Jesus, Holly, you are anything but nobody. You have absolutely no idea what you've done to my life. Y-you changed everything. I lov—"

A nagging little voice spoke up in my mind. A thought that hadn't hit me until that moment, with my eyes on the black-and-white tile of the foyer.

"You didn't tell me," I said, cutting him off.

"What?"

"*Why* didn't you tell me?" I asked, raising my voice. "Jesus Christ. You *lied* to me. After everything you know I've been through, you *lied* to me."

"I-I didn't *lie* to you, Holly. I *told* you I was a writer. You could have looked me up, you could have—"

How dare he pin this on me.

"How the fuck could you do this to me?" I looked at him, stunned that he could possibly try to turn it around, to make it *my* fault. "A-and … *God*, Brandon, what are you *doing* with me? You could have *anybody*, and you did this to *me*? What— did you see this poor, vulnerable, defenseless *babysitter* and thought she would be an easy target? Is this what you do when you're bored?"

He held onto the banister and sunk to the bottom step, holding his hand to his forehead. "Is that what you *really* think? That you were a game to me?"

"Well, what else would you call it?" I demanded, letting the sheet drop before pulling the sweater over my head. I had no idea where my bra had run off to, but he could keep it. A trophy to remember The Babysitter by.

He stared up at me, a mixture of shock and hurt painted across his face, and I chose to ignore both. "Holly, I'm telling you right now. If all I wanted was to find a quick lay, I have had my pick of them for the past five years of my life. You would not believe how many women—and men—literally *beg* me to fuck them. So, believe me, I would not have spent the past several *months* playing the most painful fucking game of hard-to-get just to sleep with you *once*." He pinched the bridge of his nose, squeezing his eyes shut. "And I sure as hell would not have fallen in love with you."

I stared at him—the famous B. Davis—as I pulled my leggings on. "Oh please, Brandon. People like you don't fall in love with people like me."

He laughed bitterly. "People like me … That's fucking hilarious." The floodgates opened up then and I watched in terrified awe as a tear trickled over his cheek. "You know how I fell in love with you? You want to know *why* it was so hard for me to tell you? Because you never treated me like I was a person *like me*," he said through gritted teeth.

"How was I supposed to when I had no idea who you were?" I spat at him before I rushed into the kitchen, immediately hit by the scent of eggplant parmesan. I caught a glimpse of our dirtied dishes still sitting in the kitchen sink as I snatched my phone from the counter.

"You never asked," I heard him mumble, and my pride remained silent as I wondered if it would have made any difference if I had.

"I meant what I said, you know," he called after me, and I spun around to see him standing in the foyer, looking up towards the chandelier.

"What?"

He shrugged helplessly, turning to walk somberly into the darkness of the living room. "I'd give it all up. The job, the house, the money, the car—everything; I'd throw it all away for you. I couldn't do that for Julia, but I *need* you, and if that's what it would take to be with you, I'd be done with it tomorrow."

I shook my head at his back. "You don't know when to quit, do you?"

He turned on his heel, walking back into the light of the foyer, appearing to me then as a soldier who had realized he was losing a battle, ready to surrender at whatever cost. The trails the tears had made over his bristled cheeks shone under the chandelier's light. "I *love* you, Holly. Do you understand what that even means? I have tried to turn it off—I swear to God—but I *can't*. Hell, maybe I could have tried harder, maybe I could have stayed away, but … Fuck …" He sniffed, pushing his sex-disheveled hair back with a hand. "I didn't ask for this to happen."

The tears that had finally begun to slow sprang back to my eyes, falling freely over my damp face. "Well, neither did I," I said, my words warbled by the downpour of tears. I turned to walk further into the kitchen, hitting Liz's number in my contacts and waited for what felt like an eternity for her to answer.

"Wait!" Brandon entered the doorway then, obviously unable to just leave me to get out of there in peace. "Let me just say one more thing, Holly, please."

I turned to face him and held the phone away from me, granting him the permission to speak with the stubborn decision already made that I wasn't going to listen to a freakin' word he had to say.

"I have only told two women that I was in love them—*two*, in almost thirty-seven years—and one of them was you. I'm fucking *begging* you, if you believe nothing else, *please* believe that."

I felt my bottom lip begin to lose control as I brought the phone to my ear. Brandon nodded once, his shoulders suddenly appearing too heavy for him to hold as he wiped a hand slowly down his face before backing out of the kitchen and heading up the stairs, his feet sounding heavy on the treads. After a moment, I heard a door slam from somewhere overhead. I winced at the sound, as though I was only then aware of how hurt he had been.

But he hid this from me, and I'm not good enough for him.

Liz seemed to be chanting my name on the other end, her voice sounding more frantic every time as she asked if everything was okay.

"Hey Liz," I said, clearing my throat. "I need you to pick me up, okay?"

And I prepared myself to walk away from a life never meant to be mine.

29

brandon

EVERY OUNCE OF MY BODY and heart told me to run after her, but my mind kept a more powerful hold on me and I watched her from my office window, getting into her sister's car. I watched through the stained glass as her face crumpled, hands tangling in the unruly hair I myself had tousled not hours before, and my fists clenched at my sides at the sight. After the countless tears I had seen her shed, I never wanted to be the cause, but there it was and it was nearly enough to send me into a craze, destroying everything within arm's reach.

I didn't bother staring as they pulled away, fearing that the pain could actually get worse if I had. I turned and sat in the chair at my desk and eyed the stack of my books on the desk, and I stared until I saw them as the enemy. My life's work that had in one way or another managed to be the destruction of not one relationship but two.

Julia flickered into my mind as I stared beyond the pile of books and into a past life. I saw the late night conversations we had shared over countless cups of coffee, talking about our shared dream of finding ourselves on the shelves of bookstores everywhere. I saw the wall of our Brooklyn apartment; plastered with the countless rejection letters we together accrued. The shared disappointment and dreams had kept us moving forward, kept us happy, but then came the letter of acceptance that should have made us both excited, and instead left one of us dragging through a dangerous swamp of jealousy.

My fingers turned white under the strain of my clenching fists, reminding myself of that final argument that sent the engagement ring into my chest. Julia, the woman I had committed myself to for over ten years, had left me at the beginning of my rise to fame with an empty house and a list of wedding guests and caterers to call. All because she had allowed her jealousy to brew into a soul-consuming hatred.

I reminded myself of how much I hated her for it. How I had sworn to whatever deity would listen that I would never put myself into that position again. This career left no room for real, honest-to-God love. I had convinced myself of that all those years ago, and what the hell had made me think it could be any different with Holly?

People like you don't fall in love with people like me. Her words echoed through my brain, accompanied by that little voice, whispering, "Another me, another life," and I saw red.

A rampage of regrettable thoughts bulldozed through my teetering mind. If I had simply kept my distance after I found myself absurdly enchanted at first sight, none of this would have happened. I never would have felt the need to hide myself, I never would have set myself back in my current work, and I never would have veered off my path of perpetual solitude. I could have spared myself the pain and torment of landing in the very position I had feared.

But I never would have known what it was like to look into her eyes, to be inside her, and know exactly how it feels to be complete.

Yes, but if I had never known her, I never would have known how fucking empty I am without her.

A flurry of sorrow-fueled rage was sent forth through my fingertips as I shoved the entire stack of books over onto the floor with a clatter that vibrated through the floorboards. My path of destruction brought my hands to the laptop next. I lifted it, shakily gripping the aluminum casing with fury sending waves of tension through my biceps, and I was ready to smash it down onto the desk's surface to destroy everything I had been working on, until I stopped myself with a single thought: *Florida.*

And just like that, my mind was made up, and I pulled my cell phone from my pocket.

Before calling my father, I hit Nick's number.

"Why the hell are you calling me?" Nick asked immediately. "Aren't you busy getting laid or something?"

His crude comment reminded me that I had texted him earlier, gushing like a teenager before embarking on my grocery store excursion with Holly. At the sound of his words, I could feel the softness of her thighs pressed on either side of my hips and her hands against my back, her nails clawing at my skin and holding on for dear life as our breath came in and out in time with each other.

Nothing in my life had ever made me feel more whole than that first time.

My eyes welled up at the thought, and I sniffed back the onset of emotion at Nick's innocently upsetting comment.

"Yeah, well, let's just say that ship has sailed."

"Oh, for crying out loud, what did you do?" Nick groaned. I could see him rolling his eyes at the now-predictable twists and turns of my life.

I wiped the tears from my eyes, willing myself to go on with the conversation. "It doesn't matter. I'm just calling to let you know I'm going to Florida for a while to stay with my parents and work on the book without any distractions."

"Jesus, are you okay?"

Ignoring him, I said, "I need someone to watch the house, okay? I'll pay you and Ashley to look after things here."

Nick sighed, and I could see him ruffling the hair on his head the way he might pet a dog if his wife would permit him to have one. "Oh, come on. You know you don't have to—"

"Well, whatever," I blurted, not in the mood to negotiate. "I'll take Tolkien with me so that you don't have to worry about her."

"How long are you going to be away? You have—let me see …" Nick flew into business mode and I heard buttons being pressed, undoubtedly flipping through my itinerary over the next few months. "You have that interview with *The Fantasy Gazette* in the middle of the month, but that's a Skype thing, so that's no problem. But next month, in mid-February, you have that anniversary party."

"I don't know if I'll make it," I said plainly.

Nick sighed his irritation as my agent/manager, but with desperation to be a good friend, he said, "Well, try. It's a big deal." I pictured him pushing his glasses onto his nose. "So, uh, again I ask, how long do you plan on being away?"

"Haven't decided yet," I replied shortly, pushing my hair back.

I wished I could have seen Nick's reaction while he was silent. The only sound through the phone speaker was his breathing and the distant sound of little girls laughing. *His kids*, I thought with a weak smile. The kids that called me Uncle. Kids that would have treated my own like their cousins.

My kids …

I held my eyes shut, and taught myself again how to breathe.

He finally spoke. "Dude, Brandon, if you need to talk …"

I bit my lip to prevent it from trembling. "I'm good, man. Seriously. I just need to get out of here for a while. Focus on what's important, you know?"

Nick sighed again. "Yeah, if that's what you need."

I hung up the phone with a "I'll let you know when I get there," and immediately called my parents to inform them that—ready or not—I was on my way within the next twenty-four hours. My father answered and while I expected excitement, the news was received with concern. I guess, with all of those times I had turned down their offer for escape, they had never expected me to one day take them up on it.

"What's going on, kid?" Dad asked in a hushed voice. I heard a door close, and imagined that he was hiding from my mom's invasive ears. "Did something happen with your girlfriend?"

"Uh, yeah, well … We just broke up," I muttered, my voice struggling on the words.

"Oh, jeez, I'm sorry, son. How are you holding up?" Dad said in his deep, soothing tone.

The little boy in me couldn't fight it any longer and I began to cry softly, the tears making new paths through the scruff on my face. "Not great," I whispered, giving up any hope of behaving as a man's man, and I allowed myself to succumb to my feelings with the comfort of my father on the other line. "I fucked up, Dad. I hid some stuff from her, and …"

"What kind of stuff?" he pried gently.

Without seeing any reason to continue the Holly Hoax any longer, I indulged my father with the tale of the relationship that never was, starting from the very beginning when a little girl ran into my leg. He gave me his full attention, only interrupting periodically to bellow at my mother that he would be out when he was good and ready. With my head in my hand, I let the memories flow freely along with my tears, reliving every moment when I could have just told her the truth. The outcome might not have been any different, I realized, remembering how insistent she was that she wasn't adequate enough to be with a person *like me*—whatever that meant.

But what could have been spared was my heart, and when I verbalized this thought to my father, he scoffed and said, "Is that really what you want, though?"

To spare my heart would have meant to have never experienced her in any possible way, and as my most vital organ reminded me that it was still somehow beating, albeit painfully, I replied, "No."

"I didn't think so," Dad said, and I could tell he was smiling. "Hey, you think there's any chance of getting back together? That can happen, you know."

"Yeah, I don't know about this time, Dad. She was pretty upset."

He sighed sadly. "Well, you're a smart kid. Maybe you'll think of a way to fix it."

I had to wonder if he was disappointed. I imagined my parents wishing for a wedding to fawn over, a daughter-in-law to fall in love with, and grandchildren to worship. And since I hadn't held up on my end of that unspoken bargain, I pictured myself to be the biggest failure in their eyes, despite single-handedly supporting them in their golden years. They never said it, but they never had to; because without the dance recitals, sonogram pictures, and bridal showers to talk about with the shuffleboard crew, what good was I?

Not surprisingly, Dad didn't bother commenting any further on the breakup. What else was there to say? "Of course, you're welcome to come down, Brandon. You know that. We'll get the guest room ready for you. Oh, and by the way, son, let's not tell your mother that you haven't been with Holly this whole time, okay? Not sure if she'd let Birdy live through that." He paused, and chuckled. "On second thought, maybe …"

"I'll get the shovel," I managed to joke, only able to twitch the very beginnings of a smile.

After hanging up, I wondered what he would tell my mother. I could just see her, wringing her hands with worry over how I was going to get myself through this one, but then thanking the Lord that I had the sense to come down to them before doing anything drastic. She could dote on me and make certain that I was treating myself right during the difficult time. Hell, I was finding that I almost looked forward to the constant home-cooked meals and the company—but, I reminded myself, I could have had that full-time with Holly had I just opened my goddamn mouth earlier when I should have.

Or if I had just been a normal fucking person, I thought angrily to myself, shutting off the phone before heading down the hall to pack my things.

30

holly

"OKAY, BUT CAN I JUST SAY SOMETHING?"

My mom, the woman who had reacted to the end of my relationship with Stephen with, "Well, I can't say I didn't see that one coming," didn't need to give me her two cents on my running out on a gorgeous multimillionaire.

"Oh, please, Kathy. Go ahead," Esther urged, lifting her cup of tea to her lips.

And you call yourself a friend, old woman.

Mom spread her hands out on the table, looking into her own mug. "I just want to point out that my daughter, my first born, slept with *B. Davis*. I just …" She closed her eyes, relishing in the details of my tornado of a romantic life. "I just can't wrap my head around that."

"He really is a hot one," Esther grinned, waggling her eyebrows at my mother.

"God, he *really* is," Mom sighed. Her eyes snapped open, looking directly at me with the heels of my palms squashing against my forehead. "How did you not know, Holly? How did you manage to talk to the guy for months without any clue of who he was? Are you living under a goddamn rock?"

"Gee, I guess so, Mom. Just installed some new moss. You should come over and check it out sometime," I grumbled, but the absurdity wasn't lost on me.

"It's almost as good as her not knowing the guy she was dating was gay, right?" Liz mumbled, peering at me over the steaming mug she held.

"Oh, low blow," Esther said with a cackle.

The meeting of the minds had been orchestrated by Liz immediately after receiving my phone call. I had assumed it to be some sort of intervention when we got to the house to find the two women sitting at the kitchen table with prepared mugs of tea waiting for our arrival. Maybe to insist that I should just stay away from men for a while, but no, Heaven forbid I assume they cared that much about my life. Because instead of an intervention, they had gathered to gawk over my apparent one-night stand with a celebrity, who just so happened to be one of my mom's favorite authors.

Seriously, how did I not know who he is?

Holly freakin' Hughes. Freakin' oblivious.

"So, when are you seeing him again?" Mom asked, rubbing her hands together, making no attempt at hiding her scheming. "I need to know so that I can bring my books for him to sign."

My hands dropped from my forehead to stare at her, throwing forth all of the disgust I could muster in one look. "You *are* kidding me, right?" She shook her head, raising her hands with confusion. "You guys are completely overlooking the fact that the guy *hid* this pretty important little bit of information from me *after* telling me he loved me, *after* having sex with me. And never mind the fact that he is way out of my league. I mean, this is all a—"

"Whoa, whoa, whoa … wait a minute. He told you that he *loves* you?" Liz's mouth fell open, so that she resembled a bug-eyed fish. "Holly … A very rich, very famous, and very—" She flashed the Google page of Brandon pictures she had been scrolling through on her phone toward me. "—very, *very* gorgeous man confessed his love for you before giving you the best sex of your life, and you *walked out* on him?"

For the record, I had never said it was the best sex of my life.

Also for the record, it really was.

"How *very* shallow of you, Liz," I said flatly, my mouth forming a tense line as my eyes narrowed.

Mom shook her head, her mug hitting the table in a declaration that she was about to say something simultaneously annoying and truthful in the way only a mother can.

"This isn't about being shallow, okay? Let's forget that he's rich, famous, and incredibly beautiful." Liz shoved the phone at her. "I get it, Elizabeth! *I'm* well aware of what he looks like, but let's just *pretend* he's not any of those things. The fact here is that, Holly, you enjoyed his company for months. You said yourself that you had feelings for him, didn't you? You had a great day with him, and he committed himself to you, and you're—what? Going to pretend that never happened because he didn't want to flaunt the fact that he's a celebrity?"

"It's really easy for you all to judge when you're not in this situation," I mumbled, staring blankly into my untouched tea.

"So, then *explain* it to us," Esther pleaded, reaching over to place a frail hand gently on my arm. "Because from where we stand, honey, you're looking like a fucking idiot."

I withdrew from her touch and she pulled back without the slightest hint of being hurt or startled. Instead of being grateful to have such a wonderful friend and family, I stood up from the table with my mug and spilled its contents out into the sink. I geared myself up for a grand exit to my room, and away from these people that were only going to shoot down any explanation I had.

Slamming the cup onto the counter, I found the sound of the ceramic against the countertop to be louder than expected and it startled even me, causing all of us to flinch. But I stood there unwavering, determined to not skip a beat as I readied myself to leave them in the dust of my anger.

"*He ... lied ... to ... me.*" I enunciated every one of the words in a tone that I hoped would scare the sense into them. "He took *advantage* of my ignorance and used the fact that I had no clue who he was against me. How can *any* of you expect me to just crawl back to him and tell him it's okay to do that to someone?" My chin wobbled fiercely with the images of his tears suddenly rushing in. He certainly hadn't looked like someone who thought it was okay, but he had done it anyway. "He ... He built me up to feeling like *someone* again, and tore me the fuck down. I'm *nobody*, and all I want is for him to know what that feels like for one fucking second and I can't even do *that*! Because there are millions of people out there who can keep that from happening to him, but it took *nothing* to remind me that I'm just a fucking speck for people to lie to and walk all over."

My feet moved me quickly from the kitchen through the living room and down the hall to my room, ignoring their pleas to come back. I stopped myself from slamming the door behind me, my conscience reminding me that Anna was still sleeping only two rooms down. I threw myself on the bed as a startled Camille jumped off and scurried underneath, peering out from the darkness to wait for the hurricane to pass. My face buried into a pillow, catching the remnants of Tobacco Vanille. Now a tainted scent, I threw it to the floor with a disgusted grunt followed by a downpour of tears.

My arms captured the memory of being wrapped around him in my bed, remembering the fragmented night of regurgitating my stupid choices while he held my hair and carried me back to bed repeatedly. I couldn't recall just how many times he brought me back to a place of calm with his gentle strokes against my back and his soothing words in my ear, but however many I remembered, I struggled to come up with any ulterior motive. And *God*, I wanted there to be one. I wanted to conjure something up that would further ruin any memory of him, but I came up empty.

I remembered what he said, that if he had only wanted a quick fuck, he had his pick of them. My stomach churned at the thought; armies of women conjuring up fantasies of doing with him exactly what I had done. I envisioned them hanging all over him, throwing themselves at him like disposable dolls, and if what he had said was true, he turned them all down, and yet …

He chose me.

Camille felt safe again, jumping up next to me and flopping herself down against my thigh. I pulled her up towards me, burying my face into her fur before hiccupping a sob against her body.

"I really am a fucking idiot," I whispered into her fur, and I wondered if my pride would ever allow me to admit that to him.

31
holly

S INCE THAT NIGHT, I HAD tried to avoid any mention of him, which I found to be difficult once I began looking.

I found his picture on the latest cover of *People*, just staring out at me from the magazine racks while I waited with Anna to pay for my daily pint of ice cream at the grocery store. The cashier had seen the look of shock as I pulled the magazine from its spot on the wire display, and she gave me a cheerful nod.

"He's gorgeous, right?" she said, gushing appropriately over the picture.

Brandon's hair had been straightened and I assumed blown out by a professional, and with his bristly chin tilted under, bright blue eyes stared up under his lowered brows with the intensity of a wolf.

"His eyes aren't really *that* bright," I said with a polite smile, while I played back a memory of that very chin grazing along the inside of my thigh.

Another night, flipping through channels, I stumbled on a repeat episode of *The Tonight Show* and just so happened to find myself staring at an interview of Brandon from sometime over the summer. He and Jimmy Fallon talked like old friends sharing a beer at a BBQ, and the thought popped into my head that, Jesus Christ, he might *actually* hang out with him.

I had turned the TV off with little desire to torture myself further and realized that there was no escaping him. Even my normal routine of going to Reade's had become contaminated. I guess I should have expected that to an extent, but I didn't expect for Bill or Jessie to gaze at me sadly, as though I were the one that got away from *them*. Scott even insisted on continuing to give me my lavender Earl Grey on the house, saying that Brandon would have wanted it that way, as though the guy had ceased to exist.

And in a way, he had. He had stopped coming to the bookstore, according to Bill and his family who asked with concern if I had seen him lately. Bill told me it wasn't like him to disappear without warning, and according to Jessie, others around town hadn't seen him either. They had worried me enough to pass by his house, just to see if his car was at least in the driveway, and it goes without saying that I had found the driveway empty. I allowed myself a moment to be troubled by his disappearing act, but only a moment, and I went back to the difficult task of forgetting him.

For all intents and purposes, it shouldn't have been all that difficult. Aside from the mentions of him at Reade's, it was almost as though he had never happened. My compadres had resorted to never bringing him up—ever. Not a mention, not a single word. I guess they assumed it would be too painful for me to be reminded of what I lost—what I gave up—but to go on as though he never was proved to be almost as difficult as forgetting about him.

But at least life brought with it some distractions. Anna provided a daily retreat from my mental torment, Esther provided her usual banter, and Liz …

Well, Liz was something else entirely.

Liz had perplexed me with some pretty mysterious behavior. Late work nights, shifty conversation, and too many phone calls locked away in her bedroom. I was growing more and more suspicious, with my mind leaning towards something romantic, and that particular night was no exception as she ran into the house after work, her heels clicking across the floor and down the hallway to her room. Not a word was spoken to either of us, and Anna and I glanced at each other, wearing the same perplexed expression over our fourth rousing game of *Candy Land*.

"What, nothing happened today? No new patients with halitosis?" I called after her suspiciously. Anna glanced up at me from the board game, and I shrugged at her before spinning the wheel. "Darn, looks like you win again, kiddo."

A knock on the front door startled us both as Anna's figure crossed the finish line to the Candy Castle. Assuming it was Esther, because who else would it be, I got up from the floor, ignoring the popping in my knees, and without bothering to look through the window, I threw the door open.

"And what the hell do you want?" I asked with a laugh as the door swung open. "O-oh, my God, I thought you were someone else. Um—Esther. I thought you were Esther."

I leaned my weight against the door frame, immediately putting the pieces of that particular puzzle together with ease. "So, Liz was the other woman, huh?" I asked, stepping aside to grant Ben and his bouquet of flowers passage into the house.

He gritted his teeth and knitted his brows together in worry. "Is this weird for you? Because I can wait outside."

I considered the question for a moment, placing a hand on my hip. The short answer was that, yes, it was incredibly weird and I was planning on having a nice chat with my sister the second I was able to. But there were grey areas, and that was what prevented me from feeling weird enough to send him out into the cold.

Just then, a gussied-up Liz appeared by my side with a grin plastered on her face. Right there in front of me, the two of them squished their lips together for a pain-staking second and Liz invited him in. She took the flowers from him and sauntered her way into the kitchen. I hastily excused myself and followed her while Anna squealed Ben's name. Apparently, she had been aware of this pairing before I even had a clue.

"So, you and Benny, huh," I said casually.

She sighed, still wearing her smile. "Okay, I know I owe you an explanation, but I didn't want to say anything because you're, um—you know, going through a breakup—"

It was the first time anybody had alluded to Brandon since that night. I swallowed hard with a deep breath, eyeing the refrigerator and imagining the beautiful box of wine inside.

"Can't be a breakup when we were never together," I mumbled, and then shook my head at the absurdity of the situation, putting myself back on track. "Wait, *that's* why you didn't say anything? Not the fact that I've, you know, seen him naked?"

Her face screwed up, as though she had just taken a big bite out of a lemon. "Well, that was weird in the beginning but it doesn't bother me anymore. He never felt anything for you."

"Oh, well, that's wonderful," I quipped. "Wait, how long has this been going on?"

"Um, well, let me think." She counted on her fingers, whispering the numbers as she went. "Two weeks, I think?"

My mouth dropped, doing the math quickly in my head. "Ben and I ended things two weeks ago," I said flatly. I grabbed a plastic cup and went to the fridge for some wine.

She shrugged, twisting her lips. She looked a touch shameful, but not enough to end things, and I couldn't blame her for that. "When you guys broke it off, he called me pretty much right away and told me how he felt."

Ben stuck his head in the kitchen. "Babe, my mom made the reservations for six and it's already a quarter to." He glanced at me. "Um, are we good here?"

Liz's eyes were also on me, and dammit, I felt like some wine drinking circus freak show; "Step right up and see the woman who can't hold onto a man to save her life!" But the longer they stared, biting the inside of their cheeks, it dawned on me that they wanted my blessing and at first, I wasn't so sure I could give it to them. I mean, why would I even want to watch these two people blossom into something perfect, and something I couldn't seem to maintain for myself?

But then with a reluctant clarity, I remembered how much Liz had done for me all of those months, and never once asked for anything in return. I remembered her years of being single, and how lonely she must have been before I landed on her doorstep. She deserved her own happiness, and she had obviously found it with Ben.

After a few moments, I nodded my approval and told him that, yeah, we were good. As though they had been holding their breath, they both sighed heavily and smiled. Not at me, but at each other, and I caught the glimmer in their eyes. The little sparkle I was so familiar with.

They were in love, and my heart ached with a cocktail of jealousy and sadness.

Goddammit, I miss Brandon.

32

brandon

THE VIEW WAS A POSTCARD picture of beauty and serenity with my gaze set on the setting sun, painting a shimmering canvas of sunlight across the ocean. The cool Florida winter breeze blew my hair back, sending the natural scent of the beach wafting up my nostrils, and I inhaled deeply.

Mom and Dad sat next to me in their beach lounge chairs, connected by their hands, looking out at the never-ending expanse of the ocean before us. They sighed happily, never tiring of the view they saw every day of their peaceful lives.

Dad reached into his cooler, pulling out another beer and then tapped me on the shoulder to ask if I wanted one.

"Why the hell not," I replied, and accepted the bottle, twisting the cap off with ease.

I caught the disapproving glance Mom shot at him as I knocked the bottle back, knowing she was probably thinking about the fourth bottle of Scotch I had brought home from the liquor store earlier that day. Dad had defended the overconsumption of alcohol, saying that it was what writers did to get the creative juices flowing, but boy, was he wrong. I had never needed to fit that stereotype before, and I seldom drank sans for a glass of something on occasion. No, drinking was what I did when I wanted to forget, but the only thing I managed to forget was that drinking never actually helped me to forget anything.

I guess I just never learned.

My arms crossed over my chest with the bottle in hand as a few young ladies walked by; their eyes interrogating my body while wearing flirtatious smiles. I suddenly felt over-exposed, wishing I had brought a shirt with me from the condo.

Dad winked at me. "They're cute, right?" He had spent the past month making attempts to get me interested in other women, to keep me from moping too much over Holly. He had since been unsuccessful, but I wasn't sure I could blame him for trying.

"Sure, if I was into cradle-robbing." I shook my head before taking another swig, pushing the salty dampness of my hair out of my face.

Dad cocked his head and peered at me over the rims of his sunglasses, reminding me of a less birdlike Nick. "Hey, when you get to be my age, you'll *wish* the girls that young still looked at you. I can't remember the last time they looked at me like—"

"Jack!" Mom smacked at him with flailing hands from her chair. "You're cut off now. You're only a pig when you drink."

I snorted at that and took another sip of the beer that had stopped tasting good two bottles earlier. My face contorted into one expressing my distaste, but I swallowed hard, and tried to remember what the hell it was I had hoped to accomplish by running away. Because all that I had managed to do was finish most of the book.

With few excuses to distract me from the task, and acting as a distraction in itself, I had worked tirelessly at getting the thing down on my laptop and out of my head, knowing it was a matter of days before I would send the manuscript off to the editor. Nick had already emailed me with the promotional details and gentle reminders that there would need to be another photoshoot (or seven, knowing their fickle tendencies), and that

I better be keeping my ass in shape in between lazy lounges on Florida's sandy shores.

January was coming to a close, and the real world was beckoning me back to it, with the anniversary party coming up in the next couple of weeks. I reluctantly accepted that I would need to return to the great Empire State sooner rather than later, and I just hoped I could successfully ignore that I knew exactly where she lived. I hoped I could continue to ignore her phone number, and that I knew where I could find her on Tuesdays and Thursdays. I would have to resist the temptation, because she had made it very clear she wanted nothing to do with me. If her walking out hadn't been enough proof of that, her lack of communication certainly was, but God, what I would have given to see that smile one more time.

My eyes took on a wistful gaze as my heart thrummed the reminder of how badly it hurt to be broken. I stared off into the fading sunset, looking past the ocean, and into the small library of memories I kept at close hand. I accessed them so often that some had even begun to fade, like an old worn blanket. Comfortable and cozy, and yet fuzzy and forgotten with wear. But others remained fresh, as though they had just happened. The scent of her hair, the taste of her skin, and the sound of her laugh could never be refreshed again, and I still would never forget. I held onto those cherished memories then, staring off in a daze, replaying them over and over again until I heard Mom whisper something, and Dad placed a hand on my shoulder.

"Hey, kid," he said, giving me a gentle shake. "Mom and I are worried about you."

I reached up to scratch the beard I had allowed to grow over the month. "You guys don't have to worry about me. I'm fine."

Mom stood up, her long sundress billowing around her legs in the light ocean breeze, and walked over to perch herself at the edge of my lounge. She placed a graceful, weathered hand on my chest, touching the healing tattoo over my heart. I winced at the touch and she apologized, immediately removing her hand from the sensitive skin and rested it on my arm instead.

"I love having you here, you know that?" she said with a smile, and I nodded. It was hard to forget when she told me a number of times throughout every day. "But I want you to leave."

"What?" I asked, laughing. "You beg me to come down here all the time, and now you're kicking me out?"

She took my hands and looked to my dad for support. He remained silent with a little encouraging wave of his hand.

"Honey, you've gotten a lot of work done, and that's great. But your father and I agree that you need to go home, and back to her. And for the love of God, this drinking has to stop. You haven't been like this since Julia."

"I was worse with Julia," I said defiantly, and in fairness, that was the truth. I hadn't yet drunken myself to the point of passing out every night for two weeks.

"I can't go back to Holly. She made it pretty clear that she doesn't want me, and I have to respect that." I dropped my half-empty bottle into the sand. "And don't worry about the drinking. I don't think I can stomach anymore of this fucking shit."

"Language," she scolded, and I raised an apologetic hand. "Anyway, B., if you love this woman *that* much to let her go, then she's worth fighting for just a little, and you haven't fought at all yet. You haven't even *called* her!"

"If she wanted to talk, she would have called me," I stated bitterly. I had often wondered why she hadn't, but wondering had proven to be nothing but another reminder that she had made her choice; she didn't want me and there was nothing I could do about it.

Dad broke his silence with a disapproving grunt. "Come on, Brandon, you're a smart man. I mean, you didn't exactly invite her into your world by dumping some heavy news on top of her. You admitted that you had kept her from it, but you didn't exactly say she could be included."

"I told her I would give it up for her," I grumbled, painfully aware of the guilt-stricken realization that flooded my veins.

"Honey, throwing your career away sounds noble, but that in itself says you can't have her *and* your job," Mom chimed in, squeezing my arm.

I bit hard against my lower lip, scraping my teeth through my facial hair. "How many times do I have to get the shit kicked out of me before I realize that my world doesn't have room for—"

"Kid, I'm saying this in the nicest way possible, but cut the shit. That was Julia. Not every woman is going to be her. So, Holly didn't call you. She needed some time to sort through this crap, but so did you. You ran just like she did, and don't you think it's time to stop running and act like a man?"

My eyes stared into the hazy sunlight, blinking in time to the whispering of my heart that sounded an awful lot like her name. It would always whisper her name, whether she was with me or not. That much wouldn't change, I knew, and if she rejected me again, then I would have to live with that. But …

I nodded slowly with my decision made and pulled myself from the lounge. "Well, guys, this has been fun."

"Where are you going?" Mom asked, watching as I picked up my warm bottle of beer from the sand.

"Well," I said, squinting up at the condo, "I figured I'd pack my shit, throw Tolkien in the car, take a nice cruise up the East Coast, and rescue my damsel."

33

holly

"CROCKPOT COMING THROUGH!"

I dodged Ben on my way to the cabinet housing the plates Liz only recently started using, since Ben decided to start bringing dinner over a couple times a week.

"It's nice to have home-cooked meals so often, right, Holly?" Liz smiled, not at me but at her knight wielding the crockpot.

I chuffed at the comment, but bit my tongue as I set the table with the help of my two little sidekicks; Kaylee was on fork duty while Anna had the utmost important task of placing a napkin next to each plate.

"Girls, time to sit down," Ben said, commanding them both with a fatherly tone, and listening intently, I pulled out my chair and sat myself down. "Very good, Holly. You get dessert."

"Oh yay!" I exclaimed, and turned to the two little girls still running circles around us and stuck out my tongue. With the mention of dessert, they scrambled to sit down, and proceeded to poke each other in the arm until they were scowling.

"Okay, enough." Liz sat down to the side of Anna and spooned a heaping serving of stew onto their two plates. "Ben, Kaylee? Stew?" Ben passed their plates to her, and I watched as they were filled, and the four set out to eat without offering me.

Holly freakin' Hughes. Invisible dinner guest.

"Stew, Holly? Oh, thank you, Holly, I'd love some," I grumbled.

I had learned over those few weeks that being the fifth wheel was worse than being the third, and truthfully, I had begun to feel as though I were walking in on these private family moments that I never should have been a part of in the first place. There were even times when I felt I should take my meals in my bedroom or at the kitchen counter, like a real member of staff would.

Liz twisted her face into an expression of apology, but before she could say anything, Ben had big news.

"So, guess what came into the office today." He put his fork down in anticipation of someone humoring him, but Liz, Anna, and Kaylee just looked at him expectantly. "Really? Nobody's going to guess?"

"Um … A wombat," I spoke up. His eyes rolled to give me a sideways look from underneath his sandy blonde brows. "No? A platypus then?"

He sighed, and I felt proud that I had already become that annoying sister-in-law, assuming that he and my sister actually did get married, which I was fully expecting.

How many people can say they've slept with their brother-in-law?

I cringed, and hoped those occasional thoughts would eventually cease to exist.

"An *Irish Wolfhound* came in today. *Huge* dog. Absolutely enormous. I can't imagine owning one of those things," he said, rambling on to himself with a shake of his head. He continued to fork his potatoes and meat as he added, "This guy could put his paws on my shoulders. Do you *know* how big that is?"

"That's a pretty big dog, hon," Liz agreed absentmindedly, turning her attention on me. "So, um, Holly … I wanted to talk to you about something. And don't freak out, because this is nothing that's going to happen for a little while, but I thought I'd bring it up now so that you can prepare yourself."

She looked worried and apprehensive, and I had to wonder if people were ever going to stop dropping bombs onto my head, or if they could maybe give me a little bit of time to overcome each explosion before giving me another to deal with.

"Are you kicking me out?" was my first reaction as I put my fork down slowly, looking into my plate of stew. The thin gravy had pooled out near the edges and I regretted momentarily not bringing over bowls instead.

Liz dropped her jaw and turned to Ben quickly for backup. He shrugged, and realizing she was on her own, she looked back to me. "Oh—no! No, that's not it. You'll leave on your own before I have a chance to kick you out."

"Oh, I wouldn't count on that," I laughed, relaxing a little.

"No, um, I found a preschool for Anna. She's starting next year, and this particular school is full-day. Dr. Martin is in the process of hiring another secretary, so I'll be changing my hours during the schoolyear to be able to pick Anna up afterward." She watched my face expectantly, waiting intently for an expression change, but all I could do was sit perfectly still as the information made itself comfortable in my brain.

"So, uh, I'm not going to need you to watch Anna after the summer," Liz quietly added with an apologetic smile.

"Yeah, I figured," I finally said, suddenly annoyed at the swirling mix of emotions that clouded my brain, preventing me from having anything productive to add to the conversation. I just nodded with a shrug, as though to say, "It is what it is," although that's not at all what I wanted to say, and took a big bite of stew-mushed potato.

"The stew is really good, Ben," I mentioned casually, dismissing any talk of my employment situation.

"Oh, thanks! It's actually my Mom's recipe, but I like to add a few of my own special ingredients to it …"

Few things in life would have made me happier than listening to Ben's riveting babble about his mother's stew recipe. I wanted nothing more than to know where it originated from and what it was exactly he did to give it that peppery kick.

Anything to keep my mind from spiraling into panic, but although I smiled and nodded with invested intrigue, I wasn't listening to a freakin' word he was saying.

I can't say I had expected to be Anna's babysitter forever. I mean, that would have been pretty ridiculous to assume—she wasn't going to *need* a babysitter forever, for crying out loud—but I had gotten comfortable and I enjoyed doing what I did, even if it wasn't the most exciting or prestigious job. I felt a pang of sadness at the thought of never going to Story Time again and not having a reason to watch annoyingly chipper toddler TV programs.

I smiled, making Ben believe I cared about his endless knowledge of peppercorns, but I was thinking about how I had initially hated watching Anna and had strictly accepted the position—or favor, really—out of necessity. The smile didn't leave my face as I thought about how much I had grown to love waking up every day knowing I was going to spend it with a fun little kid who had only once stuffed poop up her nose.

I remembered then what Brandon had said back at the diner months earlier, when he had scolded me for talking poorly about my job and insisted that enriching the life of a little girl was far more admirable than answering questions for a stupid magazine. I smiled morosely at the memory, finding that I missed him more with every passing day, but I allowed that memory to put an idea into my head, and I let myself relax with the kindling of a new hope.

***

After dinner was eaten, the table was cleared, and the dishes were washed, I excused myself before the little probable family unit jumped into making ice cream sundaes. Not because I didn't care for ice cream, because Lord knows my thighs depended on it, but because I was feeling more like an intruder and less like a member of the family as the night had gone on.

I didn't think they had made the conscious decision to ignore me, but the night felt more or less doomed the moment they began to discuss their Friday night plans of taking the girls out to the movies. This spiraled into Liz and Ben talking over me about what seemed like an intimate weekend together spent at Ben's house, and all the while I wondered if there was any possible way they'd notice if I just stabbed myself in the eye with my fork.

And I understood. Really, I did. They were a new couple and were trying to make their budding relationship bloom into something beautiful and long-lasting. But I also couldn't help feeling as though I didn't belong—because, well, I didn't.

I threw a sweatshirt on and headed over to Esther's house with a Tupperware of beef stew. Her grass was winter brown, lying dormant until spring when Ricardo would revive it to its usual lively green. I couldn't begin to imagine how annoyed that must have made her when she looked out her window every day.

"She comes bearing gifts," Esther said, throwing the door open.

Startled by her intuition, I stopped in my tracks at the first step and narrowed my eyes. "How did you know I was coming over?"

"Harry told me," she said so matter-of-factly that my jaw came unhinged and I thought that maybe it was time her son placed her in a home. A hand flew to her mu-mu clad hip and she hung her head, shaking it slowly. "Holly, take a fucking joke. I was sitting in my rocking chair and I saw you coming up the walk. Christ almighty, lighten up."

Inside the house, I smiled and waved at Harry's picture before heading into the kitchen with the Tupperware. Esther followed close behind, peering around my shoulder to see what it was I carried with me. "Beef stew," I said, putting the plastic container on the counter. "Ben brought it over in his crockpot."

She caught the unintentional bitter tone of my voice and poked me in the arm. "I thought you liked him. You said he was good for Elizabeth, and I'm inclined to agree, so what's your problem?"

I shook my head, instantly regretful. "I *do* like him," I insisted as Esther looked at me with a slight tip of her head and a pursing of her pruned lips. "But everything is happening so quickly," I blurted out. "Everything is changing. Anna is starting preschool next year, so I'll be out of a job *again*, and I feel like it's only a matter of time before Ben's moving in or Liz is moving out, and I just don't know if I'm ready to deal with all of that again so soon."

"You'll be fine," Esther said. She shuffled her slippers along the tiled floor of the dated kitchen, reaching towards a cabinet to retrieve two mugs. "Tea?"

"Yeah, sure," I muttered, turning to lean my back against the counter. "I *know* I'll be fine. I'm already thinking of what I'm going to do about work, so I'm not *really* worried. Or not much, anyway."

"Okay," she said impatiently, filling the kettle with water from the faucet. "So, I ask again, what's your problem?"

I shrugged, scrunching my face. "It's just … I guess I'm just a little resentful." Esther remained quiet, turning her back to put the kettle on. Assuming she was listening, I continued, "I *am* happy for her. She's been alone for a long time and especially after everything she's done for me, I want something good to happen for her, but I'm just tired of waiting for something good to happen for *me*." My cheeks puffed out with a sigh. "I'm such a selfish bitch."

Esther turned back to me and shook her head. "You're human, honey. You're allowed to want something good for yourself. It doesn't make you a bitch to be jealous of something your little sister has." She dropped two tea bags into the mugs. "But let me tell you something. You're never going to let yourself have anything good if you keep holding onto thinking you're not good enough for anybody, okay? You'd still—"

The sound of my phone ringing interrupted her lecture, and we both stared wide-eyed at each other with the same hopeful assumption that it was Brandon. The magic of perfect timing and all. She urged me silently to answer it, her hands flailing wildly with girly giddiness, and I reached for it anxiously only to see the number of the last person I ever expected to hear from. My finger played over the "Answer" button, stumbling over the decision to commit to hearing the voice I never thought I'd hear again, and without allowing myself to think any further, I accepted the call and rushed to the living room.

"Hello?" I asked, sitting timidly on the couch as though he were there in the room with me.

"Holly?" His voice was so distant and foreign to my ears.

"Hi Stephen," I said, surprisingly calm. "How are you?"

My mind raced with all of the reasons why he might've been calling. Maybe he had found a box of my crap somewhere in the back of a closet and wanted it out of his life. Maybe he had only three months to live and needed to make peace with everybody he had wronged—who knows. All I knew was I hoped to God he wasn't calling to ask for Camille back because dammit, she was my last hope of any sort of future. Even if that future involved a little shack in the woods surrounded by feral cats.

"Uh, good. I've been really good. Actually … I, um, I got engaged. I sent you an engagement party invitation, but you never responded, so I assumed it got lost in the mail."

Eye roll. "Oh, yeah, it must have gotten lost," I said flatly, and then not wanting him to think I really cared *that* much, I changed my tone and added, "Congratulations. I'm really happy for you."

"Oh, yeah, um … Thanks." He sounded unsure of his words, and then his sigh came as a gust of wind through the speaker, and I can't say I expected what he then said. "Holly … God, I'm so sorry for everything that happened between us. I think about it every damn day, and I just—*fuck*, I'm just so sorry."

I stared unblinking at Harry's picture above the TV. The old man in the tweed jacket seemed to smile encouragingly at me while my heart thrummed in my ears. How long had I longed to hear Stephen apologize for putting me through an emotional hell? How long had I wished for that little slice of closure? And after all that time, I hadn't thought once about what I would respond with. What was there to say, really? I couldn't just say, "It's okay, Stevie," because fuck, it *wasn't* okay, but if not that, then what?

Stephen kept talking, sounding more pained as he continued. "I was so stupid, Holly. So *fucking* stupid. You were my best friend and I never wanted to hurt you and cause you any pain, but fuck! I *cheated* on you! There was no way around hurting you after that. I just …" He released an angry noise, deriving from somewhere deep. "I just didn't want to lose you. I didn't want to lose my best friend."

"Why are you only calling *now* to tell me this?" I asked finally, twisting my fingers around the tassels of an old throw blanket.

"It's so stupid," he said, and I pictured him gnawing on his fingers the way he always did. "Anthony and I were going through our guest lists for the wedding. I kept looking at mine and I couldn't shake the feeling that you should be on it. Anthony suggested that maybe it was time to … patch things up or some shit." He laughed, although nothing was funny as far as I could tell. "I actually didn't even think you'd answer the damn phone, but I figured it was worth a shot."

I was surprised to find I didn't feel angry, but I did feel something I never thought I would have felt when talking to him again; I felt *sorry* for him. I actually felt sympathy for the man who cheated on me for half of our relationship, and I wanted to comfort him and tell him that if he had told me sooner, things would have been different. But I knew that was a lie.

"Can I ask you something?" He encouraged me to go on, and with my eyes squeezed tight, unable to look at Harry's face, I asked, "Were you always gay?" I felt ridiculous for asking, and I wasn't sure I wanted the answer.

"Yes."

The breath of relief whooshed out of me and into the speaker. "Oh, thank *God* I didn't make you gay," I laughed nervously. "How the hell was I with you for that long and not realize it?" I shook my head at the irony of my life. "I have a really bad habit of not seeing the shit right in front of me."

"Listen, that's my fault—*not* yours," he insisted. "I had been suppressing my feelings for a long time. You were the first and only woman that I felt *any* kind of attraction to whatsoever and that made me feel like you were *The One*, and I went with it. But obviously, it didn't last, and I couldn't control the urge to be who I truly was. But I should have broken things off with you before … before …" He coughed, dislodging the words from his throat. "Anyway, I'm *so* sorry that I put you through all of this, Holly. I can't say it enough. I hoped so badly that you were somewhere out there, living the fucking life after I was out of the picture. Have you been seeing anybody at least?"

I felt my walls crumble, and I spilled every last bean I had. I told him about the loss of my job at the magazine, my life at Liz's house, my friendship with Esther, the dates I had been on, my brief relationship with Ben, and then I laughed in disbelief at the short *something* with Brandon who just so happened to be B. Davis. Stephen had remained more or less a silent listener until I mentioned the name of his favorite author, and he broke out in a fanboy frenzy.

"Holy shit, you're kidding, right?"

"No, I'm not kidding," I laughed, shielding my eyes with a hand as I flopped against the pillows.

Holly freakin' Hughes and Stephen freakin' Keller. Best friends forever.

"Oh … my … *God*," he breathed. "Anthony!" I giggled like a nerve-stricken teenager as Stephen ran to gush to his fiancé about my whirlwind romance with a celebrity, and one the two of them apparently lusted over in the most surreal way. "Holly, you need to spill those details and you need to do it *right now*. But I have to warn you, whatever you say *will* be used in our bedroom later on."

I laughed as my cheeks were set on fire. "Stop it! I'm telling you nothing!"

Anthony spoke up, revealing that Stephen had at some point put me on speakerphone. "Would it help at all if we came over with a nice big bottle of Pinot? I don't mind a little train ride if you're going to paint me a very pretty picture of that man's body."

"*Ooh*, did you take pictures? Pictures would *definitely* be worth the trip," Stephen chimed in, sounding downright giddy.

"Okay, there are no pictures and as tempting as the Pinot sounds, this is still a little much for me to handle right now. Baby steps, guys," I finally said, putting a stop to the playful digging into my personal life. Too soon.

"Okay, *fine*," Stephen sighed, taking me off speakerphone, "but when this is all a very natural thing for you, you *will* share with the class. But anyway, you have to come to the wedding. *Please* let me put you on the list," he begged, and I thought about declining, regardless of the all-around good conversation we had been having for over an hour. I considered telling him, "You know what, I wouldn't mind the occasional phone call but watching you exchange vows with the man you cheated on me with? No thanks."

But it was as though our romance had never happened, leaving only the friendship that was always there, and I couldn't imagine hanging up and not anticipating the next time I would see him.

"Stevie, you don't even have to ask."

He sighed happily. "Good. Now, please, do whatever it takes to get B. Davis as your plus-one."

And with that, we said goodnight. Dropping the phone into my lap, I noticed Esther standing in the doorway with a mug in wrinkled hands. I apologized for taking the call and she shook her head with a limp wave.

"Some things are more important," she said with a solemn nod. "Now, thank Harry for making that little miracle happen."

34
holly

"COME ON, ANNA BANANA," I called down the hall. "It's time to go."

Anna ran from her room and I helped her into the coat I held. Mid-February had brought along what I anticipated to be the last of the snowfalls, judging from the warm undertone of the breeze that hit us as we stepped out with Giraffe in tow, climbing into Ol' Rusty. The two inches of snow that coated the ground had already begun the disgusting process of melting, leaving a slippery sludgy mess under the tires as we made our way to Reade's.

If I didn't think Anna would have a fit, I would have insisted we stayed home. But despite the gross weather, I was looking forward to a cup of tea and a solid hour of reading the new book in my bag—a sure-to-be delicious story about a handmaiden named Kristina and her vampire lover, Sebastian.

Holly freakin' Hughes. Broadening her horizons.

Turning the car onto Main Street, I was startled to find the shop owners already putting up their spring decorations. Cupids and hearts were being taken down from the windows to be replaced with flowers and baby animals. Valentine's Day had only just passed, but these people wasted no time moving on to the next occasion to decorate for.

At a red light, I turned to see Debbie Jefferson outside of her real estate agency. I had yet to officially meet the woman but I had heard of her enough times to know she was a snooty boorish woman who seemed to believe she was God's gift to the town. She was directing a young man on a ladder as he tacked up what appeared to be Easter egg twinkling lights along the awning above the window and door, and I suspected, judging from his face, that he would jump to meet his fate the second he had the opportunity.

Then Reade's came into view. Unsurprisingly, I saw Jessie standing outside the front entrance with her arms crossed over her chest, glaring in the direction of Jefferson Realty. With nostrils flaring, she turned with a huff to send herself flying back into the store and I could just hear the berating she was about to give Bill about staying ahead of the decorations game. He would obviously rush home the first chance he got to whittle himself an Easter Bunny out of a tree stump. I laughed out loud at the thought, turning into the parking lot to park the old rust bucket.

"So, what do you think Jessie's going to read today?" I asked Anna, making our way through the sloshy mess to the door.

She shrugged, keeping her eyes on the ground to keep herself from slipping and sliding. "I dunno," she responded, and shrugged again.

My hand was about to hit the handle when Bill swung the door open, greeting us with his usual welcoming smile. In the hand that wasn't holding the door was a stack of paper flowers he had undoubtedly cut out himself from construction paper. I noted the staple gun hanging from the tool belt on his waist, and I resisted the urge to giggle.

"Two of my favorite ladies," he said with a twinkle in his eye. He caught my glance at the paper crafts in his hand, and he held them up with pride, confirming my original assumption that he had made them himself. "Just getting ready for spring. My allergies can already feel it coming."

"You do know spring isn't for another month or so, right?" I teased, but I couldn't disagree. My eyes were already beginning to itch.

"Well, I would have kept some snowflakes up for a little while longer, but my better half has insisted we keep up with the other—*oof*!"

Jessie came up from behind, wound up, and swatted Bill on the arm with great gusto. Anna giggled at Bill's shocked expression and the look of disapproval from the short round woman with the fiery red hair.

"She has *Easter eggs*," she hissed at him. "Easter eggs! Can you believe that? Easter isn't for another two months! What in Lord's name would she be doing with *Easter eggs*? I told her it was stupid to decorate for Easter, and what does she do? She decorates for Easter!" She bounded away towards the Book Nook in an angry huff, and I hoped she wouldn't pick books with a "Kill Thy Enemy" theme.

I instructed Anna to kick the remaining snow off of her boots on the mat in front of the door, and she managed to reenact Riverdance in the process. "Good enough," I laughed, turning back to Bill to thank him for holding the door.

"Of course." He smiled, the deep lines on his face accentuating. "Now, if you'll excuse me, ladies, I have some flowers to hang before my wife kills me." He patted the staple gun at his hip, and headed off in a blur of argyle. "Maybe I should make some Easter eggs too," I heard him mumble under his breath, and I snorted a laugh.

Anna tugged me in the direction of the Book Nook, and I trailed behind her with a glance over towards the café. The familiar towering figure immediately caught my attention, and I won the game of Tug O' War as I changed our direction. At the sound of Anna's giddy squeals, Brandon turned to glance at us. The sight of his facial scruff and chiseled jaw brought the air to catch in my lungs, and I had to remind myself to breath as we approached.

"Hey Anna," he said as he smiled down at the happy little girl, and then turned his attention back to Scott.

Wow. Mature.

"Hey," I said in a small voice, and when that also went ignored, I placed my hand on his arm. "Brandon."

Scott's eyes flitted between the two of us before shoving his headphones up, making the choice to ignore us as he set to work making our drinks.

Brandon sighed, rolling his eyes down at me, but still he said nothing.

"So, are you just going to go on like none of this ever happened?" I asked, feeling the hurt as if it were a thousand-ton weight sitting on my chest. The silent treatment continued, and I squeezed Anna's hand for comfort. "Please," I begged him, "what do you want me to say?"

Scott silently handed Brandon his cup of coffee. "Thanks, man. See you this weekend," he said and turned to me finally. His forehead crumpled with agitation. "You've said plenty already, Holly," he grumbled, and began heading in the direction of the store's door.

"Talk to me, *please.*" I raised my voice, and I saw Bill look over from his decorating.

Whipping his head around as he walked, Brandon spat, "I have absolutely nothing to talk to you about."

My hand grabbed at his arm, making an attempt to stop him from leaving. "Brandon, I'm sorry!" The tears prickled at my eyes. "You have to understand—"

He jerked out of my grasp, and bent his neck to look into my eyes. I felt his passion, and hoped he couldn't kill me with a single look. "All I've ever done is understand, but you couldn't do the same for me. You couldn't even let me *talk* and explain myself, but—hey, look, I get it. You would rather be with guys who make you miserable, because you've convinced yourself that you're not worthy of anything more than that. I've been hearing you say it for months, and I have no clue why I thought I could ..." He stood to his full height, pinching his eyes shut and giving his head a quick shake. "I *knew* you'd be here, I *knew* I'd see you, and I told myself I wouldn't get angry, but— Jesus Christ ..."

It had only occurred to me then that several pairs of eyes were glued to us. We had created a scene, and I questioned why I thought it would have gone differently when I approached him. Had I expected him to be happy to see me, when I was the one to leave? Had I expected him to have a friendly conversation with me, as though nothing had changed, after everything that happened? In truth, I had no freakin' clue what I had expected, but as my body trembled and my lower lip quivered, I knew I hadn't expected him to verbally assault me with a month's supply of pent-up anger.

"Can we ... Can we just talk?" I asked, my voice traveling on a tremor.

"No," he said flatly. "No, because you want an apology from me. You want me to say that I'm sorry for hiding things from you, but to be sorry for that would mean that I'm sorry for everything else that happened between us, and that ..." He shook his head. "I could never be sorry for that."

I shook my head, as a tear trickled down my cheek. "Brandon, I don't—"

With another shake of his head, he pinched the bridge of his nose. "I shouldn't have said anything. Goddammit, I'm such a fucking idiot," he grumbled, after several moments of awkward tension-packed moments. He turned to Scott, then to Bill, and said, "I'm sorry. I shouldn't have come here yet. But, um, Saturday, right?"

Scott nodded quickly. "Uh, yeah, dude. We'll be there."

Brandon nodded, and without taking another look at me, he hurried out of the store with intent. The pain he felt stung my heart, knowing I was the one to bring him to a place of such passionate anger. Helpless, I rattled my brain with an attempt to think of an idea on how to make things right, and I grabbed at the one that had been handed to me.

"Scott," I said, as Anna and I walked towards the counter. "What's on Saturday?"

He snapped a lid onto the Earl Grey he had brewed for me. "Uh, well, there's a party to celebrate the five-year anniversary of Brandon's first book. It's a pretty huge deal."

I nodded, already scheming. "How do I get in?"

Regrettably, Scott frowned. "You can't without an invitation. The security's gonna be real tight, you know?" I sighed with another nod, taking the hint, and I grabbed the cup from him. Just as I was about to thank him, he said, "But you know, I could give you mine. That would at least get you in the place."

"You would do that for me?" I asked with a sudden wave of affection that threatened to bring tears to my eyes.

With a smile, he said, "Well, duh. All I ask is for some sort of credit when you guys finally get back together."

If we get back together.

***

I could still hear Liz's protests when I insisted on taking Ol' Rusty into the Big Apple with me that Saturday, and Lord did I wish I had listened as the thing puttered along. It wheezed a little more with every passing mile, and as I entered the Midtown Tunnel, I prayed it wouldn't decide to break down in one-way traffic surrounded by water. Out of the tunnel, it could do anything it pleased.

With my guardian angel sitting on my shoulder, I did make it, and I was surrounded by towering buildings that never ceased to make me realize how small I really was. With a gulp of anxious anticipation, I fished my phone from my bag and hit Stephen's number, putting him on speakerphone.

"Hey hon," he said after only one ring. "To what do I owe this pleasure?"

With a deep exhale, I said, "Hey, um, I'm just letting you know that I might have to crash at your place tonight. Depending on how things go, I mean."

"You better be spilling some details right now," he demanded, and I quickly ran him through my reason for the city excursion as I slowly navigated my way through traffic and carefree pedestrians. "Oh, my God, this is *so* romantic!" Stephen squealed in a way I could never remember him doing during the time we were together. "Don't worry. If this all falls through, our guest room and booze are all yours."

"Much appreciated," I laughed, and said my goodbyes.

The venue for the party was a few blocks over from Times Square, an area I had once upon a time spent a great deal of my life. It felt like a lifetime ago, when in actuality it had only been seven months, and my heart pulsed a bittersweet sadness driving past the familiar stores and sights. I hadn't realized how much I missed it all until I was being reminded, but there wasn't time for that, and I forced myself to focus.

With the parking garage found and my spot paid for, I ran as fast as I could in my heels to the roped off building. I was stopped in my tracks by the sheer amount of activity surrounding the area. Black limos, cars, and SUVS lined up, waiting their turn to drop off their inhabitants. Cameramen flashed countless pictures. Members of the media stood against the roped barricade, reaching over with microphones to grab the attention of anyone. Further down the street was a contained mass of screaming people with phones in hand, waiting for autographs, pictures, or anything they could get their hands on.

Holly freakin' Hughes. Out of her freakin' element.

I gulped, wiping my hands on the dress I wore—the same dress I thought I would be engaged to Stephen in—and I approached the nearest security guard on unsteady legs.

"E-excuse me," I said in the tiniest voice I could manage. I was obviously auditioning for a spot in the next *Chipmunks* movie. The large, burly man turned at the tap on his shoulder, and looked down at me with a menacing look in his heavy-set eyes. "Is this the anniversary party for Bran—uh, B. Davis?"

A curt nod. "Yes. Do you have an invitation?" With hands trembling, I reached into my bag, but he firmly grabbed my arm. "Don't take it out here. Come, I'll take you to the entrance." With the hand still gripping my arm, he pulled me through the intense crowd to a short man with a clipboard. "Hank, she's got an invitation."

Hank was clearly skeptical, eyeing me over the plastic board in his hands. "And you *walked*?"

"I, uh, I drove in, but I … parked my car," I said meekly. *I am not cut out for this shit.*

"Hmm," he said, cocking an eyebrow. "I see." He flipped an open palm at me. "Invitation please." I fished the piece of paper out of my bag and handed it to the man no more than an inch or two taller than me. He inspected it carefully, and nodded. "All right, then. What's your name?"

He lowered his eyes to address the clipboard in his hand as I gave him my name. Quickly scanning, he shook his head. "There's nobody with that name on the list," he replied with a flash of suspicion and anger before raising a hand. Before I could open my mouth and protest, he bellowed, "Paul!"

The big security guard was at my back again. "Yeah?"

"Not on the list," Hank sneered, glaring at me.

"Okay, out of here," Paul said flatly, gently tugging at my arm.

"Wait!" I shouted with an attempt to pull from his grasp. "Brandon knows me! I have his number in my phone! I can call him right now and get him to let me in!" They both eyed me suspiciously, but the tugging had ceased. "Or *you* can call him. Or, um, his, uh, agent. God, what's his freakin' name … The, uh, skinny guy with the beak-nose … Nick! Call Nick!" Thank God I had remembered reading about his best friend also being his agent.

Hank and Paul exchanged a look before Hank waved unceremoniously with his hand. "*Fine.* Give Nick a call, Paul.

But if he says you're not invited, you're being escorted out of here, understand?"

I nodded and thanked him before stepping to the side with Paul. He pulled a Walkie Talkie from his belt, and held it up to his mouth, eyeing me with every move.

"In case he asks, how do you know Brandon?" he asked, in a much softer voice than I anticipated.

"We're, um, friends," I said, shamefully tempted to say that we had slept together.

Nodding, he said into the Walkie Talkie, "Hey Nick, you there?"

A moment later. "Yep. What's up, Paul? Everything good out there?"

"Yeah, everything's good. Controlled. Listen, I have a woman here saying she knows Brandon. She has an invitation but she's not on the list. What do you want me to do?" Paul looked away from me, as though to pretend I wasn't right there as he discussed my situation.

A painful thirty seconds passed. "What's her name?"

Paul's eyes shifted back to me. "Name?" he asked, suddenly forgetting I had functioning ears.

"Holly Hughes."

Paul parroted back into the Walkie, and waited for Nick's reply. I pictured that tall, lanky man discussing my fate with Brandon, and I crossed my fingers that he wasn't as mad as he had been a couple days ago.

"Keep her there, Paul. I'm coming out."

I took that as a good sign.

***

Nick approached me wearing a tuxedo and a big business-like grin. "Holly! So good to see you again. I got this from here, Paul." He unclipped a velvet rope and welcomed me through before securing it back into place. When Paul had walked away to return to his post, Nick's demeanor changed to something a lot friendlier, and way more comfortable. He lowered his mouth as close to my ear as he could. "So, where the hell did you get an invitation from? Was it Scott?"

"Yeah," I breathed, stepping through the glass doors, taking in the lavish stream-lined lobby of the hotel. I could see my reflection in the marble floors, and I could have successfully cracked eggs on the sharp edges of the white leather couches. It was more luxurious than anything I had ever seen.

"He's a good guy when he's not too busy getting stoned," Nick said with a little smile and a shake of his head. "Look, Brandon doesn't know you're here and he is *freaking* out. He hates this shit. So, I'm not going to say anything yet, okay?"

"Yeah, he was pretty pissed the last time he saw me," I grimaced, remembering the incident at Reade's just a couple days earlier. Nick nodded his sympathy, and I assumed he had been told. But then, I smiled. "Wait, he gets stage fright?"

Nick laughed. "Oh, my God, yeah, and *bad*. But he doesn't throw up anymore, so I guess that's an improvement." He placed a hand on my back and pushed me along through the shining lobby. "I'll take you to the table, but then I have to get back to him. He's probably paced a groove into the floor by now."

He led me to a dimly lit ballroom clustered with at least twenty large round tables. Crystal chandeliers hung from the ceiling, tossing rainbow-colored speckles over the floor and tables. We stopped at a table with a few familiar and unfamiliar faces. Birdy, Bill, and Jessie clapped immediately at the sight of me. An older couple and a younger woman eyed me with curiosity, as Nick pulled out a chair for me.

"This is my wife Ashley," he said, placing a hand on the shoulder of the pretty young woman with auburn hair. "And over here is Jack and Carole Davis, Brandon's parents." He laid a hand on my shoulder comfortably, as though he had known me forever. "This is Holly."

The three strangers burst with excitement. Cheering and clapping as though I myself were a celebrity, and I thought the doughnut I had eaten earlier in the day was going to end up on the white tablecloth.

Nick laughed. "Okay, guys, don't scare her away. Anyway, I'm going to go keep His Highness from going insane, and I'll be back soon." With that, he was gone, walking across the large dance floor and up a wide, grand staircase, leaving me alone with the people still grinning at me.

The beautiful older woman I had learned to be Carole had her hands folded in prayer against her mouth. She sniffed, and I realized she was crying, or at least close to it. "Holly, we weren't sure we would ever meet you, with the way Brandon talked, but …"

Jack, the man Brandon clearly got his size from, put an arm around his wife's shoulders. "What she means is, we're very happy to meet the woman our son cares about so much."

With a lip trembling more than I would have liked, I said, "It's nice to meet the people who raised him." I grabbed the wine glass of water in front of me, and took a big gulp, startled by a nudge in my ribs.

Ashley smiled at me like she had known me for years. "I can't believe you're here. This is *huge*. Scott gave you his invitation?"

I nodded, and Bill chimed in. "He's a good boy when he wants to be. If only we could get him to meet a nice girl, and—"

Before I could wrap my head around what exactly was happening, a clearing throat came through the speakers, and the lights dimmed a little more. I turned my head to face the dance floor behind me, and saw a middle-aged woman wearing an expensive pantsuit. She held the microphone in both hands, smiling at the crowd with blinding-white teeth.

"Welcome, everybody," she said in a voice that suggested she started smoking at seven and never stopped. "My name is Patricia Wahlberg, publisher at S&S Publications. I want to thank you all for joining us tonight in celebrating the anniversary of a very, very special book, written by an even more special man. He has touched so many with his charm, wit, and talent, and I can see that by how many faces I'm seeing here tonight." She did a dramatic turn of her head, beaming in every direction.

Ashley leaned close to my ear as Patricia rattled on about the charities they were representing that night. "I hate this woman," she whispered, and I stifled a giggle. "Seriously, she's obnoxious."

"Now, I'd like us all to give a round of applause for the man behind the scenes. The man who helped make it all happen, Nicholas Bolton." And with that, Patricia walked to the bottom of the stairs to kiss Nick on the cheek and handed him the mic.

"Hello, hello! I'm seeing a lot of familiar faces here tonight. Ben, good to see you." Nick waved to a table near us, and I couldn't stop my gawking.

"Is that—" I whispered to Ashley.

"Ben Affleck? Yeah, he's buddies with Brandon." She laughed at my wide-eyed expression. "It takes some getting used to. Trust me, I've known these guys since elementary school. It's still weird for me sometimes."

Nick began a nonchalant walk around the dance floor, his hand stuffed into a pocket. He treated this as the most natural thing, like he was strolling down a quiet street, and I had to smile as he talked.

"Twenty years ago, I finished reading a short story that my best friend had finished writing. It was one of the most incredible things I had ever read in all of my sixteen years, and I sat there, amazed that he could create this … this *masterpiece* so effortlessly. He just shrugged, as though it were as natural as breathing or taking a dump—" The crowd interrupted with a burst of laughter, and Nick beamed with pride at his own wit. "But see, that's because it was for him, and I said, 'Dude, someday when you finish your first book, I'm going to be your agent and we're going to make you fucking famous.'"

He looked around the room with a humbled smile and a glint in his eye, and shook his head. "We've been through our share of shit over the years. Heartache, the fear of getting nowhere fast, and way more drunken nights than either of us are willing to admit in the presence of his parents, but *fuck* ..." He shook his head again. "Twenty years later, look where we are. I'm his agent, he's *still* my best friend—my brother from another mother—and he is really, *really* fucking famous." A roar of applause and cheers filled the room, and I urged myself not to cry from the overwhelming magnitude of it all.

"Anyway, you don't care what I have to say, and I've talked long enough. So, in just a minute, the man of the hour will be down here. So, excuse me while I go fetch him another Scotch, and thank you all for coming." And with that, Nick jogged back towards the stairs, taking them two at a time with his long gazelle-like legs.

I swallowed hard at the thought of seeing Brandon again— this time as his celebrity persona—and I took another gulp of my water.

Please don't hate me for being here, please don't yell at me in front of all these people, and please, please, please still be in love with me.

A waiter approached and asked if he could get any of us a drink. Brandon's mother and Birdy both asked for white wine spritzers, and his father ordered a gin and tonic. Bill and Jessie waved their hands as they declined. Ashley expressed how badly she wanted to drink, but couldn't because she was apparently nursing.

"And you, miss?" he asked, coming around the table to me.

At the risk of looking like a lush in front of his parents and closest friends, I said, "Your largest glass of any red wine you have, thanks."

And with a chuckle, he walked away while the table chatter transformed into giggles.

Ashley put a hand on my arm and smiled knowingly. "It's going to be fine," she said softly. "Even if he's pissed that you came here, he won't cause a scene in front of all these people."

"Oh, how comforting," I laughed, trying my best to sound relaxed while my nerves double-knotted themselves around every vital organ. "I can't believe how many people are here."

"It's a lot to take in," she laughed, and nudged her head into the direction of another table. "Elijah Wood is sitting at that table, and over there is George R.R. Martin ... You get used to some of it, but my God, I don't think I'll ever get used to ScarJo hanging all over my husband the way she does whenever they're together."

"You mean—" I gasped.

Ashley nodded. "Uh-huh. And I don't get it either. I mean, I love Nicky, but I'm not blind. You'd think she'd be all over B., but ..." She shrugged and took a sip of her water.

And then, the room exploded.

35
brandon

THE ROAR OF APPLAUSE BLASTED me with the force of a sonic boom, and I grinned through it with the confidence of a seasoned professional. The attention never ceased to be a humbling thing albeit nerve-racking. I slowly began my descent down the stairs, praying I could make it through everything I had to say without my nerves sending me into a fit of "uh's" and "um's."

"Ladies and gentlemen, the man of the hour—Brandon Davis!" Nick passed the microphone to me at the bottom, clapping me on the shoulder as he leaned in to my ear. "Deep breaths, dude. You got this," he whispered.

I nodded as my grip tightened around the mic, and I brought it to my mouth. "Wow," I said over the enthusiastic crowd of friends, family, and professional acquaintances. "Thank you, guys, thank you."

I turned, nodding to the room as the cheering lowered to a dull murmur, and that was my cue to begin. "You never get used to it, you know. A lot of people think that over time celebrities grow accustomed to the applause and requests for autographs, and maybe some do, but I don't. How am I supposed to get used to *this*?" I gestured out towards the room. "And all I did was write a book."

I sniffed a laugh as I began to walk around the room, allowing my eyes to scan the tables of faces looking at me. "That book has taken me places I couldn't even dream of. In fact, I received a phone call this morning from HBO with a pitch to turn that book and its sequels into a television series." A lump lodged itself in my throat at the memory of that surreal conversation; something I could never even fathom happening to me. The tables burst with yet another round of excited applause. I nodded. "I *know*. *Breckenridge* will be coming to television screens all over the world in just a couple of short years—and all I did was *write a fucking book*."

My eyes landed on the table that I knew held my parents and friends, but before I could acknowledge them, my gaze was stolen by the person I had been looking forward to seeing most of all. The person I had been banking on being there; the same person Nick informed me had taken the bait, despite how much of an asshole I was to her, and managed to find her way there. She looked panicked, like I would erupt in a fury of hatred at any moment, but I just lifted a corner of my mouth and took a deep breath.

Here goes nothing.

I sucked in a breath of air and slowly exhaled, running a hand over my ponytailed hair and cursing the hairstylist. "You know, many of you know that this day is one to celebrate, but what most people don't know is that it also weighs heavy on my heart. Because, you see, five years ago today, before I was set to attend the release party for *Breckenridge*, my fiancée left me." My walk around the room became one of passion; my arms waved theatrically as I told the story, allowing my truth to spill out all over the dance floor. "There I was, thinking my life was just beginning. A whole new world had opened up to me with this incredible job, one of success and pride. I thought we—my fiancée and I—would embark on a journey into that new world *together*, but a couple months before we were to be married, she just … threw the ring at me, told me she hated me, and left. She was jealous of everything that was happening for me, and while

I was thinking she was busy planning a wedding, she was busy building a wall of hatred around herself and I was too consumed by all of *this* to notice."

I ignored the sympathetic murmuring and looked to my feet, shaking my head. "I truly believed that she could be the only person out there for me, and so I took the beginning of my career to be the end of my love life. I threw myself entirely into my work, and closed myself off to any prospect of a relationship, and I managed on my own for nearly five years, until I met her." I pointed at Holly across the room, her jaw falling open. I watched as my mother clapped a hand over her mouth, while Birdy gripped the hands of Jessie. "It took meeting her to realize that I wasn't really managing at all, and that I desperately needed the company and affection that I soon understood could only be given by her."

I rounded the room, heading back towards her with my heart hammering in my chest. "But I fucked up. I hid things from her, out of fear of being hurt again, because this life isn't always what it's cracked up to be. I wasted the time I could have spent convincing her that she *does* deserve *this*—more than anybody—because I was too stupid to open the door and see what was right there on the other side." My feet stopped moving when I was standing in front of her, and I dropped to my knees at her feet. I placed the microphone on the table with an ear-piercing squeal through the speakers, and I reached with a hand for one of hers, gripping the cherished fingers in mine.

I brought her hand to my mouth, kissing her knuckles gently, before speaking in a low voice. "The other day didn't go at all how I wanted it to, but ... You're here, and Holly, I swear to God, I'm not letting you go again."

Her opposite hand wiped a tear away hastily. "But ... you were so mad ..."

"Baby, I was mad at myself for failing. I was mad that, after everything, you still thought you were more deserving of mediocre sex and crockpots." My eyes didn't stop watching her as she burst out with a tearful giggle. "But … you're here, and that tells me you've changed your mind about that."

I fished a hand into my suit jacket, and pulled out the box I hoped would be the beginning of the rest of my life. "Look, I know we haven't known each other for a long time, but I knew I loved you within ten seconds of meeting you. I knew I needed you to make me whole again. I knew that my life depended on being the person to make you laugh, to make you feel beautiful, and to make you feel like the most important person that has ever walked the face of this goddamn planet, because that is exactly what you are to me. And Holly, if it takes me the rest of my days to make you see that, then my time here will be well spent."

With a quivering shudder, she asked through tears, "Brandon, what are you doing?"

I smiled, my own emotions chipping away at my composure. "I was told once that I had to go to Tiffany's and check out their rings, so I did. Turns out, I liked them so much that I had to buy one." I placed the box in her hand. "I'm hoping you'll like it and want to wear it."

There was an audible gasp from my mother—the first notion in five minutes that the room belonged to anybody but the two of us. And yet, my eyes never left Holly as she slowly fell apart in front of me. A hand shakily went to open the box, and at the moment her eyes fell upon the ring sitting before her, that hand flew to her forehead as she sobbed with a laugh.

"Oh, my God," she croaked, still laughing. "I'm freakin' crying in front of Ben Affleck."

"Ben doesn't care," I laughed, pulling the ring from the box, and noticed the shaking of my own hands. I held it up to her as I reached for her hand. "Holly, please marry me?"

The room was eerily silent sans for the sound of Holly's shuddering breaths. I watched her expectantly as she focused on taking deep breaths in some attempt to pull herself together long enough to utter a response. As a few seconds turned into over a minute, I laughed, squeezing her hand. "Hey, don't leave me hanging here," I said quietly, smiling up at her.

And as though I had broken a spell, she uttered an inaudible sound that I only knew to be a "yes" by the nodding of her head. The room was engulfed by a choir of gasps as I willed my hands to be steady, sliding the ring onto her finger. It was only a little loose—an easy fix—and I gripped her hand in mine, sliding my thumb over what seemed to always belong there.

I pulled myself onto unsteady legs to see the looks of satisfied excitement on the faces of my parents and friends. There were tears streaming down my mother's face, which wasn't unexpected, but when I caught the dewy eyes of my father, I had to look away at the risk of crying myself. I pulled Holly to her feet, wrapping her in my arms as her legs wobbled, and I lowered my lips to hers. As she slung her arms around my neck, there was no fighting the tears and I let one slip, not caring that the cameras were immortalizing it for as long as it mattered to the press. I kissed her hard, holding her tight as though she might run away again if I dared to let go, but I was on borrowed time and I knew I had to cut the moment short.

With one arm still wrapped around her waist and hers still around my neck, I picked the microphone up. Clearing my throat, I said, "Okay, party's over. Thank you all for coming." And as though they thought I was joking, the crowd laughed, finally given permission to make noise. Nick reached over to take the mic, giving us his congratulations, and I knew it was only the first of many.

I leaned down to her ear, in hopes that she would hear me over the ruckus. "I love you, Holly freakin' Hughes."

She sighed tearfully, and smiled against my cheek. "I love you, Brandon freakin' Davis."

And I knew that to be the truth—the most important truth.

"Welcome to my world," I whispered, kissing her earlobe softly. "It's about to get really crazy in here," I said, pulling a cardkey out of my pocket and I slipped it into her hand. "That's a key to the room upstairs if you need a minute."

"I might just take you up on that," she said, standing on her toes to kiss me. "But first, can you introduce me to Ben Affleck?"

36
holly

I F I HAD BEEN TOLD six months earlier that I would one day be hooked on the Armani-clad arm of my fiancé in a room full of celebrities, I would have instructed you to check yourself into a psych ward.

And yet, that's exactly how I had spent that night after being proposed to. It wasn't much of a surprise to me that my social skills were lacking in the face of actors and rock stars, but that was partially because I was too busy marveling at Brandon. Despite his constant need to run a hand over his tightly ponytailed hair, he never faltered in keeping the conversation moving, whether he was talking to his mother or a member of the press. It was obvious why he was a public figure, and not just a guy hiding behind a desk writing stories.

Between being paraded around, drinking, struggling through star struck conversation, and eating some of the most lavish food I've ever eaten at a catered event, I finally found myself slumped in a seat at our table. Brandon continued to be a gracious host as I peeled my heels from my feet and laid my head on my folded arms, like a real lady.

Holly freakin' Hughes. Obvious trophy wife.

Wife. Holy crap.

Brandon's mother Carole placed a gentle hand on my arm. "Tired, honey?"

I looked up at her through bleary eyes, and it hit me suddenly that I was seeing my future mother-in-law. My heart jumped with sudden realization, and my breath caught momentarily in my throat. "Yeah, it's been a long night," I laughed, barely able to keep my eyes open, and she nodded sympathetically.

"Why don't you head up to bed?" she asked in a sweet motherly tone.

Glancing behind me at Brandon, standing with a group of men in expensive suits and drinks in hand, I turned back to her with reluctance. "But what about the party? Wouldn't it look bad if I left?"

With a wave of her hand, she said, "You've done plenty already, sweetie. Besides, I bet you have some people you want to call." She gave me a knowing smile, and I laughed despite my exhaustion.

"Yeah, I should probably call my sister and tell her that, hey, not only am I not coming home tonight, but surprise! I'm getting married." I said the words for the first time out loud. I glanced down at the ring on my hand, and grinned to myself.

Carole smiled along with me, and raised a hand, making a beckoning gesture. A few moments later, I breathed in the comforting scent of Tobacco Vanille, and I felt the large warm hands on my shoulders and a familiar kiss on my cheek.

"How's it going over here?" Brandon asked, sitting next to me.

"I think I should go lie down," I confessed regrettably. "Is that okay? I don't know what's, you know, *acceptable*."

He nodded, squeezing my knee. "Yeah, don't worry about it. This shouldn't go on longer than an hour, give or take, so I'll be up soon." He turned to his mother. "How about you and Dad? Heading to bed? I know you guys aren't used to being up past six."

She reached over to swat him playfully. "Your father is at the bar, but I'll be dragging him up to bed soon."

"And everybody else?" Brandon asked, noticing the empty table around us.

"They already headed up," I informed him.

"Well," he said, leaning in to kiss me softly, "you go ahead. As soon as I can, I'll be there." He kissed me again before standing from the table, catching the adoring smile on his mother's lips. "And hey, don't mind her. She's just thinking about all the grandkids you're going to make her. No pressure."

***

The bed was huge and exactly what I would have envisioned Heaven feeling like, or that could have been the fatigue talking. I had hung up from my last phone call for the night and told myself Esther would already be sleeping as I threw my cellphone onto the nightstand. I curled my knees to my stomach and closed my eyes, prepared to fall into a coma when the door opened and my fiancé walked in, already pulling at his bowtie and looking as though he had maybe a few too many glasses of Scotch.

He stumbled as he kicked off his dress shoes and threw his tuxedo jacket on the couch, and it hit me all at once that I was beginning the rest of my life with this incredible man who was so much more than anything I could have dreamed of.

And I deserve it. I deserve him.

He pulled his hair loose from the ponytail, shaking it out with his hands, and went to unbuckle his belt when he noticed my eyes were opened. "I figured you'd be sleeping," he said with a warm smile, coming to sit next to me on the bed. Shaking my head, I told him I had spent the past hour making phone calls. He grunted a chuckle. "And now your family is officially convinced you're insane, after accepting a proposal from the man you walked out on over a month ago?"

A stab of guilt hit my heart. "No, but I was insane for leaving, and then … God, I should have at least called, or I—"

"Yeah, and *I* should have never given you a reason to be upset in the first place." Brandon reached a hand over to cup my shoulder. Through his dark eyelashes, his piercing blue eyes looked directly into mine. "Baby, we could both talk about everything we *should* have done since we first met, but why bother? The way I see it, we got to where we were supposed to be, and right now, that's really all that matters."

"You're amazing, you know that?" Brandon shrugged his response, a little smile twitching at the corners of his mouth, and I asked the question I had been dying to get the answer to. "So, um, how long had you been planning this whole thing?"

"A week," he stated matter-of-factly.

"A *week*? You only decided you wanted to marry me a week ago?"

"Oh, no." He held a hand up before resting it on the curve of my hip. "I've known for months that I wanted to marry you, if I allowed myself to get that close, but it wasn't until I was driving back from Florida that I decided I was going to ask you to be my wife."

"Your *wife*," I repeated. I shook my head, cupping my hands over my mouth. Deep breaths. "So, how did that happen?"

"I took a detour into the city, stopped at Tiffany's, and bought the ring that spoke to me." He squeezed my hip gently, biting his bottom lip. A lustful glimmer ignited a heat in his eyes as they traveled over the curves of my body.

"But what if I had said no?"

"That was never an option," he said gruffly, his voice lowering to a whisper.

His hand came up against my cheek, stroking his thumb across to lay against my lips. My eyes closed as I kissed against the pad of his finger, and listened to the sharp inhale of his breath. I felt him lean over me, and he replaced his thumb with his lips; moving against mine softly before I opened my mouth to his whiskey tongue, reminding us both of how badly we wanted—*needed*—each other. I melted into the bed as he pulled back the blanket and groaned when he found I was naked. Through his wanton smile, he kissed along the curve of my collarbone and down between my breasts, taking a moment to suck slowly on one nipple before continuing his trail of kisses to just below my bellybutton.

I waited for him to move lower, desperately needing his mouth to relieve the built-up tension between my legs, but he stopped and I listened. I listened to the sound of his belt coming undone and listened as his pants hit the floor. My sense of touch was reignited then, as I felt his muscular build ease on top of me.

"Open," he commanded, pushing my legs apart with the width of his hips. A duet of groans filled the room as he sunk into me, surrounding himself and filling me with the desire fueled by our coupled lust and love for each other.

"Holly," he growled, and my toes curled at the sound of my own name. "Have I ever told you how fucking good it feels to be inside you?"

I grinned through a moan. "How good?" I asked between strangled breaths, gliding my hands down the length of his back to dig my fingers into the sensitive flesh of his tight ass.

Strands of his hair fell forward as his forehead pressed into mine. His eyes held me with that hypnotic intensity, like a wolf staring down its prey. "So … fucking … good." He emphasized his words with long, hard thrusts; burying himself until there was no telling where I began and he ended, pulling back until I was afraid he would leave me empty.

"How … profound, Mr. B. Davis." I smiled playfully, gazing into the depth of his darkened blue eyes. "I can see why you're a best-selling author."

His face was taken over by a lopsided smile, crinkling his eyes at the corners. "Is it that obvious?"

I took in another look of his face before my eyes rolled, closing them to the sensations that passed through his body and into mine. I reveled in the want to feel everything. The breath against my face, labored and desperate. The pumping of his blood through the veins that made contact with my skin. The long, slick strokes that brought me closer to the brink of utter bliss. The beating of my heart that seemed to say, "He's mine, he's mine, he's mine."

'Til death do us part.

"How did … you know …" I began to say, reviving a dead conversation, but I was cut off by the fullness of his tongue in my mouth.

Brandon held the kiss as he flipped onto his back, pulling me with him. I backed away, sitting up to stare down at him as I raised myself up and down, gyrating against him. "Jesus Christ." He moaned, tilting his head backward. "How did … I know … what?"

"That I would … say yes," I said, running my hands over his stomach and up to the collar of his shirt.

He looked back to me, finding my eyes in the way he always did. "Because," he said quietly, as my fingers began to unbutton his tuxedo shirt, "neither of us had made love before we found each other."

"That's so corny," I laughed, panting.

"Yeah? Okay, then would you settle for the fact that I believe we're destined to be together, and I was done throwing away time I could be spending as your husband?" His dark blue eyes stared intensely up at me.

Brandon freakin' Davis. My husband.

I laughed again through the pressure in my throat, finishing the last button. "Still corny, but I'll take it."

I opened the shirt, spreading my hands over his smooth skin, and looked down with the intention of taking in the hardness of his chest and the ridges of his stomach, but my attention was pulled to a tattoo I had never seen before. I laid a hand over the left side of his breast, and breathlessly asked when he had gotten it done.

"Florida," he replied, biting his lower lip as he dug his fingers into my hips.

I leaned forward, taking a closer look at the lettering made to look as though it were etched into stone. It read, "My heart has been taken, where it shall always be safe. My soul sings her name, with a map of her face. Strike me dead where I stand, I'll remain alive with her grace." Tears blurred my vision as I leaned in closer, pressing my lips to the inked skin.

I sat up, and Brandon noticed the pools in my eyes. "It's from the new book," he explained in a gruff voice, pulling a hand away from my waist to rest against my cheek. His face flushed a deeper shade of red. "I got it when—"

"I know," I whispered, bending into him again to press my lips softly against his, and the rise and fall of my hips met the rhythm of my mouth. "Hey, you know what?"

"Hmm," he replied, stroking his thumb against my cheek.

I lost myself in the deep blue of his eyes, and for the first time, I didn't bother holding myself back from drowning. I didn't have to. I knew I wasn't alone.

I was never going to be alone again.

"Thank God people like you fall in love with people like me," I said, brushing the hair away from his forehead.

"Yes." The corner of his mouth twitched. "Thank God."

ACKNOWLEDGEMENTS

Fᴵᴿˢᵀ ᴬᴺᴰ ꜰᴼᴿᴱᴹᴼˢᵀ, I would like to thank the people who brought me into this world, my parents. For putting up with my crap, for supporting me, and most importantly, for never doubting my ability to do great things. I hope this book makes you proud, that you consider it a great thing, and that the stuff swirling around in my head doesn't disturb you too much.

Thank you to my sisters, Karen and Kelly. Best friends forever and all that jazz. Thanks for listening to my incessant talking about this book (and others), thanks for your constant input, and thanks for simply being there when I've needed you most. You are the Liz(s) to my Holly, and forever will be.

Thank you to my partner in life, Danny. For believing in me, supporting my dreams, the endless amount of input, and mostly, for being the closest thing to a Brandon as I'll ever get. As the great Alanis Morissette once said, "You see all my light, and you love my dark … And you're still here." Thanks for still being here.

Thank you to all of my friends/editors/proofreaders/beta readers, especially Jess, Jackie, and Jo. My Three J's. Your encouragement, devotion, time, and help have been so greatly appreciated, and I truly cannot thank you enough for all you've done. Be prepared for the next book, ladies—it's coming.

To the authors I've met and befriended—Kyra Lennon, Jewel E. Ann, and Josie Brown, to name a few—thank you for your help, respect, and encouragement.

Special thanks to author, and friend, Jessica Park. I never thought that when I read *Flat-Out Love* all those years ago, I'd one day be gabbing your ear off and asking for advice. So much of this happened because of you, and when I think back on this book, I will always think of you.

Also, Diana Gabaldon, thank you for telling me to finish the book. If I'm being honest, I'm not entirely sure I'd be here, writing this, had you not said it. It's amazing what a few little words can do. I cannot say it enough … Thank you.

Last but not least—thank you, dear reader. Thank you for allowing these characters—these dear friends of mine—to come to life in your heads and hearts. Thank you for making them more real, by allowing them to exist in you. Thank you for reading, for reviewing, for loving, and for hating. You mean the absolute world to me—every single one of you. Thank you, thank you, and one more time for good measure … Thank you.

ABOUT THE AUTHOR

KELSEY KINGSLEY GREW UP IN the great state of New York, and still lives there with her family and a cat named Ethel. When she isn't writing her fingers to the bone, she enjoys a good (or bad) book, reruns of *Frasier*, ruining the lives of her Sims, and singing and dancing in the kitchen while cooking dinner. She somehow survives off a diet of tea, doughnuts, and French fries. However, she hates cheese and listening to people chew. You've been warned.

For more from Kelsey, you can find her at:
Website: http://www.kelseykingsley.com
Twitter: http://www.twitter.com/kelswritesstuff
Instagram: http://www.instagram.com/kelswritesstuff
Goodreads: http://www.goodreads.com/kelseykingsley
Facebook: http://www.facebook.com/kelswritesstuff

Made in the USA
Middletown, DE
24 October 2020

22698581R00201